Give Me Your Heart

Tales of Mystery & Suspense

Joyce Carol Oates

W F HOWES LTD

This large print edition published in 2011 by
W F Howes Ltd
Unit 4, Rearsby Business Park, Gaddesby Lane,
Rearsby, Leicester LE7 4YH

1 3 5 7 9 10 8 6 4 2

First published in the United Kingdom in 2011
by Corvus

The stories in this collection previously appeared elsewhere:
'Give Me Your Heart' in *Dangerous Women*, ed. by Otto Penzler
(Mysterious Press, 2005); 'Split/Brain' in *Ellery Queen's Mystery
Magazine*, October 2008; 'The First Husband' in *Ellery Queen's
Mystery Magazine*, January 2008; 'Strip Poker' in *Dead Man's
Hand*, ed. by Otto Penzler (Harcourt, 2007); 'Smother' in
Virginia Quarterly Review, Fall 2005; 'Tetanus' in *TriQuarterly*,
#131, 2008; 'The Spill' in *Kenyon Review*, Winter 2008; 'Bleed'
in *Shenandoah*, Spring/Summer 2008; 'Nowhere' in *Conjunctions*,
2006; 'Vena Cava' in *Portents*.

A CIP catalogue record for this book is available
from the British Library

ISBN 978 1 40747 321 5

Typeset by Palimpsest Book Production Limited,
Falkirk, Stirlingshire
Printed and bound in Great Britain
by MPG Books Ltd, Bodmin, Cornwall

To Richard Trenner

CONTENTS

GIVE ME YOUR HEART

Dear Dr K—,
    It's been a long time, hasn't it! Twenty-three years, nine months, and eleven days.
Since we last saw each other. Since you last saw, 'nude' on your naked knees, me.

Dr K—! The formal salutation isn't meant as flattery, still less as mockery – please understand. I am not writing after so many years to beg an unreasonable favor of you (I hope), or to make demands, merely to inquire if, in your judgment, I should go through the formality, and the trouble, of applying to be the lucky recipient of your most precious organ, your heart. If I may expect to collect what is due to me, after so many years.

I've learned that you, the renowned Dr K—, are one who has generously signed a 'living will' donating his organs to those in need. Not for Dr K— an old-fashioned, selfish funeral and burial in a cemetery, nor even cremation. Good for you, Dr K—! But I want only your heart, not your kidneys, liver, or eyes. These I will waive, that others more needy will benefit.

Of course, I mean to make my application as

1

others do, in medical situations similar to my own. I would not expect favoritism. The actual application would be made through my cardiologist. *Caucasian female of youthful middle age, attractive, intelligent, optimistic though with a malfunctioning heart, otherwise in perfect health.* No acknowledgment would be made of our old relationship, on my part at least. Though you, dear Dr K—, as the potential heart donor, could indicate your own preference, surely?

All this would transpire when you die, Dr K—, I mean. Of course! Not a moment before.

(I guess you might not be aware that you're destined to die soon? Within the year? In a 'tragic,' 'freak' accident, as it will be called? In an 'ironic,' 'unspeakably ugly' end to a 'brilliant career'? I'm sorry that I can't be more specific about time, place, means; even whether you'll die alone, or with a family member or two. But that's the nature of *accident*, Dr K—. It's a surprise.)

Dr K—, don't frown so! You're a handsome man still, and still vain, despite your thinning gray hair, which, like other vain men with hair loss, you've taken to combing slantwise over the shiny dome of your head, imagining that since you can't see this ploy in the mirror, it can't be seen by others. *But I can see.*

Fumbling, you turn to the last page of this letter to see my signature – 'Angel' – and you're forced to remember, suddenly . . . With a pang of guilt.

Her! She's still . . . alive?

2

That's right, Dr K—! More alive now than ever.

Naturally you'd come to imagine I had vanished. I had ceased to exist. Since you'd long ago ceased to think of me.

You're frightened. Your heart, that guilty organ, has begun to pound. At a second-floor window of your house on Richmond Street (expensively restored Victorian, pale gray shingles with dark blue trim, 'quaint,' 'dignified,' among others of its type in the exclusive old residential neighborhood east of the Theological Seminary), you stare out anxiously at – what?

Not me, obviously. I'm not there.

At any rate, I'm not in sight.

Yet how the pale-glowering sky seems to throb with a sinister intensity! Like a great eye staring.

Dr K—, I mean you no harm! Truly. This letter is in no way a demand for your (posthumous) heart, nor even a 'verbal threat.' If you decide, foolishly, to show it to the police, they will assure you it's harmless, it isn't illegal, it's only a request for information: should I, the 'love of your life' you have not seen in twenty-three years, apply to be the recipient of your heart? What are Angel's chances?

I only wish to collect what's mine. What was promised to me, so long ago. *I've* been faithful to our love, Dr K—!

You laugh, harshly. Incredulously. How can you reply to Angel, when Angel has included no last name, and no address? *You will have to seek me. To save yourself, seek me.*

3

You crumple this letter in your fist, throw it onto the floor.

You walk away, stumble away, you mean to forget, obviously you can't forget, the crumpled pages of my handwritten letter on the floor of – is it your study? on the second floor of the dignified old Victorian house at 119 Richmond Street? – where someone might discover them, and pick them up to read what you wouldn't wish another living person to read, especially not someone 'close' to you. (As if our families, especially our blood kin, are 'close' to us as in the true intimacy of erotic love.) So naturally you return; with badly shaking fingers you pick up the scattered pages, smooth them out, and continue to read.

Dear Dr K—! Please understand: I am not bitter, I don't harbor obsessions. That is not my nature. I have my own life, and I have even had a (moderately successful) career. *I am a normal woman of my time and place.* I am like the exquisite black-and-silver diamond-headed spider, the so-called happy spider, the sole subspecies of Araneidae that is said to be free to spin part-improvised webs, both oval and funnel, and to roam the world at will, equally at home in damp grasses and the dry, dark, protected interiors of manmade places; rejoicing in (relative) free will within the inevitable restrictions of Araneidae behavior; with a sharp venomous sting, sometimes lethal to human beings, especially to children.

Like the diamond-head, I have many eyes. Like

4

the diamond-head, I may be perceived as 'happy,' 'joyous,' 'exulting,' in the eyes of others. For such is my role, my performance.

It's true, for years I was stoically reconciled to my loss, in fact to my losses. (Not that I blame you for these losses, Dr K—. Though a neutral observer might conclude that my immune system has been damaged as a result of my physical and mental collapse following your abrupt dismissal of me from your life.) Then, last March, seeing your photograph in the paper – Distinguished Theologian K— to Head Seminary' – and, a few weeks later, when you were named to the President's Commission on Religion and Bioethics, I reconsidered. *The time of anonymity and silence is over*, I thought. *Why not try? Why not try to collect what he owes you?*

Do you remember Angel's name now? That name that for twenty-three years, nine months, and eleven days you have not wished to utter?

Seek my name in any telephone directory; you won't find it. For possibly my number is unlisted; possibly I don't have a telephone. Possibly my name has been changed. (Legally.) Possibly I live in a distant city in a distant region of the continent; or possibly, like the diamond-head spider (adult size approximately that of your right thumbnail, Dr K—), I dwell quietly within your roof, spinning my exquisite webs amid the shadowy beams of your basement, or in a niche between your handsome old mahogany desk and the wall, or, a delicious thought, in the airless cave beneath the four-poster brass antique bed you and the second Mrs K— share in the doldrums of late middle age.

So close am I, yet invisible!

Dear Dr K—! Once you marveled at my 'flawless Vermeer' skin and 'spun-gold' hair rippling down my back, which you stroked, and closed in your fist. Once I was your Angel, your 'beloved.' I basked in your love, for I did not question it. I was young; I was virginal in spirit as well as body, and would not have questioned the word of a distinguished elder. And in the paroxysm of lovemaking, when you gave yourself up utterly to me, or so it seemed, how could you have . . . deceived?

Dr K— of the Theological Seminary, biblical scholar and authority, protégé of Reinhold Niebuhr, and author of 'brilliant,' 'revolutionary' exegeses of the Dead Sea Scrolls, among other esoteric subjects.

But I had no idea, you are protesting. *I'd given her no reason to believe, to expect . . .*

(That I would believe your declarations of love? That I would take you at your word?)

My darling, you have my heart. Always, forever. Your promise!

These days, Dr K—, my skin is no longer flawless. It has become the frank, flawed skin of a middle-aged woman who makes no effort to disguise her age. My hair, once shimmering strawberry-blond, is now faded, dry and brittle as broom sage; I keep it trimmed short, like a man's, with scissors, scarcely glancing into a mirror as I *snip! snip-snip!* away. My face, though reasonably attractive, I suppose, is in fact a blur to most observers, including especially middle-aged American men; you've glanced at me, and through me, dear Dr K—, upon more than one recent occasion, no more recognizing your Angel than you would have recognized a plate heaped with food you'd devoured twenty-three years ago with a zestful appetite, or an old, long-exhausted and dismissed sexual fantasy of adolescence.

For the record: I was the woman in a plain, khaki-colored trench coat and matching hat who waited patiently at the university bookstore as a line of your admirers moved slowly forward for Dr K— to sign copies of *The Ethical Life: Twenty-First-Century Challenges*. (A slender theological treatise, not a mega-bestseller, of course, but a quite respectable bestseller, most popular in university and upscale suburban communities.) I knew your 'brilliant' book would disappoint, yet I purchased it and eagerly read to discover (yet another time) the puzzling fact: you, Dr K—, the man, are not the individual who appears in your books; the books are clever pretenses, artificial structures you've created to inhabit temporarily, as a crippled, deformed individual might inhabit a structure of surpassing beauty, gazing out its windows, taking pride in posing as its owner, but only temporarily.

Yes? Isn't this the clue to the renowned Dr K—?

For the record: several Sundays ago, you and I passed closely by each other in the State Museum of Natural History; you were gripping the hand of your five-year-old granddaughter (Lisle, I believe? – lovely name) and took no more notice of me than you'd have taken of any stranger passing you on the steep marble steps, descending from the Hall of Dinosaurs on the gloomy fourth floor as you were ascending; you'd stooped to speak smilingly to Lisle, and it was at that moment I noted the silly, touching ploy of your hair-combing (over the spreading bald spot), I saw Lisle's sweet, startled face (for the child, unlike her myopic granddaddy, had seen me and knew me in a flash). I felt a thrill of triumph: for how easily I might have killed you then, I might have pushed you down those hard marble steps, my hands firm on your now rather rounded shoulders, the force of my rage overcoming any resistance you, a puffy, slack-bellied, two-hundred-pound man of late middle age, might have mustered; immediately you'd have been thrown off-balance, fallen backward, with an expression of incredulous terror, and, still gripping your granddaughter's hand, you'd have dragged the innocent child backward with you, toppling down the marble steps with a scream: concussion, skull fracture, brain hemorrhage, death!

Why not try, why not try to collect what he owes me.

8

Of course, Dr K—, I didn't! Not that Sunday afternoon.

Dear Dr K—! Are you surprised to learn that your lost love with the 'spun-gold' hair and the 'soft-as-silk breasts' managed to recover from your cruelty and by the age of twenty-nine had begun to do well in her career, in another part of the country? Never would I be as renowned in my field as you, Dr K—, are in yours – that goes without saying – but through diligence and industry, through self-deprivation and cunning, I made my way in a field traditionally dominated by men and achieved what might be called a minor, local success. That is, I have nothing to be ashamed of, and perhaps even something to be proud of, if I were capable of pride.

I won't be more specific, Dr K—, but I will hint: my field is akin to yours, though not scholarly or intellectual. My salary is far less than yours, of course. I have no public identity, no reputation, and no great wish for such. I'm in a field of *service*, I've long known how to *serve*. Where the fantasies of others, primarily men, are involved, I've grown quite adept at *serving*.

Yes, Dr K—, it's possible that I've even served you. Indirectly, I mean. For instance: I might work in or even oversee a medical laboratory to which your physician sends blood samples, biopsy tissue samples, et cetera, and one day he sends our laboratory a specimen extracted from the body of the renowned Dr K—. *Whose life may depend upon the accuracy and good faith of our laboratory findings.*

Just one example, Dr K—, among many!

No, dear Dr K—, this letter is no threat. How, stating my position so openly, and therefore innocently, could I be a *threat?*

Are you shocked to learn that a woman can be a professional – can have a career that's fairly rewarding – yet still dream of justice after twenty-three years? Are you shocked to learn that a woman might be married, or might have been married, yet remain haunted still by her cruel, deceitful first love, who ravaged not only her virginity but her faith in humankind?

You'd like to imagine your cast-off Angel as a lonely embittered spinster, yes? Hiding away in the dark, spinning ugly sticky webs out of her own poisonous guts. Yet the truth is the reverse: just as there are happy spiders, observed by ento-mologists as exhibiting a capacity for (relative) freedom, spinning webs of some variety and originality, so too there are happy women who dream of justice and will make sure that they taste its sweetness one day. Soon.

(Dr K—! How lucky you are to have a little granddaughter like Lisle! So delicate, so pretty, so . . . angelic. I have not had a daughter, I confess. I will not have a granddaughter. If things were otherwise between us, Jody, we might share Lisle.)

Jody – what a thrill it was for me, at the age of

nineteen, to call you by that name! Where others addressed you formally, as Dr K—. That it was secret, illicit, taboo – like calling one's own father by a lover's name – was part of the thrill, of course.

Jody, I hope your first, anxious wife, E—, never discovered certain bits of incriminating evidence in your trouser pockets, wallet, briefcase, where, daringly, I secreted them. Love notes, childlike in expression. *Love love love my Jody. My BIG JODY.*

You're not BIG JODY very often now, are you, Dr K—?

Jody has faded with the years, I've learned. With the thick wiry gypsy-black hair, those shrewd clear eyes and proud posture, and the capacity of your stubby penis to rejuvenate, reinvent itself with impressive frequency. (At the start of our affair, at least.) For any nineteen-year-old girl student to call you Jody now would be obscene, laughable.

Now you most love being called Granddaddy! in Lisle's voice.

Yet in my dreams sometimes I hear my own shameless whisper: *Jody, please don't stop loving me, please forgive me, I want only to die, I deserve to die if you don't love me,* as in the warm bath blood-tendrils seeped from my clumsily lacerated forearms; but it was Dr K—, not Jody, who spoke brusquely on the phone, informing me, *This is not the time. Goodbye.*

(You must have made inquiries, Dr K—. You must have learned that I was found there in the bloody bathwater, unconscious, nearing death, by a concerned woman friend who'd tried to call me. You must have known but prudently kept your distance, Dr K—! These many years.)

Dr K—, not only have you managed to erase me from your memory, but I would guess you've forgotten your anxious, first wife, E—, Evie. The rich man's daughter. A woman two years older than you, lacking in self-confidence, rather plain, with no style. Loving me, you were concerned about making Evie suspicious, not because you cared for her but because you would have made the rich father suspicious too. And you were very beholden to the rich father, yes? *Few members of the seminary faculty can afford to live near the seminary. In the elegant old East End of our university town.* (So you boasted in your bemused way. As if contemplating an irony of fate, not a consequence of your own maneuvering. As, smiling, you kissed my mouth, and drew a forefinger along my breasts, across my shivery belly.)

Poor Evie! Her hit-and-run 'accidental' death, a mysterious vehicle swerving on a rain-lashed pavement, no witnesses . . . I would have helped you mourn, Dr K—, and been a loving stepmother to your children, but by then you'd banished me from your life.

Or so you believed.

(For the record: I am not hinting that I had

anything to do with the death of the first Mrs K—. Don't bother to read and reread these lines to determine if there's something 'between' them. There isn't.)

And then, Dr K—, a widower with two children, you went away, to Germany. A sabbatical year that stretched into two. I was left to mourn in your place. (Not luckless Evie, but you.) Your wife's death was spoken of as a 'tragedy' in certain circles, but I preferred to think of it as purely an accident: a conjunction of time, place, opportunity. *What is accident but a precision of timing?*

Dr K—, I would not accuse you of blatant hypocrisy (would I?), still less of deceit, but I can't comprehend why, in such craven terror of your first wife's family (to whom you felt so intellectually superior), you nonetheless remarried, within eighteen months, a woman much younger than you, nearly as young as I, which must have shocked and infuriated your former in-laws. Yes? (Or did you cease caring about what they thought? Had you siphoned enough money from the father-in-law by that time?)

Your second wife, V—, would be spared an accidental death, and will survive you by many years. I have never felt any rancor for voluptuous – now rather fattish – Viola, who came into your life after I'd departed from it. Maybe, in a way, I felt some sympathy for the young woman, guessing that in time you would betray her too. (And haven't you? Numberless times?)

I have forgotten nothing, Dr K—. While you, to your fatal disadvantage, have forgotten almost everything.

Dr K—, Jody, shall I confess: I had secrets from you even then. Even when I seemed to you transparent, translucent. Deep in the marrow of my bones, a wish to bring our illicit love to an end. An end worthy of grand opera, not mere melodrama. When you sat me on your knees naked – 'nude' was your preferred term – and gobbled me up with your eyes – 'Beautiful! Aren't you a little beauty!' – even then I exulted in my secret thoughts. You seemed at times drunk with love – lust? – for me, kissing, tonguing, nuzzling, sucking . . . sucking nourishment from me like a vampire. (The stress of fatherhood and maintaining a dutiful-son-in-law pose as well as the 'renowned theologian' were exhausting you, maddening you in your masculine vanity. Of course, in my naiveté I had no idea.) Yet laying my hand on the hot-skinned nape of your neck I saw a razor blade clenched in my fingers, and the first aston- ished spurts of your blood, with such vividness that I can see it now. I began to faint, my eyes rolled back in my head, you caught me in your arms . . . and for the first time (I assume it was the first time) you perceived your spun-gold angel as something of a concern, a liability, a burden not unlike the burden of a neurotic, anxiety-prone wife. *Darling, what's the matter with you? Are you playing, darling? Beautiful girl, it isn't amusing to frighten me when I adore you so.*

Gripping my chilled fingers in your hot, hard

fingers and pressing my hand against your big powerfully beating heart.

Why not? why not try? try to collect? – that heart. That's owed me.

How inspired I am, composing this letter, Dr K—! I've been writing feverishly, scarcely pausing to draw breath. It's as if an angel is guiding my hand. (One of those tall leathery-winged angels of wrath, with fierce medieval faces, you see in German woodcuts!) I've reread certain of your published works, Dr K—, including the heavily footnoted treatise on the Dead Sea Scrolls that established your reputation as an ambitious young scholar in his early thirties. Yet it all seems so quaint and long ago, back in the twentieth century, when God and Satan were somehow more real to us, like household objects . . . I've been reading of our primitive religious origins, how God-Satan were once conjoined but are now, in our Christian tradition, always separated. Fatally separated. For we Christians can believe no evil of our deity, we could not love him then.

Dr K—, as I write this letter my malfunctioning heart with its mysterious murmur now speeds, now slows, now gives a lurch, in excited knowledge that you are reading these words with a mounting sense of their justice. A heavy rain has begun to fall, drumming against the roof and windows of the place in which I am living, the identical rain (is it?) that drums against the roof and windows of your house only a few (or is it

15

many?) miles away; unless I live in a part of the country thousands of miles distant, and the rain is not identical. And yet *I can come to you at any time. I am free to come, and to go; to appear, and to disappear.* It may even be that I've contemplated the charming facade of your precious granddaughter's Busy Bee Nursery School, even as I've shopped for shoes in the company of V—, though the jowly-faced, heavily made-up woman with the size 10 feet was oblivious of my presence, of course.

And just last Sunday I revisited the Museum of Natural History, knowing there was a possibility that you might return. For it had seemed to me possible that you'd recognized me on the steps, and sent a signal to me with your eyes, without Lisle noticing; you were urging me to return to meet with you, alone. The deep erotic bond between us will never be broken, you know: you entered my virginal body, you took from me my innocence, my youth, my very soul. *My angel! Forgive me, return to me, I will make up to you the suffering you've endured for my sake.*

I waited, but you failed to return.

I waited, and my sense of mission did not subside but grew more certain.

I found myself the sole visitor on the gloomy fourth floor, in the Hall of Dinosaurs. My footsteps echoed faintly on the worn marble floor. A white-haired museum guard with a paunch like yours regarded me through drooping eyelids; he sat on a canvas chair, hands on his knees. Like a wax dummy. Like one of those trompe l'oeil mannequins. You know: those uncanny, lifelike figures you see in contemporary art collections, except this slouching figure wasn't bandaged in white. Silently I passed by him as a ghost might pass. My (gloved) hand in my bag, and my fingers clutching a razor blade I've learned by this time to wield with skill, and courage.

Stealthily I circled the Hall of Dinosaurs looking for you, but in vain; stealthily I drew up behind the dozing guard, feeling my erratic heartbeat quicken with the thrill of the hunt . . . but of course I let the moment pass; it was no museum guard but the renowned Dr K— for whom the razor blade was intended. (Though I had not the slightest doubt that I could have wielded my weapon against the old man, simply out of frustration at not finding you, and out of female rage at centuries of mistreatment, exploitation; I might have slashed his carotid artery and quickly retreated without a single blood drop splashed onto my clothing; even as the old man's life bled out onto the worn marble floor, I would have descended to the near-deserted third floor of the museum, and to the second, to mingle unnoticed with Sunday visitors crowded into a new computer graphics exhibit. So easy!) I found myself adrift amid rubbery dinosaur replicas, some of them enormous as *Tyrannosaurus rex*, some the size of oxen, and others fairly small, human-sized; I

17

admired the flying reptiles, with their long beaks and clawed wings; in a reflecting surface over which one of these prehistoric creatures soared, I admired my pale, face and floating ashy hair. *My darling*, you whispered, *I will always adore you. That angelic smile!*

Dr K—, see? I'm smiling still.

Dr K—! Why are you standing there so stiffly, at an upstairs window of your house? Why are you cringing, overcome by a sickening fear? *Nothing will happen to you that is not just. That you do not deserve.*

These pages in your shaking hand you'd like to tear into shreds – but don't dare. Your heart pounds, in terror of being snatched from your chest! Desperately you're contemplating – but will decide against – showing my letter to the police. (Ashamed of what the letter reveals of the renowned Dr K—!) You are contemplating – but will decide against – showing my letter to your wife, for you've had exhausting sessions of soul-bearing, confession, exoneration with her, numerous times; you've seen the disgust in her eyes. No more! And you haven't the stomach to contemplate yourself in the mirror, for you've had more than enough of your own face, those stricken guilty eyes. While I, the venomous diamond-head, contentedly spin my gossamer web amid the beams of your basement, or in the niche between your desk and the wall, or in the airless cave beneath your marital bed, or – most delicious prospect! – inside the very mattress of the child's bed in which, when she visits her grandparents in the house on Richmond Street, beautiful little Lisle sleeps.

Invisible by day as by night, spinning my web, out of my guts, tireless and faithful – happy.

SPLIT/BRAIN

In that instant of entering the house by the rear door when she sees, or thinks she sees, a fleeting movement like a shadow in the hallway beyond the kitchen and she hears a sharp intake of breath or panting, it is her decision not to retreat in panicked haste from her house but to step forward, sharply calling, *Jeremy? Is that you?* For she'd seen her sister-in-law's car parked on the shoulder of the road some fifty feet before the driveway to her house, she is certain it must be Veronica's Toyota, which Jeremy often drives; it occurs to her now that she'd expected to see Veronica at the clinic that morning but Veronica hadn't turned up – like buzzing hornets these thoughts rush at her even as she calls out more sharply, *Is that you? Jeremy?* For the boy shouldn't be here in this house at this time, uninvited; she'd left the rear door unlocked, as frequently she did, driving into town to the clinic, returning, and later in the day driving back into town to the clinic, a distance of precisely 2.6 miles, of which she has memorized each intervening property, driveway, intersecting road and street, to be played, replayed, and run backward in her mind as she drives into town, to the rehab clinic, to see her husband, and returns to the house in preparation for driving back to the clinic, which is, she has come to realize, but the preparation for returning home. For much of this morning she has been at the clinic, tries to arrive precisely at 8 A.M., when the clinic opens its front doors to visitors, for she is an early riser, both she and Jim are early risers, rarely sleep past dawn even on bitter-cold sunless winter mornings. And at the clinic at her husband's bedside usually she will remain until 7 P.M., when, exhausted, she returns home for the remainder of the day. At Jim's bedside she reads to him, checks e-mail on her laptop, and reads to Jim those messages, ever decreasing in frequency, that seem to her important for Jim to hear. With childlike logic she is thinking, *If I am a good wife, if I am good, God will spare us, God will make him well again,* and so far her prayer, which she understands is both craven and futile, has not been entirely scorned, for Jim has been transferred from the hospital to the clinic and there is the promise that one day soon he will be sent back home to recuperate and to recover his lost strength. Already he no longer needs to be fed through a tube, already the color is returning to his face, which had been deathly pale. Though still he tires easily, nods off in the midst of speaking, friends who come to visit have learned to disguise their shock and discomfort seeing Jim Gould so changed, poor

Jim who'd once been so vital, so energetic, smiling and good-natured and much loved, and now his body seems to have shrunken, he has lost more than fifty pounds, his hands are weak, legs useless, the once-powerful muscles atrophied, and now his legs are reduced to bones beneath thin hairless skin, terrible to see. And so she has learned not to see. And so she has learned to disguise her fear. And so she has learned to smile as nurses learn to smile. And when he asks her please to massage his legs, his legs hurt, she smiles and kneads the bone-hard legs, thin now as the legs of a young child; massaging these legs, she jokes with her husband, she loves him so, she would die for this man, she believes, and yet how fatigued she has grown in the past several weeks, how exasperated with her husband's demands. Jim has become unpredictable in his moods, quick to become angry. This morning, hurrying to get to the clinic, she'd forgotten to bring with her the latest issue of a professional journal for which her husband has been an advisory editor; seeing she'd forgotten it, Jim was visibly disappointed and sulky, and she'd said, *Darling, I'll drive back to get the journal, it's no trouble*, and immediately he said, *No, it isn't necessary, you can bring it next time*, and she insisted yes, of course she will drive back to get it for him, she has other errands in town that need to be done this morning. And anyway, Jim is scheduled for tests this morning. And she kisses his cheek, tells him she will return within the hour; in secret she's childishly relieved to be able to leave the clinic so soon after arriving, this dour dark dimly lighted place, the smells, don't think of the smells, the accumulated smells of decades. And the other patients, and the other visitors, who are mainly women her age and older, whom she has come to recognize at the clinic, as they have come to recognize her, and who dread the sight of one another outside the clinic. She is one of the few who takes pains with her appearance, not a vain woman but a woman well aware of her face, her body, how men regard her, or once regarded her, with more than ordinary interest. On this weekday she is wearing an attractive creamy pale yellow pantsuit that is flattering to her shapely body, she thinks, and around her throat a peach-colored Italian scarf; through her life she has been a big-boned beautiful girl yet never what one would call fat – the word *fat* is offensive to her ears, obscene. Her face is round, full-cheeked, her skin slightly flushed as if sunburned – a classic brunette beauty, her husband has called her – but now, seeing herself in the rearview mirror of her car on the way home, she is shocked by her creased fore-head, feathery white lines bracketing her eyes and at the corners of her mouth, the coral lipstick she'd so carefully applied that morning eaten off. A little cry of distress escapes her: *It is unfair! My face is wearing out, I am still young.* For she is seven years younger than the stricken man in the rehab clinic. How many years she'd been the youngest wife in their social circle. And in her heart she is the youngest still, and the one men glance at, gaze at with admiration. And turning into Constitution Hill, and onto Westerly Drive, she sees a familiar car parked at a crooked angle partly in the roadway, partly on the shoulder, her sister-in-law's black Toyota so oddly parked. This is a car her seventeen-year-old nephew, Jeremy, has been driving recently. She feels a tinge of disapproval; neither her brother nor her sister-in-law seems capable of disciplining Jeremy, who has been suspended from high school for drugs, threatening other students, threatening a teacher; she knows that Jeremy has a juvenile record for break-ins in his neighborhood near the university. Yet turning into her driveway she ceases thinking of her nephew. The driveway is a steep graveled lane bordered by a straggling evergreen hedge; with her husband so suddenly hospitalized, now in rehab, no one has tended to the property, she scarcely thinks of it, seeing that litter has been blown into the shrubbery, old newspapers and fliers scattered across the lawn, the only time she notices the condition of the property is when she's in the car, and as soon as she steps out of the car to enter the house, she will forget. Too many things to think of – it's unfair. And now pushing the rear door that opens too readily to her touch, seeing that fleeting shadow against an inner wall. And she thinks with a rush of anger, *He believes that I am with Jim, at the clinic and not here, he believes that*

24

no one is home. For it has been said of Trudy Gould that she is a saint, every day at the hospital and now at the rehab clinic, she is selfless, uncomplaining at her husband's bedside for months. She knows how people speak of her, she takes pride in being so spoken of, in fact she is terrified of the empty house, bitterly now she regrets having no children, yes but both she and her husband decided that the risk of adoption was too great, bringing a child of unknown parents into their orderly household. And now entering her kitchen with a deliberate clatter of her heels, expensive Italian leather shoe-boots with a two-inch heel, she feels a thrill of something like defiance, she will not be frightened of her own nephew, tall lanky sloe-eyed Jeremy, whom she has known since his birth. Aunt Trudy, the boy calls her, or called her until two years ago, when so much seemed to change in him. Still she thinks that Jeremy has always liked her; he would not hurt *her.* Entering the hallway now, calling in a scolding voice, *Jeremy! I see you,* and seeing now that the boy's face is strangely flushed, he is panting and his eyes are dilated and damp – he is on some drug, she thinks – yet even now, advancing upon him sharp-tongued and scolding, *Jeremy! What are you doing here! How dare you,* as he springs at her panting like a dog, knocking her back against the wall, even now she is disbelieving – *He would not hurt me, this is my house* – and somehow they are in the kitchen, they are struggling together in the

25

kitchen, a chair is overturned, in his hoarse raw boy's voice Jeremy is crying, *Shut up, shut up you old bag, old bitch,* even as she screams at him to get away, to stop what he is doing, she slaps at him, blindly Jeremy has snatched up a knife from a kitchen counter, a small paring knife, yet sharp, blindly he is stabbing at her, his aunt whom he seems not to know, does not recognize, astonished Aunt Trudy he has known all his life, staring at her now with glassy eyes narrowed to slits. Helplessly she lifts her fleshy forearms against him, her outstretched hands, to shield herself from the terrible stabbing blows; she is not scolding now, her voice is faltering, pleading now, *No no, Jeremy please no don't hurt me you don't want to hurt me, Jeremy no* as the short sharp blade flies at her like a maddened bird of prey, striking her face, her throat, her breasts straining at the now-damp creamy pale yellow fabric of her jacket top, this furious stranger who resembles her seventeen-year-old nephew will back off from her to leave her sprawled on the sticky kitchen floor to suffocate in her own blood, her lungs have been punctured, her throat is filling up with blood, in something like elation he has thrown down the bloody paring knife, *I told you! I told you! I told you Goddamn you leave me alone!* he stumbles from the kitchen, runs upstairs though it has been years since he has been upstairs in his aunt's house on Westerly Drive, wildly he rummages through bureau drawers, leaving bloody fingerprints,

26

bloody footprints, as in an antic dance in the striking baroque design of his Nike soles, man is he high, flying high, this older girl he's crazy for, a girl with whom he shares his drugs, has sex and shares drugs, he will boast to her that he hadn't planned anything of what happened in the rich woman's house, he'd acted out of sheer instinct, he'd told her he knows a house over in Constitution Hill, there's a woman who is gone all day at the hospital with her husband, he did not tell the girl that the woman was his aunt, boasting he'd be safe roaming the house as long as he wanted looking for money and for things to take, over in Constitution Hill where the houses are so large, lots so large and set off from their neighbors, no one will see him and if there's trouble no one will hear it . . . In that instant of pushing open the door she sees all this, as a single lightning flash can illuminate a nighttime landscape of gnarled and unimaginable intricacy, so in that instant she sees, sheerly by instinct she retreats from the door that has swung open too readily to her touch, in the tight-fitting Italian leather shoe-boots she runs stumbling down the gravel driveway, of course she'd seen her sister-in-law's black Toyota parked out of place by the road, she'd recognized the Toyota by the pattern of dents on the rear bumper and by the first letters of the license plate, VER; no, she will not retreat, certainly she will not retreat. Instead she turns the car into the steep gravel driveway. At the rear of the house, which is the door she and Jim always use, she sees, or thinks she sees, that the door is just slightly ajar; still there is time to retreat, with a part of her brain she knows *I must not go inside, Jim would not want me to go inside*, for her responsibility is to her husband back at the clinic, waiting for her, but this is her house, in which she has lived with her husband, Jim Gould, for twenty-six years; no one has the right to keep her from entering this house, no one has the right to enter this house without her permission, even a relative, even her shy-sullen sloe-eyed nephew Jeremy, and so with an air of defiance she pushes into the kitchen, clatter of heels on the kitchen tile in that instant seeing a fleeting movement like a shadow in the hall beyond the kitchen, she hears a sharp intake of breath or panting, in that instant a rush of pure adrenaline flooding her veins, she refuses to run stumbling and screaming down the gravel drive to summon help, a fleshy woman in her early fifties, yet still girlish, in her manner and in her speech, she will not stagger next door where a Hispanic housekeeper will take her in, in this way save her, dialing 911 as Mrs Gould collapses onto a kitchen chair, winded, panting like a terrified animal, that will not happen, she will not give in to fear, she will not flee from her own house, she will not be saved from suffocating in her own blood, it is her decision, she is Jim Gould's classic brunette beauty, she has never been a vain woman but she thinks well of herself,

28

she is not a weak woman like her sister-in-law and so she will not retreat in undignified haste from her own house, instead she will step forward with a scolding clatter of her shoe-boot heels, sharply calling, *Jeremy? Is that you?*

THE FIRST HUSBAND

1.

It began innocently: he was searching for his wife's passport.

The Chases were planning their first trip to Italy together. To celebrate their tenth anniversary.

Leonard's own much-worn passport was exactly where he always kept it, but Valerie's less frequently used passport didn't appear to be with it, so Leonard looked through drawers designated as hers, bureau drawers, desk drawers, the single shallow drawer of the cherrywood table in a corner of their bedroom which Valerie sometimes used as a desk, and there, in a manila folder, with a facsimile of her birth certificate and other documents, he found the passport. And pushed to the back of the drawer, a packet of photographs held together with a frayed rubber hand.

Polaroids. Judging by their slightly faded colors, old Polaroids.

Leonard shuffled through the photographs as if they were cards. He was staring at a young couple:

Valerie and a man whom Leonard didn't recognize. Here was Valerie astonishingly young, and more beautiful than Leonard had ever known her. Her hair was coppery red and fell in a cascade to her bare shoulders; she was wearing a red bikini top, white shorts. The darkly handsome young man close beside her had slung a tanned arm around her shoulders in a playful intimate gesture, a gesture of blatant sexual possession. Very likely this man was Valerie's first husband, whom Leonard had never met. The young lovers were photographed seated at a white wrought-iron table in an outdoor café, or on the balcony of a hotel room. In several photos you could see in the near distance a curving stretch of wide white sand, a glimpse of aqua water. Beyond the couple on the terrace were royal court palm trees, crimson bougainvillea like flame. The sky was a vivid tropical blue. The five or six photographs must have been taken by a third party, a waiter or hotel employee perhaps. Leonard stared, transfixed.

The first husband. Here was the first husband. Yardman? Was that the name? Leonard felt a stab of sexual jealousy. Not wanting to think, *And I am the second husband.*

On the reverse of one of the Polaroids, in Valerie's handwriting, was *Oliver & Val, Key West, December 1985.*

Oliver. This was Yardman's first name, Leonard vaguely remembered now. In 1985, Val had been twenty-two, nearly half her lifetime ago, and she hadn't yet married Oliver Yardman but would be marrying him in another year. At this time they were very possibly new lovers; this trip to Key West had been a kind of honeymoon. Such sensual, unabashed happiness in the lovers' faces! Leonard was sure that Valerie had told him she hadn't kept any photographs of her first husband.

'The least we can do with our mistakes,' Valerie had said, with a droll downturn of her mouth, 'is not keep a record of them.'

Leonard, who'd met Valerie when she was thirty-one, several years after her divorce from Yardman, had been allowed to think that the first husband had been older than Valerie, not very attractive and not very interesting. Valerie claimed that she'd married 'too young' and that their divorce just five years later had been 'amicable,' for they had no children and had not shared much of a past. Yardman's work had been with a family-owned business in a Denver suburb, 'dull, money-grubbing work.' Valerie, who'd grown up in Rye, Connecticut, had not liked Colorado and spoke of that part of the country, and of that 'early phase' of her life, with an expression of disdain.

Yet here was evidence that Valerie had been very happy with Oliver Yardman in December 1985. Clearly Yardman was no more than a few years older than Valerie and, far from being unattractive, was decidedly good-looking: dark, avid eyes, sharply defined features, something sulky and petulant about the mouth, the mouth of a spoiled child. In one of the more revealing Polaroids, Yardman had pulled Valerie toward him, a hand gripping her shoulder and the other hand beneath the table, very likely gripping her thigh. The man's hair was dark, thick. Faint stubble showed on his solid jaws. He wore a white T-shirt that fitted his muscled torso tightly, and tight swim trunks; his legs were covered in dark hairs. In a kind of infantile sensual delight, his bare toes curled upward.

Leonard felt a thrill of physical revulsion, anger. So this was Oliver Yardman: the first husband.

Not at all the man Valerie had suggested to Leonard.

At the time he'd thought it strange, though not disagreeably so, that Valerie hadn't asked Leonard about his past (by which is meant, invariably, a sexual past). Unlike any woman Leonard had ever met as an adult, Valerie hadn't even asked Leonard if he had ever been married.

It had been a relief, to meet a woman so confident in herself that she seemed utterly lacking in sexual jealousy. Now Leonard saw that very likely Valerie hadn't wanted to be questioned about her own sexual/marital past.

Leonard stared at the Polaroids, frowning. He should laugh, shove them back into the drawer as they'd been, taking care not to snap the frayed rubber band, for certainly he wasn't the kind of man to rifle through his wife's private things. Nor was he the kind of man who is prone to jealousy.

33

Of all the ignoble emotions, jealousy had to be the worst! And envy.

And yet: he took the photos closer to the window, where a faint November sun glowered behind banks of clouds above the Hudson River, seeing how the table at which the young couple sat was crowded with glasses, a bottle of (red, dark) wine that appeared to be nearly depleted, napkins crumpled onto dirtied plates like discarded clothing. A ring on Valerie's left hand, silver studs glittering in her earlobes, which looked flushed, rosy. In several of the photos, Valerie was clutching at her energetic young lover as he was clutching at her, in playful possessiveness. You could see that Valerie was giddy from wine, and love. Here was an amorous couple who'd wakened late after a night of love; this heavy lunch with wine would be their first meal of the day; very likely they'd return to bed, collapsing in one another's arms for an afternoon siesta. In the most blatant photo, Valerie lay sprawled against Yardman, glossy hair spilling across his chest, one of her arms around his waist and the other part hidden beneath the table, her hand very likely in Yardman's lap. In Yardman's groin. Valerie, who now disliked vulgarity, who stiffened if Leonard swore and claimed to hate 'overly explicit' films, had been provocatively touching Yardman in the very presence of the third party with the camera. Her little-girl mock-innocent expression was familiar to Leonard: *Not me! Not me! I'm not a naughty girl, not me!*

34

Leonard stared; his heart beat in resentment. Here was a Valerie he hadn't known: mouth swollen from being kissed and from kissing; young, full breasts straining against the red fabric of the bikini top, and in the crescent of shadowy flesh between her breasts something coin-sized gleaming like oily sweat; her skin suffused with a warm, sensual radiance. Leonard understood that this young woman must be contained within the other, the elder who was his wife: as a secret, rapturous memory, inaccessible to him, the merely second husband.

Leonard was forty-five. Young for his age, but that age wasn't young.

When he'd been the age of Yardman in the photos, early or mid-twenties, he hadn't been young like Yardman, either. Painful to concede, but it was so.

If he, Leonard Chase, had approached the young woman in the photos, if he'd managed to enter Valerie's life in 1985, Valerie would not have given him a second glance. Not as a man. Not as a sexual partner. He knew this.

After lunch, the young couple would return to their hotel room and draw the blinds. Laughing and kissing, stumbling, like drunken dancers. They were naked together, beautiful smooth bodies coiled together, greedily kissing, caressing, thrusting together with the abandon of copulating animals. He saw them sprawled on the bed that would be a large jangly brass bed, and the room dimly lit, a fan turning indolently overhead, through slats in the blinds a glimpse of tropical sky, the graceful curve of a palm tree, a patch of bougainvillea moistly crimson as a woman's mouth . . . Leonard felt an unwelcome sexual stirring in his groin.

She lied. That's the insult.

Misrepresenting the first husband, the first marriage. Why?

Leonard knew why: Yardman had been Valerie's first serious love. Yardman was the standard of masculine sexuality in Valerie's life. *No love like your first.* The cache of Polaroids was Valerie's secret, a link to her private, erotic life.

Hurriedly he replaced the Polaroids in the drawer. The frayed rubber band had snapped; Leonard took no notice. He went away shaken, devastated. He thought, *I've never existed for her. It has all been a farce.*

In Rockland County, New York. In Salthill Landing, on the western bank of the Hudson River. Twenty miles north of the George Washington Bridge.

In one of the old stone houses overlooking the river: 'historic,' 'landmark.' Expensive.

Early that evening, as Valerie was preparing one of her gourmet meals in the kitchen, there was Leonard leaning in the doorway, a drink in hand. Asking, 'D'you ever hear of him, Val? What was his name, Yardman . . . ,' casually, as one who has only been struck by a wayward thought, and Valerie, frowning at a recipe, murmured no, but in so distracted a way Leonard wasn't sure that she'd heard, so he asked again, 'D'you ever hear of Yardman? Or from him?' and now Valerie glanced over at Leonard with a faint, perplexed smile. 'Yardman? No.' And Leonard said, 'Really? Never? In all these years?' and Valerie said, 'In all these years, darling, no.'

Valerie was peering at a recipe in a large, sumptuously illustrated cookbook propped up on a counter, pages clipped open. The cookbook was *Caribbean Kitchen:* Valerie was preparing flank steak, to be marinated and stuffed with sausage, hardboiled eggs, and vegetables, an ambitious meal that would involve an elaborate marinade and a yet more elaborate stuffing, and at this moment involved the almost surgical butterflying of the blood-oozing slab of meat. This was a meal Valerie hoped to prepare for a dinner party later in the month; she was determined to perfect it. A coincidence, Leonard thought, that only a few hours after he'd discovered the secret cache of Polaroids, Valerie was preparing an exotic Caribbean meal of the kind she might have first sampled in Key West with the first husband twenty years ago, but Leonard, who was a reasonable man, a tax lawyer who specialized in litigation in federal appellate courts, knew it could only be a coincidence.

Asking, in a tone of mild inquiry, 'What was

Yardman's first name, Val? I don't think you ever mentioned it,' and Valerie said, with an impatient little laugh, having taken up a steak knife to cut the meat horizontally, 'What does it matter what the name is?' Leonard noted that though he'd said *was*, Valerie had said *is*. The first husband was present to her; no time had passed. Leonard recalled an ominous remark of Freud's that in the unconscious all time is present tense, and so what has come to dwell most powerfully in the unconscious is felt to be immortal, unkillable. Valerie added, as if in rebuke, 'Of course I've mentioned his name, Leonard. Only just not in a long time.' She was having difficulty with the flank steak skidding about on the wooden block, so Leonard quickly set down his drink and held it secure, while Valerie, biting her lower lip, pursing her face like Caravaggio's Judith sawing off the head of the wicked king Holofernes, managed to inset the sharp blade, make the necessary incisions, complete the cut so that the meat could now be opened like the pages of a book. As Leonard watched, fascinated, yet with a sensation of mild revulsion, Valerie then covered the meat with a strip of plastic wrap and pounded at it with a meat mallet, short deft blows to reduce it to a uniform quarter-inch thickness. Leonard winced a little with the blows. He said, 'Did he – I mean Yardman – ever remarry?' and Valerie made an impatient gesture to signal that she didn't want to be distracted, not just now. This was important! This was to be their dinner! Carefully she slid the butterflied steak into a large, shallow dish and poured the marinade over it. Leonard saw that Valerie's face had thickened since she'd been Oliver Yardman's lover; her body had thickened, gravity was tugging at her breasts, thighs. At the corners of her eyes and mouth were fine white lines, and the coppery red hair had faded. Yet still Valerie was a striking woman, a rich man's daughter whose sense of her self-worth shone in her eyes, in her lustrous teeth, in her sharp dismissive laughter like the sheen of the expensive kitchen utensils hanging overhead. There was something sensual and languorous in Valerie's face when she concentrated on food, an almost childlike bliss, an air of happy expectation. Leonard thought, *Food is eros without the risk of heartbreak. Unlike a lover, food will never reject you.*

Leonard asked another time if Yardman had remarried and Valerie said, 'How would I know, darling?' in a tone of faint exasperation. Leonard said, 'From mutual friends, you might have heard.' Valerie carried the steak in a covered dish to the refrigerator, where it would marinate for two hours. They never ate before 8:30 P.M., and sometimes later; it was the custom of their lives together, for they'd never had children to necessitate early meals, the routines of a perfunctory American life. Valerie said, '"Mutual friends."' She laughed sharply. 'We don't have any.' Again Leonard noted the present tense: *don't.* 'And you've never kept in touch,' he said, and Valerie said, 'You know we didn't.' She was frowning, uneasy. Or maybe she was annoyed. To flare up in anger was a sign of weakness; Valerie hid such weaknesses. A sign of vulnerability, and Valerie was not vulnerable. Not any longer.

Leonard said, 'Well. That seems rather sad, in a way.'

At the sink, which was designed to resemble a deep, old-fashioned kitchen sink of another era, Valerie vigorously washed her hands, stained with watery blood. She washed the ten-inch gleaming knife with the surgically sharpened blade, each of the utensils she'd been using. It was something of a fetish for Valerie, to keep her beautiful kitchen as spotless as she could while working in it. As she took care to remove her jewelry to set aside as she worked.

On her left hand, Valerie wore the diamond engagement ring and the matching wedding band Leonard had given her. On her right hand, Valerie wore a square-cut emerald in an antique setting that she'd said she'd inherited from her grandmother. Only now did Leonard wonder if the emerald ring was the engagement ring her first husband had given her, which she'd shifted to her right hand after their marriage had ended.

'Sad for who, Leonard? Sad for me? For *you*?' That night, in their bed. A vast tundra of a bed. As if she'd sensed something in his manner, a subtle shift of tone, a quaver in his voice of withheld hurt, or anger, Valerie turned to him with a smile: 'I've been missing you, darling.' Her meaning might have been literal, for Leonard had been traveling for his firm lately, working with Atlanta lawyers in preparation for an appeal in the federal court there, but there was another meaning too. He thought, *She wants to make amends.* Their lovemaking was calm, measured, methodical, lasting perhaps eight minutes. It was their custom to make love at night, before sleep, the high-ceilinged bedroom lit by just a single lamp. There was a fragrance here of the lavender sachets Valerie kept in her bureau drawers. Except for the November wind overhead in the trees, it was very quiet. *Still as the grave,* Leonard thought. He sought his wife's smiling mouth with his mouth but could not find it. Shut his eyes, and there suddenly was the brazen coppery-haired girl in the red bikini top, waiting for him. Squirming in the darkly handsome young man's arms but glancing at him. Oh! she was a bad girl, look at the bad girl! Her mouth was hungry and sucking as a pike's mouth seeking the young man's mouth, her hand dropped beneath the tabletop to burrow in his lap. In his groin. Oh, the bad girl!

Leonard had the idea that Valerie's eyes were shut tight too. Valerie was seeing the young couple too. 'I found your passport, Valerie. I found these Polaroids too. Recognize them?'

Spreading them on the table. Better yet, across the bed.

'Only just curious, Val. Why you lied about him.'

She would stare, her smile fading. Her lips would

go slack as if, taken wholly unaware, she'd been slapped.

'. . . why you continue to lie. All these years.'

Of course, Leonard would be laughing. To indicate that he didn't take any of this seriously – why should he? It had happened so long ago, it was *past*.

Except: maybe 'lie' was too strong a word. The rich man's daughter wasn't accustomed to being spoken to in such a way, any more than Leonard was. 'Lie' would have the force of a physical blow. 'Lie' would cause Valerie to flinch as if she'd been struck, and the rich man's daughter would file for divorce at once if she were struck.

Maybe it wasn't a good idea, then. To confront her.

A litigator is a strategist plotting moves. A skilled litigator always knows how his opponent will respond to a move. As in chess, you must foresee the opponent's moves. Each blow can provoke a counterblow. If Leonard confronted her with the Polaroids, the gesture might backfire on him. She might detect in his voice a quaver of hurt, she might detect in his eyes a pang of male anguish. He was sometimes impotent, to his chagrin. He blamed distractions: the pressure of his work, which remained, even for those of his generation who had not been winnowed out by competition, competitive. The pressure of a man's expectations to 'perform.' The (literal) pressure of his blood, for which he took blood-pressure pills twice daily. And his back, which ached sometimes mysteriously, he'd attribute to tennis, golf. In fact, out of nowhere such phantom aches emerged. And so, in the vigorous act of love, Leonard might begin to lose his concentration, his erection. Like his life's blood leaking out of his veins. And Valerie knew – of course she knew, the terrible intimacy of the act precluded any secrets – yet she never commented, never said a word, only held him, her husband of nine years, her middle-aged flabby-waisted panting and sweating second husband, held him as if to comfort him, as a mother might hold a stricken child, with sympathy, unless it was with pity.

Darling, we won't speak of it. Our secret.

Yet if Leonard confronted her over the Polaroids, which were her cherished sexual secret, she might turn upon him, cruelly. She had that power. She might laugh at him. She would chide him for looking through her things – what right had he to look through her things, what if she searched through his desk drawers, would she discover soft-core porn magazines, ridiculous videos with titles like *Girls' Night Out, Girls at Play, Sex Addict Holiday?* She would expose him to their friends at the next Salthill Landing dinner party; dryly she would dissect him like an insect wriggling on a pin; at the very least she might slap the Polaroids out of his hand. How ridiculous he was being, over a trifle. How pitiable.

Leonard shuddered. A rivulet of icy sweat ran down the side of his cheek like a tear.

So, no. He would not confront her. Not just yet.

For the fact was, Leonard had the advantage: he knew of Valerie's secret attachment to the first husband, and Valerie had no idea he knew.

Smiling to think: like a boa constrictor swallowing its living prey paralyzed by terror, his secret would encompass Valerie's secret and would, in time, digest it.

The anniversary trip to Italy, scheduled for March, was to be postponed.

'It isn't a practical time after all. My work . . .'

And this was true. The Atlanta case had swerved in an unforeseen and perilous direction. There were obligations in Valerie's life too. '. . . not a practical time. But later . . .'

He saw in her eyes regret, yet also relief.

Doesn't want to be alone with me. Comparing me with him, isn't she!

'. . . a reservation for four, at L'Heure Bleu. If we arrive by six, maybe a little before six, we won't have to leave until quarter to eight, Lincoln Center is just across the street. But if you and Harold prefer the Tokyo Pavilion, I know you've been wanting to check it out after the review in the *Times*, and Leonard and I have too . . .'

In fact, Leonard disliked Japanese food. Hated sushi, which was so much raw flesh, inedible.

Where love has gone, he thought bitterly.

Listening to Valerie's maddeningly calm voice as she descended the stairs speaking on a cordless

44

phone to a friend. It was nearly two weeks since he'd discovered the Polaroids; he'd vowed not to look at them again. Yet he was approaching the cherrywood table, pulling open the drawer that stuck a little, groping another time for the packet of Polaroids, which seemed to be in exactly the place he'd left it, and he cursed his wife for being so careless, for not having taken time to hide her secret more securely.

"'Oliver and Val, Key West, December 1985.'"

With that childish pride, Valerie had felt the need to identify the lovers!

At a window overlooking a snowy slope to the river and the glowering winter sky, he examined the photographs eagerly. He had seen them several times by now and had more or less memorized them, and so they were both familiar and yet retained an air of the exotic and treacherous. One of the less faded Polaroids he brought close to his face, that he might squint at the ring worn by the coppery-haired girl – was it the emerald? Valerie was wearing it on her right hand even then, which might only mean that though Oliver Yardman had given it to her, it hadn't yet acquired the status of an engagement ring. In another photo, Leonard discovered what he'd somehow overlooked, the faintest suggestion of a bruise on Valerie's neck, or a shadow that very much resembled a bruise. And Oliver Yardman's smooth-skinned face wasn't really so smooth; in fact it looked coarse in certain of the photos. And that smug, petulant mouth Leonard would have liked to smash with his fist. And there was Yardman wriggling his long toes – wasn't there a correlation between the size of a man's toes and the size of . . .

Hurriedly Leonard shoved the Polaroids into the drawer and fled the room.

'The time for children is past.'

Years ago. Should have known the woman hadn't loved him, if she had not wanted children with him.

'. . . a kind of madness has come over parents today. Not just the expense: private schools, private tutors, college. Therapists! But you must subordinate your life to your children. My husband' – Valerie's voice dipped; this was a hypothetical, it was Leonard to whom she spoke so earnestly – 'would be working in the city five days a week and wouldn't be home until evening, and can you see me as a soccer mom, driving children to – wherever! Living through it all again and this time knowing what's to come? My God, it would be so *raw*.'

Valerie laughed; there was fear in her eyes.

Leonard was astonished; this poised, beautiful woman was speaking so intimately to him! Of course he comforted her, gripping her cold hands. Kissed her hair where she'd leaned toward him, trembling.

'Valerie, of course. I feel the same way.'

He did! In that instant, Leonard did.

They'd been introduced by mutual friends. Leonard was a highly paid litigator attached to the legal department of the most distinguished architectural firm in New York City, its headquarters in lower Manhattan on Rector Street. Leonard's specialty was tax law, and within that specialty he prepared and argued cases in federal appeals courts. He was one of a team. There were enormous penalties for missteps, sometimes in the hundreds of millions of dollars. And there were enormous rewards when things went well.

'A litigator goes for the jugular.'

Valerie wasn't one to flatter, you could see. Her admiration was sincere.

Leonard had laughed, blushing with pleasure. In his heart thinking he was one in a frantic swarm of piranha fish and not the swiftest, most deadly, or even, at thirty-four, as he'd been at the time, among the youngest.

The poised, beautiful young woman was Valerie Fairfax. Her maiden name: crisp, clear, Anglo, unambiguous. (Not a hint of Yardman.) At Citibank headquarters in Manhattan, Valerie had the title of vice president of human resources. How serious she was about her work! She wore Armani suits in subdued tones: oatmeal, powder gray, charcoal. She wore pencil-thin skirts and she wore trousers with sharp creases. She wore trim little jackets with slightly padded shoulders. Her hair was stylishly razor-cut to frame her face, to suggest delicacy where there was in fact solidity. Her fragrance was discreet, faintly astringent. Her handshake was firm and yet, in certain circumstances, yielding. She displayed little interest in speaking of the past, though she spoke animatedly on a variety of subjects. She thought well of herself and wished to think well of Leonard and so had a way of making Leonard more interesting to himself, more mysterious.

The first full night they spent together, in the apartment on East 79th Street where Leonard was living at the time, a flush of excitement had come into Valerie's face as, after several glasses of wine, she confessed how at Citibank she was the vice president of her department elected to fire people because she was so good at it.

'I never let sentiment interfere with my sense of justice. It's in my genes, I think.'

Now you didn't say *fired*. You said *downsized*.

You might say *dismissed, terminated*. You might say, of vanished colleagues, *gone*.

Leonard typed into his laptop a private message to himself:

Not me. Not this season. They can't!

Another time, in fact many times, he'd typed *Yardman* into his computer. (At the office, not at home. He and Valerie shared a computer at home. Leonard knew that in cyberspace, nothing is ever

48

erased, though it might be subsequently regretted, and so at home he never typed into the computer anything he might not wish his wife to discover in some ghost-remnant way.) Hundreds of citations for *Yardman*, but none for *Oliver Yardman* so far.

He meant to keep looking.

'. . . first husband.'

Like an abscessed tooth secretly rotting in his jaw.

In his office on the twenty-ninth floor at Rector Street. On the 7:10 A.M. Amtrak into Grand Central Station and on the 6:55 P.M Amtrak out of Grand Central returning to Salthill Landing. In the interstices of his relations with others: colleagues, clients, fellow commuters, social acquaintances, friends. In the cracks of a densely scheduled life, the obsession with Oliver Yardman grew the way the hardiest weeds will flourish in soil scarcely hospitable to plant life.

Sure he knows. Knows of me: second husband. What he must remember! Of her.

Had to wonder how often Valerie glanced through the Polaroids in the desk drawer. How frequently, even when they'd been newly lovers, she'd shut her eyes to summon back the first husband, the sulky spoiled mouth, the brazen hands, the hard stiff penis thrumming with blood that would never flag, even as she was breathless and panting in Leonard's arms declaring she loved *him*.

49

Since the discovery weeks ago in November, he'd looked for other photos. Not in the photo album Valerie maintained with seeming sincerity and wifely pride but in Valerie's drawers, closets. In the most remote regions of the large house, where things were stored away in boxes. Shrewdly thinking that because he hadn't found anything did not mean there was nothing to be found.

'Len Chase!'

A bright female voice, a Salthill Landing neighbor leaning over his seat. (Where was he? On the Amtrak? Headed home? Judging by the murky haze above the river, early evening, had to be headed home.) Leonard's laptop was open before him and his fingers were poised over the flat keyboard, but he'd been staring out the window for some minutes without moving. '. . . thought that was you, Len, and how is Valerie? Haven't seen you since, has it been Christmas, or . . .'

Leonard smiled politely at the woman. His open laptop, his document bag and overcoat on the seat beside him – these were clear signals he didn't want to be interrupted, which the woman surely knew, but she had come to an age when she'd decided not to see such signals in cheerful denial of their meaning: *Please leave me alone, you are not of interest to me, not as a woman, not as an individual, you are nothing but a minor annoyance.* Melanie Roberts was Valerie's age, and her frosted hair was razor-cut in Valerie's style. Very likely Melanie was a rich man's daughter as well as a rich man's wife, but the advantage she'd held as a younger woman had mysteriously faded, even so. Melanie seemed to think that her neighbor Leonard Chase might wish to know that she'd had lunch with friends in the city and gone to see the Rauschenberg exhibit at the Metropolitan Museum and then she'd dropped by to visit her niece at Barnard. Melanie was watching Leonard with sparkly expectant eyes in which dwelled some uneasiness, a fear of seeing in Leonard's face exactly what he was thinking. He had to concede, he saw in Melanie Roberts's face that he might still be perceived as an attractive man; in his seated position he appeared moderately tall, with a head of moderately thick hair, graying, but attractively graying; his skin tone was slightly sallow, but perhaps that was just the flickering Amtrak lighting; his face was dented in odd places, and loosely jowly in others; his nostrils looked enlarged, like pits opening into his skull; his eyes behind wire-rimmed bifocal glasses were shadowed and smudged; yet he would seem to this yearning woman more attractive than paunchy near-bald Sam Roberts, as others' spouses invariably seem more attractive, since more mysterious, than our own. For intimacy is the enemy of romance. The dailiness of marriage is the enemy of immortality. Who would wish to be immortal if it's a matter of reliving just the past week?

Melanie Roberts's smile was fading. Amid her chatter, Leonard must have interrupted. '. . . hear you, Len? It's so noisy in this . . .'

51

The car was swaying drunkenly. The lights flickered. With a nervous laugh Melanie gripped the back of the seat to steady herself. Another eight minutes to Salthill Landing – why was the woman hanging over his seat! He yearned to be touched, his numbed body caressed in love, so desperately he yearned for this touch that would be the awakening from a curse, but he shrank from intimacy with this woman who was his neighbor in Salt-hill Landing. On his open laptop screen was a column of e-mail messages he hadn't answered, in fact hadn't read, as he hadn't for most of that day returned phone messages, for a terrible gravity pulled his mind elsewhere. *The first husband. You cannot be first.* Melanie was saying brightly that she would call Valerie and maybe this weekend they could go out together to dinner, that new seafood restaurant in Nyack everyone has been talking about, and Leonard laughed, with a nod toward the window beside his seat where some distance below the oily dark sprawl of the Hudson River was lapsing into dusk: 'Ever think, Melanie, that river is like a gigantic boa constrictor? It's like time, eventually to swallow and digest us all?'

Melanie laughed sharply as if not hearing this, or hearing enough to know that she didn't really want to hear more of it. Promising she'd tell Sam hello from him and she'd call Valerie very soon, with a faint, forced smile lurching away somewhere behind Leonard Chase to her seat.

He would track down the first husband, he would erase the man from consciousness. He would erase the man's memory, in which his own wife existed. Except he was a civilized human being, a decent human being, except he feared being apprehended and punished, that was what he would do.

Early November when he'd discovered the Key West photos. Late February when his CEO called him into his office in the tower.

The meeting was brief. One or two others had been taken to lunch first, which had not been a good idea; Leonard was grateful to be spared lunch. Through a roaring in his ears he heard. Watched the man's piranha mouth. Steely eyes through bifocal glasses like his own.

Downsized. Stock options. Severance pay. Any questions?

He had no legal grounds to object. Possibly he had moral grounds, but he wouldn't contest it. He knew the company's financial situation. Since 9/11 they'd been in a tailspin. These were facts you might read in the *Wall Street Journal*. Then came the terrible blow, unexpected – at least, Leonard believed it to be unexpected – the ruling in Atlanta: a federal court judge upheld a crushing $33 million award to a hotel-chain plaintiff plus $8 million in punitive damages. The architectural firm for which he'd worked for the past seven years was hard hit. Conceding yes, he understood. Failure was a sickness that burned like fever in the eyes of the afflicted. No disguising that fever, like jaundice-yellow eyes.

Soon to be forty-six. Burned out. The battlefield is strewn with burned-out litigators. His fingers shook, cold as a corpse's, yet he would shake the CEO's hand in parting, he would meet the man's gaze with something like dignity.

He had the use of his office for several more weeks. And the stock options and severance pay were generous. And Valerie wouldn't need to know exactly what had happened, possibly ever.

'. . . seem distracted lately, Leonard. I hope it isn't . . .'

They were undressing for bed. That night in their large, beautifully furnished bedroom. Gusts of wind rattled the windows, which were leaded windows, inset with wavy glass in mimicry of the old glass that had once been, when the original house had been built in 1791.

'. . . anything serious? Your health . . .'

From his corner of the room Leonard called over, in a voice meant to comfort, that of course he was fine, his health was fine. Of course.

'Damned wind! It's been like this all day.'

Valerie spoke fretfully, as if someone were to blame.

Neither had brought up the subject of the trip to Italy in some time. Postponed to March, but no specific plans had been made. The tenth anniversary had come and gone.

In her corner of their bedroom, an alcove with a built-in dresser and closets with mirrors affixed to their doors, Valerie was undressing as, in his corner of the bedroom, a smaller alcove with but a single mirrored door, Leonard was undressing. As if casually, Leonard called over to her, 'Did you ever love me, Valerie? When you first married me, I mean.' In his mirror Leonard could see just a blurred glimmer of one of Valerie's mirrors. She seemed not to have heard his question. The wind buffeting the house was so very loud. 'For a while? In the beginning? Was there a time?' Not knowing if his voice was pleading or threatening. If, if this woman heard, like the frightened woman on the train she would laugh nervously and wish to escape him.

'Maybe I should murder us both, Valerie. 'Downsize.' It could end very quickly.'

He didn't own a gun. Had no access to a gun. Rifle? Could you go into a sporting goods store and buy a rifle? A shotgun? Not a handgun; he knew that was more difficult in New York State. You had to apply for a license, there was a background check, paperwork. The thought made his head ache.

'. . . that sound, what is it? I'm frightened.'

In her corner of the room Valerie stood very still. How like an avalanche the wind was sounding! There had been warnings over the years that the hundred-foot cliff above Salthill Landing might one day collapse after a heavy rainstorm, and there had been small landslides from time to time, and now it began to sound as if the cliff might be disintegrating, a slide of rock, rubble, uprooted trees rushing toward the house, about to collapse the roof . . . In his corner of the room Leonard stood as if transfixed, his shirt partly unbuttoned, in his stocking feet, waiting.

They would die together, in the debris. How quickly, then, the end would come!

No avalanche, only the wind. Valerie shut the door of her bathroom firmly behind her; Leonard continued undressing and climbed into bed. It was a vast tundra of a bed, with a hard mattress. By morning the terrible wind would subside. Another dawn! Mists on the river, a white wintry sun behind layers of cloud. Another day Leonard Chase would enter with dignity, he was certain.

2.

'Dwayne Ducharme, eh? Welcome to Denver.'

There came Mitchell Oliver Yardman to shake Leonard's hand in a crushing grip. He was 'Mitch' Yardman, realtor and insurance agent, and he appeared to be the only person on duty at Yardman Realty & Insurance this afternoon.

'Not that this is Denver, eh? Makeville is what this is here – you wouldn't call it a suburb of anyplace. Used to be a mining town, see. Probably you never heard of Makeville back east, and this kind of scenery, prob'ly you're thinking ain't what you'd expect of the West, eh? Well, see, Dwayne Ducharme, like I warned you on the phone: this is east Colorado. High desert plain. The Rockies is in the other direction.'

Yardman's smile was wide and toothy yet somehow grudging, as if he resented the effort such a smile required. Here was a man who'd been selling real estate for a long time, you could see. Even as he spoke in his grating mock-western drawl, Yardman's shrewd eyes were rapidly appraising his prospective client Dwayne Ducharme, who'd made an appointment to see small ranch properties within commuting distance of Denver.

So this was Oliver Yardman! Twenty-one years after the Key West idyll, the man had thickened, grown coarser, yet there was the unmistakable sexual swagger, the sulky spoiled-boy mouth.

Yardman was shorter than Leonard had expected, burly and as solid-built as a fire hydrant. He had a rucked forehead and a fleshy nose riddled with small broken veins, and his breath was meaty, sour. He wore a leathery-looking cowboy hat, an expensive-looking rumpled suede jacket, a lime-green shirt with a black string tie looped around his neck, rumpled khakis, badly scuffed leather boots. He seemed impatient, edgy. His hands, which were busily gesticulating in twitchy swoops like the gestures of a deranged magician, were noticeably large, with stubby

57

fingers, and on the smallest finger of his left hand he wore a showy gold signet ring with a heraldic crest.

The first husband. Leonard's heart kicked in his chest; he was in the presence of his enemy.

In the office, which was hardly more than a storefront and smelled of stale cigarette smoke, Yardman showed Leonard photographs of 'ranch-type' properties within 'easy commuting distance' of downtown Denver. In his aggressive, mock-friendly, yet grudging voice, Yardman kept up a continual banter, peppering Leonard with facts, figures, statistics, punctuating his words with *Eh?* It was a verbal tic that Yardman seemed unaware of or was helpless to control, and Leonard steeled himself waiting to hear it, dry-mouthed with apprehension that Yardman was suspicious of him, eyeing him so intimately.

'. . . tight schedule, eh? Goin' back tomorrow, you said? Said your firm's relocating? Some kinda computer parts, eh? There's a lot of that in Denver, 'lectronics, chips, these are boom times for some, eh? Demographics're movin west, for sure. Population shift. Back east, billion-dollar companies goin' down the toilet, you hear.' Yardman laughed heartily, amused by the spectacle of companies going down a toilet.

Leonard said, in Dwayne Ducharme's earnest voice, 'Mr Yardman, I've been very—'

'Mitch. Call me Mitch, eh?'

'Mitch. I've been very lucky to be transferred to

58

our Denver branch. My company has been downsized, but—'

'Tell me about it, man! Downsize. Cut back. Ain't that the story of these United States lately, eh?' Yardman was suddenly vehement, incensed. His pronunciation was savage: *Yoo-nited States*.

Leonard said, with an air of stubborn naiveté, 'Mr Yardman, my wife and I think of this as a once-in-a-lifetime opportunity. To relocate to the West from the crowded East. We're Methodist Evangelicals, and the church is flourishing in Colorado, and we have a twelve-year-old boy dying to raise horses, and my wife thinks—'

'That is so interesting, Dwayne,' Yardman interrupted, with a rude smirk. 'You are one of a new pioneer breed relocating to our wide-open spaces and relaxed way of life and lower taxes. Seems to me I have just the property for you: six-acre ranch, four-bedroom house for the growin' family, barn in good repair, creek runs through the property, fences, shade trees, aspens, in kinda a valley where there's deer and antelope to hunt. Just went on the market a few days ago. Dwayne Ducharme, this is serendip'ty, eh?'

Yardman locked up the office. Pulled down a sign on the front door: CLOSED. When he wasn't facing Leonard, his sulky mouth retained its fixed smile.

Outside, the men had a disagreement: Yardman wanted to drive his prospective client to the ranch, which was approximately sixteen miles away, and

59

Leonard insisted on driving his rental car. Yardman said, 'Why'n hell we need two vehicles, eh? Save gas. Keep each other company. It's the usual procedure, see.' Yardman's vehicle was a new-model Suburban with smoke-tinted windows, bumper stickers featuring the American flag, and a dented right rear door. It was both gleaming black and splattered with mud like coarse lace. Inside, a dog was barking excitedly, throwing itself against the window nearest Leonard and slobbering the glass. 'That's Kaspar. Spelled with a *K*. Bark's worse 'n his bite. Kaspar ain't goin' to bite you, Dwayne, I guarantee.' Yardman slammed the flat of his hand against the window, commanding the dog to 'settle down.' Kaspar was an Airedale, purebred, Yardman said. Damn good breed, but needs discipline. 'You buy this pretty li'l property out at Mineral Springs for your family, you'll want a dog. 'Man's best friend' is no bullshit.'

But Leonard didn't want to ride with Yardman and Kaspar; Leonard would drive his own car. Yardman stared at him, baffled. Clearly, Yardman was a man not accustomed to being contradicted or thwarted in the smallest matters. He said, barely troubling to disguise his contempt, 'Well, Dwayne, you do that. You in your li'l Volva, Volvo, Vulva, you do that. Kaspar and me will drive ahead, see you don't get lost.'

In a procession of two vehicles they drove through the small town of Makeville in the traffic of early

60

Saturday afternoon, in late March. It was a windy day, tasting of snow. Overhead were massive clouds like galleons. What a relief, to be free of Yardman's overpowering personality! Leonard hadn't slept well the night before, nor the night before that; his nerves were strung tight. In his compact rental car he followed the military-looking black Suburban through blocks of undistinguished storefronts, stucco apartment buildings, taverns, X-rated video stores, and onto a state highway crowded with the usual fast-food restaurants, discount outlets, gas stations, strip malls. All that seemed to remain of Makeville's mining-town past were the Gold Strike Go-Go, Strike-It-Rich Lounge, Silver Lining Barbecue. Beyond the highway was a mesa landscape of small stunted trees, rocks. To get to Yardman Realty & Insurance at 661 Main Street, Makeville, Leonard had had a forty-minute drive from the Denver airport through a dispiriting clog of traffic and air hazier than the air of Manhattan on most days.

He thought, *Can he guess? Any idea who I am?*

He was excited, edgy. No one knew where Leonard Chase was.

Outside town, where the speed limit was fifty-five miles an hour, Yardman pushed the Suburban toward seventy, leaving Leonard behind. It was to punish him, Leonard knew: Yardman allowed other vehicles to come between him and Leonard, then pulled off onto the shoulder of the road to allow Leonard to catch up. In a gesture of genial contempt, Yardman signaled to him and pulled out onto the highway before him, fast. In the rear window of the Suburban was an American flag. On the rear bumper were stickers: BUSH CHENEY USA; KEEP HONKING, I'M RELOADING.

Yardman's family must have been rich at one time. Yardman had been sent east to college. Though he played the yokel, it was clear that the man was shrewd, calculating. Something had happened in his personal life and in his professional life, possibly a succession of things. He'd had money, but not now. Valerie would never have married Yardman otherwise. Wouldn't have kept the lewd Polaroids for more than two decades.

If he guessed. What?

The Suburban was pulling away again, passing an eighteen-wheel rig. Leonard could turn off at any time, drive back to the airport and take a flight back to Chicago. He'd told Valerie that he would be in Chicago for a few days on business, and this was true: Leonard had a job interview with a Chicago firm needing a tax litigator with federal court experience. He hadn't told Valerie that he'd been severed from the Rector Street firm and was sure that there could be no way she might know. He'd been commuting into the city five days a week, schedule unaltered. His CEO had seen to it. He'd been treated with courtesy: allowed the use of his office for several weeks while he searched for a new job. Except for one or two unfortunate episodes, he got along well with his old colleagues. Once or twice he showed up unshaven, disheveled; most of the time he seemed unchanged. White cotton shirt, striped tie, dark pinstripe suit. He continued to have his shoes shined in Grand Central Station. In his office, door shut, he stared out the window. Or clicked through the Internet. So few law firms were interested in him, at forty-six: 'down-sized.' But he'd tracked down Yardman in this way. And the interview in Chicago was genuine. Leonard Chase's impressive resumé, the 'strong, supportive' recommendation his CEO had promised, were genuine.

Valerie had ceased touching his arm, his cheek. Valerie had ceased asking in a concerned voice, *Is anything wrong, darling?*

This faint excitement, edginess. He'd been in high-altitude terrain before. Beautiful Aspen, where they'd gone skiing just once. Also Santa Fe. Denver was a mile above sea level, and Leonard's breath was coming quickly and shallowly in the wake of Yardman's vehicle. His pulse was fast; he was elated. He knew that after a day, the sensation of excitement would shift to a dull throbbing pain behind his eyes. But he hoped by then to be gone from Colorado.

Mineral Springs. This part of the area certainly didn't look prosperous. Obviously there were wealthy Denver suburbs and outlying towns, but this wasn't one of them. The land continued flat and monotonous, and its predominant hue was the hue of dried manure. Leonard had expected mountains, at least. In the other direction, Yardman had said with a smirk – but where? The jagged skyline of Denver, behind Leonard, to his right, was lost in a soupy brown haze.

The Suburban turned off onto a potholed road. United Church of Christ in a weathered wood-frame building, a mobile home park, small asphalt-sided houses set back in scrubby lots in sudden and unexpected proximity to Quail Ridge Acres, a 'custom-built,' 'luxury home' housing development sprawling out of sight. There began to be more open land, ranches with grazing cattle, horses close beside the road lifting their long heads as Leonard passed by. The sudden beauty of a horse can take your breath away; Leonard had forgotten. He felt a pang of loss that he had no son. No one to move west with him, raise horses in Colorado.

Yardman was turning the Suburban onto a long bumpy lane. Here was the Flying S Ranch. A pair of badly worn steer horns hung crooked on the open front gate, in greeting. Leonard pulled up behind Yardman and parked. A sensation of acute loneliness and yearning swept over him. *If we could live here! Begin over again!* Except he needed to be younger, and Valerie needed to be a different woman.

Yet here was a possible home: a long, flat-roofed wood-and-stucco ranch house with a slapdash charm, needing repair, repainting, new shutters, probably a new roof. You could see a woman's touches: stone urns in the shape of swans flanking the front door, the remains of a rock garden in the front yard. Beyond the house were several outbuildings, a silo. In a shed, a left-behind tractor. Mounds of rotted hay, dried manure. Fences in varying stages of dereliction. Yet there was a striking view of a sweeping, sloping plain and a hilly terrain – a mesa? – in the distance. Pierced with sunshine, the sky was beautiful, a hard glassy blue behind clouds like gigantic sculpted figures. Leonard saw that from the rear of the ranch house you'd have a view of the hills, marred only by what looked like the start of a housing development far to the right. If you stared straight ahead, you might not notice the intrusion.

As Leonard approached the Suburban, he saw that Yardman was leaning against the side of the vehicle, speaking tersely into a cell phone. His face was a knot of flesh. Kaspar the purebred Airedale was loose, trotting excitedly about, sniffing at the rock garden and lifting his leg. When he sighted Leonard, he rushed at him, barking frantically and baring his teeth. Yardman shouted, 'Back off, Kaspar! Damn dog, *obey!*' When Leonard shrank back, shielding himself with his arms, Yardman scolded him too: 'Kaspar is all damn bark and no bite, din't I tell you? Eh? C'mon, boy. Fuckin' sit. *Now.*' With a show of reluctance, Kaspar obeyed his red-faced master. Leonard hadn't known that Airedales were so large. This one had a wiry, coarse tan-and-black coat, a grizzled snout of a muzzle, and moist dark vehement eyes like his master.

Yardman shut up the cell phone and tried to arrange his face into a pleasant smile. As he unlocked the front door and led Leonard into the house, he said, in his salesman's genial blustery voice, 'Churches, eh? You seen 'em? On the way out here? This is strong Christian soil. Earliest settlers. Prots'ant stock. There's a Mormon population too. Those folks are serious.' Yardman sucked his fleshly lips, considering the Mormons. There was something to be acknowledged about *those folks*, maybe money.

The ranch house looked as if it hadn't been occupied in some time. Leonard, glancing about with a vague, polite smile, as a prospective buyer might, halfway wondered if something, a small creature perhaps, had crawled beneath the house and died. Yardman forestalled any question from his client by telling a joke: '. . . punishment for bigamy? Eh? Two wives.' His laughter was loud and meant to be infectious.

Leonard smiled at the thought of Valerie stepping into such a house. Not very likely! The woman's sensitive soul would be bruised in proximity to what Yardman described as the 'remodeled' kitchen with the 'fantastic view of the hills' and, in the living room, an unexpected spectacle of left-behind furniture: a long, L-shaped sofa in a nubby butterscotch fabric, a large showy glass-topped coffee table with a spiderweb crack in the glass, deep-piled stained beige wall-to-wall carpeting. Two steps down into a family room with a large fireplace and another 'fantastic view of the hills' and stamped-cardboard rock walls. Seeing the startled expression on Leonard's face, Yardman said with a grim smile, 'Hey, sure, a new homeowner might wish to remodel here some. Renovate. They got their taste, you got yours. Like Einstein said, there's no free lunch in the universe.'

Yardman was standing close to Leonard, as if daring him to object. Leonard said, in a voice meant to be quizzical, 'No free lunch in the universe? I don't understand, Mr Yardman.'

'Means you get what you pay for, see. What you don't pay for, you don't get. Philos'phy of life, eh?' Yardman must have been drinking in the Suburban; his breath smelled of whiskey and his words were slightly slurred.

As if to placate the realtor, Leonard said of course he understood: any new property he bought, he'd likely have to put some money into. 'All our married lives it's been my wife's and my dream to purchase some land, and this is our opportunity. My wife has just inherited a little money – not much, but a little' – Dwayne Ducharme's voice quavered, in fear this might sound inadvertently boastful – 'and we would use this.' Such naive enthusiasm drew from Yardman a wary predator smile. Leonard could almost hear the realtor thinking, *Here is a fool, too good to be true.* Yardman murmured, 'Wise, Dwayne. Very wise.'

Yardman led Leonard into the master bedroom, where a grotesque pink-toned mirror covered one of the walls, and in this mirror, garishly reflected, the men loomed overlarge, as if magnified. Yardman laughed as if taken by surprise, and Leonard looked quickly away, shocked that he'd shaved so carelessly that morning: graying stubble showed on the left side of his face, and there was a moist red nick in the cleft of his chin. His eyes were set in hollows like ill-fitting sockets in a skull, and his clothes – a tweed sport coat, a candy-striped shirt – looked rumpled and damp, as if he'd been sleeping in them, as perhaps he had been, intermittently, on the long flight from New York to Chicago to Denver.

Luckily, the master bedroom had a plate-glass sliding door that Yardman managed to open, and the men stepped quickly out into fresh air. Almost immediately there came rushing at Leonard the frantically barking Airedale, who would certainly have bitten him except Yardman intervened. This time he not only shouted at the dog but struck him on the snout, on the head, dragged him away from Leonard by his collar, cursed and kicked him until the dog cowered whimpering at his feet, its stubby tail wagging. 'Damn asshole. You blew it. Fuckin' busted now. Every one of 'em in the fuckin' family, ain't it the same fuckin' story.' Flush-faced, deeply shamed by the dog's behavior, Yardman dragged the whimpering Airedale around the house to the driveway where the

Suburban was parked. Leonard pressed his hands over his ears, not wanting to hear Yardman's furious cursing and the dog's broken-hearted whimpering as Yardman must have forced him back inside the vehicle, to lock him in. He thought, *That dog is his only friend. He might kill that dog.*

Leonard walked quickly away from the house, as if eager to look at the silo, which was partly collapsed in a sprawl of what looked like fossilized corncobs and mortar, and a barn the size of a three-car garage with a slumping roof and a strong odor of manure and rotted hay, pleasurable in his nostrils. In a manure pile a pitchfork was stuck upright, as if someone had abruptly decided that he'd had enough of ranch life and had departed. Leonard felt a thrill of excitement, unless it was a thrill of dread. He had no clear idea why he was here, being shown the derelict Flying S Ranch in Mineral Springs, Colorado. Why he'd sought out Mitch Yardman. The first husband, Oliver Yardman. If his middle-aged wife cherished erotic memories of this man as he'd been twenty years before, what was that to Leonard? He was staring at his hands, lifted before him, palms up in a gesture of honest bewilderment. He wore gloves, which seemed to steady his hands. He'd been noticing lately, these past several months, that his hands sometimes shook.

Just outside the barn, Yardman had paused to make another call on his cell phone. He was leaving a message, his voice low-pitched, threatening and yet seductive. 'Hey babe. 'S me. Where the fuck are ya, babe? Call me. I'm here.' He broke the connection, cursing under his breath.

At the rear of the barn, looking out at the hills, Yardman caught up with Leonard. The late-afternoon sky was still vivid with light, massive clouds in oddly vertical sculpted columnar shapes. Leonard was staring at these shapes, flexing his fingers in his leather gloves. Yardman swatted at his shoulder as if they were new friends linked in a common enterprise; his breath smelled of fresh whiskey. 'Quite a place, eh? Makes a man dream, eh? Big sky country. That's the West, see. I lived awhile in the East, fuckin' hemmed in. No place for a man. Always wanted a nice li'l ranch like this. Decent life for a man, raise horses, not damn rat-race real estate . . . Any questions for me, Dwayne? Like, is the list price negotiable? Or—'

'Did you always live in Makeville, Mr Yardman – Mitch?' Dwayne Ducharme had a way of speaking bluntly yet politely. 'Just curious!'

Yardman said, tilting his leathery cowboy hat to look his client frankly in the face, 'Hell, no. The Yardmans is all over at Littleton. Makeville is just me. And that's temp'ry.'

'Yardman Realty & Insurance is a family business, is it?'

'Well, sure. Used to be. Now just me, mostly.'

Yardman spoke with an air of vaguely shamed

regret. *Burned out*, Leonard was thinking. Yardman's sulky mouth seemed about to admit more, then pursed shut.

'You said you lived in the East, Mitch . . .'

'Not long.'

'Ever travel to, well – Florida? Key West?'

Yardman squinted at Leonard, as if trying to decide whether to be amused or annoyed by him. 'Yah, I guess. Long time ago. Why're you askin', friend?'

'It's just, you look familiar. Like someone I saw, might have seen once, I think it was Key West . . .' Leonard was smiling; a roaring came up in his ears. As in court, he sometimes had to pause to get his bearings. 'Do you have a family? I mean, wife, children . . .'

'Friend, I know what you mean,' Yardman said grimly. 'Some of us got just as much family as we need, know what I'm saying?'

'I'm afraid that—'

'Means my private life is off-limits, Dwayne.' Yardman laughed. His face crinkled. 'Hey, man, just kidding. A wife's a wife, eh? Kid's a kid? Been there, done that. Three fucking times, Dwayne. Three strikes, you're out.'

He'd been married three times? Divorced three times? Risky for naive Dwayne Ducharme to say, with a provocative smile, 'No love like your first. They say.'

'No fuck like your first. But that's debatable.'

71

Leonard froze. Had Valerie been Yardman's first? One of the first, maybe. Leonard believed this must be so.

Now Yardman meant to turn the conversation back to real estate: in his hand was a swath of fact sheets. Any questions? Mortgages, interest rates? 'There's where Mitch Yardman's expertise kicks in.'

'Yes. I have questions.' Leonard's voice quavered; his mouth had gone dry. For a moment his mind had gone blank. Then, pointing: 'Those hills over there? Is that area being . . . being . . . developed? On the way in I saw some bulldozers . . .'

Yardman scowled, shading his eyes. As if he'd never seen such a sight before, he said, shrugging, 'Seems there might be something going on there, that ridge. But the rest of the valley through here, and your own sweet li'l creek that your boy will be crazy for wading in, running through it, see? – that's in pristine shape.'

Yardman swatted Leonard's shoulder companionably as he turned to lead his credulous client back to the driveway. It was that touch, that suggestion of brotherly solicitude, that made Leonard recoil. A thrill of pure loathing, revulsion, hit him like adrenaline.

Swiftly it happened: the pitchfork was in Leonard's hands, leather gloves gripping tight. So this was why he'd taken care to wear leather gloves! Without so much as grunting with the effort, Leonard had managed to wrench the heavy pronged implement out of the hardened manure

72

pile, and in the next instant, as the garrulous man was about to step outside, Leonard came up behind him and shoved the prongs against his lower back, knocking him violently forward, off-balance; and as Yardman turned in astonishment, desperate to grab hold of the thrusting prongs, Leonard shoved the pitchfork a second time, and a third, at the man's unprotected throat.

How quickly then what happened, happened. Afterward Leonard would have but a dazed and fragmented memory, as of a fever dream.

Yardman on his knees, terror shining in his eyes, and perplexity – what was happening to him? And why? Now fallen and flailing on the dirt floor, straw and bits of manure floating in swirls of dark blood. Leonard thought, *Earth is dark, blood is dark – it will soak in, it won't be noticed.* As Leonard circled Yardman, striking at him with the pitchfork, the wounded man was fighting to live, bleeding from numerous wounds, now pleading for his life. Yet Leonard had no mercy – he hadn't come thousands of miles to exact mercy! With the unexpected strength of his shoulders, he drove the prongs into Yardman's bleeding chest, Yardman's forearms raised to protect his face. Several feet away the leather cowboy hat lay, thrown clear.

Leonard stood over the dying man, panting. So strange that his fury hadn't abated but seemed to have burst from him into the very air: 'Laugh now! Make a joke now! What's funny now? Yardman.'

The man's name was flung from his mouth, like spittle.

Emerging then from the barn. Uncertain of his surroundings, and he was very tired, arms like lead. Where was this? He'd last slept – couldn't remember; on the plane? Jolting and unsatisfying sleep. And when he'd called home, the phone had rung in the empty house in Salthill Landing, and when he'd called Valerie's cell phone, there had been no answer, not even a ring.

There in the driveway was the Suburban, parked where Yardman had left it. At the rear window the Airedale barked frantically. The heavy pitchfork was still in Leonard's hands; he'd seemed to know that there was more effort to be made. Once begun, such an effort was not easily stopped. Though his hands in the blood-splashed leather gloves ached as if the bones had cracked, he had no choice; Yardman's dog was a witness, could identify him. Slowly he approached the Suburban. The Airedale barked louder, slobbering against the window. Leonard cautiously opened one of the rear doors, speaking to the dog in Yardman's commanding/cajoling way, but the vehicle was built so high off the ground it was awkward for Leonard to lean inside, virtually impossible for him to maneuver the pitchfork, to stab at the dog. Leonard glanced down at himself and saw in horror that his trousers were splattered with dark liquid. The maddened dog was smelling blood. *His master's blood. He knows.*

74

It was becoming increasingly difficult for Leonard to think clearly. A mist seemed to have pervaded his brain. 'Kaspar? Come here . . .' But the panicked dog had leapt into the front seat of the SUV and so with a grunt Leonard managed to climb into the rear of the vehicle, again trying to maneuver the pitchfork, to strike at the dog, but unable to get leverage, and in an instant, quick as an adder's thrust, the Airedale managed to sink his teeth into Leonard's exposed wrist, and Leonard cried out in surprise and pain and hastily climbed out of the vehicle, dragging the pitchfork behind him. For he must not surrender the pitchfork, he knew. Standing dazed in the driveway in this place he couldn't now clearly recall, which seemed to be tilting beneath him as in a mild earthquake. The flesh at his right wrist was torn, bleeding? A dog had attacked him? Why?

He glanced around to see a dust-colored pickup approaching from the road. A male figure wearing a cowboy hat in the driver's seat, a female figure beside him, staring. Seeing the bloodied pitchfork in Leonard's hands, they stared. There came a man's hoarse voice: 'Mister? You in need of help?'

STRIP POKER

That day at Wolf's Head Lake! Nobody ever knew.

Of my family, I mean. Not even Daddy. I did not tell Daddy.

It was late August. Humid-hot August. At the lake you'd see these giant thunderhead clouds edging across the sky like a mouth closing over, and in the mountains, streaks of heat lightning that appear and disappear so swiftly you can't be sure that you have actually seen them. For kids my age, nothing much to do except swim – unless you liked fishing, which I did not, or boating, but we didn't own a boat – and the only place to swim for us was on the far side of the lake at the crowded public beach, since the lake on our side was choked with weeds so slimy and disgusting only young boys could swim through it. That day we're over at the beach swimming, trying to dive from the diving board at the end of the concrete pier, but we're not very good at diving; mostly we're just jumping from the high board – twelve feet, that's high for us – seeing who can jump the most times, climb the ladder dripping wet, run out on

76

the board and grab your nose, shut your eyes, and jump, reckless and panicky and thrilled, striking the water and propelling beneath and your long hair in a ponytail trailing up, bubbles released from your dazed lips, closest thing to dying – is it? Except sometimes you'd hit the water wrong, slapped hard as if in rebuke by the lake's surface, which looks like it should be soft, red welts across my back, murky water up my nose so my head was waterlogged, ears ringing, and I'm dazed and dizzy, staggering around like a drunk girl, all of us loud-laughing and attracting disapproving stares. And there comes my mother, telling me to stop before I drown myself or injure myself, trying not to sound as angry as she's feeling, and Momma makes this gesture – oh, this is mortifying! makes me hate her! – with her hands to suggest that I might injure my chest, my breasts, jumping into the water like that, as if I give a damn about my breasts, or anything about my body, or if I do, if I am anxious about my body, this is not the place, the public beach at Wolf's Head Lake on an afternoon in August, for Momma to scold me. I'm a tall lanky-lean girl almost fourteen years old with small-boned wrists and ankles, deep-set dark eyes, and a thin curvy mouth that gets me into trouble, the things I say, or mumble inaudibly; my ashy blond hair is in a ponytail straggling like a wet rat's tail down my bony vertebrae; except for this ponytail you'd think that I might be a boy, and I hoped to God that I would remain this way forever, nothing so disgusting as a grown woman in a swimsuit, a fleshy woman like Momma and her women friends that men, adult men, actually looked at like there was something glamorous and sexy about them.

Momma is glaring at me, speaking my full, formal name, Annislee, which means that she is disgusted with me, saying she's driving back to the cottage now and I'd better come with her and Jacky, and I'm stubborn, shaking my head, no, I am not ready to leave the beach, where it's still sunny and maybe will not storm, and anyway my bicycle is at the beach. I'd biked to the beach that morning, so I'd have to bike back. And Momma says all right, Annislee, but if it starts storming, you're out of luck. Like she hopes it will storm, just to punish me. But Momma goes away and leaves me. All this while I've been feeling kind of excited and angry, and sad – why I've been jumping from the high board not giving a damn if I do hurt myself – this fiery wildness coming over me sometimes. *Why should I care if I hurt myself, if I drown!* Missing my father, who isn't living with us right now in Strykersville, and resenting that my closest cousin, Gracie Stearns, went away for the weekend to Lake Placid in the Adirondacks, staying with a new friend of hers from Christian Youth, a girl I hardly know. People at Lake Placid are likely to be rich, not like at Wolf's Head Lake, where the cottages are small and crowded together and the boats at the marina are nothing special. All this day I've been feeling mean, thinking how could I hurt Gracie's feelings when she came back, our last week at the lake before Labor Day and I wouldn't have time to spend with Gracie, maybe.

This guy I met. Wants me to go out with him. He's got a boat, wants to teach me to water-ski.

There was no guy. The boys I went swimming with, hung out with, were my age, or younger. Older kids at Wolf's Head I scarcely knew. Older guys I was scared of. Mostly.

At the lake we stayed with my mother's brother Tyrone and his family. Momma and my younger brother, Jacky, and me. Uncle Tyrone's cottage, which wasn't on the lake but a hike through the woods and a haze of mosquitoes and gnats and the lake off-shore choked with weeds and cattails and I wasn't comfortable sleeping three to a room, Momma and Jacky and me, anxious about my privacy, but Wolf's Head Lake was something to look forward to, as Momma was always saying now that my father was out of the picture.

Out of the picture. I hate such a way of speaking. Like Momma can't bring herself to say exactly what the situation is, so it's vague and fading, like an old Polaroid where you can't make out people's faces that have started to blur. As if my father weren't watching over his family somehow or anyway knowing of our whereabouts every day of our lives you can bet!

Him and Momma, they were still married. I was

sure of that. This time Daddy said, I will lay down my life for you, Irene. And the kids. Just tell me if ever you wish it.

Momma doesn't even know how true that statement is. Momma will never know.

There was a time when I was seven, Daddy had to go away. And Momma got excitable then. We were cautioned by Momma's family not to upset her. Not to make loud noises playing and not to get up at night to use the bathroom if we could help it, Jacky and me, because Momma had trouble sleeping and we'd wake her and might scare her. Momma kept a knife under her pillow in case somebody broke into the house; sometimes it was a hammer she kept by her bed, but never any kind of gun, for Momma hated guns – she'd seen her own brother killed in a hunting accident. She made Daddy keep his guns over at his brother's house, his two rifles and his shotgun and the handgun called a revolver with a long mean-looking barrel, which he'd won in a poker game in the U.S. Army stationed in Korea at a time when I had not yet been born. That made me feel shivery, sickish, for my parents did not know me then and did not know of me and did not miss me. And if they had not married each other, it would be that they would never miss me.

So we were told not to upset Momma. It is a scary thing to see your mother cry. Either you run away (like Jacky) or you do something to make your mother cry more (like me). Just to show that it's you your mother is crying about and not something else.

'Ann'slee – what kind of name's that?'

This older guy, must be in his late twenties, named Deek – what sounds like Deek – oily dark spiky haircut and scruffy whiskers and on his right forearm a tattoo of a leaping black panther so it's like him and me are instantly bonded 'cause I am wearing over my swimsuit a Cougars T-shirt (Strykersville High's mascot is a cougar), a similar big cat leaping and snarling. Just the look of this Deek is scary and riveting to me, him and his buddies, all of them older guys and strangers to me, hanging out at the marina pier, where I've drifted to instead of heading back to the cottage, where Momma expects me.

I'm embarrassed telling Deek that Annislee is some weird name derived from a Norwegian name – my mother's grandmother was Norwegian, from Oslo – but Deek isn't hearing this, not a guy who listens to details, nor are his beer-drinking buddies with big sunburned faces and big wide grins like they've been partying a long time already and it isn't even suppertime. Deek is near-about a full head taller than me, bare-legged in swim trunks and a Harley-Davidson T-shirt, winking at me like there's a joke between us – or am I, so much younger than he is, the joke? – asking how'd I like to ride in his speedboat across the lake, how'd I like to play poker with him and his buddies? I tell Deek that I don't know how to play poker, and Deek says, 'Li'l babe, we can teach you.' Tapping my wrist with his forefinger like it's a secret code between us.

Li'l babe. Turns out that Deek is Rick Diekenfeld, owns the flashy white ten-foot speedboat with red letters painted on the hull, *Hot Li'l Babe,* you see roaring around Wolf's Head Lake raising choppy waves in its wake to roil up individuals in slower boats, fishermen in stodgy rowboats like my uncle Tyrone yelling after *Hot Li'l Babe,* shaking his fist, but *Hot Li'l Babe* just roars on away. There's other girls hanging out with these guys. I am trying to determine if they are the guys' girlfriends, but I guess they are not. Seems like they just met at the Lake Inn Marina Café, where you have to be twenty-one to sit by the outdoor bar. These girls in two-piece swimsuits, fleshy as Momma, spilling out of their bikini tops. And the guys in T-shirts and swim trunks or shorts, flip-flops on their big feet, and the names they call one another are harsh and staccato as cartoon names, sounding like Heins, Jax, Croke. And there's Deek, who seems to like me, pronouncing and mispronouncing my name, *Ann'slee,* running the tip of his tongue around his lips, asking again how'd I like to come for a ride in his speedboat, quick before the storm starts, how's about it? Deek has held out his Coors can for me to sip out of, which is daring – if we get caught, I'm underage by eight years – but

82

nobody's noticing. Lukewarm beer that makes me sputter and cough, a fizzy sensation up inside my nose provoking a sneeze-giggle, which Deek seems to find funny, and something about me he finds funny, so I'm thinking, *What the hell.* I'm thinking, *Daddy isn't here, I am not even sure where Daddy is. And Gracie isn't here. This will be something to tell Gracie.*

This guy I met. These guys. Riding on the lake, and they taught me to play poker.

So we pile into *Hot Li'l Babe,* these four big guys and me. There's lots of people around at the marina, nothing to worry about, I am thinking. Or maybe I am not thinking. Momma says, *Annislee, for God's sake, where is your mind?* Well, it looked like – I thought – these other girls were getting into the speedboat too, but they changed their minds, saying the clouds were looking too threatening. *What if you're struck by lightning?* the girls are saying with shivery little giggles. In fact there's only just heat lightning (which is harmless – isn't it?) way off in the distance beyond Mount Hammer, miles from the lake, so I'm thinking, *What the hell, I am not afraid.*

'Hang on, Ann'slee. Here we go.'

This wild thumping ride out onto the lake, full throttle taking off from the marina, and the looks on the faces of boaters coming in – a family in an outboard boat, a fisherman in a rowboat – register such alarm, it's hilarious.

83

Everything seems hilarious, like in a speeded-up film where nothing can go seriously wrong, nobody can get hurt. Deek steers *Hot Li'l Babe* with one hand, drinks Coors with the other. I'm hanging on to my seat, crowded between two of the guys (Jax? Croke? or is this big guy panting beside me Heins?), trying not to shriek with fear – in fact I am not afraid, am I? Can't get my breath the wind is coming so fierce and there's a smell of gasoline in the boat and in the pit of my stomach that sickish excited sensation you get on the downward plunge of a roller coaster. Overhead it's a surprise, the sky is darkening fast, the giant mouth is about closed over the sun, and the way the thunderclouds are ridged and ribbed makes me think of the inside of a mouth, a certain kind of dog that has a purplish black mouth, oh God. Just these few minutes, there's nobody else on Wolf's Head Lake that I can see. The boat engine is roaring so hard, these guys are so loud, a beer can I've been gripping has spilled lukewarm beer onto my bare legs, can't catch my breath, telling myself, *You are not going to die, don't be stupid, you are not important enough to die.* Telling myself that Daddy is close by, watching over me, for didn't Daddy once say, *My little girl is going to live a long, long time – that is a promise.*

To a man like Daddy, and maybe Deek, is given a certain power: to snuff out a life, as you might (if you were feeling mean, and nobody watching) by grinding a broken-winged butterfly that's

84

flailing beneath your foot, or to allow that life to continue.

'Made it! Fuckin' made it! Record time!' Deek is crowing like a rooster; we're across the lake and okay. Deek cuts the motor bringing the speedboat to dock. It's a clumsy-shaped boat, it seems now, banging against the dock; Deek has to loop a nylon rope over one of the posts, cursing *Fuck! fuck! fuck!* He's having so much trouble, finally Heins helps him, and they manage to tie up the boat. We're in an inlet here in some part of Wolf's Head Lake that isn't familiar to me, short stubby pier with rotted pilings, mostly outboard-motor and rowboats docked here. Getting out of the boat, I need to be helped by one of the guys, slip and fall, hit my knee, one of my sandals falls off, and the guy – Croke is the name they call him – big-shouldered in a T-shirt, thick hairs like a pelt on his arms and the backs of his hands, and a gap-toothed grin in a sunburned wedge-face sprouting dark whiskers on his jaw, grabs my elbow, hauls me up onto the dock: 'There ya go, li'l dude, ya okay?' Greeny-gray eyes on me; in that instant he's being nice, kindly, like I'm a kid sister, somebody to be watched over, and I'm grateful for this, almost I want to cry when people are nice to me, that I can't believe I deserve it because I am not a nice girl – am I? *Damn, I don't care. Why should I care?* The fact is, these new friends of mine are smiling at me, calling me Ann'slee, Ann'slee honey, c'mon with us. Next thing I know the five of us

85

are swarming into a convenience store at the end of the dock, Otto's Beer & Bait, where Momma has stopped sometimes but which direction it is to Uncle Tyrone's cottage, and how far it is, I could not say. The guys are getting six-packs of Coors and Black Horse Ale and Deek tells me to get some eats, so I select giant bags of taco chips, Ritz crackers, and Cheez Whiz and at the deli counter some cellophane-wrapped ham sandwiches and dill pickles. Out of the freezer a six-pack of chocolate ice cream bars; I'm leaning over and the frost-mist lifts into my warm face, so cool it makes my eyes mist over, so one of the guys, I think it's Jax, pokes his finger toward my eye meaning to wipe away a tear, I guess, saying 'Hey, li'l dude, you okay?' This guy is so tall, my head hardly comes to his shoulder. Maybe he works at the quarry; those guys are all so big, muscular and going to fat. The quarry at Sparta was where my father was working last time I heard. Up front at the cashier's counter there is this bleach-hair bulldog woman older than Momma staring at the five of us taking up so much space in the cramped aisles, not cracking a smile though the guys are joking with her, calling her Ma'am, trying to be friendly. A thought cuts into me like a blade: *This woman knows me, she will call Momma.* How I feel about this possibility, I'm not sure. (Do I want to be here, with these guys? Is this maybe a mistake? But girls hook up with guys at Wolf's Head Lake – that is what you do at Wolf's

Head Lake, isn't it? What people talk about back at school next month? And Labor Day in another week.) The cashier woman doesn't seem to know me, only just regards me with cold curious eyes, a girl my age, young even for high school, with these guys who must be ten, fifteen years older, guys who've been drinking beers for hours (you can tell: you can smell beer on their breath, their reddened eyes are combustible), speaking to the girl in a kind of sly teasing way but not a mean way so I'm feeling a stab of something like pride, maybe it is even sexual pride, my flat boy-body and dark eyes and curvy mouth and my thick ashy blond hair springing from a low forehead like my Daddy's, prone to brooding. *Ann'slee* is like music in these guys' mouths, this name that has made me cringe since first grade. Hearing *Ann'slee honey, Ann'slee babe* makes me grateful now. Deek tugs my ponytail and praises the eats I've brought to the counter and pays for everything with a credit card.

Next we hike through a marshy pine woods, clouds of mosquitoes, gnats, those fat black flies that bite before a thunder-storm. A sultry wind is blowing up, yet the sun is still shining, rifts in black clouds hot and fiery so you think there might not be a storm, the clouds might be blown away. In the woods are scattered cottages linked by a rutted lane. Loud voices, kids shouting. Bathing suits and towels hanging on drooping clotheslines. Most of the cottages are small like my uncle

Tyrone's, with shingleboard siding or fake pine or maple, crowded close together, but Deek's uncle's cottage is at the end of the lane, with nothing beyond but trees, bushes grown close against the cottage so neighbors can't see into the windows. Deek tries the front door but it's locked, dumps his groceries on the porch and goes around to the back of the cottage to jimmy off a window screen, Heins is excited, asking what the hell is Deek doing, doesn't he have a key for the cottage? 'This is breaking and entering,' Heins says, but Deek only laughs, saying, 'Din't I tell you? This is my uncle's fuckin' place I'm welcome in, any fuckin' time.'

When Deek gets the screen off the window, he turns to me, grabs me around my middle, and lifts me like you'd lift a small child, not a girl weighing eighty pounds and five feet three, which is tall for my age, saying for me to crawl inside and open the door, I am a better fit through the window than he is. Deek's fingers on me are so hard almost I can't catch my breath, squirming to get free like a captured bird, but a bird so scared it isn't going to struggle much, and next thing I know Deek has shoved me through the window with a grunt, headfirst I'm falling, might've broken my neck except I'm able to grab hold of something, scrambling up on my hands and knees, panting like a dog and my heart pounding fast as the guys are cheering behind me, and the skin of my buttocks, inside the puckered fabric of my swimsuit bottom, is tingling from the palms of Deek's hard hands shoving me.

It's no problem opening the front door of the cottage, just a Yale lock. The guys come whooping and laughing inside, dropping six-packs and groceries on a dingy counter. Seems like more than four of them in this small room. It's one of those cottages that is mostly just a single room with two small rooms at the back for sleeping. In the main room are mismatched pieces of furniture, a rickety Formica-topped kitchen table, chairs with torn seats, against a wall a narrow kitchen counter, a tiny sink, and a tiny two-burner gas stove, cupboards and one of those half-sized refrigerators you have to stoop to reach into. Smells here of cooking, old grease, plain old grime. Looks like it hasn't been cleaned or even swept for months – there are cobwebs everywhere, dust balls and husks of dead insects on the floor-boards, ants on the sticky Formica-topped table on the counter, tiny black ants that move in columns like soldiers. Deek is looking through a stack of magazines on an end table, whistling through his teeth and laughing: 'Oh, man. Sweet Jesus.' The guys crowd around Deek, looking at the magazines while I'm ignoring them, removing the groceries from the bags, wiping down the sticky Formica-topped table and counters with wet paper towels, trying to get rid of the ants. Damn nasty ants! And the smell in here. The way the guys are carrying on over the magazines, the crude things they are saying – I'm edgy, embarrassed. Deek sees me, the hot flush in my cheeks, laughs and says, 'C'mere, Ann'slee. Look here.'

But Jax says quick and sharp, 'This ain't for her, Deek. Fuck off.'

Deek is laughing at me, saying not to be looking so mean, but I'm turned away, sullen and uneasy, not smiling back at him, saying maybe I don't want to play poker after all, my mother is probably wondering where I am, I can walk back to our cottage, I won't need a ride. Deek says, 'Okay, li'l babe,' dumping the magazines into a trash can, and one of the guys has opened a Coors for me, icy cold from Otto's Beer & Bait. They are trying to be nice now, so I'm thinking maybe I will stay for a while, learn to play poker – it's nowhere near dark. Nothing waiting for me at the cottage except helping Momma and my aunt prepare supper and if it's raining just TV till we go to bed. Here I'm entrusted with setting out food for these big hulking hungry guys, there's a feeling like an indoor picnic, finding paper plates in the cupboard, a plastic bowl to empty chips into, unwrapping the mashed-looking ham sandwiches. The storm hasn't started yet, maybe there won't even be a storm, the thunder is still far away in the mountains. I'm thinking that Deek really likes me, the way he looks at me, smiles. It's a special smile like a wink, for me. Pushing me through

the window. *He touched me! He touched me there –
did he?*

I won't need many beers to become giddy-
drunk.

That buzzing sensation in the head when your
thoughts come rushing past like crazed bats you
can't be sure even you've seen, blink and they're
gone.

Deek says: Name of the game is five-card draw.

Deek says: Poker isn't hard, is it? Not for a smart
girl like you.

Hard to tell if Deek is teasing or serious. These
first few games, I seem to be doing well. Deek's
chair is close beside mine so that he can oversee
my cards as well as his own. Like we're a team,
Deek says. Telling me the values of the cards,
which isn't so different from gin rummy, euchre,
and truth (which is the card game my friends and
I play). Royal flush, straight flush, flush, five-of-
a-kind hand (when the joker is wild), and it is all
logical to me, common sense I'm thinking, except
maybe I'm not remembering, Deek talks so fast
and there's so much happening each time cards
are dealt. In the third game, Deek nudges me to
'raise' with three eights, two kings; Deek whispers
in my ear that this is a full house – I think that's
what he said, 'full house' – and the cards are strong
enough to win the pot: fifteen dollars! This is
amazing to me; I'm laughing like a little kid being
tickled, and the guys are saying how fast I am

catching on. Heins says, 'Li'l dude is gonna pull in all our money, wait and see.'

Deek has been the one to 'stake' me, these early games. Five one-dollar bills Deek has given me.

In his chair close beside mine, Deek is looming over me, twice my size, breathing his hot beer-breath against the side of my face, hairs on his tattoo-arm making the hairs on my arm stir when his arm brushes near. Like we are young kids whispering and conspiring together. I am thinking that poker isn't so hard except you have to keep on betting and if you don't stay in the game you have to 'fold,' and if you 'fold' you can't win no matter the cards in your hand and so you have to think really hard, try to figure out the cards the other players have, and if they are serious raising the bet or only just bluffing. Deek says that's the point of poker, bluffing out the other guy, seeing can you bullshit him or he's going to bullshit you.

Doesn't it matter what your actual cards are, I ask Deek, if they are high or low? Deek says sort of, scornfully, like this is a damn dumb question he will answer because he likes me. 'Sure it matters, but not so much's how you play what you're dealt. What you do with the fuckin' cards you are dealt, that's poker.'

Through the beer-buzz in my brain come these words: *What you do with what you're dealt. That's poker.*

These first few games, when good cards come to me or Deek tells me how to play them, it's like riding in the speedboat across the choppy lake, gripping my seat, squealing and breathless, and the boat thump-thump-thumping through the waves like nothing could stop it ever – such a good feeling, a sensation in my stomach that is almost unbearable, Deek casting his sidelong glance at me, stroking his whiskery jaws, saying, 'Okay, Ann'slee honey, you are on your own now.' A flashing card-shuffle in Heins's fingers and the cards flicked out and I'm fumbling my cards, blinking and trying to figure out what they mean. The guys keep opening cans of Coors for me; could be I am drunk and not knowing it, biting my lower lip and laughing. Goddamn I am clumsy, dropping a card (an ace!) that Croke can see, and the guys are waiting for me, seems like I've lost the thread of what is going on so Deek nudges me, saying, 'You have to bet, Ann'slee, or fold.' I'm frowning and moving my lips like a first grader trying to read; what's it mean – ace of hearts and ace of spades and four of diamonds and four of clubs and a nine of clubs, should I get rid of the nine, I guess I should get rid of the nine. My thoughts seem to be coming in slow motion now as I toss down the four of clubs – no! Take it back, it's the nine of clubs I don't want. Heins deals a replacement card to me and I fumble turning it over. My face falls; it's a nine of spades – I'm disappointed, should I be disappointed? The guys are trying to be patient with me. I am itchy and sweaty inside the Cougars T-shirt, and my

93

swimsuit beneath, halter top with straps that tie around the neck and puckered fabric bottom, still damp from the lake, and my ponytail straggling down my back still damp too. Momma says we should shower and shampoo our hair after swimming in that lake water; there's 'impurities' in it – sewage draining from some of the cottages, diesel fuel leaked into the lake from motorboats. Some people, Uncle Tyrone says, no better than pigs. Must be. The guys are waiting for me to make a decision (but what decision should I be making? I've forgotten). Deek leans over to take hold of the nape of my neck, gripping me the way you'd grip a dog to shake it a little, reprimand it – 'C'mon, babe, you in or out?' – and I try to ease away from him, I think it's meant as a joke, and not some kind of threat, and Heins says, 'She's just a kid, Deek. Why'd you want to play with a kid?' and Deek turns on him: 'Fuck you, Heinie! Ann'slee and me, we're a *team*.'

This is warming to me, to hear. *Team – we are a team*. So I say, 'I'm *in*,' toss another bill onto the pile. Croke mulls over his cards, decides to fold, Jax folds, Heins raises like he means to provoke Deek. By now my bladder is pinching so hard I have to pee again, itchy and nervous, uncertain what to do, guess I will 'fold' now, should I 'fold'? A single dollar bill is left of all my winnings. The winning hand is Heins's, though maybe in fact Heins's cards are weaker than my two pair, but damn it's too late, I'm out. I folded, and I lost.

Could cry, my winnings are gone so fast, it's like the dollar bills Deek staked me were my own, now gone. A childish hurt opens in me like an old, soft wound.

'Too bad, li'l dude. This is poker.'

The guys laugh at me, I'm wanting to think fondly. The way you'd laugh at a pouting child who doesn't have a clue what is going on around her.

Outside, the sky is mostly clouds. But a hot steamy sun is shining through. This smell in the air, it's like there is a lightning storm somewhere else.

Heins is dealing. Heins says, 'Cut, babe.' Somehow, I'm betting my last dollar bill. Something tells me I am going to win this time – win all my money back! – but the cards are confusing to me, can't remember what Deek was telling me, straight, flush, full house, two pair – I'm staring at my cards, king of hearts, ten of hearts, eight of hearts, five of diamonds, and two of diamonds, get rid of the two of diamonds, that's a low card – should I? or is this a mistake? – the replacement card Heins deals me is a six of spades, I'm disappointed, *Ohhh damn*, in my confusion thinking that the black spade brings down the value of the red cards, that's how it looks to me, so my last dollar bill is taken from me when I'm too scared to bet and say instead 'Fold,' laying down my cards, and Jax peers at them, saying, 'Shit, babe, you coulda done better.' Anyway I am relieved to be out of the game, needing to use the bathroom bad, swaying on my feet (bare feet? where are my sandals?), the floor is sticky against the bottoms of my feet, feels like it's tilting, I'm losing my balance, falling into somebody's lap, but manage to get to the bathroom and shut the door behind me, feeling so strange, like on a roller coaster, where I'd be frightened except everything seems funny to me, even losing my dollar bills, *my* dollar bills you'd think I had brought with me to the poker game, only just makes me laugh. In the murky mirror above the cruddy sink, there's my face, dazed and sunburned, and my eyes (that Momma says are my father's eyes, hazel/dark-brown beautiful eyes but you can't trust them) are threaded with blood, that's a little scary but still I can't stop laughing. These guys like me, the way Deek looks at me, pulls my ponytail, slaps my rear, maybe I am a pretty girl after all. Giggling leaning to the mirror, pursing my lips so they get wrinkly, kissing my mirror-lips, whispering *Ann'slee honey! Li'l dude!* Nobody has ever called me that before.

I will tell Gracie. Nobody else.

Thinking how I loved it when Daddy tickled me when I was a little girl. Daddy spreading his big fingers and, walking, pretending they were daddy longlegs come to tickle me, making me kick and squeal with laughter. I was seven, in second grade, when Daddy went away up to Follette, and the woman from Herkimer County Family Services asked Did your father ever hurt you, Annislee? – and I said No! He did not. Daddy did not. You would

96

think that when you answered such a question that would be the end of it, but repeatedly the question would be asked, as if to trick you. Asking did your daddy hurt you or your brother or your mother, try to remember, Annislee, and I was angry, saying in a sharp voice like a fingernail scraped on a blackboard, *No, Daddy did not.*

'Hey, Ann'slee – didn't fall in, did you?'

One of the guys rapping on the door, making the latchkey rattle.

At the table the guys are devouring ham sandwiches in two, three bites. Big fistfuls of chips. Cans of Black Horse Ale opened, and the ale smell is sharp and acrid. Heins is shuffling cards, pushes them across the table for me to cut. Am I still in this game? With no dollar bill to toss into the pot? They're asking where am I staying at the lake and I tell them. Where do I live and I tell them: Strykersville, which is about twelve miles to the south. Is your family with you at Wolf's Head, Deek asks me, and I tell him yes, except for my father, who isn't there. Deek asks where is my father, and I hesitate, not wanting to tell him that I am not sure. Last I knew, Daddy was living in Sparta, but he's one to move around some. Not liking to be tied down, Momma says.

Croke asks do I have any brothers, his greeny gray eyes on me in a way that's kindly, I think. I say Yes, Jacky, who's nine years old and a damn pain in the neck.

Why'd I say this? To make the guys laugh? You'd think that I don't love my little brother, but truly I do.

Seems like the guys want me back in their game. Deek is allowing me to put up my Cougars T-shirt 'for collateral.' Since washing my face, I'm feeling more clearheaded – I think! – wanting to win back the dollar bills I've lost. Maybe this is how gamblers get started – you are desperate to win back what you've lost, for there is a kind of shame in losing.

But the cards don't come now. Or anyway, I can't make sense of them. Like adding up a column of numbers in math class, you lose your way and have to begin again. Like multiplying numbers – you can do it without thinking, but if you stop to think, you can't. Staring at these new cards, nine of hearts, nine of clubs, king of spades, queen of spades, four of diamonds. I get rid of the four of diamonds and I'm excited, my replacement card is a jack of spades, but my eyes are playing tricks on me, what looks like spades is actually clubs, after raising my bet I see that it's clubs and I've made a mistake, staring and blinking at the cards in my hands that are kind of shaky like I have never seen a poker hand before. Around the table the guys are playing like before, loud, funny-rude, maybe there's some tension among them, I can't figure because I am too distracted by the cards and how I am losing now, nothing I do is right now, but why? When

Croke wins the hand, Deek mutters, 'Shi-it, you goddamn fuckin' asshole,' but smiling like this is a joke, a kindly intended remark like between brothers. I'm trying to make sense of the hand: Why'd Croke win? Why's this a winning hand? What's a full house? Wondering if the guys are cheating on me, how'd I know? The guys are laughing at me, saying, 'Hey, babe, be a good sport – this is poker.'

Croke says, '*My* T-shirt now!' Pulls the Cougars T-shirt off over my head, impatient with how slow I am trying to pull it off. There's a panicked moment when I feel the guys' eyes swerve onto me, my halter top, my small breasts the size of plums, anxious now like undressing in front of strangers, but I am trying to laugh, it's okay – isn't it? – just a game. 'This is poker,' Deek says. This is Wolf's Head Lake in August, the kinds of wild things you hear about back at school, wish you'd been part of. And now I am.

In just my swimsuit now, and barefoot. Feeling kind of shivery, dizzy. Picked out the swimsuit myself at Sears, so can't blame Momma. It's like a kid's sunsuit, too young for me: bright yellow puckered material, a halter top that ties around my neck and a matching bottom and both of them kind of tight and itchy and damp-smelling from the lake. Croke is clowning with the T-shirt wrapped around his head like a turban, saying that li'l babe owes him one more thing: 'This is strip poker, honey. You raised that bet, din't you?

99

There's two damn bets here. My T-shirt, and now something else.'

Croke is teasing, isn't he? All the guys are teasing? The way they are looking at me, at my halter top, I'm starting to giggle, can't stop giggling, like being examined by the doctor, icy-cold stethoscope against my chest, and I'm half naked, trembling on the edge of an examination table, so scared my teeth start chattering and the doctor gives up, disgusted, calls for Momma to come in. Jax is saying, 'She's drunk. We better sober her up and get her out of here.'

Right away I mumble *I am not drunk!* which makes the guys laugh.

Deek says, leaning over me, brushing my arm with his to make the hairs stir, 'Thass a cute li'l swimsuit, Ann'slee. You're a hot li'l babe, eh?'

Jax says, disgusted, 'She's just a kid. Ain't even in high school, I bet.'

Deek says, 'Shit she ain't. How old're you, Ann'slee?'

Eighteen, I tell him. Can't stop laughing, wanting to hide my face in my hands. Thirty-eight! (Thirty-eight is Momma's age, so *old*.)

Jax says, 'I told you, she's wasted. No way she's more'n fifteen.'

Deek says, 'Fifteen is hot. This is a hot li'l babe.'

Heins says, 'Want the cops to bust us? Asshole.'

Deek says, 'How's that gonna happen? This li'l honey is my girl.'

My girl is such a warm thing to say. *My girl my*

girl. Nobody has ever said that to me except my daddy till now.

'Strip, li'l dude! C'mon.'

'Got to be a good sport, Ann'slee. That's poker.'

Deek is teasing me, but he's serious too. And Croke.

'*I'll* strip. Lookit me.'

Deek yanks off his T-shirt that's grimy at the neck, suddenly he's bare-chested, coarse black hairs like a pelt over his chest which is hard-muscled, but at the waistband of his swim trunks his flesh is bunchy and flabby. 'Shi-it,' Croke says, loud like a cross between yawning and yodeling, with a flourish yanking off his T-shirt, baring his heavy, beefy, pimple-pocked chest like a TV wrestler; Croke's chest is covered with hairs like slick seaweed, and oily with sweat. There's a strong smell of underarms. Jax and Heins make crude comments. I'm saying that I don't want to play poker anymore, I guess, I want to go home now, need to get home where my mother is waiting for me, and Croke says, bringing his fist down hard on the table like he's drunk, 'Not a chance, babe. Ain't goin' anywhere till you pay up.'

Deek says, 'When you won the pot, we paid up, din't we? Now you got to pay, Ann'slee. That's poker.'

In just my swimsuit, what can I do? Can't take off the halter top, but for sure can't take off the bottom.

My sandals! Maybe the guys would let me substitute my sandals.

Except I don't see my sandals on the messy floor.

Maybe I lost them in the other room? Climbing through the window?

The guys are pounding the table: 'Strip! Ann'slee's got to strip! Top or bottom, you owe us. That's poker.'

Deek is practically on top of me. Not just his underarms smell, but his oily spiky hair that's cut mini-hawk-style. Big yellow crooked teeth, breath in my face like fumes. Deek is saying, like you'd talk to a young child, or some animal like a dog that needs to be cajoled, 'Take off your top, li'l dude, thass all, thass a damn cute li'l top, show us your cute li'l boobies, you ain't got nothin' we ain't seem already, wanta bet?' All this while I'm hunched over trying to shield my front with my arms, but my arms are so thin, and Deek is pressing so close, slides his arm around my shoulders and I'm on my feet, panicked, trying to run to the door. But Croke grabs me like it's a game we are playing, or him and Deek are playing, like football, Ann'slee is the football, captured. Croke's big fingers tear at the halter straps, Croke manages to untie the straps and pulls off the halter, *Ohhhh, lookit!* – the guys are whistling and stamping their feet, teasing, taunting like dogs circling a wounded rabbit, and I'm panicked like a rabbit, trying to laugh, to show this is just a joke, I know it's a joke, but I'm desperate to get away from them, stumbling to the bathroom, the only place I can get to, shutting the door behind me, fumbling to latch the door, had a glimpse before I shut it of Croke (I'd thought was my friend) with the halter top on his head, tying the straps beneath his chin like a bonnet.

Somewhere not too far away Momma is looking at the clock, fretting and fuming: Where is that girl? Where the hell has Annislee got to this time?

They wouldn't hurt me – would they?
They like me – don't they?
How long I am crouched in the bathroom in terror of the guys breaking in, how long I am shivering and trembling like a trapped rabbit, I won't know afterward, and even at the time what is happening is rushing past like a drunken scene glimpsed from a speeding car or boat on the lake. My right breast is throbbing with pain, must've been that Croke squeezed it, an ugly yellowish purple bruise is taking shape.

Croke I'd thought liked me. Helping me out of the boat.

Back in grade school already we'd begun to hear stories of what guys can do to girls if they want to hurt them, though we had not understood why. And sometimes the girls are beaten, strangled, left for dead, it isn't known why.

'Hey, Ann'slee.'

There's a rap on the plywood door. I'm not going to open it.

One of the guys rattling the door so hard it slips open. It's Jax leaning in, seeing me crouched against the wall so frightened my teeth are chattering, says, like he's embarrassed, 'Here's the swim top. Nobody's gonna hurt you.'

I'm too scared to reach up and take the halter top from him. Jax shoves it at me, muttering, 'Put the damn thing on.'

Jax shuts the door. With trembling fingers I refasten the top.

Avoiding my reflection in the mirror. That greasy smudge where I'd kissed my own lips.

When I emerge from the bathroom, stiff and numbed, my eyes blinking back tears, the guys are still at the table, still drinking. Seems like they're between poker games. Or maybe they're through with poker for the night. Their eyes swerve onto me in that way that reminds me of excited dogs. Deek says, 'Li'l dude! There you are. C'mon back, sit on Deek's lap, eh? You're my girl.'

A glint like gasoline in Deek's bloodshot eyes and a way his big teeth are bared in a grin without warmth or mirth warns me that I am still in danger. Through the plywood door I'd heard Deek mutter what sounded like *Ain't done with her yet, so don't fuck with me.*

Outside, all I can see of the early-evening sky is massive bruise-colored clouds. Still there is heat lightning way in the distance.

'Here y'are, Ann'slee. Shouldna been so scared.'

Croke tosses the Cougars T-shirt at me. I'm so

grateful for the shirt, smelly from where Croke wiped his sweaty face with it, I'm stammering, 'Thank you!'

There is a break in what the guys are doing, I can feel it. Or maybe they've been waiting for Ann'slee to emerge from the bathroom, uncertain what they would do with me, or whether they would do anything with me: like turning a card, possibly. It just might be the card that makes you win big, or it might be the card that assures you will lose. It might be a card that will mean nothing in your life. Or everything. It might even be a card you won't need to request – the card will come flying at you.

Now I'm wearing my Cougars T-shirt over my swimsuit top again, I am not feeling so exposed. It's a baggy shirt, coming down practically to my thighs.

I will pretend I haven't heard Deek. How he's staring at me with a loose wet smile, running the tip of his tongue around his lips.

Things a guy can do. You don't want to know.

My heart is beating hard, hidden inside the T-shirt. My voice is calm-sounding, telling the guys, 'There's other kinds of stripping, not just taking off clothes. There's this card game we play called truth – you ever heard of truth?'

'Truth? Some kids' game? No.'

I'm a little distance from the nearest of them, who happens to be Heins. The way I'm standing is to let them know that I am not going to make a run for the front door as I tried to do earlier; I am not panicked now, or desperate. I am smiling at them, the way a girl might. I am trying to smile. The heat pumping off these guys is a sex-heat so palpable you can feel it yards away. Like the charged air before a storm. I don't want to think it's the dogs' instinct to lunge, tear with their teeth, they can't help it.

I tell the guys maybe we can play truth. 'It's a little like poker, except you don't bet money, instead of paying a bet you pay in truth. There's high cards and low cards and a joker that's wild. If you lose, you reveal a truth about yourself that nobody else knows.'

Nobody seems very interested in learning this game, I can see. Deek says disdainfully, 'How'd you know what a person said was true? Any old bullshit, how'd you know?'

'You would want to tell the truth – wouldn't you? If it was the right time.'

Croke says, '*You* tell us, li'l dude. Make up for how you been acting, like you're scared of us.'

Quickly I say, 'I'm not scared of you! I love being here, coming across the lake on Deek's boat . . . There's nobody I know has a boat like Deek's.'

At this, Deek smiles. Then the smile freezes.

'You bullshittin' me, babe? Wantin' a ride back acrost the lake, that's it?'

No! I'm smiling at Deek, keeping my distance from him. Between us there is Heins, slouched at the table, idly shuffling the pack of cards. I tell

106

Deek I wouldn't lie ever, not to him and his friends. I would tell only the truth, which is stripping the soul.

Jax shoves a chair out for me beside him at the table. So I sit down. There's a little distance between Deek and me. One of the guys has opened an ale for me; I will pretend to sip.

I'm not drunk now – am I?

Drawing a deep breath. This truth I have to reveal.

'Two years ago this August, my father was driving back with me from his cousin's place down in Cattaraugus, this town called Salamanca on the Allegheny River. It was just him and me, not my mother or my brother Jacky. Driving back to Strykersville from Salamanca and Daddy wants to stop at a tavern in this place outside Java. Daddy was living away from us then, like he does now, and this was my weekend to be with him. At the tavern, which was on a lake where people had rowboats and canoes, Daddy bought me some root beer and french fries, and I was sitting at a picnic table while Daddy was inside at the bar. There were kids in the park, people were grilling hamburgers and steaks, some girls playing badminton asked me if I'd like to play with them, so I did, but after a while they went away and I was by myself and thought that I would walk around the lake. It wasn't a big lake like Wolf's Head, and I thought that if I walked fast, I would get back before Daddy came out of the tavern.

107

But the path around the lake wasn't always right beside the lake and was sort of overgrown, so I wasn't sure if I should keep going or turn back. I was worried that Daddy would come out of the tavern before I got back and see I wasn't there and be anxious. These years he'd been away, at Follette, he'd got so he worried about things more, like his family, he said, he'd had a lot of time to think—'

Deek interrupts: 'Follette? That's where your father was?'

'Yes.'

Not like I am ashamed, just this is a fact: Daddy served four years of a nine-year sentence for aggravated assault and was released on parole for good behavior when I was eleven years old. Follette is the men's maximum-security prison up north at the Canadian border, the facility in the New York State prison system where nobody wants to go.

The guys' eyes are on me now. The guys are listening, and I continue with the story, which is a true story I have never told any living soul before this evening.

'So I'm hoping that I am not lost, I'm on a kind of wood-chip trail and there's a parking lot nearby and a restroom, I'm thinking that I can use the women's room, except out of the little building there comes this man zipping up his trousers and he's seeing me, he's in these rumpled old clothes and his face is boiled-looking and hair sticking up around his head, older than my daddy, I think,

108

and he's coming right at me, saying, 'H'lo, honey, are you alone way out here?' and I tell him no, my daddy is right close by, so he looks at the parking lot but there's no cars there, but he says, 'Well! Too bad, this time' – I think that's what he said, he might've been talking to himself.

'I wasn't listening and walked away fast. And I waited for him to go away and I thought he did and I went inside the women's room which was hard to see in, there wasn't any light and the sun was about setting, and I'm inside one of the toilet stalls, and there's a scratching noise, and this guy – it must be this guy – has followed me into the women's room! Where a man is not ever supposed to be! He's poking a tree branch beneath the stall door, to scare me, saying, 'Li'l girl, d'you need help? Need help in there? Wiping your li'l bottom? I can wipe, and I can lick. I'm real good at that.' I'm so scared I am crying. I tell the man Go away please go away and leave me alone, my daddy is waiting for me, and he's laughing, telling me the kinds of things he was going to do to me, things he'd done to girls that the girls had 'liked real well' and nobody would know, not even my daddy. But there was a car pulling up outside, and a woman comes into the restroom with a little girl, so the man runs out, and when I come outside he's gone, or anyway I think he's gone. The woman says to me, 'Was that man bothering you? D'you want a ride with me?' and I said no, I was going back to my daddy's car and would wait for him there. Why I told the woman this, I don't know. I thought that the man was gone. I headed back to the tavern the way I'd been coming. Now the sun is setting, it's getting dark. I'm walking fast, and I'm running, and there's the man with the boiled-looking face, almost I don't see him squatting by the path, he's got a rope in his hands, a rope maybe two feet long stretched between his hands he's holding up for me to see, so I panic and run the other way, back to the parking lot, and the man calls after me, 'Li'l girl! Don't be afraid, li'l girl, your daddy sent me for you!' Things like that he was saying. I found a place to hide by some picnic tables, and for a long time, maybe twenty minutes, the man is looking for me, calling, 'Li'l girl!' He knows that I am there somewhere, but it's getting dark, and then there's headlights, a car is bumping up a lane into the parking lot, and I can't believe it, it's my daddy. Just taking a chance he'd find me, Daddy would say afterward, that I'd be on this side of the lake – he'd asked people if they had seen me and somebody had and he'd come to the right place, at just the right time. He caught sight of the man with the boiled face. I told Daddy how he'd been following me and saying things to me, wanting to tie me up with a rope, and Daddy runs after him and catches him. The man is limping and can't hardly run at all, and Daddy starts hitting him with his fists, not even saying anything but real quiet – Daddy does things real quiet. It's the man who is crying

110

out, begging for Daddy to stop, but Daddy can't stop, Daddy won't stop until it's over . . . Daddy says when a man uses his fists it's self-defense. Fists or feet, nobody can dispute 'self-defense.' Use a deadly weapon, like a tire iron – like Daddy used fighting another man in Strykersville, which got him arrested and sent to Follette – and you're in serious trouble, but just your fists and your feet, no. What Daddy did to that man who'd wanted to tie me up and hurt me, I didn't see. I did not see. I heard it, or some of it. But I did not see. And afterward Daddy dragged him to a ravine, where there'd be water at some times of the year but was dry now, and pushed him over, and I did not see that either. And Daddy comes back to me excited and breathing hard and his knuckles are skinned and bleeding but Daddy doesn't hardly notice. He grabs me and hugs me and kisses me. Daddy is so happy that I am safe. 'You never saw a thing, honey. Did you?' And I told Daddy no, I did not, and that was the truth.'

Listening to my story, the guys have gotten quiet. Even Deek is sitting very still, listening to me. The look on his face, like he's waiting to laugh at me, bare his glistening teeth at me in a mock-grin, is gone. Fresh-opened cans of Black Horse Ale on the table the guys have not been drinking. Must be they are waiting for me to continue. But my story is over.

Hadn't known how it would end. Because I had not told it before. Even to myself, though it is a

111

true story. I wouldn't have known that I had the words for it. But you always have words for a true story, I think.

I am not going to tell Deek, Jax, Croke, Heins how there was never any article in any newspaper that I saw about the man with the boiled-looking face if he'd been found in Java State Park in that ravine. What was left of that man, if anything was left. Or maybe he'd gotten all right again, next morning crawled out of the ravine and limped away. That is a possibility. I didn't see, and Daddy never spoke of it afterward. Daddy drove us back to Strykersville that night. It was past midnight when we got home, and Momma was waiting up watching TV, and if she'd meant to be angry with Daddy for keeping me out so late, by the time we got to the house she was feeling different, and kissed us both, saw that I was looking feverish and said, *Annislee, go to bed right now, it's hours past your bedtime*. That night Daddy stayed with Momma.

Off and on then Daddy stayed with us. Then that fall something happened between him and Momma, so Daddy moved out; that's when he began working at the stone quarry at Sparta. But Sparta is only about fifty miles from Strykersville, and Daddy and Momma are still married, I think. *Till death do us part* Daddy believes in, and in her heart Momma does too.

I'm smiling at these guys crowded at the battered old table in Deek's uncle's cottage, so close I can

112

see their eyes, and the irises of their eyes, and as far into their souls as I need to see. Saying, 'I feel lucky – I'd like to try poker again, a few hands. I think I'm catching on now.'

SMOTHER

*O*nly a doll, Alva! Like you.

That's what they told her. Their voices were a single voice.

She was very young then. It had to be 1974, because she was in second grade at Buhr Elementary School, which was the faded red-brick building set back from the busy street; she has forgotten the name of the street and much of her life at that time but she remembers the school, she remembers a teacher who was kind to her, she remembers Rock Basin Park where the child was smothered.

This was in Upper Darby, Pennsylvania. A long time ago.

Now it begins: this season of the year.

Early warm spring. Why?

Can't sleep. Can't concentrate. Questions put to her, can't hear. Can't seem to walk more than a few feet without swaying. Fear of losing her balance in some public place, falling. Strangers' hands on her.

It's worse this year. Must be airborne pollen, can't breathe.

Can't breathe. Smother!

Is it a buried child she remembers? Or only a smothered child?

Is it a child? Or a baby?

Only a doll, Alva. You can see.

Is it a girl? Or . . .

She's desperate, ridiculous. Praying, *Dear God, don't let it be a girl.*

She is an adult now. She is not a child. Somehow she has become thirty-seven years old.

An orphan! Thirty-seven years.

Can't sleep. Can't breathe. Hurriedly dresses, leaves for the arts college. On the bus her head rattles. A man is peering at her from behind a raised newspaper, eyes she feels crawling on her, disrobing her, poking fingers, prying open. *Cut* is a nasty word she first heard at the faded red-brick school long ago. No idea what it meant. No idea why the older boys laughed. No idea why she ran away to hide her face. No idea why her teacher spoke so carefully to her: *Alva, have you been hurt? Alva, have you been touched?* Holding out her left arm, where the purplish yellow bruise had blossomed in the night.

Alva pulls the cord. Next stop! Can't breathe in the crowded bus. Eyes crawling over her like lice.

She has disguised herself in swaths of muslin, like a nun, like a Muslim woman, wrappings of saffron material, mist-colored, soiled white. And her waist-long hair that needs washing, spilling from a makeshift velvet cowl.

Alva's long narrow bony feet. In need of washing.

Venus de Milo, it's been said of Alva, unclothed.

Botticelli Venus, in a voice of (male) marveling.

Tells herself she is twelve hundred miles from Rock Basin Park. She is thirty-seven years old, not seven.

Thirty-seven, Alva? You must be joking.

Alva doesn't joke. Taking cues from others, Alva is able to laugh on cue – a high-pitched, little-girl, startled sound like glass breaking – but she doesn't understand the logic of jokes.

Alva sometimes laughs if (somehow) she's tickled. Breasts and abdomen palpitated by an examining gynecologist at the free clinic, echo exam where the technician moves a device around and around, and pushes against, the thinly flesh-cushioned bone protecting the heart.

Yet why is it you can't tickle yourself? Alva wonders.

Sometimes even in mirrors nobody's there.

Can't be more than, what – twenty-five?

Alva won't contest the point. Alva doesn't lie, but if people, predominately men, wish to believe that she's younger than her age, as young as she appears, Alva won't protest.

The transparent tape they'd wrapped around her

head, over her face, to smother her, to shut her mouth and eyes, shut her terrified screams inside, Alva hadn't protested. Too exhausted, when finally the tape was torn off.

Tearing off eyelashes, much of her eyebrows, clumps of hair.

Hadn't protested. Never told. Who to tell?

Alva has learned: to modulate her voice like wind chimes, to smell like scented candles, to shake her long streaked-blond hair like a knotted waterfall past her slender shoulders. Her smile is shyly trusting. Her eyes are warm melting caramel. Men have fallen in love with that smile. Men have fallen in love with those eyes. The exotic layers of cloth Alva wraps herself in, gauze, see-through, thin muslins, sometimes sprinkled with gold dust. An unexpected glimpse of Alva's bare flesh (is she naked, beneath?) inside the swaths of fabric, midriff, inside of a forearm, creamy translucent breast.

Men follow Alva. Alva knows to hide.

Smother! A man's gritty palm closing over her mouth, clamping tight to keep her from screaming.

Momma! Make him stop! Don't let—

The scream had to be swallowed. There was no choice.

Almost she can see the man's face.

A perspiring face, red-flushed face, furious eyes.

Never tell! What we did to her, we'll do to you.

For a long time she forgot. Now she's remembering. Why?

She's twelve hundred miles from Rock Basin Park and Upper Darby, Pennsylvania. Has not returned in many years. Maybe the man who claimed to be her father has died. Maybe it's her mother who continues to send checks, whose signature Alva avoids looking at.

Guilt money, this is. But Alva needs money.

Lately she can think of nothing else except *Only a doll, Alva. Like you.* Can't sleep, can't breathe. These terrible days of early warm spring when everyone else walks in the sunshine, coatless and smiling. Airborne pollen, maple seeds madly swirling in the wind, a rich stupefying scent of lilac.

Lilac! In Rock Basin Park. Where she ran. Where she hid. Maybe he'd crushed her face in it: lilac. If not Alva's face, the other girl's.

Alva has never had a child. Alva has never been pregnant.

Men have tried to make Alva pregnant. Many times.

Children frighten Alva; she looks quickly away from them. If by accident she glances into a stroller, a baby buggy, a crib, quickly she turns her gaze aside.

It's just a doll, Alva. Like you.

Amnesia is a desert of fine white sun-glaring sand to the horizon. Amnesia isn't oblivion. Amnesia isn't memory loss caused by brain injury or neurolog-

118

ical deterioration, in which actual brain cells have died. Amnesia is almost-remembering. Amnesia is the torment of almost-remembering. Amnesia is the dream from which you have only just awakened, hovering out of reach below the surface of bright rippling water.

Amnesia is the paralyzed limb into which one day, one hour, feeling may begin suddenly to flow.

This Alva fears. Amnesia has been peace, bliss. Waking will be pain.

Alva, dear, is something wrong? Alva, tell me, please?

. . . know you can trust me, Alva. Don't you?

Alva is childlike and trusting, but in fact Alva is not childlike and not trusting. Alva certainly isn't one to tell. Not any man, of the many who've befriended her.

Teachers. Social workers. Psychologists. Therapists. Older men eager to help Alva, who so mysteriously seems unable to help herself. *Some secret in your life, Alva? That has held you back, kept you from fulfilling your promise?*

This is true. This is true! Alva knows. Long ago she was a promising young dancer. She has been promising as a student, a singer, an actress. Promising as a spiritual being, and promising as an artist/sculptor/jeweler. Alva's most ambitious project was stringing together glass beads – hundreds, thousands of beads! – into exotic

'Indian' necklaces and bracelets sold at a crafts fair in Grand Rapids, Michigan. Alva has received payment for intermittent work in Christian campus groups, in feminist centers, Buddhist centers, organic food co-ops, neighborhood medical clinics. She has worked in photo shops, frame shops. She has passed out fliers on street corners. She has worked in cafeterias. She has waitressed. She has been a model.

Alva never accepts money. On principle.

Alva will accept money sometimes. Only if necessary.

If desperate, Alva will accept meals, winter clothing, places to stay. (Alva never stays in one place for long. Alva slips away without saying goodbye.)

Like exotic glass beads, Alva's life. But there is no one to string the glass beads together.

Men who've loved Alva have asked, *What is it — a curse, a jinx, something in your childhood? Who are your parents? Where are you from? Are you close to your mother, your father . . . ?*

Alva is mute. Alva's head is wrapped in transparent tape. Alva's screams are shut up inside.

Alva removes the envelope from the post office box. Opens it, tosses aside the accompanying letter, keeps only the check made out to Alva Lucille Ulrich. Guilt money, this is. But Alva needs money.

Alva needs her medications. Alva has qualified for public health assistance, but still Alva must pay a minimal fee, usually ten dollars, for her meds.

Alva takes only prescription drugs. Alva has been clean for years.

You saw nothing. You are a very bad little girl.

Hiding in plain view. Nude model. The girl who'd been morbidly shy in school. Calmly removing her layers of exotic fabric, kicking off her sandals, slipping into a plain cotton robe to enter the life studies room. Taking her place at the center of staring strangers, at whom she never looks.

The instructor, usually male. Staring at Alva too. At whom Alva never looks.

Venus de Milo, it's been remarked of Alva. *Botticelli Venus.* Alva scarcely hears what is said of her at such times, for it isn't said of her but of her body.

Alva prefers large urban university campuses. Alva prefers academic art departments, not freelance artists or photographers.

Alva is an artist's model. Alva is not available for porn – 'erotic art.' Alva is not sexual.

Saw nothing. Bad girl.

It's early May. It's a sprawling university campus close by the Mississippi River. Far from Rock Basin Park. Far from Upper Darby, Pennsylvania.

Early May, too warm. Even Alva, naked, is warm. Students have shoved windows up as high as they can in the third-floor room in the old building on

University Avenue. Alva has been sleepless; Alva has had difficulty breathing. Alva is uneasy; these windows open to the sky. There are noises from the busy street outside, but still there is airborne pollen, swirling maple seeds, a smell of lilac from somewhere on campus.

Smother!

Alva shudders. Alva stares into a corner of the ceiling. Alva holds herself so very still seated on the swath of velvet draped over a chair, Alva doesn't appear to be breathing.

The child! In a soiled pink eyelet nightgown smelling of her panicked body. Eyes open and staring, sightless. Where the hand has clamped there is the reddened impress of fingers in the ivory skin. A bubble of saliva tinged with blood glistens at the small bruised mouth. They are wrapping her in the blanket that had been Alva's. They are wrapping her tight so that if she comes awake, if she comes alive again, she won't be able to kick and struggle. At dusk they will drive to Rock Basin Park, they will abandon her in a desolate place where there are no footpaths and lilac is growing wild.

'Alva—'

The model slumps suddenly. So rigidly she'd been holding herself, blank features like a statue, blind eyes; now abruptly she has slumped to the floor, unconscious.

Waking dazed and confused on the bare floorboards. Someone is wrapping her in the velvet

122

cloth. Hiding her nakedness. Sprawled awkwardly on the floor, shocked strangers staring at her, Alva is no classic Greek figure but a stricken woman no longer young.

The art instructor, Doyle, has called Alva's name. To hear 'Alva' uttered with such urgency is to understand that the man has strong feelings for Alva that he has managed to disguise until now.

Lifting Alva to her feet. Alva is weakly protesting that she's all right and wants to continue the sitting. But Alva is led away, to a quieter place. Doyle brings Alva's clothes and sandals to her, he brings a wet facecloth, a bottle of spring water.

'Your face went dead white, Alva. Just before you fainted.'

Alva shudders, remembering. The amnesia is lifting, like sun burning through a sky of clotted cloud.

Doyle is middle-aged, divorced. Doyle is stocky and bald, a gold stud in his left earlobe. A part-time faculty member in the art department. Painter, sculptor. Alva has never seen Doyle's work. Alva has scarcely glanced at Doyle until now. Though knowing – the kindness in his manner, the way he smiles at her, as he doesn't so readily smile at others – he has been intensely aware of her.

'Your beautiful face.'

Three days later, by chance Alva sees the headline in a newspaper Doyle has left spread open on his kitchen table.

By purest chance, since Alva rarely glances at newspapers.

In a state of mounting panic, Alva reads.

The unidentified child. Approximately two years old. Body abandoned in a park in Upper Darby, Pennsylvania. A girl 'tightly swaddled' in a grimy blanket. A girl in a soiled jumper with 'a border of pink bunnies' on it. A girl bruised about the face and torso, believed to have been smothered.

Alva learns that the 'Pink Bunny Baby' case was one of the most notorious murder cases of the decade in the North-east. Hundreds of thousands of fliers were posted; thousands of tips were received by police; hundreds of individuals were questioned, investigated, released. The Pink Bunny Baby was never identified. No photograph of her was ever publicly released, only police sketches of a beautiful doll-like face with widened, thick-lashed eyes. Alva has been staring at the sketch in the newspaper. 'My sister!' Alva begins to speak excitedly. Alva laughs, a rising crescendo. When Doyle stands beside her, Alva points to the sketch of Pink Bunny Baby's face. Beneath, the caption reads 'Never-identified 2-year-old murder victim, 1974.'

'I saw. I saw who killed her. My sister. I was a witness.'

★   ★   ★

124

Phone rang. Friday evening. Believing it to be a friend, she lifted the receiver without checking the ID.

The voice was a stranger's. Low-pitched, somehow insinuating.

'Mrs Ulrich?'

Here was the wrong note. To her students and younger colleagues at the institute she was Dr Ulrich. To friends and acquaintances, Lydia. No one called her Mrs Ulrich any longer. No one who knew her.

She felt a stab of apprehension. Even as she tensed, she spoke warmly and easily into the phone: 'Yes, who is it?'

By the age of sixty-one she'd acquired a social personality that was warm, easy, welcoming. You might call it a maternal personality. You would not wish to call it a manipulative personality. She was a professional woman of several decades. Her current position was director of a psychology research institute at George Mason University. She'd been a professor at the university for eighteen years, much admired for her collegiality and ease with students. Her deepest self, brooding and still as dark water at the bottom of a deep well, was very different.

'. . . of the Upper Darby police department. I have a few questions to ask you, preferably in person.'

Upper Darby! She'd moved away nearly twenty-five years ago.

Lydia, her husband, Hans, and their young daughter, Alva.

Her friendships of that time, when she'd been an anxious young wife and mother, had long since faded. Her husband had had professional ties in the Philadelphia area, but long ago.

'But – why? What do you have to ask me?'

'Your husband is deceased, Mrs Ulrich? Is that correct?'

This was correct. Hans had died in 2000. Already four years had passed. For seven years in all, Lydia and Hans had not been living together. They had not divorced or even formally separated, because Hans had not believed in any outward acknowledgment of failure on his part.

The detective, whose name Lydia hadn't quite heard, was asking if he and an associate could come to her residence in Bethesda to speak with her the following day, at about 2 P.M. They would drive from Upper Darby for an interview of possibly forty minutes, or an hour.

The next day was Saturday. This was to have been a day of solitude. When she needn't be Dr Ulrich. In the evening she was going out with a friend; through the long hours of the day she intended to work, with an afternoon break for a long, vigorous walk. As a professional woman, she had learned to hoard her privacy, her aloneness, while giving the impression in public of being warmly open and available.

It was difficult to keep the edge out of her voice.

126

'Why must it be in person? Can't we speak over the phone?'

'Mrs Ulrich, we prefer not on the phone.'

Again Mrs Ulrich. Spoken with an insinuating authority. As if the police officer knew Mrs Ulrich intimately, it was Mrs Ulrich he wanted.

In this way Lydia understood: the subject of the inquiry would be family. Whatever it was, it would have nothing to do with her professional identity and reputation.

She could not avoid asking this question, with dread: 'Is this . . . about my daughter?'

Lydia strained to hear, behind the detective's low-pitched voice, background voices, muffled sound. The man was calling from Upper Darby police headquarters. His intrusion into her life, into the solitude and privacy of her apartment (a tenth-floor condominium overlooking a shimmering green oasis of parkland), was impersonal, as if random. He didn't know her, had no care of her. He was pursuing a goal that had nothing to do with her. And of course it couldn't be random but was calculated. He'd acquired her (unlisted) home telephone number in Bethesda, Maryland. He knew about Hans's death. This meant he probably knew other facts about her. That he might know facts about Lydia Ulrich she didn't know about herself caused her to feel dizzy suddenly, as if a net were being closed around her.

The detective hadn't said yes, nor had he said no. Was this call about Alva?

'Is Alva in trouble? Is she . . . ill?'

127

Has she been arrested, is she in police custody, has she overdosed on a drug, is she in a hospital, is she . . .

Since answering the phone, Lydia had been placating herself with the thought that, so far as she knew, Alva was in Illinois, not Pennsylvania. Since they'd moved from Upper Darby, Alva had never been back. Lydia was sure.

The detective whose name Lydia hadn't caught was telling her, in a voice that didn't sound friendly, that their daughter was not ill, so far as he knew. But the subject of his inquiry had to do with her, Alva Ulrich, as a possible witness in a criminal investigation.

Criminal investigation! Lydia's heart stopped.

It would be drugs. Since the age of fourteen Alva had been involved with drugs. Like malaria, the disease persisted. Lydia jammed her fist against her mouth. The detective's words had struck her like an arrow. Damned if she would cry out in pain.

No doubt many more times than her parents knew, Alva had been arrested for drug possession. She'd been taken into police custody, briefly jailed, discharged to rehab, discharged 'clean.' Drifting on then to the next state, another sprawling university campus. Another improvised fringe life in pursuit of some sort of artistic career . . . The last time a call as jarring as this had come from a stranger, years ago, when she and Hans had been living in Georgetown, their thirty-year-old daughter, from whom they'd long been estranged, had been hospitalized in East Lansing, Michigan, after a drug overdose. She'd been comatose, near death. Dumped by her druggie friends on the pavement outside the ER one night in winter 1997.

Immediately Lydia had flown to East Lansing. Hans had refused to accompany her.

The detective was asking, wasn't Lydia in contact with her daughter? Lydia wondered if the question was a trick, for already he knew the answer, from Alva. Quickly Lydia said yes, of course she was in contact with her daughter: 'Alva is an art student, a painter, at . . .' But was it Illinois State University at Carbondale or Springfield? Alva had provided Lydia with post office box numbers in both cities recently. 'I just wrote to her about two weeks ago. I sent her a check, as I often do, and she seems to have cashed it. Please tell me if something has happened to my daughter.'

'When is the last time you spoke with her, Mrs Ulrich?'

Lydia could not answer. She was being humiliated, eviscerated.

Yet the stranger at the other end of the line continued, with a pretense of solicitude. Asking, hadn't Lydia a street address for her daughter either? – so Lydia was forced to admit no, 'Just a post office box. It's been that way since she left home. Alva has wanted her privacy. She's an artist . . .'

Lydia's voice was weak now, faltering. Not the self-assured voice of Dr Lydia Ulrich, director of the Pratt Institute for Research in Cognitive and Social Psychology at George Mason University, but the broken, defeated, bewildered voice of Hans Ulrich's wife.

'Springfield, is it? Alva is studying art there . . .'

The detective murmured something ambiguous. Maybe yes, maybe no.

'. . . don't seem to have her street address, officer. Maybe, if you know it, you could tell me?'

'Sorry, Mrs Ulrich. Your daughter has requested that we not inform you of her exact location at this time.'

'Oh. I see.'

This hurt. This was unmistakable. An insult. Shame.

Not my fault. How is it my fault! I tried to love her. I do love her.

Now Lydia was broken, defeated. Quickly now she gave in. Of course the detectives could come to see her next day. The net was tightening; her breath came short. Before they hung up Lydia heard herself ask, 'If a – a crime has been committed . . . Alva isn't in danger, is she? Alva is being protected – is she?'

The detective's answer was terse and enigmatic; she would ponder its meaning through much of the night: 'At the present time, ma'am, it appears, yes she is.'

Of course, Alva was in Carbondale, not Springfield! Lydia knew this.

A few minutes after her conversation with the Upper Darby detective, she realized.

She would cancel her plans for the weekend. Both Saturday and Sunday. She knew, seemed to know, that the Upper Darby detectives would not be bringing her good news.

'My daughter. Alva. Something has happened. She has become involved in a criminal case out in Illinois, I think. She's a witness . . .'

Witness to what? Lydia shuddered to think.

She was rehearsing what she would say, telephoning friends. To cancel their plans for dinner, a play. To explain her state of mind. (Agitated, anxious.) In the turbulent years of her marriage to a demanding and difficult man, Lydia hadn't had time for the cultivation of friends, but now that her life was spacious and aerated as a cloudless sky, she'd acquired a circle of remarkable friends. Most of them were women her age, divorcées, widows. A few remained married. Their children were grown and gone. All were professional women nearing retirement age but, like Lydia, in no hurry to retire. They did not wish to speak of it.

Not yet! Not yet! The women clung to their work, at which they excelled, with a maternal possessiveness.

Their children had not only grown and gone but in some cases had disappeared. Like Alva, they were of the legion of walking wounded, drifting into a drug culture as into a vast American inland sea. The women did not speak of these children except in rare, raw moments. Lydia's friends knew about Alva, and knew not to ask after Alva. The son of Lydia's closest friend had committed suicide several years ago in a particularly gruesome way; only Lydia knew among their circle of friends. But never spoke of it.

The women had come to these friendships late in life, but not too late. Theirs was the most precious sisterhood: no blood ties between them.

Genes are the cards we're all dealt. What we do with the cards is our lives.

This was a remark of Hans Ulrich's, frequently cited in intellectual journals.

'I tried. I have never given up on . . .'

He had given up. The father.

And how painful for Lydia to realize that long after Hans had coolly detached himself from their daughter, refusing even to hear from Lydia what Alva's latest problems, crises, predicaments were, Alva still preferred him to Lydia: the powerful, elusive father.

Seductive even when elusive. Especially when absent.

'But where is Daddy, why isn't Daddy with you? Are you keeping Daddy from me? Are you lying to Daddy about me? Does Daddy know that I almost died? I don't want you here, I want Daddy. *I don't trust you, I hate you.*'

It was a child's accusation. Hateful, unthinking, intended purely to hurt.

In the hospital in East Lansing, at Alva's bedside, Lydia had tried to disguise her horror, seeing her daughter so haggard and sallow-skinned, her eyes bloodshot, sunk deep into their sockets. Alva had been too weak to sit up, to eat solids, to speak except in a low hoarse broken voice, almost inaudible and terrible to hear. Lydia wanted to believe it was Alva's sickness that spoke, not Alva. For how could Alva hate *her*!

'Darling, I'm your mother. I love you, I'm here to help you . . .'

'You're wrong. You're stupid. It's Daddy I trust. His judgment.'

Lydia was stunned. Thinking, *Even in her sickness, she knows.*

Not Lydia's judgment but Hans's judgment was to be trusted. Hans's moral repugnance at what he called the slow train wreck of their daughter's life. Not a mother's unconditional love and forgiveness the wounded daughter craved, but a father's righteous fury, unforgiving.

You disgust me. You and your kind. If your mother can stomach you, good for her. Not me.

Hans had refused to go with Lydia to East Lansing, and he would refuse to discuss the arrangements Lydia made for Alva to be admitted to a drug rehabilitation clinic after her discharge from the hospital. He was departing for Europe. Medical conferences in Berlin, Rome. Hans Ulrich

133

was a consultant to the UN and would be named to the president's advisory board on matters of health and public welfare. His life was a worldly one; he'd become one of the preeminent epidemiologists of his generation. Not the effluvia of family life but the grandeur of public life would define him. Not fatherhood, not marriage. Not love, but professional achievement and renown. Hans was a man who, when he died (prematurely, aged sixty-one, of cardiac arrest, thousands of miles from Lydia), would be eulogized in prominent obituaries for his 'seminal' work in this crucial field. *Survived by wife, daughter* was the most perfunctory afterthought.

In the hospital in East Lansing, at her daughter's bedside, Lydia had seemed finally to understand. It had to be a fact others knew, to which Lydia had come late: to love unconditionally is fraudulent, a lie. There is a time for love, and there is a time for the repudiation of love. Yet Lydia protested, 'I can't change my love for you, Alva, even if . . .'

Even if you don't love me.

Alva grimaced and shut her eyes. A shudder passed over her thin body. She could not have weighed more than ninety pounds. Her skin looked jaundiced but was coolly clammy to the touch. An IV tube drained liquid into her bruised forearm. The hair that had been a beautiful ashy blond through Alva's girlhood was coarse, matted, threaded now with silver like glinting wires. A sour odor lifted from her; Lydia would carry it away from the hospital in her clothing, her hair. She thought this must be the odor of dissolution, impending death.

She returned to her hotel room. She showered, washed her hair. She left a message for Hans with his assistant. *You must try to come! Our daughter may be dying.*

But Alva had not died. Another time Alva recovered.

So quickly that one day she checked out of the hospital and eluded her mother. It was a bleakly comic scene Lydia would long recall: her astonishment at Alva's vacated bed, her naive query put to one of the floor nurses: 'But didn't my daughter leave any word for me?'

No word. Only the hospital bill.

A considerable bill, for eight full days.

That had been the last time Lydia had seen her daughter, or spoken with her. Terrible to realize, when the detective from Upper Darby called her, that it had been more than seven years.

Seven years. A child's lifetime.

Genes are the cards we're all dealt. What we do with the cards is our lives.

Hans Ulrich was denounced in some circles as cold, unfeeling, a statistician and not a medical man. In other circles, politically conservative, he was honored as a seer.

In fact it had been more than seven years that

Lydia had been sending checks to Alva in care of post office boxes in the Midwest. After dropping out of college for the third and final time, Alva had drifted westward, to Ohio, Indiana, Iowa. To Michigan, Minnesota. To Missouri, to Illinois. Impossible to determine if Alva traveled alone or with others; if she'd acquired, in her itinerant life, some sort of family; if she'd even married, and if so if she'd remained with her husband or drifted away from him as she'd drifted away from her parents. Lydia sent checks, and Alva cashed them. At the outset, Lydia and Hans were still living together in Georgetown, where both had academic appointments; Hans disapproved, but never interfered so long as the money Lydia sent was clearly her own, from her salary. With the checks Lydia never failed to enclose a handwritten letter or card. She would wish one day that she'd kept a record of these, as a kind of journal or diary of her own life, the crucial facts of her life offered to her daughter in a relentlessly upbeat tone, for words are the easiest of deceits, so long as they aren't spoken aloud. To write a thing is to make it true, Lydia thought.

Alva rarely replied to Lydia's letters, except from time to time to notify her of another change of address, on the printed form provided by the post office. But Alva never failed to cash the checks.

'She reads my letters, at least. That's how we keep in touch.'

This had to be so. Lydia would explain to the prying detectives.

'Not an interrogation, Mrs Ulrich. An interview.'

Mrs Ulrich. The wife, the mother. She was their subject.

Lydia's nervous offer of coffee? tea? soda? was politely declined. A woman whose home is entered, a woman who can't provide some gesture of hospitality, is a woman disoriented, disadvantaged, like one suffering from that infection of the inner ear that determines our ability to keep our balance.

Lydia's offer of a smile was politely declined.

Their names were Hahn and Panov. Lydia stared at the cards handed to her. Already she had forgotten which man was which.

Hahn, Panov. Was Hahn the elder? He led the interview.

'. . . won't mind, will you, if we tape this . . .'

Lydia invited them to sit down. It must have been choreographed: the detectives took seats in chairs facing her but at a little distance from each other. Lydia would glance at one of the men, and at the other; back to the first, and again the other. While Hahn questioned her, Panov studied her in profile.

Alva was in danger, Lydia thought. It had to be drug-related, and it had to be a serious crime.

How she, the mother, was connected, Lydia could not imagine.

Wanting to cry, *Please tell me! Don't torment me.*

It was unnerving to think that these strangers glancing about casually at Lydia's attractive living room flooded with May sunshine, making no comment on it, as other visitors would naturally have done, seemingly not very impressed, knew something about Alva, and something about Lydia, that Lydia didn't know.

Unnerving to think that these men, who'd driven from the Philadelphia area to Bethesda to speak with Lydia, had flown to Carbondale, Illinois, to speak with Alva.

Yet more unnerving, Alva had been the one to contact the detectives. Alva, who feared and despised figures of authority like police, social welfare officials, judges!

Lydia was told that her daughter had been encouraged to contact the Upper Darby Police Department by a therapist whom she'd been seeing as well as a faculty member at the state university, because in recent weeks she had been haunted by memories of having witnessed a violent crime as a child. Alva had come to believe that she had crucial information to offer police, to aid in the investigation of a homicide of 1974 that had recently been reopened by Upper Darby police.

Homicide! Lydia was astonished.

'This can't be. Alva couldn't have been more than seven at that time.'

Not drugs? Not Illinois?

Lydia smiled nervously. Looking from Hahn to

138

Panov, from Panov to Hahn, thinking this had to be a misunderstanding. Surely not a joke?

Alva had never been one to joke. You couldn't reason with Alva by speaking playfully. Couldn't coax her, even as a little girl, out of a mood by making her laugh, because Alva couldn't be made to laugh. Instead, Alva would stare at you. Blankly.

So the detectives regarded Lydia, not exactly blankly but with professional detachment, a kind of clinical curiosity. They were seeing a sixty-one-year-old woman who looked much younger than her age, a widow, a professional woman, obviously educated and well-spoken and not the Mrs Ulrich they might have expected, having first met her daughter.

They were seeing a woman who needed to be assured that her daughter wasn't ill, wasn't in danger. 'For some reason I have only a post office address for Alva in Carbondale. I would so appreciate it if you could give me her street address before you leave.'

A reasonable voice. Not exactly begging. A mother concerned for her child, though the child is thirty-seven.

'She moves so often, that's why I seem to have lost . . .'

Lydia had forgotten that she'd been told that Alva didn't want her to know her street address. You'd have thought she had forgotten.

Neither Hahn nor Panov acknowledged her remark. Lydia wanted to think, *They're being kind, they feel sorry for me. They are on my side.*

139

So you yearn to think when investigators enter your home.

The detectives would have recognized Alva at once: one of the walking wounded, casualties of the drug culture. Young people whose early promise had been destroyed by drugs as by a virulent disease.

They would recognize Lydia, the brave left-behind mother.

'. . . a witness, you say? Alva? As a child of . . .'

Lydia spoke respectfully of her daughter, though also skeptically. She would not suggest that her daughter had to be fantasizing, as so often, through the years, Alva had done.

Hahn was telling Lydia that the newly reopened case was a notorious one: 'Pink Bunny Baby.' Did she remember it?

A very young child, believed to be about two, had been found dead in a remote area of Rock Basin Park. She'd been tightly swaddled in a blanket, bruised but not visibly injured, having been smothered to death. The little girl wore an article of clothing with pink bunnies on it, and so in the media she was the Pink Bunny Baby. A police sketch of her doll-like face as it must have been before her death had been replicated many thousands of times in the press, for weeks, months.

Pink Bunny Baby had never been identified. Her murderer or murderers had never been identified.

Lydia was stunned. Whatever she'd been expecting, it could not have been this.

'Of course I remember. That nightmare. We lived only a few miles from Rock Basin Park. Alva was in second grade at the time. We tried to shield her from . . .'

It came back to Lydia, the clutch of fear she'd felt then. A mother's fear that something terrible might happen to her child.

When your child is an infant, you're in terror that somehow she will die, simply cease breathing; you must check her constantly, compulsively. When she's older and often out of your sight, you worry that a madman might steal her away.

Though it was widely believed that Pink Bunny Baby had been killed by a parent or parents, not a roving madman. For who else would wish to kill a child so young, except a deranged parent? That was the nightmare.

Lydia spoke slowly at first, with a kind of recalled dread. By degrees she began speaking more rapidly, as if a mechanism had been sprung in her brain.

'For months, every day it was Pink Bunny Baby in newspapers, on TV. There were fliers and posters. Everyone spoke of it. You couldn't escape it. We censored everything that came into the house and we never let Alva watch TV alone, but still she was badly frightened by older children at school. She was a high-strung, nervous child. Extremely intelligent, with a talent for drawing and music, but too restless to sit still for more than a few minutes. Today she would be diagnosed as ADD, but in the 1970s no one had identified attention deficit disorder, and the only medication for hyperactive children would have been tranquilizers. We took Alva – that is, I took her – to pediatricians, child psychiatrists, neurologists. Hans was outraged when she was diagnosed as borderline autistic – we knew this couldn't be accurate, Alva was a bright, communicative, verbal child who could look you in the eye when she wanted to. Even before the child's body was found she'd had nightmares, and these got worse. She did astonishing crayon drawings of the 'little pink baby' she called her baby sister. She begged us to let her sleep with us at night – but she was too old, Hans insisted. She begged us to take her to the place where Pink Bunny Baby was found.'

Words spilled from Lydia, leaving her breathless. The detectives listened without comment and without the usually encouraging smiles and head signals that accompany conversation.

This wasn't a conversation, of course. This was an interview.

The elder detective asked, 'And did you take your daughter to the park, Mrs Ulrich?'

'Of course not! You can't be serious.'

'Did your husband take her?'

'Certainly not.'

'Neither of you ever, alone or together, took your daughter to Rock Basin Park?'

Lydia looked from one detective to the other. Hahn, Panov.

She was confused; she was speaking in-coherently. Wanting to plead with them: *What did my daughter see? What has she told you about me?*

'Well, yes. Before the child's body was found. But not to that terrible place.'

'You knew where the place was, then? You were familiar with that part of the park?'

Lydia hesitated. It had been so long: thirty years.

'Only just from the newspaper. There were countless stories, photographs of the park. Even maps.'

'How long did you live in Upper Darby, Mrs Ulrich?'

'Five years. Hans had an academic appointment at—'

'In all those years you'd never been to that part of Rock Basin Park where the child was found? Yet you could recognize it from the newspaper?'

Lydia tried not to speak sharply. As an adminis-trator, knowing that a sudden break in civility, a breach in decorum, can never really be amended. 'Yes, probably we'd been there. It was a hiking area, wasn't it? A very beautiful part of Rock Basin Park – a stony creek, wild-growing lilac, wood-chip paths through a pine forest, massive outcroppings of granite . . . When I took Alva to the park by myself, which was most of the time, while Hans was working, we kept to the playground area, where there were other children, but when Hans was with us, on Sundays usually, he wanted to hike along the creek. Once, when Alva was about

143

four, very bright and precocious, she slipped away from Hans and me and we'd thought she was lost, or abducted. We were searching for her everywhere, calling for her, terrified she might have drowned in the creek, but it turned out that Alva was only hiding from us – a kind of demon got into her sometimes – she was hiding from us inside a hedge of lilac, she was feverish-looking, giggling at us, and when Hans caught up with her he was furious, lost control and grabbed Alva by the shoulders and shook her hard, like a rag doll, shouted into her face, she was paralyzed with fear. I wasn't able to stop Hans in time. I think . . .' Lydia paused, trembling. She had never told anyone this. She had never entirely acknowledged this. Between Hans and her there had been patches of blankness, lacunae to which no language accrued, therefore no knowledge. Perhaps Hans had hurt Alva; the child was white-faced with terror, mute. That Daddy had turned on her, Daddy whom she adored. And the truth was, Lydia hadn't dared intervene; she'd been frightened of Hans herself. Wondering afterward if Alva had known how her mother had failed her at that crucial moment. 'I tried to hold her, comfort her, but . . . Ever afterward, if I took Alva to the park, to the playground area, she was anxious, frightened. She began to have a thing about dolls – not her own dolls, Alva hadn't wanted dolls, but dolls left behind in the playground, lost and broken dolls. She was fascinated by them and frightened. 'Look at the baby, look at the baby' – she'd laugh, hide her mouth with her hand as if there were something naughty, something obscene, about the doll, or about seeing it, and I would say, 'Alva, it's only a doll, you know what a doll is, Alva – don't be silly, it's only a doll.' And this went on for years.' Lydia paused, not liking her anxious, eager voice. She stared at the tape recorder. The slowturning cassette inside. What was she revealing, to strangers, that could never be retracted? 'But none of this has anything to do with the little girl found in the park in 1974. This happened years before. Alva was seven when the child was found. She was in second grade at Buhr Elementary. As I said, she became morbidly fascinated with Pink Bunny Baby. At this time Hans began traveling often. He's a – he was a – prominent scientist, and ambitious. When he was away, Alva became particularly anxious. It was 'Daddy, Daddy, where is Daddy, is Daddy coming back?' As if Alva could foresee, many years later, that Daddy would leave us – leave me. Of course Hans was flattered by our daughter's fixation on him, but he couldn't tolerate any sort of house-hold upset. Emotions have very little to do with science, I mean with the methods of science. If you're a psychologist, like me, you might study emotions – but not in an emotional way. As I grew out of being a mother, I grew into being a scientist. But not a scientist like Hans Ulrich. Not of his originality, genius. Not of his stature. Hans

145

was a quintessential male scientist – he needed a domestic household, he needed a wife who was in no way a rival. He'd been born in Frankfurt, and he was contemptuous of the ways in which Americans spoil their children. Not all Americans – just the affluent, the privileged. He hadn't been a child of privilege, and he didn't want a child of his to be one either. So he wasn't the sort of father to indulge a child as imaginative and headstrong and sensitive as Alva. He believed that she was exaggerating her fears – her nightmares – to manipulate us. Especially Daddy. I found it hard to discipline Alva, even to scold her. Like tossing a lighted match onto flammable material! I was afraid my daughter wouldn't love me. Maybe Hans was right, I wasn't a good mother – something went terribly wrong. Already in middle school she began to grow away from us, and in high school the drugs began. So Alva left me, anyway. Whatever I did, it must have been a mistake.'

Lydia paused. She was breathless, agitated. Yet awaiting assurance: *Of course you aren't to blame, how wrong you are to blame yourself, obviously your daughter has a biochemical imbalance, you are wrong to blame yourself, Mrs Ulrich!* But the detectives from Upper Darby, Pennsylvania, allowed the moment to pass.

Is it a cliché of speech, a sinking heart? Yet Lydia felt a sinking sensation in her chest at this moment. *They aren't kind men. They don't feel sorry for me. They are not on my side.*

Now the interview must conclude, for Lydia had told the detectives all she knew.

'Mrs Ulrich, your daughter was adopted, yes?'

'No, Alva isn't adopted. I'm sorry.'

Sorry my daughter misled you. Sorry my daughter wishes not to be my daughter.

She went away to bring the birth certificate to show the detectives. Moving stiffly, like one with knee or spinal pain. Moving stiffly, like an elderly woman.

The detectives studied the document without comment. Alva Lucille Ulrich. Parents Lydia Moore Ulrich, Hans Stefan Ulrich. The certificate had been signed by an obstetrician at the University of Pennsylvania Medical School Hospital, Philadelphia, PA, February 19, 1967.

'. . . a common fantasy, adoption. In imaginative children. It isn't considered pathological unless carried to extremes. Just a fantasy, a kind of comfort. That you've been adopted, your real parents are . . .'

Somewhere else. Someone else.

Lydia recalled the birth pains. Excruciating labor that had lasted nearly ten hours. She had wanted, she'd thought, a natural childbirth, what's called, bluntly, 'vaginal.' Her obstetrician and her husband had not thought this a very good idea. And so it had not been a very good idea.

In the end, Lydia had had a C-section. An ugly

147

razor scar in the pit of her now sagging belly, which she might show to the detectives if they were skeptical of her credentials as a biological mother.

'Alva asked if she'd been adopted. We told her no. Yet the fantasy persisted. Except as an adult she should have grown out of it.'

They were asking Lydia if she'd adopted another child. A younger child. Or had she had another child, younger than Alva?

A younger sister to Alva. Who had died.

'No. I did not.'

It was bewildering to contemplate the shadow figure who was somehow Mrs Ulrich in Alva's imagination. Mrs Ulrich, whom the detectives were pursuing.

While she, Lydia, recalled through a haze of pain someone bringing her a squirming wet red-faced baby, *hers*. The astonishment of this baby so naturally in her arms, sucking at her milk-heavy breast. It had seemed to transpire in a dream. The dream could not have been her own, for it was too wonderful for Lydia to have imagined. Out of the massive labor, the exhilaration of the baby, the nursing. The eager young father who'd loved her then.

Detectives' questions are circular, tricky. Another time Lydia was asked if she'd adopted a child, any child, and Lydia explained no, never. And another time she was asked if she'd had any other children apart from Alva, and she said no.

148

Any other children apart from Alva who had died.

'No. I'm sorry.'

In their marriage it was Lydia who had wanted more children and Hans who had not. All marriages are fairy tales, *Once upon a time there was a man and a woman*, and the Ulriches' tale was of a man who'd pursued a career and a woman who'd delayed her career to be a devoted mother to a difficult daughter who would repudiate her and break her heart. In fact, Lydia hadn't really wanted another child. She had allowed Hans to think so; in a way it was flattering to Hans to think a woman would wish to have a second child with him after the stresses of the first, perhaps a son this time, to perpetuate the Ulrich name, but truly, in the most secret recesses of her heart, Lydia had not wanted another child, not a son, certainly not another daughter, after the first.

Wishing in secret, in weak moments, *If Alva had never been born.*

Lydia's own mother had suggested an abortion when Lydia was newly pregnant. Before Hans had known. For Lydia and Hans weren't yet married. They had not even been living together. Hans was finishing his doctorate at Penn; Lydia was only midway in her graduate studies. She was twenty-three. She was a very young twenty-three. She was a brilliant but self-doubting student whose professors had encouraged her to continue, but she'd fallen in

149

love with Hans Ulrich – how difficult not to fall in love with Hans Ulrich, though her mother warned her she was too young to be a mother, she had so much life before her, children might wait, marriage might wait, to another man perhaps, for Hans Ulrich was not a man to give comfort but only to take comfort – and in the spell of sexual enchantment she'd defied her mother, married Hans Ulrich and had his child.

He had loved her then. Lydia, and their daughter.

For Alva had been a beautiful child at first.

The child of Lydia's destiny. That seemed clear.

Really, Lydia couldn't imagine her life without Alva. Never!

Very easily she could imagine her life without Alva. The life she was living now, if you subtracted all thoughts of Alva in the way that, despairing over being able to wash clean a grimy wall, you simply painted it over.

Lydia's friends who were mothers like herself, some of them grandmothers, never spoke of such things. They spoke of other things but never this. No one dared to acknowledge a lost life, if she had not married and had children exactly as she had. You did not speak of it. You dared not speak of it. In fact, it was pointless to speak of it.

You did not even think of it, with children near. For children hear what is not said more keenly than what is.

Only a doll, Alva. Like you.

As a research psychologist, Dr Ulrich had tested numberless subjects. She was particularly interested in the relationship between consciousness and the brain: 'self-identifying.' There is a magical period of self-recognition in two-year-olds, utterly missing in younger children. To recognize the self (in a mirror, in reflective surfaces, in photographs) is taken for granted in normal individuals. Self-identity resides in a certain region of the brain that, if destroyed, can't be replaced. The self is in the brain: the soul is in the brain cells. To be an academic scientist is to test hypotheses. You perform experiments, you tally results, you publish papers; by degrees you accumulate a public career. Dr Ulrich, the psychological tester, was without affect. In her role as tester she smiled cordially, to manipulate and comfort. But no one could read her heart. Subjects are to be manipulated; otherwise there is no experiment and there is no accumulated wisdom. Now the detectives from Upper Darby, Pennsylvania, were the testers and Dr Ulrich, seated on an ottoman in her own living room, was the subject. She understood the detectives' cordial expressions. The steely calculation in their eyes.

To be innocent of wrongdoing is to be as vulnerable as one whose skin has been peeled back. To stand so naked, exposed. Every word sounds like an admission of guilt.

But guilt for what, Lydia had no idea.

Forty minutes into the interview – forty minutes!

it had seemed like hours – as the detectives were asking her another time to tell them what she could remember of her daughter's medical record as a child living in Upper Darby, the telephone rang. Lydia had intended to remove the receiver from the hook but had forgotten. Now she was grateful for the interruption. This summons to another life.

Within earshot of the detectives, she said, in a voice her friend would not have identified as anxious, 'Dolores, I'm sorry, I will have to call you back in about twenty minutes.'

Wanting the intruders to hear. Twenty minutes. No more.

Wanting them to hear. *My life. My real life. To which you have no access.*

It was then that they told her.

Why they'd come to speak with her. Why her daughter had called the Upper Darby PD. What claims her daughter was making that involved her and her husband in the smothering death of the unidentified child found in Rock Basin Park.

Stunned, Lydia looked from one detective to the other. Their names were lost to her now. Their faces were as blurred as faces reflected in water.

Lydia began to stammer. 'I don't understand – my daughter has accused my husband and me—'

Smothering? Murder? A baby sister? The child in the tightly swaddled blanket, the soiled jumper said to be decorated with a row of pink bunnies?

'. . . the murder? That murder? The little girl? In Rock Basin Park? My daughter Alva has . . .'

Now the net was tightening around her, she could not breathe. A band tightening around her forehead. She was stammering, trying to speak. To deny, to explain. *My daughter is sick. My daughter has blamed me. I don't know why.* But she could not explain. She could not speak. One of the detectives caught her arm – she'd begun to faint. The other went quickly to bring her a glass of ice water.

Ice water! At such a time, the detective had brought her ice water. Seeing that Lydia had, in her compact kitchen, a refrigerator that dispensed ice cubes.

'I . . . don't believe this. Can't . . .'

She would not recall afterward what they'd said. What they'd said next. She had assured them she was fine, she would not faint. She could hear their voices, at a distance. She could see them as if through the wrong end of a telescope. Her vision was bizarrely narrowed, edged in black. For part of her brain, its visual field, had darkened. *My daughter hates me. Blames me. But . . . I am blameless.*

Her voice was begging. Her voice was near inaudible.

'Please, I want to speak with her. My daughter. Please . . .'

But she could not speak with her daughter, for

her daughter did not wish to speak with her. So it was explained to Mrs Ulrich another time.

'. . . a misunderstanding! My daughter isn't well. If you've spoken with her, you must know. Alva has a history of . . .'

But she could not accuse her daughter, could she?

These men on a mission. Regarding her steely-eyed, assessing.

A sixty-one-year-old woman. A professional woman. Accused of having smothered a child thirty years before. A child who'd possibly been her own daughter. Unless an adopted daughter. Two-year-old younger sister of the seven-year-old daughter. Unless the seven-year-old was also adopted. Unless Mrs Ulrich had not herself smothered the child but had aided and abetted Hans Ulrich. Conspired with Hans Ulrich to commit the murder. Thirty years ago.

'Why? Why now? Why on earth now? I've just sent her a check, Alva cashed. For five hundred dollars. I have the canceled check, it's one of many. I can show you. I've saved all the checks. Thousands of dollars. Why would she turn on me, her mother? Why now . . .'

She was terrified to think, *These are men on a mission. Mrs Ulrich is their prey.*

Pink Baby Bunny was a high-profile cold case. Suddenly you are hearing of 'cold cases' revived and solved everywhere in America. As crime rates decline. As old unsolved cases are reactivated. Older detectives, some of them coming back from retirement, are reactivated. Reinspired. Mrs Ulrich was in their gun sights.

'If I could just talk with Alva, if you could arrange for me to talk with her, please. In person . . .'

'Your daughter doesn't want to talk with you, Mrs Ulrich. We've explained.'

'But . . .'

Men with a mission. Pitiless, professional. You could see.

Or did they pity her? The trembling sixty-one-year-old woman whose life was shattering around her.

Yet she was in their gun sights, she was their prey. Mrs Ulrich. A trophy.

They had driven in pursuit of her this morning from Upper Darby, Pennsylvania, to Bethesda, Maryland. As they'd flown, last week, to Carbondale, Illinois. To interview her accuser. To tape the accuser's statement.

Her life shattered. Her professional life destroyed. Now she would retire: forced to retire. Even if not arrested, not formally accused. Her photograph in the papers, on TV. *Lydia Ulrich. Director of. Questioned by police. Smothering murder, 1974. Two-year-old victim. Body left in park.*

Was she arrested? She was not arrested. Not yet.

Should she call a lawyer? That was up to Mrs Ulrich.

Still her vision was radically diminished: a tunnel

rimmed with black. The detectives' blurred faces at the end of the tunnel. If one day you open your eyes and can't see one side of the room, it's a brain tumor you have. Tunnel vision, it's panic.

Panic that your life is being taken from you. Tattered and flapping like flags in the wind.

Body left in park. Believed younger daughter of. Smothered.

The detectives were saying that they would play the tape of her daughter's statement, recorded the previous week in Carbondale. If Mrs Ulrich wished.

Yes. No. She could not bear it.

She would call a lawyer, she would save herself. As Hans would have fought to save himself.

Her life passing before her eyes, something tattered and torn flapping in the wind. Pitiful.

The detectives were regarding her with pity. Suspicion, but also pity. Perhaps they would be kind. Perhaps they did not want to destroy her. In their mission to solve the notorious cold case, in their zeal for TV celebrity, they would not want to destroy an innocent sixty-one-year-old woman.

Not arrested. Not arrested. Not yet!

Her heartbeat was rapid but weak. It could not pump enough blood to her brain.

If Hans were here! It was Hans they sought. The smotherer.

If Hans were here, as soon as the detectives entered the apartment, even as he was shaking

156

their hands, he would allow them to know *This is my home; I am the authority here.*

As a mother she'd taken the sorrow of her life and transformed it into love for her daughter. By an act of pure will she'd transformed it. Evidently it hadn't been enough.

She would explain. She could explain.

There were no words. Language was being taken from her.

The infant greedily sucking at her breast. Tugging at the raw nipple. Oh! it had hurt, as if the infant girl had teeth. But how lovely, the most sensual experience of Lydia's life.

A woman's secret, erotic life. A mother's life.

Hans had not known. Hans would have been astonished and revulsed if he'd known. But Hans had not known.

'. . . the tape of your daughter's statement, Mrs Ulrich? Would you like to hear?'

She could not accuse her daughter, could she? Her daughter she loved; she could not.

Could not plead, *She is cruel, she hates me. Blames me, I don't know why. My only child. She is evil.*

The history of her nightmares. The history of her fantasizing. Delusions, hallucinations. Accusing others. Blaming others. Sexual molestations, rape. Threats against her life. Stalking. Plundering of her soul.

She wasn't sure she could bear it, hearing her daughter's voice. The voice she hadn't heard in

157

years. Gripping her daughter's thin clammy-cold hand in the hospital room in East Lansing. Vowing to save her. Not to abandon her, as Hans had done. *Trade my life for yours if I could.*

History of nightmares. How was it the mother's fault?

History of accusations. Causing wreckage in lives, then moving on. How was it the mother's fault?

Not under arrest. Her name would not (yet) be released to any news media. Certainly she might call an attorney. Cooperation with the investigation was advised.

Witnesses would be interviewed. Records and documents would be checked. Mrs Ulrich might provide names. Mrs Ulrich might take a polygraph if she wished. The body of Pink Bunny Baby would very likely be exhumed for DNA analysis.

A match to Mrs Ulrich?

Unless the child had been adopted.

Unless the child had been abducted.

'. . . never spoke of this, Mrs Ulrich? That you can recall?'

'Spoke of . . . ?'

'Having seen your husband smothering a child. Telling your daughter it was only a doll.'

'Of course not.'

'This is entirely new to you.'

'Yes! It is.'

Wanting to scream at him. The enemy.

Lydia was speaking more calmly now. A sob in her voice.

She would not cry. Swiping at her eyes, which stung as if she'd been staring into a blinding sun.

They would be impressed with Lydia's integrity. Her honesty.

She'd taken a seat on the ottoman. Backless, because her posture was so impressive. *She would not cry.*

'She began taking drugs in high school, I think. She was fourteen, wouldn't come downstairs to dinner one evening when Hans was home. He called her, insisted that she come eat with us. There was a wild stomping on the stairs – Alva had wound transparent tape around her head, over her face, she'd made a grotesque mask of her own face, distorted, hellish, she was laughing and flinging herself around as if she wanted to hurt herself. Hans and I were terrified . . . She'd taken methamphetamine – we'd hardly known such a drug existed. Hans couldn't deal with it. I had to calm Alva, try to calm her – her skin was burning. I managed to unwind and cut the horrible tape away from her head, her eyebrows and eyelashes, clumps of hair, were pulled out – what a nightmare! Hans, the most agnostic of men, who hadn't a shred of belief in anything supernatural, said of our daughter, 'A devil gets into her,' sometimes 'A devil is in her.' But he never hurt her. Except once, that time in the park. The lilac bushes were in bloom – it should have been a beautiful time.

Stands of lilac growing wild. That rich smothering smell, there's a kind of madness in it. Hans hadn't meant to hurt her. She was a torment to us. 'A devil, a devil is in her.' But after that he rarely touched her, even to hug her, kiss her. He was frightened, I think. Of what he might do to her. I was the one who loved her. I've never given up.'

Yes, she would be calling an attorney. This very day.

Yes, she would cooperate with their investigation, for she had no reason not to cooperate. Her daughter's charges were absurd. Her daughter was mentally unstable. There was a medical history, there were medical records.

The good that came of this would be, Alva would receive medical treatment. In Carbondale, or here in Bethesda. Lydia would make arrangements.

Would not cry, Would not be destroyed.

Yes, she would hear the tape of her daughter's accusations. She was prepared for the shock of it. She believed.

Then, as one of the detectives moved to change the cassettes, Lydia asked him to wait a minute. She would be right back.

Rising shakily to her feet. One of the detectives helped her.

How brittle her bones felt! For the first time, she was feeling her age.

In her bathroom Lydia ran cold water from a faucet, distracted by the stricken face in the

160

mirror. Perhaps she did look sixty-one. Perhaps the detectives had not been surprised. The capacity to recognize the self is located in the left brain hemisphere, but in Lydia, so wounded, the capacity seemed to be damaged. *Why is that woman so old? I remember her young.*

She could not bear it, the woman's eyes.

In the medicine cabinet were numerous little bottles of pills. Old prescriptions she'd never thrown away. You never know when you might need sleeping pills, painkillers. She'd amassed a considerable quantity.

More than enough. If necessary.

Running water, Lydia opened the bathroom door stealthily.

She'd hoped that in the mirror, which would pick up a reflecting surface in the dining room, she could see slantwise into the living room, where the detectives were. By now one was probably on his feet, stretching. Perhaps both. In lowered tones they would be speaking of their suspect. The mask-faces were animated now. They were alive now, scenting their prey. Their teeth were bared in ex-hilaration. Yet they were uncertain of the woman; she was nothing like they'd expected. The daughter's story was so far-fetched. Much of it was unverifiable. Much of it was common know-ledge, widely reported in the media. The defense attorney would rebut their case. There was the daughter's medical history; they would investigate.

But Lydia couldn't see into the living room. The

glass door of a breakfront reflected only a doorway, a wall.

Lydia was thinking of the famous experiment in childhood truth-telling and deception. Pandora's box, some called it. Several children of about the age of three were left alone together in a room, emphatically instructed not to look into a shut box. With a hidden camera, the children were videotaped. Nearly 90 percent of the children looked into the box, but when questioned, fewer than 33 percent confessed to having looked. When five-year-olds were tested, nearly 100 percent disobeyed and tried, often very convincingly, to deceive. Demonstrating that as children mature, their capacity for deception increases.

Curious, Hans had wanted to test Alva at age two. Her disobeying, and her insistence upon her innocence afterward, had been so charming, Hans had only laughed. His beautiful little girl, so precocious! In a variant of the test, Hans offered a chocolate treat to Alva if she 'really, really' told the truth. Some children, stricken with doubt, would have demurred at this. Not Alva.

Lydia had laughed with Hans, though saddened by the child's precocious duplicity. And, somehow, the innocence of it. But Hans had been charmed. *In* Homo sapiens *the talent for deception is our strongest evolutionary advantage*.

No trust. Preemptive war. The only wisdom.

Summoning her strength to walk back into the living room, even to smile at her tormentors, Lydia saw that, as she'd envisioned, one of the detectives was strolling about, admiring the view from her windows. 'Twelfth floor? Must be nice.' Gently Lydia corrected him: 'Tenth floor.'

They asked Lydia if she was prepared to hear her daughter's statement and Lydia said yes.

TETANUS

iaz, César. Like an upright bat, quivering wings folded over to hide its wizened face, the boy was sitting hunched over the table beneath glaring fluorescent lights, shaved head bowed, rocking back and forth and humming frantically to himself. Arresting officers had banged him a little, torn his filthy T-shirt at the collar, bloodied his nose and upper lip. His eyes, wetly glassy, frightened and furtive, lurched in their sockets. He was breathing hard, panting. He'd been crying. He'd sweated through his T-shirt, which was several sizes too large for his scrawny body. He was talking to himself now, whispering and laughing. Why was he laughing? Something seemed to be funny. Spittle shone at the boy's red fleshy lips, and the nostrils of his broad stubby nose were edged with bloody mucus. He took no notice of the door to the windowless room opening, a brief conversation between two individuals, adults, male, Caucasian, figures of authority, of no more apparent interest to him than the tabletop before him. He was eleven years old; he'd been taken into Trenton police custody on a complaint by his mother for threatening her and his younger brother with a fork.

'César? Hello. My name is . . .'

Zwilich spoke with practiced warmth, calm. Pulling out a chair at the counseling table, at his usual place: back to the door. Outside were Mercer County guards. Mercer County Family Services shared cramped quarters with the Mercer County Department of Parole and Probation and was adjacent to the Mercer County Youth Detention Center, which was an aggressively ugly three-story building made of a stony gray material that looked as if it had been pissed on over a period of many years, in jagged, whimsical streaks. You came away thinking that these walls were covered in graffiti, though they were not.

Early evening, a Friday in late June. Parole and Probation had shut for the weekend, but Family Services was open for business, and busy.

One of those days that, beginning early, swerve and rumble forward through the hours with the numbing, slightly jeering repetition of an endless stream of freight cars. Even as Zwilich's life was falling into pieces he was speaking in his friendly-seeming and upbeat voice to *Diaz, César*, whose latest arrest sheet lay before him on the table, beside a folder stamped 'Mercer County Family Services: Confidential.'

'. . . and I'm here just to ask you a few questions, César. You've been in counseling with Family Services before, I think. This time we need to clear up some problems before you can go home. Can you hear me?'

The batlike boy sneered, smirked. You had to think that he was very frightened, yet his manner was hostile, insolent. He was rocking from side to side, gripping his scraped elbows. He was muttering to himself and laughing, and Zwilich, an adult male in his mid-thirties, old enough to be César Diaz's father and wishing to project a fatherly or older-brotherly manner, wishing to convey to César Diaz that he sympathized with him, respected him, he was on his side and not on the side of the enemy, had no doubt that if he could hear the obscene words the boy was muttering, a hot flash would color Zwilich's cheeks above his patch of whiskers and his heart would kick in revulsion for the boy, but luckily Zwilich couldn't hear.

He would tell Sofia, It's been one of those days. Which? Which days?

A day of temptation. Terrible temptations.

And did you succumb?

Goddamn, he was not going to succumb. He'd had a few drinks at late lunch to buoy his spirits, and the prospect of a few drinks this evening, alone or with another, somewhere improvised, filled him now with a gassy sort of elation, like a partly deflated balloon someone has decided, out of whimsy or pity, to inflate.

Zwilich spoke. Kindly, with patience. Such evil in him, his secret little cesspool glittering deep inside the well of his soul; it was his task, a sacred task, to keep the lid on. Yet the boy resisted. Staring, stubborn and unyielding, at a bloody smear on the table before him, where he'd wiped the edge of his hand after having wiped a skein of bloody mucus from his nose. Zwilich was thinking that César Diaz, exposed in pitiless fluorescent lighting, might have been drawn, with finicky, maniacal exactitude, by Dürer or Goya. No mere photograph could capture his essence. His forehead was low and furrowed in an adult expression of anguish indistinguishable from rage. His bony boy's head had been shaved, as if to expose its vulnerability, breakable layers of skull bone upon which a scalp, reddened with rashes and bumps, seemed to have been fitted tight as the skin of a drum. A very ugly head, an aborigine head, crudely sculpted in stone and unearthed from the soil of centuries. The arresting officers had pegged César Diaz as possibly gang-affiliated, but Zwilich thought that wasn't likely; the kid was too young and too scrawny – no gang would want him for a few years. The shaved head was more likely Mrs Diaz's precaution against lice.

Zwilich suppressed a shudder. Itchy scurrying sensation at the nape of his neck, his jaws beneath the whiskers. He'd caught lice from clients in early years. But not for years.

According to César Diaz's mother, he'd been sniffing glue with other boys earlier that day, and coming home he'd caused a 'ruckus' in their building, he'd been 'violent,' 'uncontrollable,' 'threatening.' Glue sniffing! It was an epidemic among boys César's age, in certain Trenton neighborhoods. If Zwilich hadn't been assured that César had been examined by a doctor, passed back into police custody, and delivered to Family Services for evaluation, he'd have thought the boy was still high, or deranged. Sniffing airplane glue was the cheapest, crudest high, scorned by serious junkies (meth, heroin) for causing the quickest brain damage. The boy's bloodshot eyes shone with an unnatural intensity, as if about to explode, and a powerful odor of unwashed flesh, sweat, grime, misery wafted to Zwilich's nostrils.

It would be traumatic for César to be kept overnight in detention, but there, at least, he'd be made to take a shower. A real shower. As in a slow-motion dream sequence, Zwilich could imagine the bat-boy cringing beneath hot rushing water, layers of filth gradually washing off his skinny body, in swirls at the drain beneath the boy's bare feet. The darkish Hispanic pallor emerging, a startling beauty, out of encrusted dirt.

He felt a sudden pang of tenderness for the boy. As if he'd glimpsed the boy naked and vulnerable and begging for love.

'César? Will you look at me? Your mother has said—'

Now César looked up sharply. 'Mama? She here?'

'Not just yet, César. Your mother is very upset

with you, and worried about you. She's hoping that we can—'

'Mama comin' to take me home? Where's she?'

The bloodshot eyes widened, excited. The bony shoulders twitched like broken wings.

'Your mother might – possibly – be coming to take you home tonight. Or it might be better for you to stay overnight at the—'

'Mama here! Ma*ma!* Goddamn fuck Ma*ma!*'

'César, hey, calm down. Sit still. If the guards hear you and come in, our interview is over.'

Zwilich frequently saw young offenders, as they were called, not only handcuffed but their cuffs chained to waist shackles; not infrequently, since adolescents were the most desperate of all offenders, their ankles were shackled too. Trooping in and out of the detention center next door, kids in neon orange jumpsuits, cuffed and shackled, and it was an unnatural and obscene vision that passed over by degrees into being a familiar vision, one that induced a sensation of extreme fatigue in the observer, like simply wanting to give up: die.

As if reading Zwilich's wayward thoughts, César bared his yellow teeth in a taunting smile. 'Hey, man? You be cool? I goin' home. Mama come? Mama sorry now?'

'Maybe. We'll see.'

'Mama sorry. Yes.'

The boy spoke with such vehemence, Zwilich didn't doubt that yes, Mama was very sorry.

The wan, stale odor of sorrow blew through air vents in the old State Street building. Some smells, in the first-floor men's lavatories, were feculent, sulfurous, a prefiguring of the farthest-from-daylight pit of hell.

Six years on the staff at Family Services, Zwilich would have been promoted to supervisor by now except for budget cuts through festering New Jersey, and departmental resentments. Inevitable that he'd provoke resentment, being overqualified for his job and inclined, beneath his courteous manner, to exasperated patience, irony. Most days he wore black jeans and a white cotton dress shirt and sometimes a necktie – sometimes a lead-colored necktie. He wore expensive silver-threaded Nikes, in cool weather a black leather bomber jacket to align himself with, not his colleagues, still less his superiors, but his clients. His bristly sand-colored whiskers were trimmed into a goatee; his still-thick hair, receding at his temples, was trimmed in a crew cut that gave him, in these uncertain years approaching forty, an air of youthful vitality and waywardness that at times Zwilich still felt. He hadn't quit his job as Sofia had quit hers, in disgust, dismay. He had plans still. Environmental law, a Ph.D. in social psychology. He wasn't old. He wasn't broken. Maybe inclined to sarcasm – can't be helped. He didn't want to think that without a clear future, a vision of some sort of happiness, the present becomes unendurable in a very short time.

He asked César, How'd you like some pizza? A Coke? and César shrugged okay cautiously, as if suspecting a trick; it's a world in which, if you're eleven years old, some older guy, or could be a girl, holds out a pizza slice for you, a can of Coke, and when you reach for it slaps your hand away, laughs in your face. Zwilich made a quick call on his cell phone, the pizzeria across the street where sometimes he ordered takeouts. Poor kid was probably starving. The least Zwilich could do, feed him.

It was Zwilich's task to interview the detained juvenile and make a recommendation to his supervisor, who, in the flurry of late Friday, and in his trust in Zwilich's judgment, would do no more than glance at the report and pass it on: whether to release César Diaz into an adult relative's custody or keep him overnight, or longer, in the juvenile detention facility. Zwilich disapproved of keeping kids as young as César Diaz even overnight in detention, where the oldest boys were sixteen. Inmates were segregated according to age and size, but still, a boy like César would be abused.

Probably something like that had already happened to César. Not once but many times.

On Monday, a Family Court judge would rule on César's case. Probation and outpatient therapy were most likely, unless, if Family Services recommended it, he were incarcerated in a juvenile facility. A kid's life in Zwilich's hands, like dice to

be tossed. A wild thought came to him: take César
Diaz home.

A call to Sofia to come back, see what I've done.

Except Sofia wasn't answering his phone
messages to her. Where was she staying, with
whom, in Trenton or possibly in Philadelphia:
Zwilich had suspicions but no clear knowledge.

. . . love you but frankly I'm afraid of you, terrified of going under with you, drowning.

He'd been shocked: Drown? With him?

As if Zwilich were a depressed man, was that it?
Sofia was fearful of the contagion?

He'd hated her in that moment. He'd wanted to
slap her beautiful, selfish face.

If they'd had a child. By now, children. When
two adults cohabiting fail to have children, they
remain perpetual children themselves.

'Well, César. See you've been busy.'

Zwilich whistled through his teeth looking
through the boy's file. He'd been taken into police
custody five times, twice within the past three
months. Vandalism, petty thefts, disturbances at
school and at home, glue sniffing. A previous case-
worker had noted that one of the vandalism
episodes included 'desecration of a cemetery' and
another the torture of a stray dog. It was noted that
an older neighborhood boy had tied a rope around
César's neck and yanked him around, causing him
to faint, when he'd been nine; another time, César
had fashioned a noose and stuck his own head into
it; yet another time, more recently, he'd forced a

noose over his six-year-old brother's head. He'd been picked up with two older boys for stealing from a 7-Eleven store, and not long afterward he'd been arrested for vandalism in the rear lot of the 7-Eleven store. He'd been several times suspended from school. Following these incidents he'd been assessed by Family Services psychologists and counselors and given sentences of 'supervised probation' with required therapy from Family Court judges who hadn't wanted to incarcerate so young a child. But Zwilich thought the next judge wasn't going to look kindly on all this.

The prosecutor for the case had told Zwilich that he intended to ask the judge to incarcerate the boy in juvenile detention for thirty days minimum. César Diaz required psychiatric observation as well as treatment for the glue sniffing, and it was 'high time' for the boy to learn that the law is serious. Sour, prim as a TV scold, Zwilich's colleague said, How're kids going to respect the law if there aren't any consequences to their behavior?

Zwilich sneered: Who respects the law? Whose behavior has consequences? Politicians, megacorporations?

He'd said, 'Hell, this is a child who's been arrested. Look at him, he's so small.'

Now, in the counseling room, Zwilich wasn't so sure. Fury quivered in César's tightly coiled little body; halfway you expected him to spring up at you, like a snake baring its fangs.

'. . . want to hurt your mother, César? Your little brother? You love them, don't you? Tell me.'

'Din't hurt nobody! Shit what Mama says.'

'I think you love them. Sure you do. Why'd you want to scare them, César? Tell me.'

César shrugged, sniggered. *You tell me.*

In César's file it was noted that his father, Hector Diaz, was deceased. Zwilich said, in a confiding voice, 'My father died when I was a little boy, César. I was just six. I know what it's like.'

César looked interested, briefly. His eyes shifted with caution, a kind of adult shyness, wariness. As if, like the offer of pizza, this might be some sort of trick.

Zwilich said, 'I still miss my father, César. But I talk to him, in a way. Every day I talk with him.' Zwilich paused, wondering if this might be true. He certainly talked with someone, in a continuous tape loop of improvised, pleading speech; but that someone seemed not to be listening. 'Do you talk with your father too?'

César shrugged, evasive now, down-looking, wiping at his leaking nose. Zwilich had several times offered him tissues, but the boy disdained them, preferring to wipe bloody snot on his fingers and his fingers on the table. Zwilich tried another father question, but the boy wasn't responding. You had to suppose that this was a misguided tactic: probably the kid hadn't even known his father, or, if he'd been told that somewhere he

174

had a father, he'd been told that the father was dead.

Father *deceased*. One problem out of the way.

When Zwilich proceeded to ask César about the thefts from the 7-Eleven store, the boy become animated, agitated. Now he began to chatter incoherently in an aggrieved voice. The 7-Eleven clerk must have been an Indian; César muttered a racist slur. There was indignation in his little body, and he eyed Zwilich insolently, as if to say, *So what, man?*

The boy was mimicking older boys he admired, neighborhood punks, dope dealers, the slatted rat-eyes, jeering laugh, junior macho swagger. In a boy so young the effect was as comical as a cartoon that, upon closer inspection, is pornographic.

Zwilich knew these kids. Some were 'juvies,' others were adolescents, 'youths.' Their souls' deepest utterances were rap lyrics.

He pitied them. He was sympathetic with them. He detested them. He feared them. He was grateful for them: they were his 'work.'

You would wish to think that César Diaz, so young, could be saved from them. Removed from his neighborhood, which was poisoning his soul, and placed – where? In a juvenile facility? But the youth facilities were overcrowded, understaffed. Zwilich admired some of the administrators of these facilities, for he knew of their idealism – their initial idealism, at least – but these places were in effect urban slum streets with walls around them.

César continued to chatter, agitated and aggrieved. Zwilich glanced at his watch, worn with the dim digital clock face on the inside of his wrist as if the exact time were a secret Zwilich didn't wish to share: 6:55 P.M. The date was June 30, 2006.

Each day, each hour. Equal to all others. If God is in one of these, God is in all of these.

He believed this! He wanted to believe.

Yet: *If God is absent from just one of these, God is absent from all of these.*

The pizza would be arriving soon, the Cokes; these would help. One of the guards would rap on the door: 'Mr Zwilich? Delivery.' César would observe the counselor paying for the meal, bills removed from Zwilich's wallet in a gesture of easy generosity. Sharing a meal with a client, in these cramped quarters, was a technique of Zwilich's, a friendly maneuver, intimate yet not overly familiar. You felt the urge to feed, to nurture, a kid like César, who had to be famished.

At the thought of pizza, Zwilich felt a mild stirring of nausea. Beer fat, whiskey fat, in flaccid flesh at his waist, a secret fat, for Zwilich was a lean, lanky, still-young-looking man, five feet ten inches, one hundred seventy pounds, given to small gestures of vanity – smoothing the bristly hairs of his beard, running his fingers through his brushlike hair, checking to see if – yes? was it

176

evident? – the deep bruised indentations beneath his eyes suggested insomniac nights, or late-drinking nights, restlessly surfing TV. The first mouthful of gummy pizza cheese, greasy Italian sausage, and scorched but doughy bread would repel him, and his thirst wasn't for syrupy-sweet Coke.

She loved him, she'd said. But didn't want to go down with him, and he'd said, But I thought you loved me, in the most piteous voice, and she'd said, backing away so he couldn't touch her, pull her off-balance toward him as in a clumsy dance, I love you! But I goddamn don't intend to drown with you. Alcohol – addictions of any kind, including nicotine, the most common painkillers – were more difficult for women to overcome than for men; it must be biochemical, genetic. Zwilich hated it, that his wife feared him, when first time he'd met her, at a bar in New Brunswick, in a gathering of medical students, Sofia had been drinking whiskey, straight. He'd been stunned by her beauty, her strong sensual mouth and vivid physical presence. The sight of a woman drinking whiskey aroused Zwilich, for it was rare in his experience and often the prelude to a sexual encounter, as it would prove with this woman after she'd become his wife.

Nine years! Since he'd first met her. Of these nine years, they'd been married seven.

If they'd had a baby. Babies. What then? Zwilich had no idea but couldn't think that having babies

177

was the solution to a riddle that taunted you every time you looked into a mirror: You? *Why?*

Here was César Diaz, a young woman's baby. It had to have seemed that little César was someone's answer, a temporary answer, to the riddle *Why?*

Freely César was speaking, boasting of his friends. Lots of friends, César's friends, to look out for him. If he went 'inside' – if he was 'kept here.' No clear transition then to a story about someone who'd fired a gun into the air, they be drinkin' this guy brother home from Ee-rock he in the army he have this gun shoot this gun, bullet go high in the air then fall, hit some old guy, poor old guy next-door back yard he hit, poor old guy he have bad luck the bullet hit him neck, he don't get to the hospital he die in ambulance you see on TV? Everybody talkin' about it but nobody know who shoot the gun. César grinned, laughed. He'd been tapping his neck to indicate a bullet entering, shaking his head, laughing. Nobody know.

Zwilich was listening now. He knew of this incident, which had been widely reported in the Trenton area: a random bullet fired into the air that had fallen and killed an elderly man in the Straube Street project back in April, and the shooter had never been identified. Zwilich tried to interrupt the chattering boy to ask who the shooter was – an Iraqi war veteran? – but César laughed, saying it wouldna happen if God din't

178

want it that way, nobody damn fault how the gun go off, how you blame it?

'César, did you tell your mother about this?'

César sniggered, vastly amused. Had to be Mr Zwilich was a real asshole to ask that.

'An elderly man dies, nobody cares? What if this man was your grandfather, César?'

'Hey man, he *not.*'

Zwilich felt a throb of dislike for the boy. The mimicry of older boys, men, in his voice, his vocabulary, his mannerisms, the contortions of his small body. Zwilich would be meeting with César's mother, not the next day, nor the next, but sometime on Monday, at which time César would appear before a Family Court judge, in the company of a court-appointed public defender. He saw in César's file that Gladys Diaz, twenty-eight, had moved to Trenton four years before from Camden, New Jersey; she was a diabetic who received Mercer County welfare payments for her sons and for herself; in Camden she'd been arrested for trying to cash forged checks and had been sentenced to two years' probation. At 3:30 P.M. on June 30,2006, Mrs Diaz had called 911 to report that her son César was 'threatening' her with a fork – not an eating fork but a long, two-pronged fork like you use for turning meat – screaming he was going to kill her and his six-year-old brother. He'd been sniffing glue; Mrs Diaz couldn't control him. But when Trenton police officers arrived at the Straube Street apartment and César ran away, panicked, crawling to hide beneath a bed, Mrs Diaz relented, saying maybe they shouldn't take her son away, then she'd relented again, saying yes! they should! this time she wasn't going to come with him to the precinct, César is on his own this time, though again changing her mind as the officers hauled the boy, shrieking and stumbling, to the street, to the waiting patrol car, wrists cuffed behind his back, and the officers would note on their reports a strong smell of red wine on Mrs Diaz's breath. César was speaking excitedly of Mama as if Zwilich must know her. César was furious with Mama but César was desperate for Mama. César was saying Mama been wantin' to scare him, now Mama sorry. Callin' the damn police, Mama done that before, sayin' she gonna call them to scare him, and his brother too, lots of times, to scare them. Mama afraid to beat him now, he too big, damn police come for him at school too but he'd never been 'kept in' this place; he'd be let go now, Mama comin' to take him home. Why this was funny, Zwilich didn't know. The boy's laughter was sharp like shattering glass and getting on his nerves. If the boy was made to spend a single night in the juvenile facility, he'd be punished for that shriek of a laugh. He'd be punished for his runny nose, and for his smell, and for being a runt, a loser.

César was demanding to know where's Mama? was Mama here yet? and Zwilich said his mama wasn't here, and César said, his voice rising, Where's Mama? I want Mama to take me home, and he wasn't laughing now, tears of indignation shone in his eyes, and Zwilich said, 'César, your mama told us to take you and keep you here as long as we want to. Your mama said, "I don't want César in the house anymore, I'm done with César, you keep him."'

Zwilich was a perfect mimic of Mama's furious voice. Fixing his somber counselor's eyes on César's face.

In fact Mrs Diaz *had* said something like this. The mothers of kids brought into juvenile custody invariably said something like this, or more extravagant despairing things, but Mrs Diaz had also said she hoped her son could come back home that night, she wanted to take him to stay with a relative in New Brunswick, get him out of the neighborhood for a while, and Zwilich, who'd spoken to the distraught woman on the phone, said yes, that sounded like a good idea.

César stared at Zwilich now in stunned silence, his mouth quivering. César couldn't be more respectful than if Zwilich had slapped him on both cheeks, hard. You didn't tell an eleven-year-old that his mama didn't want him, not in Zwilich's profession you didn't, but the impulse had come to him, not for the first time in circumstances like these, but for the first time with a child so young, an impulse as strong as sex, overpowering, irresistible, a wish to create something – even misery, even self-disgust – out of nothing. Zwilich felt a sick thrill. Zwilich smiled. Zwilich was overcome by shame. Luckily, the interview wasn't being taped, no surveillance camera in this airless cubbyhole, and outside in the corridor the Mercer County guards, stupefied with their own boredom, hadn't the slightest interest in what transpired in the room unless there'd been a call for help, an adult's cry for intervention and restraint.

Zwilich relented. 'César, hey.' Stood and approached the stricken boy. César's eyes shone with tears, which gave him the look of a fierce little dog. When Zwilich touched him, to comfort him, the boy cringed. 'César, your mama didn't mean it. She called us – just a while ago she called and left a message for me. "I love my—"'

So swiftly it happened then, Zwilich would live and relive the assault and never quite comprehend how César grabbed his right hand and bit his forefinger before Zwilich could shove him away. Bit down hard, tendons taut in his grimy neck; in an instant he'd become a deranged animal. Zwilich struck him with his free hand, his fist, on the side of the head, knocked the boy from his chair and onto the floor, yet he wasn't able to pry the boy's jaws open to free his finger. Zwilich was shouting, screaming in pain, oh God the pain was terrible, the mad boy had bitten Zwilich's forefinger to the bone, at the first joint. Only when the guards rushed at him did the boy release his pit-bull jaws and Zwilich stagger away. The guards cursed the boy trying to crawl beneath the table; he was lifted, thrown down, scrambled frantic and crablike on the floor, shrieking as if he were being murdered. Quickly now the guards subdued him, cursing him, laughing at the size of him, couldn't weigh more than seventy-five pounds, they had him on his belly on the linoleum floor, on his face, wrists behind his back and cuffed and lifted for maximum pain, wouldn't cease struggling so the guards cuffed his ankles too, marveling *Jesus! The size of the little bastard!* Zwilich showed the guards his wounded finger, which was bleeding thinly down his hand, down his arm to his elbow, and seemed somehow to have become smeared on the front of his white shirt. He hadn't known he'd been shouting for help. Trying to laugh it off: the kid was quick as a snake, Zwilich hadn't seen the attack coming. He was white-faced, dazed. In a state of shock and his heart pounding crazily. The panic rush, the adrenaline rush, had to be as powerful as any heroin rush Zwilich had had, years ago, when he and Sofia had experimented with injecting heroin into their veins, not seriously but just to see what it was like, and they'd backed off from it almost immediately, at least Zwilich had, and never tried it again. Zwilich was stammering at the guards, telling them to take César Diaz away, he couldn't bear the sight of the boy any longer. The evaluation would note the abrupt termination: 'assault on a Family Services counselor.'

In the skirmish Zwilich had nearly lost control of his bladder. Jesus! The guards would've been witnesses – he'd never have outlived such a professional humiliation.

Now you're fucked, little cocksucker, for life.
Not for life, surely: only remanded to juvenile detention for thirty days.

Pitiless glaring lights in the medical center, where in a cubicle screened off from more serious traumas Zwilich's wounded forefinger was given a thorough cleansing, disinfecting. The young Korean resident doctor examined the finger as if he'd never seen anything so curious. 'You can see teeth marks all around. These are human teeth?'
Human teeth had the ring of a joke punch line. Zwilich laughed, a hot flush in his face. He was still shaky, edgy. But yes, he had to concede, human teeth.
'Small, though? A child? Child teeth?'
'Not so small – the child is eleven.'
Zwilich waited for the young doctor to inquire if the child was Zwilich's own child – it seemed a natural question; Zwilich was a normal man yet might be the father of a crazed demonchild – but already the doctor was deftly bandaging the finger. Strangely, for all the pain, which still throbbed like flashing neon, the wounded finger hadn't bled much.
In a staff lavatory at Family Services Zwilich had

184

run cold water on the wound, washing away the blood and numbing the finger. He'd have improvised a clumsy gauze bandage for the finger out of a near-depleted first aid kit in the office, but his supervisor insisted that he go to the medical center immediately to get professional medical attention for the bite. For insurance reasons, Zwilich supposed: if such a wound became infected – if, for instance, the finger had to be amputated – Family Services would be liable for a large settlement.

Before Zwilich left the clinic holding his thick-bandaged finger at chest level to minimize the throbbing, the young Korean doctor insisted that he have a tetanus shot.

Zwilich laughed irritably. He was fine; he didn't need a tetanus shot, he was sure. Or rabies.

The doctor said somberly, 'Yes, but the inside of a human mouth can be as dangerous as an animal's mouth. Teeth caries contain infectious microorganisms. You'd be surprised.'

Zwilich thought, *Would I!* In his dazed state, nothing could surprise him.

The needle bearing the transparent tetanus vaccine entered Zwilich's left bicep cleanly, with little pain, but shortly afterward, as he left the clinic, his arm began to throb. And the clumsy bandaged forefinger throbbed with pain. A jeering sort of pain, it seemed to Zwilich, recalling the demon-child's look of feral hatred. If he'd been able, César Diaz would have torn out Zwilich's

185

throat with his teeth. Zwilich shuddered, stumbling as if he'd been drinking. He badly needed a drink and so stopped by the Dorsey Hotel, the romantic seedy bar – like the interior of a cave, Sofia had said, and that cave undersea and muted – where frequently he'd met up with her after work. For a while Sofia had been a therapist at the hospital a half-block away; her specialty was pediatric oncology. Wistfully she'd said, If we're going to start a family . . . , and her voice had trailed off and he'd said quickly, We can. Soon. We will. When things are more in control. He'd meant to say (hadn't he?) under control. When things are more under control. His father had often used the expression, to placate Zwilich's mother. When things are more under control.

In this way months pass. Years.

At the bar, in perpetual twilight, a ghost figure barely visible in the mirror behind rows of glittering bottles, Zwilich drank a beer, and a second beer with a shot glass of whiskey, drinking with calculated slowness, telling himself that he was early, Sofia wasn't late, he was waiting for her to appear, this pleasant interim of merely waiting, Sofia would be breathless from having hurried, a smell of rain in her loose hair. Sofia's hand on his shoulder, a light claiming touch: 'Hey.' And the pressure of her wide, warm mouth against his, which quickened his heart, which was shriveled to the size of a peach pit, with hope. 'Hey. Where've you been?' Already he'd forgotten the interview, the assault, the evaluation, abhorrent to him, he would not remember, an aberration in Zwilich's life not to be shared with Sofia, not ever. Half consciously counting four men at the bar beside himself and there was the bartender, and it's a law enforcement officer's habit, you see that their hands are in sight, and you see where the entrance, exits are, where you might need to take cover in an emergency. For such things can happen; you can't foresee. One of the older drinkers at the bar had the large gravely heraldic head of Zwilich's father, who'd been a rich Hartford, Connecticut, stockbroker who'd died not when Zwilich had been six but when he'd been twenty-six and so long estranged from his father and in so undefined a phase of his life, geographically as well as otherwise, that Zwilich hadn't known that his father had had a massive stroke and had died pleading to see his son until several days after the death, when Zwilich's distraught mother had finally been able to locate him in an outlying district of Brooklyn where he'd been, temporarily, 'living with friends.' Zwilich must have been staring at this man, unlike Zwilich's late father unkempt, unshaven, for at last the man squinted over at Zwilich with a faint frowning smile, as if trying to determine who Zwilich was, and a sensation of cold terror washed over Zwilich: *I am not one of you, I don't belong here.* Hurriedly Zwilich paid the bartender what he owed him and fled.

Another Trenton bar, on lower State Street, Zwilich looked into: but Sofia wasn't there. Nor was Sofia at the Bridge House, where the bar was crowded, the air dense and combative, and Zwilich called the bartender: 'Has Sofia been in here tonight?' And the bartender cupped his hand to his ear amid the din, and Zwilich raised his voice: 'I'm looking for my wife, has my wife been in here tonight?' and there was a momentary hush. The Bridge House is a tavern in which there is a moment of respect when a man in a blood-spattered white shirt and with a bandaged finger announces in a raw uplifted voice that he's looking for his wife. Yet still the bartender said no, hadn't seen Sofia that night, in fact hadn't seen Sofia for some time. Zwilich thanked him and departed, and now at sunset, crossing the Delaware River to Morrisville, Pennsylvania, hot rain splashing against the windshield of his car, Zwilich is possessed by the thought that he will drive to Philadelphia; he's convinced that he knows where Sofia might be staying, and with whom. Driving across the familiar bridge, he's made to notice the strangeness of the fading sky; below the bridge there is mostly darkness, but much of the sky remains in patches of light, the sun melting into the horizon like a broken egg yolk. The effect has to be the result of chemical pollution, yet it's luridly beautiful. Below are the old shuttered mills, warehouses, the decaying Trenton waterfront, but at the Pennsylvania shore a string, as far as Zwilich can see upriver, of glittering

188

house lights. His heart beats with a forlorn eager hope: sun spilling its light onto the bridge, onto the river, like a slow-motion detonation in which, though many thousands are destroyed in a fiery holocaust, no one feels any pain.

THE SPILL

1.

Once, a farm family named Braam lived on fifty acres of land abutting the Black River in a steeply hilly, densely forested part of Herkimer County, New York, known as the Rapids. This was in the foothills of the Adirondack Mountains, when my mother was very young.

Walter Braam was a part-time farmer whose primary income came from working as foreman at the enormous stone quarry at Sparta, a small city twelve miles to the south. Walter's sons Calvin and Daniel also worked at the quarry. When Walter's first wife, Esther, died of a rapid and unspeakable (ovarian?) cancer, Walter grieved wildly for a year and then abruptly remarried, with no warning to his family. His second wife was a young woman named Lizabeta who'd worked in a Sparta rooming house as a cleaning girl; Lizabeta was fourteen years younger than Walter, brought to the Rapids at the age of twenty-four to be a stepmother to eighteen-year-old Calvin and twenty-year-old Daniel, who still lived at home, and to care for, tirelessly, without complaint, Walter's elderly, arthritic mother and his yet more elderly and more arthritic aunt. Lizabeta had three children with Walter: Agnes, who was six in October 1951; Melinda, who was three; and thirteen-month-old Alistair. Also in the Braam household was Walter's twenty-three-year-old nephew, John Henry, whom Walter had taken in because John Henry's mother, Walter's oldest sister, Dorothy, claimed she 'couldn't keep him' – she'd 'given up on him.'

So many Braams! Lizabeta woke sweating and shivering in the night, having dreamed of a great mouth, always hungry, that had to be fed. She, Lizabeta, was the one to feed this mouth.

It was like a fairy tale, one of the cruel ones. A giant had to be fed each night or he would devour the servant girl whose task it was to feed him; unless maybe – Lizabeta wasn't certain – the giant did finally devour the girl. Lizabeta would read to her children only those fairy tales that ended *And they lived happily ever after*, and before beginning any story she checked the end to see how it turned out.

When Walter first brought Lizabeta to the Rapids, shortly before he married her, Lizabeta expressed astonishment that the narrow gravel road leading past the Braams' property was called Braam Road. 'A road named for *you!*' she'd exclaimed naively. Walter explained: the road had been named for his grandfather Wilhelm, who'd been one of the first settlers in this part of Herkimer County, in the 1890s. At the time Walter told Lizabeta this they were driving in Walter's pickup truck and Walter's hard, scarred hand was on Lizabeta's fleshy thigh, squeezing as you might squeeze a child who has said something charming but foolish. A gentle reprimand, but unmistakable.

In the Rapids, Lizabeta would learn to say little. In her former life in Sparta, she hadn't been encouraged to say much either.

On the narrow Braam Road, the Braams had no near neighbors. The Rapids was a remote region, sparsely settled. The farms Lizabeta glimpsed were small and the farmhouses modest, but the Braam house had a weatherworn stone facade that gave it a look of austere dignity. It was two stories high, and on each floor tall narrow windows without shutters seemed to hint at mysterious lives within. The roof was shingled, steep. At the highest peak was a copper weathervane in the shape of a cock.

On sunny days the cock gleamed brightly, as if strutting. On overcast days, much of the winter in the foothills of the Adirondacks, the cock emitted a wan, sullen glare.

That weathercock! No matter how many times you'd seen it, always you glanced upward, to the peak of the roof. Always you were taken in, imagining the copper cock to be alive.

John Henry too seemed always to be noticing the weathervane cock for the first time, calling, whistling to it, laughing and waving in a pretense that the copper cock was a living bird and in fact one of the 'garden angels' sent to earth to 'keep an eye' on him.

Behind the Braam house was a large barn with a stone foundation, unpainted plank walls, and a steep, rusting tin roof. There were sheds, a chicken coop, a silo in need of repair, a few remaining farm animals (two horses, several Guernsey cows, Rhode Island Red chickens, barn cats, and a dog named Bessie). Needing continual upkeep was the barnyard, which stank of muddy manure and rotting hay, and the miles of barbed wire fencing, tasks that fell mostly to John Henry.

I live in a stone house. I am married now, and my husband doesn't need to farm, he is foreman at the quarry.

It was a boast put to Lizabeta's family, who'd sent her away at fifteen to live by herself in Sparta, years before. Her mother, her sisters, her girl cousins living out beyond Star Lake in the mountains, whom she hadn't seen in a decade and had no expectation of seeing again.

It was so; most of the fifty acres were uncultivated now. Walter planted a few acres in corn, wheat, hay to feed the animals. But his workdays were spent at the quarry, not on the farm. Close beside the house, John Henry plowed and helped maintain a half-acre garden (tomatoes, pole beans, peppers, sweet corn, tangled vines yielding squash, pumpkins) for Lizabeta.

'Aunt Liz'beta' she was called by John Henry in his sing-song, grating voice.

John Henry's quick shy eyes lighting on her, and away in nearly the same instant. John Henry's wormy lips moving, working as if with words that teased him, impossible to utter. John Henry's narrow muscled shoulders slouching, as if at his height of more than six feet, at least five inches taller than Lizabeta, he might make himself smaller, unobtrusive.

Aunt Liz'beta was the murmur, John Henry's horsy face darkened with the blood of surprised excitement, arousal.

John Henry was so good with the children, though: adored Agnes, Melinda, Alistair as if they were his own little brother and sisters, whom he'd protect with his life.

Or maybe – for who could fathom what went on in John Henry's head, buzzing like a swarm of hornets? – John Henry thought that the young children in the household were not Uncle Walter's children but somehow, who knows how, *his*.

He would never hurt them. He would never. He is so goodhearted. And the children love him. Never complains, such a good worker! My husband's nephew. He lives with us. He has no other home on this earth.

The Spill. It would happen at the Spill, in October 1951.

194

When Melinda was three years, two months old. When Agnes was six and big for her age. Sharp-eyed, inquisitive. A restless child, with Walter Braam's pale, slightly protuberant eyes and his air of willfulness. *Never go anywhere near the Spill,* Agnes had been warned repeatedly. *Something terrible could happen to you at the Spill.*

These were Lizabeta's words. There was no need to warn Melinda, who was still too young even to trail after her sister out into the fields and woods and hills.

Lizabeta hadn't known of the Spill until she'd been living in the Rapids for several months as Walter Braam's wife. Hadn't seen it until the following spring, when water came rushing across the rock formation in a single frothy, churning stream like a river, to empty into the Black River below.

It was Calvin who'd shown her. He'd driven her into town, to buy groceries in the Rapids, and on the way back he'd driven past the Braam house, another half-mile or so, to point out the Spill to her, from the road.

'The Spill. I can see why it's called that.'

'Dan and me, we'd play there. When we were little. Pa would've warmed our asses if he knew. A boy from school, Duncan Welleck – the Wellecks live a few miles away – he'd come with us, climbing up the Spill. Once he fell and split his damn head open, bled like a pig, but we got him home okay and Pa never knew.'

It wasn't like Lizabeta's stepson to confide in

her. It wasn't like any of the Braams to confide in her, or to speak of Walter in such a way. Another woman, a more imaginative or cunning step-mother, would have seen her advantage and asked Calvin more about disobeying his father at the Spill, or anywhere; but Lizabeta was shy, un-certain. When you must remember to keep your lips pursed shut when you smile, not to reveal your chunky, stained teeth, you are inclined to be shy and uncertain.

The Spill was two things: the contorted rock formation, like a small humpbacked mountain, and the water that streamed down it from the Adirondacks. Much of the year, several small streams rushed down the Spill to enter the Black River below, but after heavy rains, and during the spring thaw, the shallow streams converged into a single whitewater stream that rushed across the rock face to spill over a twenty-foot drop into the river. (The Black River. Lizabeta had no sense of where this river went, or where it came from: higher in the mountains? She supposed. It was an accident that Lizabeta even knew what the river was named; people in the Rapids referred to it only as 'the river,' which had a stretch of jagged rocks and a turbulent whitewater rapids just beyond the Rapids bridge. One day Lizabeta would see a map of New York State and discover how the Black River turned like a great snake, traversing Herkimer County at a diagonal to empty into Lake Ontario, seventy miles to the west. On this map the Spill was far too small to be marked.)

In late summer the streams of the Spill had become so shallow that most of its rocks were exposed, harmless. In a severe drought, the Spill was dry. Anyone sure-footed and unafraid of heights could make his way carefully across the Spill, a distance of about fifty feet. (Almost, Lizabeta could imagine herself clambering across the rocks herself. Except she was pregnant at the time. Seems like, looking back on those years, Lizabeta was pregnant much of the time.)

It was when the water level rose, often rapidly during a rainstorm, and the several shallow streams converged into a single rushing stream that the Spill was treacherous.

Beautiful to observe at a distance. Treacherous to approach.

That day, Calvin said, 'It's just some freak of nature, Pa says, why it got shaped like it did. In school they tell you it was glaciers. A glacier is an ice field – ice mountain. This was a long time ago, a hundred thousand years ago.' Calvin paused importantly, to let the weight of such a figure sink in. 'See, the way this is, the things we see, where we live, it wasn't always like this. How things were exactly, nobody knows. Nobody could remember that far back. Except the Spill, that's some old freak thing from that time. That wouldn't ever happen again, now the glaciers are gone.'

All this while Lizabeta was staring at the

waterfall, and a stream of glittering water cascading down a steep hill, or hills, that rose up above them, blotting out half the sky like a mountain shoved close. Lizabeta knew, though she couldn't see from her seat in the pickup, that the water was falling into the river, hidden from sight by underbrush. Lizabeta's dry lips had parted; her heartbeat had quickened. Calvin seemed to be imparting some message to her, but what? She could not think of a thing to say in reply. Oh, she hated being so clumsy with words, when words meant so much! Calvin leaned his arms on the steering wheel, staring through the pickup windshield at the Spill. Calvin was a lanky boy of nineteen with tufted dark hair, a blunt profile, slightly stubbled jaws. Stepmother and stepson sat in the old Ford pickup staring at the Spill a short distance from the road – falling, frothy, splashing water, glittering with light like broken shards of glass – for how many minutes Lizabeta could not recall afterward, until Calvin backed the pickup around on the gravel Braam Road and drove back to the house.

'Don't tell Pa I took you to see the Spill,' Calvin said, with a mirthless little laugh. 'He don't like us wasting gas.'

You was the most her stepsons would call her. Not *Ma*, and not *Lizabeta*. There was just no name for her, their father's second, young, hugely pregnant wife.

★   ★   ★

Some of these facts about the Spill would be stated in the newspapers. The granite outcroppings, the shallow streams that rose rapidly to form a single rushing stream after a heavy October rainstorm, the Black River, where, three miles downstream, caught in concrete rubble beneath the Constableville bridge, the body would be found, naked, so badly broken, the face so battered it was scarcely recognizable.

2.

'God knows – he didn't give me the strength.'

Dorothy Chrisman spoke literally, it seemed. Lizabeta's sister-in-law from Sparta, who'd 'given up' on her son John Henry and sent him away to live with her family in the Rapids.

In Dorothy's husky smoker's voice there was an air of reproach that meant *God knows – he did this wrong thing*. As in Dorothy's ruddy, coarse-skinned face there was a small grim look of satisfaction. So you were led to be agreeable, as Lizabeta was, to sympathize with the aggrieved woman. To take Dorothy Chrisman's side against God, who'd done the wrong thing to Dorothy.

There was this tendency in the Braams, Lizabeta had noticed, to be resigned to something gone wrong, even as, with their brooding and reproach, they knew where blame was located.

'You'd think God gave you a damn hard burden

deliberately, he'd give you the strength to bear it, eh? You'd think.'

Quickly Lizabeta murmured, Yes. You would think!

Outside, John Henry was calling – crying, it sounded like – *Chick chick chick CHICK, chick chick chick CHICK,* scattering seed for the red-feathered chickens, two dozens hens and two roosters, which was one of John Henry's farm chores he performed twice a day, always efficiently but always noisily. You could hear John Henry talking to the chickens, a stream of excited, warm, friendly chatter, interrupted by John Henry's laughter, though his words were muffled. His mother, Dorothy Chrisman, listened, exhaling cigarette smoke through wide, dark, outraged nostrils, and said nothing, pointedly.

It was one of Dorothy's rare visits. Once or twice a year, at unexpected times. Braam relatives often visited the farm and were welcome to stay as long as they wished, or almost; but Dorothy, who'd grown up in the Rapids, seemed to have acquired a distaste for it. She worked as a nurse's aide at the hospital in Sparta and had 'no man to support' her. Stating this fact, Dorothy looked pointedly at Lizabeta, who, as Walter's wife, clearly had a man to support *her.*

John Henry called his mother *Mama.* In a pleading, childlike voice incongruous with his height, spindly arms and legs, and age: '*Mama!*'

In her mid-forties, Dorothy looked a decade

older. She was a short, mannish woman with a habit of wincing as she laughed and the fine-creased skin of the longtime smoker. Red lipstick on her mouth shone like grease; the rest of her face was bare of makeup, raw-looking and singed. It was mysterious how John Henry seemed to know that his mother was coming for one of her rare visits when Lizabeta herself didn't know. (For Walter never informed her. Nor was it clear that Walter informed his mother, elderly Mrs Braam, who was Dorothy's mother and did not like surprises and upsets in the routine of her invalid life.) 'Why can't you tell us that Dorothy is planning to come home with you?' Lizabeta dared to ask Walter, in a pleading voice so that he might not take offense, and Walter said how could he tell anyone, he didn't always know himself. His sister hated to be 'pinned down.'

Walter laughed, acknowledging that yes, his sister could be a bitch.

What was cruel was that Dorothy planned her visits to be short: she arrived with Walter, un-announced, had supper, stayed one night, and returned to Sparta at seven o'clock the next morning, when Walter left for work.

John Henry's Ma*ma* no sooner arrived than John Henry's Ma*ma* departed.

Dorothy never brought a gift for her sister-in-law Lizabeta, just inexpensive little drugstore gifts (bath powder, fancy soaps) for her mother and her aunt and 'supplies' for John Henry. In the young man's presence Dorothy was distracted and grudging, and the actual number of minutes she spent with him was brief. There was John Henry chattering away excitedly, hoping to entertain his unresponsive mother, telling her more than she wanted to know of his farm chores for Uncle Walter and his 'special pets' among the farm animals and the 'garden angels' who watched over him and spoke to him in a secret language (in thunder, in rain, in wind; in the creaking limbs of the giant elms about the house; in the cries of birds and wild animals in the night). The more Dorothy frowned, the wilder John Henry's claims grew. A fever seemed to come upon him in his mother's company. Unless Dorothy restrained him, John Henry began to rock from side to side, head, neck, torso bobbing as if he were a rubber doll; his eyes glittered, his lips gleamed with spittle. You could not be certain when John Henry spoke in this way whether he was being as fanciful as a young child, testing the credulity of adults, or whether he was serious. Maybe there was no difference. In another part of the house Lizabeta felt pity for him, poor John Henry, hearing his bleated, repeated 'Ma*ma*, Ma*ma*,' which sounded as if he were pleading with his mother.

Yet no matter his mental age, which seemed to oscillate wildly, John Henry exercised the tact of an adult, thanking his mother profusely for the 'supplies' she brought him, unwrapped, in a Sears shopping bag: socks with reinforced toes and heels, thick cotton underwear, flannel pajamas, khaki work trousers, a coarse-knit sweater too small for John Henry's stooped, muscular shoulders. Some of these items didn't appear to be new purchases but appeared secondhand, worn or even soiled; Lizabeta wondered if her sister-in-law, a nurse's aide at the Sparta hospital, pilfered them from the rooms of patients who'd left them behind or had died. But John Henry never betrayed the slightest disappointment with his mother's gifts, thanking Ma*ma* and trying to hug her around the neck and kiss her cheek even as Dorothy chided him for God's sake not to 'squeeze the life out' of her.

Lizabeta, who adored her young children and was anxious for their well-being virtually every minute of her waking life, could not comprehend her sister-in-law's cruelty to her own son. Seeing Lizabeta's face, Dorothy said to her, smirking, 'If you had a special case like John Henry, you'd know how it is.'

Lizabeta thought no, she would not. She could not imagine behaving in such a way with any child of hers.

Lizabeta was never easy in her sister-in-law's presence, as she was never easy in the presence of any of her husband's family. Elderly Mrs Braam thought nothing, in her rambling monologues, of comparing her son's 'new wife' to Esther, who'd been a 'saint,' and even the grown boys, Calvin and Daniel, who were polite to Lizabeta, seemed frequently to be exchanging glances in her presence as if amused by her, or scornful. Dorothy, who was critical of all of the family, including even her brother Walter, was given to telling Lizabeta, in a pretense of sisterly intimacy, as if she couldn't confide in any of the others, 'Just hope that someday God doesn't pull the same trick on you, Lizzie.' ('Lizzie' was the pretense, Lizabeta knew. But she smiled weakly, to acquiesce.) 'It's a man's world,' Dorothy continued, with her angry wincing laugh. 'Hank Chrisman, the boy's father – *he* walked out. *He* keeps his distance. Can't blame him, eh?'

To this Lizabeta had no reply. Blankly she stared at the ashes her sister-in-law was letting spill over the side of the ashtray.

'Well, *you* can't understand. Only the mother can know.'

Lizabeta felt the rebuke. A hot, heavy flush rose into her face.

Lizabeta had been born with a rosy, smudged mark on the lower right side of her face, so that her cheek had the look of having been slapped. At such times she felt the birthmark burn and darken. She felt her sister-in-law's eyes move upon her, bemused.

Walter had told Lizabeta that his oldest sister had been the only girl in the family to leave the Rapids and to train for a job. She'd been a nurse's aide in Sparta, where she'd met and married this Chrisman when she was nineteen and had John Henry when she was twenty-two. Chrisman

204

worked for the railroad and was often out of town, and in recent years it wasn't clear – for not even Walter wished to ask Dorothy – if the two were still married after more than a decade of living apart. Lizabeta had noted how in his rapid chatter to his mother, John Henry never asked about his father, or anything about his Ma*ma*'s life in Sparta. Did he lack the mental capacity to imagine Ma*ma* somewhere else? Or had John Henry, after several years of living in the Rapids, forgotten Sparta?

As Lizabeta was forgetting. And good riddance!

If Calvin and Daniel were in a mood – playful-mean, taunting-teasing – to suggest to John Henry that his father was on his way to the farm, John Henry immediately became excited and anxious, hunching his shoulders to make himself smaller, shaking his head and whimpering, 'Is *not. Is not.*'

It seemed clear that John Henry did remember his father. Remembered something about his father. Lizabeta tried to intervene, to assure him that his father was not coming, his cousins were only teasing.

'Is *not. Is not!*'

Once an idea got into John Henry's head, it was difficult to dislodge it. John Henry, usually docile, could become not just frightened but angry like a dog that has been baited, in danger of snapping, biting.

Only rarely did John Henry scuffle with his cousins. Calvin and Daniel knew better than to seriously torment him. Of course, it was forbidden to tease John Henry at all, in any cruel way to upset him: if Walter were home, the boys wouldn't have dared. John Henry liked to be teased gently, as you'd tease a young child to make him laugh, not cry. To make him feel loved, not mocked.

It was often said by Braam relatives that John Henry wasn't what the Herkimer County school district had labeled him – 'retarded' – but was 'just pretending.' (Why? No one could say.) Some of the Braams even believed, as John Henry seemed to, that he was watched over by a higher power, his 'garden angels' or God. The boy was smart enough in his own way, wasn't he? But Dorothy didn't see it this way. Dorothy, who was John Henry's exasperated *Mama*, who'd worked for twenty-five years at Sparta General Hospital, said bluntly that John Henry was a 'birth accident.'

Lizabeta wanted to protest. John Henry, who lived with them, who loved them, a *birth accident!* She hoped that, outside with the chickens, John Henry couldn't have overheard such a terrible remark.

Dorothy said smugly, '*You* don't know, Lizzie. You'd have to be the mother to know.'

The twist of Dorothy's lips as she uttered the name Lizzie, you could see that she found it faintly comical.

Sometimes, goaded by her sister-in-law's stiff silence, Dorothy began to speak freely, carelessly. Her coarse face became enlivened. She gave off an odor of yeasty female flesh, something harshly antiseptic beneath. She moved her hands about, gesturing, her hands that resembled her son's: large, broad, with long spatulate fingers. Her eyes, like John Henry's, were pale blue, and inclined to water. Except Dorothy's eyes darted about with malicious curiosity while John Henry's eyes were eager, yearning, hopeful. Where John Henry quivered like a puppy wanting only to be liked and petted, Dorothy quivered with disdain and a wish not to be touched. As a hospital worker, she'd seen too many 'nasty' – 'damned nasty' – things. She told Lizabeta frankly that she'd long ago lost her 'respect' for suffering. She'd come to a place where you start to blame people for their damned bad luck. Sick, dying, miserable people were Dorothy Chrisman's work; she laughed, saying you'd have to pay her to give a damn about them. When she'd first begun working at Sparta General, a girl of nineteen who'd never seen anyone die, she'd been brimming over with sympathy, but now she had to bite her tongue not to come out with 'So? So what? What'd you expect from life? Open your eyes.'

Lizabeta laughed nervously, wanting to think that her sister-in-law was joking.

'Every day of my life I thank God that Walter took John Henry in. Else John Henry would be in some state home behind bars. *I* couldn't keep him. You see John Henry now, he's calmed down some – Walter works him like a horse out here, so John Henry can't get so restless and excitable, the way he was growing up. Not just his brain but his thyroid had some defect. He'd never sleep through a night, not once. Wandering the house at night talking to angels, and outside in the street and in neighbors' yards in any weather so they'd call the police. More times than I could count, John Henry was beat up bad. Scars on his face, you've seen them – damn lucky his eye didn't get put out, kids kicking him. He wouldn't be toilet-trained till he was seven or eight. Wouldn't talk until he was six, and then he wouldn't shut up. See, John Henry was born after a long labor. Twenty hours and I was awake for all of it. Trying to get that damn baby out of me, I was screaming and sweating like a hog. It was a forceps delivery – his head got squeezed. There's a kind of dent in his head, like at the side, here, where the bone is soft. John Henry will always be the mental age he is, he won't grow up. Don't let him get into that rocking he does, back and forth, side to side, when he's excited. He can stop himself if he tries. Don't let him pick at his nose, or stick his fingers in his ears or where he shouldn't be sticking them, or scratching, or, you know,' Dorothy said, with a look of distaste, 'touching himself. John Henry has been trained about dirty habits – he knows better. His father was the one to discipline him, before he walked out. John Henry is trained. He knows not to touch other children, not ever.' Dorothy paused. Her words suggested that she thought of

208

John Henry as a child, not a fully mature young man in his twenties, who towered over her. 'What he does in private is his own business. You can't stop some things. Dirty habits, it's how boys are. Like even a trained dog will do what it wants to do if it thinks its master isn't watching.'

Dorothy, a chain smoker, ground out one of her Chesterfields in a saucer. Lizabeta shuddered, thinking, *She is trying to befriend me. She thinks that I am as cruel as she is.*

When Dorothy left that morning, Lizabeta stood stiffly in the doorway and made no move to embrace her. John Henry, waiting outside, tried to hug her and was repelled, and trotted after Walter's pickup the full length of the long driveway, waving his arms and crying plaintively, 'Bye-bye, *Mama!* Bye-bye, *Mama!*' until the pickup turned into Braam Road and disappeared from view.

This was the last visit of Dorothy Chrisman to the Braam farm in the Rapids, in early September 1951.

If he'd never come to live with us. If there might have been some other way.

'He's here now. He will be living with us now.'

In this way, Walter brought John Henry into their lives. The tall, gangling, shaved-headed boy with his eager smile, eager frightened eyes, gripping an overstuffed, badly worn duffel bag against his chest, ushered into the kitchen by Walter.

'My sister's son, John Henry. He's come to help out on the farm and around the house. He can have the room behind the kitchen.' Walter paused, seeing the look in Lizabeta's face of shock, incomprehension. Yet he did not acknowledge the look, for this wasn't Walter Braam's way. Calmly he supplied Lizabeta's name to John Henry, enunciating his words. 'John Henry, this is my wife, Lizabeta. Your aunt.'

Quickly John Henry nodded his strange shaved head, which seemed too small for his body, as if to suggest that this was a fact he knew: 'Liz'beta. Aunt.'

Walter corrected him: 'Aunt Lizabeta. You will say "Aunt Lizabeta."'

'Aunt Liz'beta.'

John Henry's voice was as high-pitched as a boy's. His watery blue eyes were fixed not on Lizabeta's stained smile but somewhere lower, her heavy breasts or her hard, swelling belly, which was partly hidden by a ratty cardigan sweater.

At this time Lizabeta was six months pregnant with their second child, and the pregnancy was a difficult one. She moved about dazed and dizzy, and her legs (of which, in her shy way, she'd been sometimes vain) were popping ugly varicose veins; soon she'd be wearing flesh-colored support hose like the older Braam women. Yet she managed to stammer, 'John Henry. Why, he*llo*.'

Lizabeta's smile could not have been more forced, pained. She could feel the rosy smudged birthmark on her cheek throbbing with blood. She was thinking that the room behind the kitchen was mostly a storage room, poorly heated, that contained a ruin of an old iron bedstead and a terribly stained mattress upon which Lizabeta's elderly father-in-law was said to have died years before; she would have to prepare it for John Henry, at least minimally, but when? Walter would want supper shortly. He'd spoken to Lizabeta matter-of-factly, but his tone suggested *You will accept this. You will not question me.*

At this time, in March 1948, John Henry was twenty years old but looked both younger and older. His face was boyish and yet nicked, scarred, singed-looking, like the face of a mistreated doll; his arms and legs were long and spindly, not yet filled out with muscle; he was Walter's height but slouched his shoulders to make himself smaller, less obtrusive. His hands were unusually large, paddle-hands, with long fingers and broken nails edged with grime. Lizabeta saw with alarm that John Henry appeared to be covered in a film of grime: the webs of skin between his fingers were shadowed with grime; grime in creases on his neck, the bony knobs of his wrists. His baggy overalls were stiff with grime. On his badly scuffed workboots were what looked like tar stains. He smelled of his young male body, eager and rancid. Lizabeta fought a sensation of faintness, thinking, *Another. I'm not strong enough.*

She would be, though. She had no choice.

'Is he – what you'd call mentally retarded?'

That night, upstairs in their bedroom, undressing for bed, Lizabeta dared to ask Walter this question. Walter responded with a vague annoyed grunt, neither no nor yes but a signal that he wasn't in a mood to answer her questions. Lizabeta persisted. 'He isn't dangerous, is he? He can be trusted around children?' In her flannel nightgown, she stood barefoot with her weight on her heels; the small of her back ached from the weight of the hard, swelling belly like a melon jutting out before her, which exuded a pulsing heat. Walter stood on the other side of the bed, his back to Lizabeta, pulling off his white foreman's shirt, pulling off his undershirt, letting the soiled clothes fall. Trousers Walter took care to lay across the back of a chair. His shoes were usually placed side by side in front of the chair, where he would sit in the morning to put them on.

It was Walter Braam's habit to undress in this way, distractedly, as if lost in thought and unaware of what he did, in full confidence that, as the previous, saintly wife, Esther, must have done, his newer wife, Lizabeta, would pick up after him, shirts and undershirts, shorts and socks, pajamas. It was what a woman did, what Braam women did, one of the easy tasks among others not so easy. Lizabeta said in a breathy rush of words, as if her anxiety might be alleviated by such information, 'He – John Henry – seems very . . . kind. He's shy with us, but he made friends with Agnes right away. She was laughing so at him! So I think – I hope . . .' Lizabeta's voice trailed off tentatively. Walter hadn't answered her, but Walter was listening, Lizabeta knew. It was true that at supper, though John Henry had been clumsy and self-conscious with the adults, he'd whispered and laughed with Agnes as if the two were old friends. It was clear that Agnes adored her strange shaved-headed cousin from Sparta, who, as Agnes's father had told her in his terse way, had 'come to live with us' now.

Barefoot and flat-footed, slightly short of breath, Lizabeta observed her silent husband across their bed: the man's broad, muscled, faintly scarred back, which was very pale and going to fat at the waist; his dark, thick-tufted hair, which was nonetheless thinning at the crown of his head. Walter was forty-three years old and had a foreman's air of authority. In the Braam household, as at the Sparta quarry, it was rare for him to be questioned. Lizabeta loved him, and was fearful of him. You did not love a man who didn't inspire fear, though you might fear a man – many men – whom you did not love. Walter was unpredictable in his moods. He was known to be a generous man, and yet he was quick-tempered, he could be cruel. As a father, he was a strict disciplinarian; his sons respected him, resented him, and seemed, Lizabeta thought, to love him, though not wildly, as their little half-sister, Agnes, loved him. He never went to church yet could not abide anyone speaking disparagingly of God, religion, as he could not abide profanity in the household and yet, when he became angry, he lashed out with the most obscene words Lizabeta had ever heard, which frightened her, suggesting such violent disgust with the human body and with sex, which meant, as a wife must acknowledge, with *her*. Through the Rapids, Walter Braam was admired as a loyal friend and neighbor, one who leased acres of farmland to other, poorer farmers for modest fees, yet Walter never forgave an enemy and maintained feuds with other men for decades; his 'oldest enemy,' as Walter called him, had been in Walter's eighth-grade class at the Rapids school, at the time Walter had dropped out of school to work on his father's farm. Lizabeta had the idea that he disapproved of his sister Dorothy, yet how readily he'd taken in Dorothy's cast-off son, John Henry. Lizabeta thought, *He is a good man – he can be strong enough for both of us.*

Lizabeta had fallen in love with Walter Braam within minutes of his having noticed her: he'd smiled at her, not greedily or mockingly but in a kindly way, and called her Lizabeta. How beautiful this name sounded in Walter Braam's mouth! While in the mouths of other men the name had sounded clumsy, foolish. Lizabeta had worked in a Sparta rooming house as a chamber-maid, but she'd also worked in an adjoining tavern from time to time, and men who noticed her, who approached and spoke to her, hadn't always been kind. Men who'd touched her, put their hands on her, bought her drinks, told her how 'good-looking' she was – how 'sexy, like Jane Russell' – and laughed at her, hurt her and zipped up their trousers afterward and walked away whistling. Sometimes the men had left tips for her, sometimes not. Sometimes they were friends of the man who owned the rooming house and the tavern, and sometimes not. Then there was Walter Braam, who left tips for Lizabeta out of kindness. Asking her full name, which was Lizabeta Torvich, which no one knew, or cared to know. A widower, Walter Braam. An older man with nearly grown sons and farm property out in the Rapids who worked in town, as foreman at the stone quarry. *God, let this man love me. God, let him want me. God, I will be a good person all the days of my life, God, have mercy on me.* Lizabeta had not ever known why Walter Braam had singled her out for his attention, still less why, soon afterward, he'd asked her to marry him; years later, after Lizabeta had had their first child, Agnes, while Lizabeta was pregnant with their second child, she would not have been astonished if he'd decided abruptly that he didn't want to be married to her any longer and told her to go away. (But would Lizabeta be allowed to take Agnes with her? Or would Walter insist upon keeping his daughter? In her fantasy of self-abasement, Lizabeta hadn't fully worked out the plot of this cruel fairy tale.) For the house on Braam Road was elderly Mrs Braam's house, after all, which Walter would inherit when his mother died.

Lizabeta had come around the bed to touch Walter now, to hesitantly stroke his bare, muscled arm as you might stroke the neck, the rippling sides, of a horse, to placate the horse, that his terrible bulk and strength would not turn against you. She'd annoyed him, she knew, by her questions. For there was the implication in such questions that Walter Braam might have acted rashly and without regard for his family, which could not be so. For Walter Braam cared passionately about his family, and his manhood was bound up with this care and his pride in himself as the protector of his family, Lizabeta knew, or should have known; yet her concern for Agnes and for the baby to be born – yes, and her concern for herself: *It is yourself you are thinking of, John Henry's eyes on you* – had caused her to speak impulsively, recklessly. And so Lizabeta would placate her husband now, stroking his arm, laying the side of her head against his shoulder, just lightly, as might a child who has roused a parent to anger half purposefully, to be forgiven. Lizabeta's milk-heavy breasts swung loose inside the flannel nightgown; she'd seen with a fascinated repulsion how swollen they'd become, how the

216

once tight, taut little flesh-colored nipples had turned brown and widened to the size of half-dollars, and the skin of her distended belly was a strange waxy white, stretched tight as the skin of a drum, and her pubic hair seemed to have become drier, and scratchier, and the soft marble-white flesh of her thighs, which had grown heavier, rubbed together now in a damp slapping way that was perversely arousing and left her short of breath. In these early years of their life together, the sexual feeling was still strong between them, despite Lizabeta's pregnancies, but now Walter stiffened and pushed her away without looking at her, saying another time, for the final time, 'John Henry is living with us now.'

And so it was, and would be.

3.

He worked.

Eager to work as a work dog, restless and uneasy and doubtful of being loved when not working, saying, 'What d'you want done?' in his anxious high-pitched voice.

'Aunt Liz'beta? Ma'am? What d'you want done? *O-kay!*'

O-kay had the tone of a phrase of pop music, something breezy and cheery John Henry must have overheard on the radio. *O-kay* was one of John Henry's numerous code sounds, which signaled yes, John Henry knew what such code sounds meant, just as you did. *O-kay!* was sometimes accompanied by a salute of John Henry's right hand to the right side of his forehead, as he'd seen soldiers in uniform do. *O-kay, Aunt Liz'beta!*

Watered and fed the barn animals. Mucked out their filthy stalls, cleared away filth and debris from their drinking pond at the center of the barnyard. Groomed the horses, milked the cows. Carried on animated if one-sided conversations with the horses, the cows, the barn cats, the lame mixed-breed Labrador. And the chickens. Gathered eggs each morning from the hens' nests. Separated sick chickens from others not yet afflicted. Braved the roosters' angry pecking at his hands, legs. Shoveled hay. Shoveled manure. In winter shoveled snow from the long driveway and from the paths. In spring yoked the horses to plow the half-acre garden behind the house. Helped his aunt Lizabeta, whom he adored in a puppy's way of craven affection, to hoe, rake, seed, and water the garden and with the thinning of plants, weeding, and harvesting. Repaired the falling-down fences, for a farm's fences are in continual need of repair. Hacked down tall grasses with a rusted scythe. Nailed tarpaper strips to the sheds' roofs, amid the hammering talking and laughing to himself, for such work, the rhythm of such work, repetitions of such work, is deeply comforting. Heavy lifting, carrying. Clearing out the cellar after torrential rainstorms, leakage. Helping his aunt Lizabeta with housework, though Lizabeta was hesitant to put John Henry to work indoors for, oh! John Henry was clumsy with household things, 'ladies' things' John Henry called them – he dropped and broke plates, collided with furniture, became confused sorting cutlery into a drawer (a task that little Agnes could do unfailingly), and skulked away deeply ashamed. And if John Henry volunteered to carry a stepladder indoors for his aunt to use while dusting the high corners of a room, he was likely to ram the ladder against a doorway and gouge the wood; carrying a ladder upstairs, John Henry was likely to miss a step and fall backward, landing on his back, stunned and breathless and the damned ladder on top of him, so Lizabeta had to stoop over him to help him scramble out from under it, frightened that poor John Henry had injured himself, guilty as if she'd caused the accident herself. Oh, why didn't John Henry go away somewhere and leave her alone? He made her so anxious. Except Lizabeta loved John Henry, of course, everyone had come to love John Henry, who was so good-hearted, such a good worker, far more reliable and capable than, for instance, Walter's sons Daniel and Calvin, so good with children, and children loved John Henry, very young children especially. John Henry loved to observe the new baby, Alistair, being bathed, though he could not help with the bathing; John Henry loved to watch over Agnes and Melinda outdoors and was happiest when called upon to rescue a child from a hornet, for instance, or from one of the angry red roosters rushing to peck at a child's soft bare legs so the girls squealed *Oh! oh! oh! John Hen'y, help!* and John Henry clapped and whistled and chased the bad rooster away. In the village of Rapids, where, usually on Fridays, Lizabeta shopped for groceries and took the girls with her, there was a notorious black dog that stood in the road and barked and snarled menacingly, and John Henry had the power to calm this dog by talking to him at length in a calm voice, explaining afterward that the dog was Big Fred he'd used to know and was a friend of his.

John Henry is so good with children; it's because John Henry is a child himself.

Older children were uncomfortable with John Henry's antics, and some of them, the boys, were scornful and cruel, but luckily, Lizabeta's girls were still young enough to be beguiled by their cousin John Henry, who told such elaborate, fantastical tales of angels, talking animals, and special messages that came for him in wind, in rain, in thunder, and in the forlorn cries of nighttime birds. Both girls shrieked with laughter when John Henry waved and called to the 'rooster angel' on the highest roof of the house, carrying on in such a contagious way the girls insisted they could see the copper rooster moving, looking down at them.

'Know who he is? That rooster? He's a garden angel, he's there to watch *me. O-kay!*'

Everybody laughed, John Henry was so funny. Lizabeta laughed with the girls. Yet she felt uneasy at times. She knew that John Henry was only pretending – wasn't he? – but she wasn't sure that the children understood. When she told them that the rooster was 'just a weathervane' and 'not real,' Agnes said, with childish disgust, 'Oh Mama, we know that.' But Melinda smiled uncertainly, squinting up at the copper rooster and jamming her fingers in her mouth.

Melinda was the sensitive child, just three years old in this drought-stricken summer of 1951. Agnes was brash and confident and clearly took after her father. Melinda was inclined to shrink back, a wan, almost-pretty girl with lank brown hair and mistrustful brown eyes. For Melinda the distinction between *real* and *not-real* that meant so little to Agnes wasn't so clear-cut, for you could have a dream that spilled over into the room – couldn't you? wasn't that what a nightmare was? – or you could get so sleepy you felt sickish and your eyelids could shut and in that instant a dream could come up out of nowhere and scare you and make you cry, it's so *real*.

Lizabeta thought, *Anything we can think, it is real in some way*.

This was not a reassuring thought. There were the cruel fairy tales with the terrible endings.

John Henry dreamed with his eyes open, maybe. Lizabeta thought maybe that was what was wrong with him.

221

She did love him! She didn't hate him. Who could hate John Henry? It was like hating a puppy who adored you and wanted only to lick your hands like a deranged lover, lick your face with its pink wet soft squirmy tongue.

A child himself. Why he's so good with children.

When John Henry had first come to live with the Braams, after finishing his farm chores he'd sometimes wandered off in the direction of the small village of Rapids, on the banks of the Black River, about three miles to the east. There John Henry bought his favorite soda at the general store, a sickish-sweet carbonated cherry Coke in a bottle; if he saw anyone working outdoors, in a garden for instance, he went over to introduce himself as John Henry Braam. (Which was not John Henry's legal name. But he seemed to have forgotten his legal name.) Most people seemed to like him; John Henry was so friendly and child-like. He boasted to Lizabeta that he had many 'kind friends' there. In the Rapids, John Henry visited the one-room schoolhouse on Cobb Road that, in the late afternoon and early evening, when he dropped by, was empty of students and locked up; eagerly he tried the front door, peered into the windows, drifted about the small playground as if looking for someone or something. Like a lost dog, or a ghost, observers reported to the Braams. Poor John Henry!

From his mother, Lizabeta knew that as a boy of eleven, John Henry had been told that he

222

couldn't return to school because he'd been kept back in fourth grade two years in a row and was deemed 'unteachable' from that point onward. There were no special education classes in the Sparta school district at this time. There were no accommodations for 'retarded' or 'disabled' students. John Henry had never done well in school, but he'd liked his teachers and classmates and was baffled to be forbidden to return even to the playground; he couldn't comprehend that he'd become older than his classmates, and at five feet six towered over them. 'John Henry asked me why he couldn't go back to school and I told him, because they don't want you, and he asked why they didn't want him, and I said, because they don't like you, and he asked why they didn't like him, and I said, because in their eyes you are not normal like them, you are a freak.' Lizabeta's sister-in-law spoke with an air of grim satisfaction, as if to indicate that in her dealings with her son, she was never less than absolutely truthful.

Lizabeta shuddered, remembering. Poor John Henry!

Not everyone in the Rapids was so friendly to John Henry. As he'd been in Sparta, John Henry was sometimes tormented by boys and young men who shouted crude, cruel names (Freak! Idiot! Loony!) and threw stones at him, chasing him like a pack of dogs until he retreated to the Braam farm to hide. Once, Lizabeta saw him limping into the barn and found him huddled in the hay in the corner of the barn where the horses were stalled, shivering, hugging his knees to his chest. 'John Henry! Did someone hurt you? Who has hurt you?' Lizabeta asked, but John Henry refused to answer, only muttering, 'Bad thing! Bad thing!' Lizabeta said, incensed, 'Tell me who hurt you, John Henry. I'll tell your uncle Walter and he'll see that it doesn't happen again,' but John Henry just repeated, stubbornly, 'Bad thing! Bad thing!' Lizabeta was incensed on John Henry's part, yet more as Walter Braam's wife, for it seemed to her an insult, an insult against the Braam family, that anyone in the area should dare to torment Walter's nephew, knowing who John Henry was and where he lived. Lizabeta stooped to touch John Henry's shoulder, but John Henry recoiled from her with a whimper, as if her touch scalded.

He wants to be alone, Lizabeta thought. Like a wounded animal, to lick his wounds.

Among most of the Braams it was believed that John Henry didn't feel pain, or cold, or heat, as other people did. John Henry had to be called indoors sometimes, so he wouldn't freeze his fingers and toes shoveling snow after a blizzard, and John Henry had to be prevented from working in an open field or repairing roofs in blistering hot sunshine. If John Henry injured himself in a fall or cut himself and bled all over his clothes, he was likely to chatter and joke about it – 'Bad thing! Bad thing! *O-kay!*' – as if he were embarrassed by his own clumsiness and eager to change the subject; for John Henry understood that his value was in his work, and in his willingness to work, and his place with the Braams was a matter of work. On his face, hands, and forearms were numerous scabs, scars, burn marks. His shaved, stubbled head bore scars and dents. His pale blue eyes leaked moisture that ran in grimy rivulets down his face but were somehow not 'real' tears, for John Henry didn't cry, not as a 'normal' person might cry.

John Henry had to be called John Henry, and both these names had to be equally sounded, for if you called him just John – or teased him, as Walter's sons sometimes did, with variants of his name like John-John or Hen-ree – John Henry would become anxious and agitated, as if he'd been scolded. Why this was, no one seemed to know. Or why John Henry only ate hot oatmeal, which he prepared himself, for breakfast, morning following morning; or why John Henry could not bear to see any animal killed, and shuddered at the sight of meat, and refused to eat any meat, just vegetables, potatoes, coarse brown bread. John Henry favored certain of the farm animals but not others, as if there were personal animosities and feuds among them that only John Henry and the animals could understand. Many times John Henry got into quarrels with animals and chickens; you could hear his high-pitched voice at a distance. (Was John Henry serious or just pretending? Lizabeta wondered if he might be both simultaneously.) You could tease

John Henry if you teased him gently: 'John Henry! The moon is looking in the window at you.' Or, 'John Henry! There's one of your 'garden angels' checking up on you.' (An ugly black crow on a fence railing, which did seem to be tilting its head and fixing a yellow eye on John Henry.) You could cajole credulous John Henry into seeing things with his watery eyes that weren't there: human faces, human figures, animals, angels in the foliage high overhead, in contorted rock formations, in clouds. Especially clouds fascinated John Henry in their unpredictable variety, in the way they appeared out of nowhere and seemed to move in the sky of their own volition – coming from where, and going where? Slack-jawed, head flung back, John Henry was capable of staring at the sky for long entranced minutes, claiming afterward that he'd been watching 'God's thoughts' which had gotten loose from 'inside God's head.' More entrancing even than clouds were airplanes passing overhead, a relatively rare sight: John Henry dropped whatever chore he was doing to run into an open field and crane his neck, gape and wave excitedly and cry what sounded like 'Me! Me! Me! Me!' (For one of John Henry's wishes was to be an airplane pilot someday.) In the village, Lizabeta was embarrassed and annoyed by John Henry's noisy excitement when trucks of a certain size and heft passed by on the country highway, and by John Henry's enthusiasm for the Buffalo & Chautauqua freight train that thundered through on an erratic schedule, drawing him to the railroad embankment, where he waved and shouted as the cars rattled past. Lizabeta said, 'John Henry, it's dangerous to get too close to a train – you know that, don't you?' and John Henry fixed her one of his quivery looks, smiled, and said, 'Aunt Liz'beta, that train knows *me*.'

Lizabeta laughed. For John Henry was so funny, wasn't he. And he adored her, and the children. *So good with children, a child himself.*

Except John Henry was clumsy with what he called 'ladies' things' – breakable objects, or objects that involved some sort of ritual or fuss. His big paddle-hands couldn't be trusted with lifting little Alistair, though John Henry loved to watch the baby being bathed by his aunt Lizabeta, afterward dried tenderly in a soft towel and powdered with special white baby powder; John Henry never minded taking away soiled diapers to drop into a bucket of strong-smelling ammonia, in preparation for being washed. (No disposable diapers in those days, in the Rapids!) John Henry was thrilled to be asked to 'watch over' Agnes and Melinda when they played outdoors; inside the house, Lizabeta could hear the three of them chattering together, and John Henry's voice occasionally lifted in a mimicry of her scolding voice: 'Mama says *no*. Mama says *no*.' There was a rowdy game played by Agnes, John Henry, and Bessie the Labrador retriever that resembled tag; Melinda, whose legs were still too short to carry

227

her with much speed or strength, had to watch from the sidelines. Lizabeta noted disapprovingly that her elder daughter, Agnes, shouted at John Henry as if they were the same size and age; Agnes was bratty, and bossy. Lizabeta dreaded her hurting John Henry's feelings by calling him a cruel name that Agnes might have overheard him called. John Henry adored his little cousins, was eager to carry them on his shoulders or give them piggyback rides, amid much squealing and laughter. Once, to her horror, Lizabeta happened to glance out a kitchen window to see John Henry crawling on his hands and knees in the grass and Agnes straddling his back, thumping his head and neck with her fists, crying, 'Giddyup, horsie! Giddyup, horsie!' as John Henry winced with pain. Lizabeta called from the window for Agnes to stop at once!

She knew that John Henry would insist it 'never hurt.' Nothing done to him, especially by children, ever registered as hurt with John Henry.

It was in the dry, scorching heat of August 1951 when Lizabeta was hanging out laundry that she happened to see, on the far side of the back yard, little Melinda pulling off her pink cotton T-shirt because she was too hot, and getting her head caught in the neck so that she staggered in circles shrieking for help, and there came John Henry to Melinda's rescue, stooping over the struggling little girl and removing the pink top, in the same gesture trying to force it back down over Melinda's head, for John Henry had seemingly been trained, as Dorothy would grimly say he'd been disciplined, *not ever* to remove clothing from a child, any more than from himself, except in the absolute privacy of his bedroom or in the bathroom. Melinda was flailing her arms in protest, tearing at the T-shirt in a fit of temper, managing to pull it off again and this time tossing it onto the ground. No.

Lizabeta saw John Henry staring at the three-year-old girl's bare, smooth chest, the tiny flat breasts, tiny nipples; John Henry was unsmiling, hunched over Melinda, his strained face gleaming with sweat and his hands uplifted, not touching the child, not daring to touch the child, but staring at her, unmoving. In that instant a cold rush of panic coursed through Lizabeta like an electric current, and the conviction came to her with the force of a truth already known but not acknowledged: *He can't live here. He can't stay with us. He will have to leave.*

4.

'Stay here! *Don't* follow me.'

Lizabeta snatched at a jacket hanging on a peg by the kitchen door and stepped outside. Bareheaded in the wind, breathless and shivering with a strange sort of exhilaration, and dread.

It was early October. At last the drought had broken. Six days of pelting rain and intermittent gale-force winds had made the old Braam house quake and shredded and splintered limbs from the ancient elms that towered over it. The Black River was said to have risen more than a foot, and the Spill once again rushed with a single churning whitewater stream cascading into the river. Restless from being trapped indoors for so long with fretting children and elderly invalids, before even the sky cleared on the final day of rain Lizabeta hurried outside.

Especially Lizabeta was worn down by Agnes, who'd been running and shrieking like a demon on the stairs, 'playing' by making a racket and tormenting her younger sister, refusing to eat, refusing to take her nap in the afternoon, throwing off Lizabeta's restraining hands with little cries of insolence. *Hate Mama! Hate Mama!*

Lizabeta hadn't heard. A mother does not hear. All you can do is ignore. A child like Agnes, a fever that will pass.

For the past six days school had been suspended. Part of the Braam Road had been washed out. Traveling to Sparta to work in the early morning, returning from Sparta at dusk, Walter and his sons had to drive fifteen miles out of their way on partially flooded roads. Walter had brought home a few groceries from Sparta; there hadn't been any deliveries to the general store in the village, where Lizabeta usually shopped. Nor had Lizabeta been able to get into the village, in any case.

Elsewhere in Herkimer County, on lower

ground, there'd been serious flooding. Roads, bridges washed out, houses destroyed, several deaths. Yet it was a time of exultation! For now the October sun shone through dripping foliage with a fierce blinding light that made Lizabeta's eyes hurt in the way that, at times, Agnes's fierce insolent face made Lizabeta's eyes hurt.

Choked with rage, wanting to whisper to the child, 'Yes, and I hate you too. Bad, bad girl.'

Her younger daughter she loved. Melinda, who smiled at her mother with love and the neediness of love. And little Alistair she loved. But not Agnes. No longer.

It would pass, this feeling. It was a fever that would pass. As Lizabeta's mother-in-law, Mrs Braam, had told her, the willful little girl would 'come round.'

Of course. Lizabeta understood. Six-year-old Agnes was not a demon but an energetic little girl, a bored and restless and fretful little girl who didn't really hate her Mama but loved her Mama.

Yet Lizabeta had to escape, for just a few minutes. Alone, so that she could breathe, for just a few minutes. In the bright gusty damp air, riddled with droplets of water from the trees that fell on her bare head and face like rain, Lizabeta walked swiftly, blindly. She would hike along the lane, through the fields, and to the riverbank; there was a path there. On rocky soil she would hike to the Spill, then return, a half-hour perhaps, had to breathe and had to be alone, oh but she was out of breath, panting for breath; since the baby, since the babies, Lizabeta had gained weight, her belly and her breasts were slack, fatty thighs no longer a girl's supple muscled thighs but the thighs of an older woman creased and puckered and it disgusted her, made her want to scream, how the fleshy insides of her thighs rubbed together now, a damp slapping sound, a sound Lizabeta was sure others could hear, her stepsons Daniel and Calvin, her husband's nephew John Henry, whose habit it was in Aunt Liz'beta's presence to quickly avert his eyes from her even as he chewed at his lower lip.

Those raw yearning boy's eyes. She'd seen from the start.

Wanting to scream at them, as at the children: *I am more than this, my body. A woman is more than her body.*

As she neared the hay barn, her feet in ratty sneakers already soaked through, Lizabeta heard a cry behind her and turned to see Agnes on the back porch, calling something after her in a petulant, high-pitched voice. Lizabeta shouted at her: 'Get inside! I said – get inside! *Don't* follow me! Bad girl!' Her voice was choked with rage, she hadn't known how much rage, shaking her fist at the child and threatening to go back to hit her.

When Agnes hesitated, Lizabeta ran a few steps in her direction with her fist raised.

You wouldn't. Would not ever. Strike that child. Not ever.

With a final defiant shriek, Agnes ran back inside the house.

Lizabeta hoped that no one was watching: elderly Mrs Braam, or Mrs Braam's sister. The shades at their first-floor windows were drawn, which was a good sign. Walter and his sons were at work, and where was John Henry? Somewhere outside, clearing away storm debris.

Lizabeta walked on. She heard one of the horses wicker in the barn; a rooster was crowing querulously. There was storm debris everywhere: broken tree limbs, mud sloughs, a barnyard glittering with reeking puddles. Liquid manure, floating manure, the manure of horses and cows, and the special stench of rain-rotted hay, the stench of rotting flesh, for something must have died, drowned and died and was rotting now somewhere close by. Lizabeta averted her eyes, tried not to breathe until she was past the barnyard.

Not ever. Would not. Strike a child. I would not.

It may have been that Mama had slapped fretful little Agnes. In a sudden fit of frustration, despair. Not in dislike of the child. Not in hatred of the child.

No one had seen. Agnes had cried, screamed, kicked and thrashed in childish rage, but Agnes had already been screaming and thrashing, and no one had seen, and no one would know. Except Agnes, who would learn to respect her mother.

Discipline was necessary with willful children, the Braams believed. Certainly Walter thought so.

Even now Walter sometimes threatened his grown sons with blows, or did in fact hit them, or shove them, if they provoked him; you could see the flush of resentment in the young men's faces, you could see their clenched fists, but neither ever struck his father in return. They were likely to slink away, abashed and sullen. But they respected their father, Lizabeta knew.

But not me. Not ever.

Lizabeta walked hurriedly, stumbling in soft, spongy earth, her hair whipping in the wind. Her heart pounded with a kind of frantic jubilation. The air shone with moisture; everywhere she looked there was a wet, glittery beauty; patches of sumac were beginning to turn, vivid orange, red-orange, assaulting the eye. Only vaguely was she aware of branches slapping at her face, thorns catching at her clothing. Somehow the back of her left hand was threaded with blood; she'd been scratched without noticing. Fear touched her, suffused her. So swift the sensation came and departed, she was left with only its memory, glancing down at herself, the bulky jacket, which reminded her of her swollen belly, the heaviness of her pregnant body.

Why she'd fled the house: it wasn't just the children, nor the elderly ailing women, damned leaking ceilings, so much housework to be done, and that evening's meal to be prepared, but she was in terror that she was pregnant again. And Alistair only thirteen months old!

For the past week, in a daze of apprehension, Lizabeta had been counting days on the calendar. The lightest of pencil marks, so that no one glancing at the large glossy International Harvester calendar that hung on the kitchen wall would notice. Repeatedly she'd counted, backward and forward. And the days were becoming too many: thirty-two, thirty-three, thirty-four. *Can't be. No!*

She could not bear it, the moment of telling. Approaching the man, the father. A woman believes that she is pregnant and must inform the man who is the father of the child, and this man, who is the father, will respond visibly to her words. The look in his eyes, the tightening in his jaws.

'Jesus! Don't tell me.'

This time, he might say, 'Lizabeta! Goddamn, this can't be.'

Walter hadn't wanted a third child, not at his age. Yet he'd come to love his baby son, it seemed. Not that Walter spent much time with his baby son, or with his young daughters. But he loved them, as Braam men loved their children, at a distance. The care and love of children was women's work exclusively.

Your son, isn't he beautiful?

You love him, don't you? And you love me?

This time, this fourth pregnancy, so soon after the third, Lizabeta could not imagine speaking of, which words she must choose, how Walter would react – she could not.

Lizabeta walked swiftly away from the house. Hardly knowing where she was going. Only she had to hurry: to run! She had never once resisted Walter's wish to have sex with her, she would not have imagined for a moment that any wife might resist her husband. Their lovemaking was apt to be abrupt, impulsive. Walter sometimes 'took care' – as he called it – but more often, if he'd been drinking and had come home late from Sparta, he did not. To a man like Walter Braam, sex was a weakness: to indulge in it was a concession to weakness, not to love or tenderness. Walter would accept responsibility for this fourth pregnancy in seven years, for Walter Braam was a man to accept responsibility; yet at the same time he would blame Lizabeta. She knew.

Lizabeta paused to glance about: where was she? Her feet, the lower parts of her legs, were wet; she was chilled, uneasy. The sun that had been so bright a few minutes before was now partly obscured by clouds and had taken on a wan, sullen glare. The autumnal air had turned colder. Lizabeta had been following the partly overgrown path beside the river, away from the house. Away from the farmyard. If this land was still Braam property, it no longer resembled farmable land but, hilly and rocky, with outcroppings of shale or granite in layers like gigantic steps, it had the look of a great, ancient ruin. Close by, the river rushed swollen and mud-colored, the highest Lizabeta had ever seen it. 'Black River' – Lizabeta shaped the name aloud. For no one in the Rapids ever called the river by its map name. There was nothing of blackness in it now; after a week of rain the river more resembled a massive flooded ditch. Ahead, just visible through a stand of badly shredded, peeling birch trees, was the series of steep misshapen hills, the rock formations known locally as the Spill. Lizabeta could see rock strata and glittering falling water in a noisy stream, spilling into the river below. Lizabeta smelled the water, she smelled mud. Her nostrils were assailed by a rich, stupefying odor of decay.

Corpses of dead, drowned creatures in the river. Amid storm debris the swollen and obscene carcasses of dogs, sheep, ground-hogs, deer, rushing past as in a lurid pageantry.

Could die here. No one would know. No one would know why.

There came a cry: 'Aunt Liz'beta!'

John Henry, breathless and excited. He must have sighted Lizabeta and followed her along the river. Early that morning Walter had sent John Henry out to clear away storm damage in the area around the barns and to begin the work of repairing fences; he'd been gone much of the day. His coveralls were splotched with mud and wet to the knee, his battered boy's face shone with sweat and seemed flushed as if with sunburn. As a dog is pleasurably excited to unexpectedly discover its master out-of-doors, so John Henry seemed pleasurably excited to see Lizabeta in this unexpected place. Lizabeta felt a stab of dismay – *Don't look at me. Go away and leave me* – but of course John Henry was looking at Lizabeta, staring and blinking, his teeth bared in a big smile. His head was bobbing, that shaved head covered in bluish stubble like smudged coal dust.

John Henry's shaved head! All of Lizabeta's repugnance, her despair, her hurt, her frustration, and her rage, her terror at her predicament, seemed to spring at her from the pathetic sight of the retarded boy's shaved head.

Years ago Lizabeta had learned why John Henry's head had to be shaved every few weeks: to prevent John Henry from 'catching' head lice. (As a boy in Sparta, John Henry had 'caught' lice often and had become terrified of the brutal delousing procedure, with a rough haircut and head shave and kerosene scrubbed into the exposed scalp, followed by a scrubbing with lye soap, which had been performed, Lizabeta could imagine with what fury and disgust, by John Henry's nurse's aide mother, Dorothy.) And Lizabeta had soon learned whose task it would be to keep John Henry's head shaved once he'd moved to the Rapids: hers.

John Henry's poor battered head needed shaving now. Somehow, in those days of pelting rain, John Henry's head had been overlooked.

John Henry was telling his aunt Lizabeta something about the flooded river, the 'angels' in the river, when Lizabeta impatiently interrupted: 'Melinda is missing! She ran away – she's gone to the Spill.'

238

John Henry ceased chattering. His mouth came open, slack in astonishment. Like a deaf man straining to hear, John Henry stared and blinked at Lizabeta and was for a moment speechless. Melinda? The Spill?

For abruptly it came to Lizabeta, how the three-year-old had run from her and was lost to her, not the six-year-old whom she'd shouted at, Mama with an upraised fist, Mama livid with rage, but Melinda, the child who was beloved, whose loss meant something: 'She's got away from me, John Henry. She woke from her nap, she slipped outside, it's the Spill she headed for, Melinda is gone to the Spill.' Lizabeta spoke rapidly yet with the air of one trying to remain calm, to keep from screaming. As John Henry gaped at her, Lizabeta repeated: 'The Spill! Melinda! Your cousin Melinda! John Henry, Melinda is gone to the Spill, we must save her.'

'M'linda? The Spill? *Is*?'

John Henry smiled uncertainly. His teeth were badly discolored, broken. For John Henry could not be taken to Sparta to any dentist, even if his uncle had wished to pay for his dental work, just as John Henry could not be taken to any eye doctor, even if his uncle had wished to pay for prescription glasses for his weak, watery eyes. His low forehead creased like an old man's: Was Aunt Liz'beta teasing? Was this one of the Braams' jokes? It was not like any woman to tease John Henry. Aunt Liz'beta, her voice lifting in alarm, a silvery voice, a voice like a bird's cry, a voice that pierced John Henry's heart like a knife blade, did not appear to be teasing him, and yet – could you know for sure? So often words were surprises, like nudges in the ribs or slaps against the back of the head. Words were shouts, so loud you couldn't hear. What was strangest was how close up, or at a distance, inside a house or out-of-doors, wearing different clothes, at different times of day and in different moods, individuals whom John Henry knew the names of and recognized the faces of, he could not be certain that he really knew. Few things scared John Henry (for John Henry was beloved of God, who dwelled in the sky and watched over him, most days), but this scared John Henry, for it had to be a mistake of his own. There was his uncle Walter, who had taken John Henry in to live with him, who was sometimes kind to him and sometimes impatient with him, greeted him with a smile, a nod of his head, *Good work, John Henry*, and sometimes stared at him in surprise and disgust, *Damn clumsy sod, look at this. Done wrong.* And John Henry shrank away in shame like a kicked dog. But a kicked dog is called back in time. For a kicked dog is forgiven by those who have taken him in. John Henry's young aunt Lizabeta seemed to have forgiven him; John Henry was grateful for this. Couldn't recall what he'd done wrong but so grateful to be forgiven. Aunt Liz'beta was speaking to him, leading him to the Spill, where Melinda had run to only a few minutes before, and so it seemed to John Henry, yes, he'd seen his little cousin running along the path beside the river, running from her mama, who stood now on the bank of the frothy stream where spray was blown into their faces, staring and pointing: 'John Henry! Look! There's Melinda over there – by that big boulder – d'you see her?' John Henry crouched on the bank craning his neck, gaping open-mouthed, uncertain what he saw or wasn't seeing, for his eyes were blurred with moisture, a din of churning water. Faintly he could make out something wedged between rocks, might've been a broken tree limb, raw greenish pale wood of a broken willow, or might've been a drowned crea-ture, or a live, struggling little girl flailing her arms as John Henry's aunt Liz'beta cried for him to hurry! hurry! before it was too late, hurry! and John Henry obeyed, stepping into the water, which was colder than he expected, needing to grab onto rocks, desperate to grab onto rocks, anything he could grab onto, managing with effort to pull himself up, sharp-edged shelves of granite like gigantic steps in the earth, on all sides misshapen rocks and boulders flung down from the sky by a furious God and barely visible in the sky thin drifting clouds, angels riding those clouds leaning over to spit on John Henry's baldie-head and laugh at him though they'd been his friends just that morning, John Henry was hoping that his aunt Liz'beta didn't hear, how ashamed John Henry would be if any of the Braams knew how his garden angels had turned against him another time. It seemed that only a few days ago John Henry had clambered across the Spill when the streams of water were shallow trickles amid the rocks and he hadn't been afraid then though he'd slipped once or twice on slimy moss, cut the palm of his hand in a fall, but managed to clamber across the Spill and back again and an angel whistling at him from a tall birch had seemed to be praising him for being light-footed and graceful as a cat, but now the angels were withholding their judgment, now John Henry was crouched, now squatting, making his way with painstaking slowness across the the lower part of the Spill, like a great clumsy cockroach making its way, a great scuttling crab, hunched over, grabbing at rocks to haul himself toward, to reach out for Melinda, to take Melinda's hand, but the water came so fast, so blinding fast and so cold, John Henry's hands were becoming numb, John Henry's hands were bleeding from a dozen cuts, recklessly he lunged forward, he could hear Melinda crying *John Henry! John Henry!* as the water overcame him, splintered into myriad glittery particles like broken glass and each of these water particles a miniature rainbow, there came an unexpected voice, a harsh voice, a din of harsh accusing voices *John Henry don't touch yourself John Henry you disgust me damn clumsy sod dirty boy freak blow your damn nose in a tissue not your damn fingers don't stick fingers in your nose keep out of your damn mouth your ears you smell of your body you don't wipe yourself your father is going to discipline you going to cut off your disgusting thing why don't you go away why don't you die nobody wants you* he'd swallowed water, coughing, choking, his foot slipped on slimy moss and this time he fell, in astonishment falling, too astonished to cry out in pain, the stubbly head struck a sharp-edged rock and in that instant cracked like an egg, the life pent-up inside the head began to leak from him, how like a broken egg, a messy broken egg cracked in a clumsy hand, stricken in shame John Henry fell, the mad rushing frothy stream took him as he was propelled forward and down falling as if thrown from a height, his neck was broken, the knobby bones of his vertebrae were broken, his left eye gouged out, he wasn't John Henry now, no one knew his name now, amid a desolation of broken and shredded tree limbs and underbrush he was spinning, taken down, over the edge of the Spill and into the river below, borne away and lost in the swollen rushing mud river below.

Lizabeta ran.

In terror of what she'd seen, what she'd caused to happen at the Spill, Lizabeta ran.

Ran blindly, stumbling in the wet earth. Ran without looking back and without knowledge of what had happened, what had happened to John Henry, where the Spill had taken him. She hadn't

243

seen, immediately she'd backed away, turned, and ran. Seeing how on the path before her the six-year-old Agnes had dared to follow her, but now Lizabeta seized Agnes in her arms, trying awkwardly to run with the frightened child until her arms gave out, she had to let the struggling Agnes down, and now mother and daughter ran together, white-faced Lizabeta clutching at Agnes's small hand as they ran away from the Spill and back to the house a half-mile away.

5.

Days later the body was found, three miles downstream in the rubble beneath the Constableville bridge. Walter Braam identified the remains of his nephew John Henry Chrisman, and the body was taken away and quickly buried. In local papers there was no explanation for the 'storm accident' in the Spill, to be counted as one of several fatalities resulting from the October 1951 flooding in the western Adirondacks.

In June 1952 Lizabeta Braam had a fourth child, the last of Walter Braam's six children: a boy named Henry. By this time Lizabeta had become an intensely religious Christian who attended both Sunday morning and Wednesday evening services at the First Methodist Church of Rapids. Though Lizabeta suffered from ill health for the remainder of her life – migraine, lightheadedness, female ailments – everyone who knew her, or knew of her, was emphatic in describing her as a saintly woman like no one else of their acquaintance, utterly selfless, loving, devoted to her family and relatives, and so it seemed she was, in the memories of her numerous grandchildren.

Grandma Braam, who adored us.

It was my mother's older sister, Agnes, who told this story of John Henry Chrisman, in the years after Lizabeta died. A story told and retold, so it seemed sometimes that I had known John Henry myself. My mother, Melinda, could not have remembered John Henry very clearly, yet she insisted that she did. Fifty-five years after her cousin John Henry died in the Spill, my mother would say, with an inscrutable expression that might have been tenderness, or merely wonderment: 'I can see John Henry plain as day, standing in front of me. His face – his face is a blur. But his shaved head I can see. His hands – his big raw scraped-looking hands that had something in them, for me. John Henry is what we called him.'

NOWHERE

1.

*M*y mother, I wish . . .

   The first time no one heard. So softly Miriam spoke. In the din of raised voices, laughter. In the din of high-decibel rock music. She was into the beat, sweating with the percussion. Shaking her head from side to side and her eyes closed. Leaking tears but closed. *My mother, I wish someone would . . .* At the crowded table no one noticed. It was the Star Lake Inn, the deck above the lake. Music blared from speakers overhead. Had to be the Star Lake Inn, though it didn't look familiar. The moon was rising in the night sky. She'd lost her sandals somewhere. Couldn't remember who'd brought her here, six miles from home. Then she remembered: the boy from the marina driving the steel-colored Jeep. Not a local guy. He'd been flirting with her all week. Her heart skidded when she saw him. Big-jawed boy with sun-bleached hair, had to be mid-twenties, father owned one of the sleek white sailboats docked at the marina, but Kevin wasn't

246

into taking orders from the old man like a damn cabin boy, he said. Anger flared in his pale eyes. He was from downstate: Westchester County. Half the summer residents at Star Lake were from Westchester County. He'd thought Miriam was older than fifteen, maybe. Gripping her wrist, not her hand, helping her up into the Jeep. A stabbing sensation shot through her groin.

Had to be past 11 P.M. The moon continued to rise in the sky above Mount Hammer. She'd gotten off work at the boathouse at 6 P.M. In the Jeep she'd called home on her cell phone. Left a message for her mother: she'd run into friends from school, wouldn't be home until late.

Please don't wait up for me, Mom. Makes me nervous, okay?

The boy in the Jeep didn't know Miriam's brothers, hadn't known Miriam's father. *Orlander* meant nothing to him. Maybe to his father, who owned one of the new A-frames on East Shore Drive, *Orlander* meant something. In the Adirondacks there were local residents and there were property owners from downstate. If you were a local male, you worked for the downstate property owners: carpentry, roofing, plumbing, hauling away trash. You paved driveways, you exterminated vermin. You fenced off property to keep out deer hunters like yourself. The expensive new lakeside houses were always in need of upgrading: redwood decks, children's rooms, saunas, tennis courts. Les Orlander had been a roofer. His brother-in-law

247

Harvey Schuller siphoned out waste from buried septic tanks and dug new septic fields. YOUR SHIT SMELLS SWEET TO ME was a joke bumper sticker Miriam's father had had printed up, but Harvey kept it displayed in his office, not on his truck. If you were a local female, you might work inside the summer residents' houses: cooking, caring for children, cleaning. You served at their parties. You picked up after their drunken houseguests. Uncomplaining, you wore rubber gloves to retrieve from a stopped-up toilet a wadded Kotex or baby diaper someone had tried to flush away. You wore a nylon uniform. You smiled and hoped for a generous tip. You learned not to stack dirty dishes from the dinner table but to remove each plate ceremoniously, murmuring *Thank you!* as you took the plate away, *Thank you!* you murmured as you served dessert and poured wine into glasses. *Thank you!* mopping up spilled wine, on your hands and knees picking up shattered glass. Your employers called you by your first name and urged you to call them by their first names, but you never did. Ethel laughed to show she thought it was funny, such bullshit. Not that she was a bitter woman, for truly Ethel was not.

Beggars can't be choosers, right?

Miriam's mother thought this was an optimistic attitude.

Three years of his five-to-seven-year sentence for assault Miriam's father served at Ogdensburg men's facility, and during those years of shame her mother worked for summer residents and for a Tupper Lake caterer. Often Ethel stayed overnight at Tupper Lake, twenty miles away. It began to be said in Star Lake that she met men there, at the resort hotels. She took 'gifts' from them. At this time Miriam was in eighth grade and deeply mortified by both her parents. Her father she loved and missed so badly, it was like part of her heart was locked away in the prison. Her mother she'd used to love but was beginning now to hate. *Wish! Wish to God something would happen to her.* When Miriam's oldest brother, Gideon, confronted their mother one day, Ethel shouted at him that her life was her own, not her damn children's. Her 'money life' and her 'sex life' she said were her own business, not some damn loser inmate's who'd let his family down. Shocked then by the fury of the words roiling from her, Ethel had tried to laugh, saying it was a joke, some kind of joke, anyway isn't everything some kind of joke, the way life turns out? But Gideon would never forgive her.

Quit roofing, moved to Watertown and impregnated a woman he never married, and a few months later enlisted in the U.S. Marines and got sent to Iraq.

Even when their father was paroled and returned to Star Lake to live, Gideon avoided the family. Every time Miriam came home she steeled herself for news of him: he'd been killed in that terrible place. Or for the sight of Ethel, disheveled, lying on her bed in the waning hours of the afternoon.

I wish. Why don't you. Why, when you're so unhappy!

'Looking lost, Miriam? Where's your rich boyfriend?'

Miriam was a girl to be teased. A hot blush rising into her face. Her eyes were warm glistening brown with something shrinking and mocking in the droop of the eyelids. Her hair was streaked blond-brown, the commonest color. Before meeting Kevin after work she'd hurriedly brushed out her hair, pursed her lips, applying dark red lipstick to make her appear older, sexier. Now it was hours later and the lipstick was eaten off and her hair was in her face and so many guys were looking at her, laughing at her, all she could do was shake her head, blushing and embarrassed.

Oz Newell, who'd been Gideon's closest high school friend, was calling down the table: 'What'd he do, the fucker, take a leak and fall in? Want me to break his head?'

Nervously Miriam laughed, shaking her head. She was scared of something like this. Older guys relating to her like she was their kid sister, wanting to protect her, and somebody getting hurt.

Her brothers had gotten into fights at places like the Star Lake Inn. Her father.

Star Lake Resident Pleads Guilty, Assault
Reduced Charges Lead
to 5–7 Years at Ogdensburg

The kind of work men did here in the Adirondacks, a belligerent attitude was natural. Drunk Friday night was natural. It was sheer hell to take orders from foremen, bosses. Rich men from downstate, like Kevin's father. 'Manual laborer.' By age forty-five you'd be limping. By age fifty your back was shot. Natural to want to break some fucker's head. Miriam thought, *I had fists like theirs, I'd feel the same way.*

Must've been Miriam had wandered past their table looking lost. Looking like a girl who's been dumped by her boy-friend, trying not to cry. Also she's underage. Also she's never had sex. Also she's been feeling sick, gagging in the restroom in one of the smelly toilet stalls, but nothing came up. Whatever he'd given her: *Baby, you need loosening up.* In the Jeep, a joint they shared that made her cough, choke, giggle insanely. At the Star Lake Inn, vodka and cranberry juice for Miriam. She was confused about where Kevin had gone, exactly where they'd been sitting, couldn't find the table, someone else had taken the table, but maybe Kevin was inside at the bar, maybe Kevin was looking for her? Cigarette smoke made her eyes sting and blur, she couldn't see. Somebody grabbed at her arm, grinning faces lurched at her: 'Miriam? Miriam Orlander? What're you doing *here*?'

251

So she was sitting with them. Practically on Brandon McGraw's lap. Like she was their little-girl mascot. Maybe because she wasn't beautiful. She was fleshy, warm-skinned, but not beautiful. These were older guys in their twenties who'd gone to school with her brothers or who'd worked with them. One or two of them might've worked with Miriam's father. And one or two of them with Miriam's uncle Harvey Schuller. Where their girl-friends and wives were, Miriam wondered. When she asked, they told her it was boys' night out. She figured they'd come to the Star Lake Inn immediately after work to begin drinking. In summers you worked late, until 7 P.M. Miriam's father and brothers worked even later. The table was strewn with dirty plates, empty bottles. The remains of hamburgers, deep-fried shrimp, pizza crusts. Onion rings, coleslaw, ketchup. A grease sheen on the Formica surface. The table was outdoors, above the lake; still the air was heavy with smoke from their cigarettes. They were drinking beer, ale, whiskey. They were drunk, high, stoned. Miriam saw the red-rimmed eyes she knew to associate with drugs: speed, crystal meth. These guys weren't into smoking dope like the kids she knew. Beyond wanting to feel mellowed out and restful, like they could love mankind. She shivered to hear: raw male laughter like the praying of coyotes. Their young faces were reddened, coarse, and prematurely lined from outdoor work. Their shoulders, necks, upper arms were thick with muscle. Their hair was buzzcut short or straggling past their collars. Martin had worn his straggly hair tied back in a kind of pigtail. The loggers and tree trimmers, who worked with chain saws, were likely to be scarred or missing fingers. If Miriam got drunker/sillier, she'd count how many fingers were missing from the table. Sex energy lifted from the men's heated skins, frank as sweat. Most girls would be uneasy in the company of so many men, but not Miriam Orlander, who'd grown up in a household with three older brothers she'd adored.

Well, mostly. Mostly she'd adored them.

And her father, Les Orlander, she'd adored.

'Drown the fucker in the lake, who'd know? His rich daddy can drag the lake for his corpse.'

This was Hay Brouwet. The subject seemed still to be whoever it was who'd brought Miriam to the Star Lake Inn, then abandoned her.

'What d'you say, Miriam? Pick out which one he is.'

Quickly Miriam said, 'He isn't here now. I don't see him.'

Hay cupped his hand to his ear, not hearing. The rock music was so loud. The braying at the table so loud. Miriam caught her breath, seeing the smooth shiny stub of Hay's right forefinger. Hay was a logger, must've had a chain-saw accident. Miriam felt faint imagining having to kiss that stub. Suck that stub in her mouth. *If he asks me to, I will.*

In the Jeep, in the parking lot, Kevin had made some joke about Miriam sucking him off; Miriam pretended not to hear. In the tussle she'd lost her sandals. He hadn't meant to hurt her, she was sure. *Hey, baby, I'm sorry – just joking.*

Except Hay was married, wasn't he? One of the older guys at the table, had to be thirty. Seeing Miriam's eyes on him, winking.

'You see the asshole, let me know, okay?'

It was pretty clear Hay was high on something. That mean-happy red-eye-glittering look, and he'd sweated through his shirt.

Crystal meth. Each of Miriam's brothers had instructed her individually never to try it. Not ever! Miriam was scared but intrigued. She knew that Stan, who was twenty-three, had had something to do with a methamphetamine lab – a cook-shop, it was called – but he'd never gotten caught, and now he lived up in Keene. Ice was for older guys, not a fifteen-year-old girl whose hope was to go to nursing school at Plattsburgh State. An immediate high, wired straight to the brain. Her brother Martin was back in rehab at Watertown. *Fries your brain like nothing else. Makes you shiny and hard. Why's that bad! What's better you got to offer!*

Ethel had slapped him; he'd been yelling and laughing and stomping in the house so hard the windowpanes shook like a army bomber from Fort Drum was passing too low over the roof. Martin had hardly felt the blow, only brushed Ethel away like you'd brush away flies.

254

A few minutes later they heard him outside. A noise of breaking glass.

'Miriam, what the hell? You crying?'

It was the smoke. Making her eyes water. Her eyeballs burned in their sockets. She was annoyed, shaking her head, *no*, why'd she be crying? She was having a great time.

Her left wrist where Kevin had grabbed and twisted was reddened in overlapping welts. Half consciously she was touching the skin, caressing.

'He do that? Your wrist?'

'No.'

Brandon McGraw's blood-yellow eyes were peering at Miriam's wrist. His bristly eyebrows nearly met over the bridge of his nose, which was large, red-flushed, with deep, stretched-looking nostrils.

A look of shocked tenderness in Brandon's face so you'd almost want to laugh. Like the look she'd seen once on her father's face as he squatted in the driveway to stare at something small, wriggling, dying, a fledgling robin blown out of its nest.

'Like hell, Miriam. This looks like a guy's finger marks.'

'Really, no. I'm just clumsy.'

Miriam drew her arm away. Shrank both arms against her chest.

How she'd got there she didn't know. Six miles from home. Too far to walk in the dark. Missing her shoes. She was drunk, she'd been sweating so. *Miriam! I've been sick with worry.*

255

She hated Ethel. Couldn't bear to see Ethel.

Alone. The two of them. In the house on Salt Isle Road. Ethel, Miriam. Where there'd been six people, now reduced to two.

These guys felt sorry for her, Miriam knew. Seeing her, they were thinking *Orlander: bad luck.*

'He didn't hurt me. I don't care about him. See, I'm having a great time. I want to dance.'

Dance! Miriam wanted to dance! Stumbling and almost falling. The floor tilted beneath her like the deck was a boat. Were they on a cruise boat, on the lake? Choppy waves?

Through the speakers blared heavy metal rock. Maybe you could dance to it. Was anybody dancing? Miriam wasn't the girl this was happening to. Miriam wasn't the type. How she'd got here to the Star Lake Inn, which was a biker hangout on the marshy side of the lake, she didn't know. Underage but looking eighteen at least. No one asked her for ID. The kind of place the bartenders stayed inside and there were no waiters. You pushed your way in, got drinks from the bar, pushed your way back out onto the deck. Lights on tall poles. Insects swirling around the lights like demented thoughts. Miriam's brothers had come here. She'd been eating cold french fries from one of the greasy plates. Hadn't eaten since lunchtime. None of this was remotely like Miriam Orlander. At the boathouse, she was the girl who blushed easily. The girl who didn't flirt with men. Had not wanted to waitress, so she worked in the store, where she was the youngest salesclerk and got stuck with the hardest work, like unpacking the merchandise, stocking the shelves. What embarrassed her was the female employee uniform she had to wear. Red T-shirt with white letters, AU SABLE BOATHOUSE, straining against her breasts. Worse yet the white cord miniskirt trimmed in red. The miniskirt rode up her thighs. Sitting, she had to keep her knees pressed tightly together. Walking, she had to tug at the skirt, uncomfortably aware of her thighs rubbing together. Men stared. Some smiled openly. Miriam was a healthy girl: five feet six, one hundred thirty pounds. Ethel had crinkled her face at the uniform. *Miriam! I don't think this is a good idea.* She'd wanted to come with Miriam to the boathouse to speak with Andy Mack, who'd hired Miriam and provided the uniform for his girl employees, but Miriam had screamed at her and run out of the house.

Now Miriam was dancing. Wild and tossing her body like it's impaled on a hook she's got to wriggle, wriggle, wriggle to get free. Oz Newell was dancing with her, and for a while Hay Brouwet. For such burly muscled guys, they got winded fast. Miriam laughed at them. Miriam loved how the music poured like something molten into her veins. The beat was so fast her heart raced to keep up. Maybe it was ice he'd given her; maybe this was the ice rush, and she loved it. Breathing through her mouth, panting.

Bare feet, kind of pudgy pale feet, toenails painted dark to match the sexy lipstick, she's picking up splinters in the tender soles of her feet from the raw floorboards but doesn't feel any pain. Not a glimmer of pain. No more pain! Maybe it doesn't matter if she isn't beautiful, the way Oz Newell is looking at her. His eyes on her breasts in the tight red T-shirt, his eyes on her soft rounded belly, her hips and thighs in the tight white miniskirt trimmed in red. Rivulets of sweat trickle down Oz's sunburned face. Oz does construction work for Herkimer County. Oz had some kind of disagreement with Gideon; they didn't part friends. Miriam is weak with sudden love for him. Laughs to think how surprised Oz would be if she slipped her bare arms around his neck and tongued his face, licked away the sweat droplets like tears. Oz is twenty-five or -six. Ten years older than Miriam. Gideon's age. Not a boy but a man. His hair is a blond buzzcut. Eyebrows and lashes so pale you almost can't see them. Gray eyes like pinwheels, spinning.

Hay Brouwet is back, and another guy, fattish and drunk-silly, grimy baseball cap on his head advertising WATERTOWN RACEWAY. The dancing, if you can call it dancing, is getting out of control. Hay is shaking his shiny stub-finger in Miriam's face, gyrating his hips like some stoned rock star, collides with an older man carrying beers, two beers in the stretched fingers of each hand, and the beers go flying, there's a comical scene like

258

something on TV, Miriam is helpless, laughing, panting, and breathless, and almost wets herself. There's a feeling like fire: wildfire. The guys' eyes on her, the heavy-metal vibrations thundering inside her head. Like, with a fire, the wind blows it in one direction and not another – it's the difference between somebody's property going up in walls of roaring flame and somebody else's, only a few hundred feet away, untouched. There are controlled burns in the Adirondacks. You have to get permission from the county. And there are uncontrolled burns – lightning, campers' fires, arson.

Arson. There's times you are so angry, so beaten down, you need to start a fire. Toss a match, evergreens dead and dried from acid rain, it's like a fireball exploding. Miriam remembers one of her brothers saying this. *Hey – just joking.*

Miriam's father had been a volunteer fireman for Au Sable township. There'd been years of the excitement and dread of hearing the siren, a high-pitched wail from the firehouse a mile away, seeing Daddy roused to attention, hurriedly dressing if it was night, running out to his pickup. Often they'd smelled smoke, seen smoke rising above the tree line, heard sirens. Those years Miriam had taken for granted would go on forever. But after Ogdensburg, Les hadn't rejoined the volunteers. Maybe there was a law against ex-convicts being volunteer firemen, Miriam hadn't wanted to ask.

Abruptly the deafening rock music stopped. For

a moment Miriam didn't know where she was. Her eyeballs were burning as if she'd been staring stupidly into a hot bright light. Inside her tight-fitting clothes she was slick with sweat like oil. Damn miniskirt had ridden up to practically her crotch. Like a child, Miriam wiped her damp face on her T-shirt. Somebody's arms came down heavy on her shoulders, somebody stumbling against her, a big guy, soft fleshy belly, a smell of whiskey and heat pouring off his skin. Quick as a cat, Miriam disentangled herself and backed away. Ran barefoot to the edge of the deck, where, overlooking lapping water just below, it was quieter, smelling of the lake. Miriam recalled as if through a haze that she was at Star Lake: six miles from home. The way the moon was slanted in the sky, now east of Mount Hammer, it had to be late. *Worried sick about you. You're all I have.*

Star Lake was dark, glittering by moonlight. Said to be in the shape of a star, but up close you couldn't see any shape to it, only glittering water and opaque wedges of shadow that were trees and, on the far shore, the east side, lights from the new houses, not visible from the shore road. Miriam had never been in any of these houses; she had no friends who lived in them. Mostly these were summer people who kept to themselves. Their houses were architect-designed A-frames, split-levels, replicas of old Adirondack log lodges. The last months of his life, Miriam's father had worked for a roofing contractor on several of those houses.

He'd been disbelieving, the prices people from downstate were paying. *Like another world*, he'd said. *It's another world now.* He had not seemed especially grieving that day. Quiet and matter-of-fact, informing his daughter as if it were something she should know.

'Hey, baby. Where you goin'?'

A hand came down on Miriam's shoulder. Fingers kneading the nape of her neck beneath her damp crimped hair. Miriam felt a stab of panic even after she saw it was Oz Newell. Now the music had stopped, she wasn't so sure of herself. *I don't want this. This is a mistake.* Miriam managed to twist away from Oz but grabbed his hand, as a girl might do, to pull him back to the others, to the table. Oz slung his arms around her shoulders and nuzzled her hair, called her baby, as if he'd forgotten her name. Miriam felt weak with desire for the man, unless it was fear. 'I miss Gideon. Damn, I miss your dad.' Oz's voice sounded young, raw, clumsy. He had more to say but couldn't think of the words. Miriam murmured, 'I do too. Thanks.'

Halfway back to the table Miriam saw the jut-jawed young man from the marina weaving through the crowd. It was a shock to see him; she'd taken for granted he'd dumped her. Was Kevin his name? Was this Kevin? Miriam hadn't remembered him wearing a Yankees cap, but she remembered the arrogant jut-jawed face, the streaked blond hair. He was walking unsteadily and hadn't seen her. Or, seeing her, had not recognized her. He was alone, appeared to be looking for someone. Miriam wondered if maybe he'd been in the men's room all this while, being sick to his stomach. His face looked freshly washed and not so arrogant as he'd seemed with just him and Miriam in the Jeep, when he'd bragged of his father's sailboat and twisted Miriam's wrist. Miriam pointed him out to Oz: 'That's him.'

2.

Did it to himself.

This was a way of speaking. It was the way she knew they were speaking. It was a way of wonderment, and of accusation. It was a way of consolation. In Au Sable County and Star Lake and where Les Orlander had been known. A way of saying, *Nobody else is to blame, no one of us. Nobody did it to him, he did it to himself.* Yet it was a way of admiration too. It was a way of saying, *He did it to himself, it was his free choice.* A way of acknowledging. *He did it to himself, he had the guts for it, and not everybody has.* In the Adirondacks, a man's guns are his friends. A man's guns are his companions. Les Orlander had not been a fanatic gun collector, like some. Like some of his relatives and in-laws. Shotguns, rifles. Legal weapons. Les had owned only a shotgun and a rifle, and these were of no special distinction. *Did it to himself, used his rifle*, was a tribute to the man's efficiency. *Did it to himself, out alone in the woods.* A gun is a man's friend when friends can't help. A friend to protect him from shame, from hurt, from dragging through his life. A gun can make a wounded man whole. A gun can make a broken man stronger. No escape, except a gun will provide escape. *Did it to himself* had to be the legacy he'd leave his family.

3.

You know I love you, honey. That will never stop.

He'd said that. Before he went away. Miriam was staring out the school bus window. Her breath steamed faintly on the window. Her eyes were glazed, seeing little of the landscape: trees, fields, roadside houses, mobile homes on concrete blocks at the end of rutted driveways.

. . . come see me, okay? Promise?

There came the tall, clumsy Ochs girl lurching toward her. As the school bus started up, lurching along the aisle, staring and grinning at Miriam. She was at least two years older than Miriam: fourteen, one of the special education students at school. Her face was broad and coarse and blemished in dull red rashes and bumps. Her small cunning eyes had a peculiar glisten. Lana Ochs wasn't retarded but was said to have 'learning disabilities.' Her older sister had been expelled for fighting in the school cafeteria. On the bus, no one wanted Lana to sit

263

with them: she was so large-boned, fidgety, and smelled like rancid milk. Miriam's backpack was in the seat beside her. She was saving a seat for her friend Iris. Miriam stared out the window as Lana approached, thinking, *Go away! Don't sit here.* But Lana was hunched over her, grinning. She asked, 'This seat taken?' and Miriam said quickly, 'Yes, it is.' For Iris Petko, who was in Miriam's seventh-grade homeroom, would be getting on the bus in a few minutes, and Lana Ochs knew this. Still she hung over Miriam, swaying and lurching in the aisle, as if about to shove Miriam's backpack aside. In a whiny, insinuating voice she said, 'No it isn't. It isn't taken, Miriam.' Miriam was sitting halfway to the rear of the bus. There were several empty seats Lana might take. In another minute the bus driver would shout back at her to sit down; it was forbidden to stand in the aisle while the bus was in motion. Miriam said, 'It's for Iris. You can sit somewhere else.' Her eyes lifted to Lana Ochs's flushed face, helpless. Lana's hair was matted and frizzed. Her lips were fleshy, smeared with bright red lipstick. Older boys on the bus called Lana by an ugly name having to do with those lips. Lana leaned over Miriam, saying in a mock whisper, 'Hey, Miriam – your father and my father, they're in the same place.' Miriam said, 'No they're not.' Lana said, 'Yes they are. That makes us like sisters.' Miriam was staring out the window now, stony-faced. She was a shy girl but could be stuck-up, snotty. In seventh grade she had that reputation. Her friends were popular girls. She received high grades in most subjects. She'd had three older brothers to look after her, and there had been a certain glamour accruing to the Orlander boys, who'd preceded their sister in the Star Lake public schools. Now the youngest, Martin, a sophomore at Star Lake High, no longer rode the school bus but got a ride into town with friends. Miriam was vulnerable now, not so protected. She could smell Lana Ochs leaning over her, saying in a loud, aggrieved voice for everyone to hear, 'You got no right to be stuck-up, Miriam. Your father is no better than my father. You think you're hot shit but you're not.' Miriam said, 'Go away. Leave me alone. I hate you,' and Lana said, 'Fuck you!' swinging her heavy backpack against Miriam, striking her on the shoulder. Now the driver, who should have intervened before this, braked the bus and shouted back at them, 'Girls! Both of you! Stop that or you'll get out and walk.' Lana cursed Miriam and swung past the seat, sitting heavily behind her. Miriam could hear her panting and muttering to herself. Miriam fumbled to open her math book: algebra. Her heart was beating frantically. Her face burned with shame. Everyone on the bus had been watching, listening. Some she'd thought were her friends but were not. Wanting to scream at them, *Go away! Leave me alone! I hate you.*

At this time, Les Orlander had been incarcerated

at the men's maximum-security prison at Ogdensburg for just six days.

4.

Ogdensburg. Almost as far north as you could drive in New York State. And there was the St Lawrence River, which was the widest river Miriam had ever seen. And beyond, the province of Ontario, Canada.

Miriam asked Ethel could they drive across the bridge to the other side someday, after visiting Les, if it was a nice day and not windy and cold, and Ethel said, distracted, glancing in the rearview mirror, where a diesel truck was bearing close upon her on Route 37, 'Why?'

It added something to the prison, Miriam wanted to think, that it had once been a military fort. Built high on a hill above the river, to confound attack. From the access road the prison was too massive to be seen except as weatherworn dark gray stone, like something in an illustrated fairy tale of desolation and punishment. Beside the front gate was a plaque informing visitors of the history of the prison: 'Fort La Présentation was built in 1749 by French missionaries. It was captured by the British in 1760 and its name changed to Fort Oswegatchie. After the Revolution, it was the site of several bloody skirmishes in the War of 1812. In 1817 its name was changed to Ogdensburg, and in 1911 it was converted into the first state prison for men in northern New York State. In 1956 –' Ethel interrupted irritably, 'As if anybody gives a damn about history who'd be coming here.' Miriam said, stung, 'Not everybody is like you, Mom. Some people actually want to learn something.' Miriam made it a point to read such plaques when she could. So much was shifting and unreliable in her life; at least history was real.

It was a way too of telling Ethel, *You aren't so smart. You didn't graduate from high school. As I am going to do.*

Probably Ethel was right, though. Visitors to Ogdensburg had other things on their minds.

Everywhere were signs. PRISON PERSONNEL ONLY. Restricted area. Trespassers subject to arrest. VISITORS' PARKING. VISITING HOURS. PENALTIES FOR VIOLATION OF CONTRABAND RESTRICTIONS. A ten-foot stone wall topped with coils of razor wire surrounded the prison. Once you got through the checkpoint at the gate, you saw an inner electrified six-foot wire fence, angled sharply inward. Whenever she saw this fence, Miriam felt a clutch of panic, picturing herself forced to climb it, like a frantic animal scrambling and clawing to twist over the top, cutting her hands to shreds on the glinting razor wire. Of course she'd have been shocked unconscious by the electric voltage.

No one had escaped from Ogdensburg in a long time.

Ethel was saying with her bitter-bemused laugh,

267

'Damn prisons are big business. Half the town is on the payroll here. Guards run in families.'

Once you passed through the first checkpoint, you were outdoors again, waiting in line with other visitors. It was a windy November day, blowing gritty snow like sand. The line moved slowly. Most of the visitors were women. Many had children with them. Many were black, Hispanic. From downstate. A scattering of whites, looking straight ahead. *Like sisters*, Miriam thought. No one wanted to be recognized here. Miriam dreaded seeing someone from the Ochs family who would know Ethel. She hadn't told Ethel what Lana Ochs had said on the bus that everyone had heard. *Your father and my father. In the same place.*

Miriam didn't know why Lana's father was in prison. She supposed it had to do with theft, bad checks. Though it might have been assault.

It wasn't uncommon for men in the Star Lake area to get into trouble with the law and to serve time at Ogdensburg, but no one in the Orlander family had ever been sent to prison before. Miriam remembered her mother screaming at her father, *How could you do this, so ashamed, ruined our lives, took our happiness from us and threw it into the dirt and for what!*

Miriam had pressed her hands against her ears. Whatever her father had answered, if he'd shouted back or turned aside, sick and defeated, Miriam hadn't known.

It was true: Les had taken their happiness from

them. What they hadn't understood was their happiness, because they'd taken it for granted, not knowing that even ordinary unhappiness is a kind of happiness when you have both your parents and your name isn't to be uttered in shame.

Les had been incarcerated now for nearly eighteen months. Gone from the house on Salt Isle Road as if he'd died. *Doing time.*

Miriam had constructed a homemade calendar. Because you could not buy a calendar for the next year and the next and the next, at least not in Star Lake. On the wall beside her bed she marked off the days in red. *Wishing-away time* was what it was. Miriam overheard her mother saying on the phone, *You wish away time, like wishing away your life. Goddamn if I'm going to do that.*

Miriam hadn't understood what Ethel meant. She'd understood the fury in her mother's voice, though.

Les Orlander's sentence was five to seven years. Which could mean seven years. Miriam would be nineteen when he was released and could not imagine herself so old.

'Move along. Coats off. Next.'

They were shuffling through the second checkpoint, which was the most thorough: metal detector; pockets and handbags emptied onto a conveyor belt; coats, hats removed, boots. Ethel was flushed and indignant, struggling to remove her tight-fitting boots. Each visit to Ogdensburg was stressful to her. She seemed never to accept

269

the authority of others to peer at her, examine her belongings, query her. She was an attractive woman of whom men took notice, if only to stare at her, then dismiss her: a face no longer young, a fleshy, sloping-down body. Breasts, hips. Since her husband's arrest and imprisonment she'd gained weight. Her skin seemed heated. Her dark hair was streaked with gray as if carelessly. In the parking lot she'd smeared dark lipstick onto her mouth, which was now down-turned, sullen. The black female security guard was suspicious of her. 'Ma'am? I'm asking you again, all the contents of that bag *out*.' Ethel's hands were shaking as she fumbled to comply. Miriam was quick to help. Under duress, she immediately became Ethel's daughter. She would side with her mother against others, by instinct.

Orlander, Ethel, and *Orlander, Miriam,* were checked against a list. A guard directed them into another crowded waiting room. Hard not to believe you were being punished. Related to an inmate, a criminal, you deserved punishment too.

Everywhere they looked were glaring surfaces. Rooms brightly lit by fluorescent tubing. Linoleum floors, pale green walls. Where a surface could be buffed to shine, it shone. Miriam had never smelled such harsh odors. Disinfectant, Ethel said. 'One good thing, there's no germs in this damn place. They'd all be killed.'

'I wouldn't be too sure, Mom. We'd be killed before that.'

'God, I hate it here. This place.'

'Think how Daddy feels.'

'Daddy.' Ethel's voice quavered with contempt.

Don't hate Daddy! Miriam wanted to beg. *We are all he has.*

The night before, Miriam hadn't been able to sleep. Misery through the night. She could feel her skin itching, burning. Her sensitive skin. Rehearsing what she would tell her father that would make him love her. That was all it was, trying to make Daddy love her. When she'd been a little girl, the baby of the family, it had been so easy; Daddy had loved her, and Mommy, and her big brothers, who'd adored her when they had time for her. Then something happened. Miriam had gotten older; Daddy wasn't so interested in her or in his family. Daddy was distracted; Daddy was in one of his moods. Drinking, Miriam knew. That was it. Part of it. He'd had disagreements with the roofing contractor for whom he worked. He'd tried working on his own, but that brought problems too. Ethel said, *Things change, people change. What's broke can't be made whole again,* but Miriam didn't want to believe this.

Driving to Ogdensburg that morning, Ethel had been unusually quiet. That week she'd worked at Tupper Lake for two days, two nights and so she'd had that drive and now the drive to Ogdensburg and she was tired. She was tired, and she was resentful. Not one of Miriam's brothers was coming this time, which meant Ethel had to drive both ways. Miriam was only thirteen, too young for a driver's permit. Ethel had her own life now. In Tupper Lake. At home, the phone rang for her and she took the portable out of the room, speaking guardedly. Miriam would hear her laugh at a distance. Behind a shut door.

She's seeing men. Les better not know. Miriam's brothers were uneasy, suspicious. Gideon hadn't yet confronted Ethel. Miriam was frightened, preferring not to know.

Her skin! Her face. Broken out in hives and pellet-hard little pimples on her forehead; her fingernails wanted to scratch and scratch.

'Miriam, don't.'

Ethel caught Miriam's hand and gripped it tight. What had Miriam been doing, picking at her face? She was stricken with embarrassment. 'Do I look really bad, Mom? Will Daddy notice?' Ethel said quickly, 'Honey, no. You look very pretty. Let me fluff your bangs down.' Miriam pushed her mother's hands away. She was thirteen, not three. 'I can't help it, my face itches. I could claw my ugly face off.' Miriam spoke with such vehemence, Ethel looked at her in alarm.

'Yes. I know how you feel. But don't.'

At last they were led into the visitors' room, where Inmate Orlander was waiting. Ethel poked Miriam in the side. 'Smile, now. Give it a try. Look at Momma – I'm smiling.'

Miriam laughed, startled. Ethel laughed. Clutching at each other, suddenly excited and frightened.

* * *

272

'Go on, honey, Your daddy wants to see you.'

Ethel urged Miriam in front of her, like a human shield. The gesture was meant to be playful, but Miriam knew better. Ethel would hold back while Miriam talked with Les; she wasn't so enthusiastic about seeing him as Miriam was. They had private matters to discuss. Their transactions were likely to be terse, tinged with irony and regret.

Miriam smiled and waved at her father, who was standing stiffly behind the Plexiglas partition waiting for his visitors. Les Orlander in olive-drab prison clothes, one inmate among many.

Here was the shock: the visitors' room was so large, and so noisy. You wanted the visit to be personal, but it was like TV, with everyone looking on.

And the plastic partition between. You had to speak through a grill, as to a bank teller.

Les was frowning. Seeing Miriam, he smiled and waved. Miriam didn't want to see how he glanced behind her, looking for Miriam's brothers and not seeing them.

Third visit in a row, not one of Les's sons.

'Sweetie, hi. Lookin' good.'

He would look at her, smile at her. He wouldn't ask about the boys in Miriam's hearing.

'. . . got something for me there?'

They brought Les things he couldn't get for himself: magazines, a large paperback book of maps, *Civil War Sites*. These Miriam was allowed to give to her father, with a guard looking on.

Harmless items, printed material. Les seemed genuinely interested in the Civil War book, leafing through it. 'We'll go to Gettysburg. When I get out.'

It was unusual for Les to allude to getting out to Miriam. There was a kind of fiction between them, in this place, of timelessness; so much energy was concentrated on the present, cramming as much as you could into a brief visit, there wasn't time to think of a future.

'So – what's new, honey? Tell me about school.'

School! Miriam couldn't think of a thing.

For visiting Daddy she'd cultivated a childish personality not her own. Like auditioning for a play, reading lines with a phony forced enthusiasm and smiling with just your mouth. Bad acting and everyone knew, but it had to be done, for you could not read in your own flat, raw voice. To sound sincere you had to be insincere. Miriam told her father about school. Not the truth but other things. Not that this past year her teachers seemed to feel sorry for her, or that she hadn't many friends now, in eighth grade; she'd lost her closest girlfriends, like Iris Petko, whom she'd known since first grade, guessed their mothers didn't want them to be friendly with Miriam Orlander, whose father was incarcerated in a maximum-security prison. Miriam supposed that Les didn't know what grade she was in or how old she was exactly, for he had other things on his mind of more importance. Still, he seemed to want to hear her news, leaning forward cupping his hand to his ear. In prison he'd become partially deaf in his right ear; the eardrum had burst when someone (guard? inmate?) had struck him on the side of the head shortly after he'd arrived at the prison. Les had not reported the injury, as he hadn't reported other injuries and threats, saying that if he did, next time it would be his head that was busted, like a melon.

Miriam's father was a stocky, compact man in his late forties. He'd had a hard-boned good-looking face, now battered, uncertain. Scars in both his eyebrows like slivers of glass. His dark hair had been razor-cut military style, leaving his head exposed and vulnerable, the tendons in his neck prominent. He was prone to moods, unpredictable. His eyes were often suspicious, guarded and watchful. Miriam loved him but also feared him, as her brothers did. So much of her life had been waiting for Daddy to smile at her, to single her out from the others in his sudden, tender way; as if Daddy's feeling for Miriam overcame him, caught him by surprise.

Hey, sweetie – love ya!

He'd been wounded by life, Miriam knew. The hurt he'd done another man had rebounded to him, like shrapnel. Les had the look of a trapped creature. You never wanted to antagonize him; he had a way of striking out blindly.

At Ogdensburg, Les was assigned to the metal shop. Making license plates, dog tags. His pay was $1.75 an hour.

Again he was thanking Miriam for the Civil War book. The Civil War was one of Miriam's father's interests, or had been. Les had never been in the army, but his father, Miriam's grandfather she'd never known, had been an army corporal who'd died in his second tour of Vietnam, long ago in 1969. Les's feeling for his father was a confusion of pride and anger.

'We'll go, baby. I promise. When I get out. I'll be up for parole in . . .' Les tried to calculate when, how many months.

It was time for Ethel to talk to Les. Ethel's hand on Miriam's shoulder, to release her.

Miriam waved goodbye to her father, smiling hard to keep from crying. Les mouthed, *Love ya, baby!* as Miriam backed away.

In the visitors' lounge there were vending machines, a scattering of vinyl chairs. Everyone who visited an inmate at Ogdensburg seemed to be hungry. Cheese Stix, potato chips, candy bars, doughnuts, soft drinks. Mothers were feeding children from the machines. Children sat hunched and eating like starving cats. Miriam was faint with hunger but couldn't eat here.

She never wanted to hear what her parents talked about. Never wanted to hear that low quivering voice in which Ethel spoke of financial problems, mortgage payments, insurance, bills, work needing to be done on the house. *How can I do this without you. How could you leave us. Why!*

There was no answer to *why*. What Miriam's

father had done, in a blind rage: use an ax (the blunt edge, not the sharp: he had not killed the other man, only beaten him unconscious) against a man, a homeowner, who owed him money for a roof-repair job, and Les had been charged with attempted murder, which was dropped to aggravated assault, which was dropped to simple assault, to which he'd pleaded guilty. If Les had been convicted of attempted murder, he might have drawn a ten-to-fifteen-year sentence.

Everyone said, *Les is damn lucky the bastard didn't die.*

'*Hey* – want some?'

A fattish boy of about seventeen surprised Miriam, thrusting out a bag of Cheese Stix at her, which Miriam declined. Out of nowhere the boy seemed to have stepped. He had a blemished skin, a silver ring clamped in his left nostril. He wore a jungle fatigue jumpsuit with camouflage spots that looked painted on the fabric, crude as cartoon spots. He was a head taller than Miriam, looming close. 'Hey – where're you from?' Miriam was too shy not to answer truthfully, 'Star Lake.' The boy whistled, as if Miriam had said something remarkable. 'Star Lake? Oh man, where's it? Up by the moon? That's where I'm headed.' Miriam laughed uneasily. She guessed this was meant to be funny. She hadn't ever quite known how girls her age met boys outside of school, what sorts of things they said. Miriam knew from overhearing her brothers how cruel, crude, jeering, and dismissive boys could be about girls to whom they weren't attracted or didn't respect, and she wasn't able to gauge others' feelings for her. '. . . your name?' the fattish boy asked, and Miriam pretended not to hear, turning away.

Wishing she'd asked Ethel for the car key so that she could wait for her outside. She needed to get out of this place, fast.

'We could go outside, have a smoke. I got plenty.' The fattish boy persisted, following Miriam. He seemed amused by her, as if he could see through her pretense of shyness to an avid interest in him. Asking again if she wanted a smoke, tapping his thumb against a pack of cigarettes in his shirt pocket with a suggestive leer. Miriam shook her head: no, she didn't smoke. She was aware of the boy's shiny eyes on her, a kind of exaggerated interest, like something on TV. Was he flirting with her? Was this what flirting was? Miriam was only thirteen, but already her body was warmly fleshy like her mother's, her face roundly solid, not beautiful but attractive sometimes. When her skin wasn't broken out in hives. The boy was saying, 'I saw you in there, hon. Talking to who's it, your old man?' Miriam backed away, smiling nervously. She was becoming confused, wondering if somehow the boy knew Les, or knew of him. He was saying, mysteriously, 'There's something nobody ever asks in here – who's an inmate,' and Miriam said quickly, 'I have to go now, I have to meet my mother.' Again the boy spoke mysteriously, 'Not what you think, hon. What nobody ever asks.' Miriam was trying to avoid the boy, making her way along the wall of vending machines where people were dropping in coins, punching buttons, but the boy followed her, eating from his bag of Cheese Stix. 'We're up from Yonkers visiting my brother, he's gonna max out at six years. Know what that is? 'Max out'? Six years. What's your old man in for? Involuntary manslaughter – that's my brother.' The boy laughed, sputtering saliva. 'Like my brother didn't intend what happened, that's the deal, only know what, hon? That's bullshit. Bullshit he didn't. You max out, you don't get no fucking parole officer breathing down your neck.' Miriam was walking more quickly away, not looking back, trying not to be frightened. They were back at the entrance to the lounge, where another corridor led to restrooms. The boy loomed over her, panting into her face. 'Hey, hon, nobody's gonna hurt you. Why you walking away? Think somebody's gonna rape you? Any guy tries to talk to you, think he's gonna rape you? That is so sick, hon. What d'you think, Baby Tits? Your ass is so sweet, a guy is gonna jump you, the place crawling with guards?' The fattish boy spoke in a loud, mocking drawl. Miriam heard the anger beneath. She hadn't understood; something was wrong with this boy. Like the special-ed students at school you tried to avoid because they could turn on you suddenly, like Lana Ochs.

A female guard approached them. 'Miss, is this guy bothering you?' Miriam said quickly, 'No.' She hurried to the women's restroom, to escape.

Igneous. Sedimentary. Metamorphic.

Miriam was underlining words in her earth science workbook in green ink, writing in the margin of the page. Beside her, driving, Ethel seemed upset. Wiping at her eyes, blowing her nose. Each time they visited Les at Ogdensburg, Ethel came away upset, distracted. But today seemed worse. Miriam pretended not to notice.

Miriam hadn't told Ethel about the fattish boy in the camouflage jumpsuit. She would recast the experience, in her imagination, as a kind of flirtation. He'd called her hon. He'd seemed to like her.

Ethel said suddenly, as if the thought had just surfaced, in the way of something submerged beneath the surface of the water that suddenly emerges, 'I wanted to go to nursing school at Plattsburgh. You know this, I've told you. Except that didn't happen.' Ethel spoke haltingly, with an embarrassed laugh. 'Seems like my life just skidded past. I loved Les so much. And you, and the boys. Except I'm *not old.*'

Miriam could make no sense of her mother's words. She dreaded hearing more.

They were headed south on Route 58, nearing Black Lake. A windy November day, gray sky spitting snow. Ethel drove the old Cutlass at wavering speeds.

280

Miriam especially dreaded to hear why Ethel had dropped out of high school at seventeen to marry twenty-year-old Les Orlander.

'Miriam, I told him.'

Now Miriam glanced up from her textbook. 'Told him – what?'

'That I've been seeing someone, and I'm going to keep seeing him. I have a friend now. Who respects me. In Tupper Lake.'

Ethel began to cry. A kind of crying-laughing, terrible to hear. She reached out to touch Miriam, groping for Miriam's arm as she drove, but Miriam shrank away as if a snake had darted at her.

Ethel said, 'Oh God. I can't believe that I told him . . . and he knows now.' Repeating, as if her own words astonished her, 'He knows.'

Miriam shrank into herself; she had nothing to say. She was stunned, disgusted, and frightened. Her brain was shutting off; she wasn't a party to this. Maybe she'd known. Known something. Her brothers knew. Everyone knew. Les Orlander, whose relatives visited him at Ogdensburg, had probably known.

'. . . nothing to do with you, honey. Not with any of you. Only with him. Your father. What he did to us. 'I don't know what happened. What came over me,' he said. My own life, I have to have my own life. I have to support us. I'm not going to lose the house. I'm not going down with him. I told him.'

A heavy logging truck had pulled up behind the

Cutlass and was swinging out now to pass, at sixty-five miles an hour on the two-lane country highway. Ethel's car began to shudder in the wake of the enormous truck. Miriam felt a sudden desire to grab the steering wheel, turn the car off the road.

I hate you. I love Daddy, and I hate you.

'Can't you say something, Miriam? Please.'

'What's there to say, Mom? You've said it.'

The rest of the drive to the house on Salt Isle Road passed in silence.

5.

. . . in silence for much of the drive to Gettysburg. And hiking in the hilly battlefield, and in the vast cemetery that was like no other cemetery Miriam had ever seen before. *All these dead,* Les marveled. *Makes you see what life is worth, don't it*! He hadn't seemed depressed or even angry, more bemused, shaking his head and smiling as if it were a joke, the grassy earth at his feet was a joke, so many graves of long-ago soldiers in the Union Army, dead after three days of being slaughtered at Gettysburg: a 'decisive' battle in the War Between the States.

They would question Miriam about that day. Afterward.

The long drive in the car with Les, what sorts of things he'd said to her. What was his mood, had he been drinking. Had he given any hint of how unhappy he was, of wanting to hurt himself . . .

Wanting to hurt himself. The words they used. Investigating his death. *Hurt*, not *kill*. Les's relatives, friends. Miriam's brothers could hardly speak of it, what he'd done to himself. At least, not that Miriam heard. And Ethel could not; there were no words for her.

Les had been paroled five months when they'd made the trip to Gettysburg they'd been planning so long. Five months out of Ogdensburg and back in Star Lake picking up jobs where he could. The roofing contractor he'd worked for for years wasn't so friendly to him now. There was a coolness between Les and his brother-in-law Harvey Schuller. Les had served three years, seven months of his sentence for assault. In Ogdensburg he'd been a model prisoner, paroled for good behavior, and this was good news, this was happy news, the family was happy for Les, the relatives. If they were angry with him for what he'd done, bringing shame to the family, still they were happy he'd been paroled, now his drinking was under control, his short temper. Though Ethel had her own life now, that was clear. Take it or leave it, she'd told Les; those were the terms he'd have to accept if he wanted to live with her and their daughter. *I am not going to lie to you, I don't lie to any man, ever again*. By this time Ethel had been disappointed with her man friend in Tupper Lake. More than one man friend had disappointed her; she'd acquired a philosophical attitude at age forty-seven: You're on your own, that's the bottom line.

No man is going to bail you out. Ethel had gained weight, her fleshy body a kind of armor. Her face was a girl's face inside a fleshy mask through which Ethel's eyes, flirty, insolent, yearning, still shone. Miriam loved her but was exasperated by her. Loved her but didn't want to be anything like her. Though Ethel had a steady income now, comanaging a local catering service, no longer one of the uniformed employees. Ethel didn't need a husband's income, didn't need a husband. Yet she'd taken Les in; how could she not take Les in, the property was half his, he'd built most of the house himself, they'd been married almost thirty years, poor bastard, where's he going to live? Nowhere for Les to take his shame; his wife had been unfaithful to him and, worse yet, hadn't kept it a secret, his wife barely tolerated him, felt pity for him, contempt. Maybe she loved him, maybe that was so – Ethel wasn't sentimental any longer; all that was drained from her when Les lifted the ax to bring the blunt edge down on another man's skull – but what kind of love was it, the kind of love you feel for a cripple; Ethel didn't mince words. Take it or leave it, she'd told him, things are different in this house now. So far as the Ogdensburg parole board knew, Les Orlander was living at home with his family, P.O. Box 91, Salt Isle Road, Star Lake, NY. *Makes you see what life is worth*, Les said. *Dying for a good cause.*

It was early June. A few days after Memorial Day. Everywhere in Gettysburg Cemetery were

284

small American flags, wind-whipped. Miriam had never seen so many graves. And such uniformity in the grave markers, in the rows of graves. Row upon row of small identical grave markers it made you dizzy to see. Miriam imagined a marching army. Ghost army of the doomed. She felt a shudder of physical revulsion. Why for so long had she and Les planned to come here?

For an hour, an hour and a half, they walked in the Civil War memorial. It was a cool bright windy day. Warmer in southern Pennsylvania than it would have been in Star Lake, in the Adirondacks. Of course there were other visitors to the memorial. There were families, children. Les was offended by their loud voices. A four-year-old boy clambering over graves, snatching at miniature flags. Les said something to the child's father that Miriam didn't hear, and the young father pulled at his son's hand, rebuked. Miriam held her breath, but there was nothing more.

Stocky and muscled, in a hooded pullover, jaws unshaven, and a baseball cap pulled down low over his forehead, Les wasn't a man another man would wish to antagonize, unless that man was very like Les himself. Was your father angry about anything, did he seem distracted, what was his mood that day, Miriam would be asked.

As if, after her father's death, Miriam would betray him!

She did tell Ethel what was true: on the drive down, Les had been quiet. He'd brought tapes

285

and cassettes and a few CDs of music he wanted to hear or thought he wanted to hear, rock bands with names new to Miriam, music of a long-ago time when Les had been a kid, a young guy in his twenties just growing up. Miriam was disappointed: some of the songs Les listened to for only a few seconds, then became impatient, disgusted. Telling Miriam to try something else.

It was awkward in Les's company. Just Les alone, not Ethel or one of Miriam's brothers. She had to suppose it was the first time they'd ever been alone together in the car like this, though she could not have supposed it would be the last time. Somehow the trip to Gettysburg had come to mean too much. They'd planned it for so long. It seemed to have something to do, Miriam thought, with her father's memory of his own father. Not that Les said much about this. Only a few times, in the way of a man thinking out loud. If Miriam asked Les what he'd said, he didn't seem to hear. She was sitting beside his right ear, which was his bad ear. You didn't dare to raise your voice to Les; he took offense if you did that. Even Ethel knew better than to provoke him, for sometimes he seemed to hear normally and other times he didn't; you could not predict. And so sometimes he talked without hearing, without listening. In the cemetery at Gettysburg, the wind blew words away. Miriam saw how Les walked stiffly, like a man fearing pain. Maybe one of his knees. Maybe his back. His shoulders were set in a posture of labor; he'd done manual labor most of his adult life. Roofers are particularly prone to neck and spine strain. Miriam watched her father walk ahead of her, along the rows of grave markers, hands jammed into the deep pockets of his jersey pullover. He seemed to her a figure of mystery, still a good-looking man though his face was beginning to look ravaged, his skin sallow from prison. After he shot himself to death with his deer rifle a few weeks later, in a desolate stretch of pine woods beyond the property on Salt Isle Road where he'd used to hunt white-tailed deer and wild turkey with Miriam's brothers, Miriam would be asked if he'd said much about the cemetery at Gettysburg, or about his father, or Gideon, who was stationed in Iraq, and Miriam said evasively she didn't remember.

Les hadn't said much about Gideon. He hadn't seen Gideon in nearly a year. He was bewildered and angry that Gideon had enlisted in the army without consulting him. Iraq was a dirty war, a sham war like they'd said of Vietnam. Like Gideon had wanted to put distance between himself and Star Lake, was that it? Between himself and his family.

Miriam was walking fast to keep pace with Les. She'd thought he was going to head back toward the parking lot, but he seemed to be walking in the opposite direction, back into the cemetery. Overhead, clouds were shifting in the sky like soiled sailcloth. Miriam didn't want to think that the trip to the Gettysburg memorial had gone wrong somehow. Maybe it was too late. Les should have gone with the family, all of them, years ago, when Miriam's brothers were young and Miriam was a little girl. Somehow the trip had come to be too important to Les and Miriam; there was a strain to it, like the strain of a balloon being blown bigger and bigger until it threatens to burst. And then it bursts.

There was a tall plaque beside the roadway. Miriam read aloud, in fragments: "'. . . Lincoln's Gettysburg Address, November 19, 1863, the greatest speech of the Civil War and one of the greatest speeches ever given by any American president. *Four score and seven years ago. All men are created equal. Brave men, living and dead, who struggled here. The world will little note, nor long remember, what we say here, but can never forget what they did here*—"' and Les interrupted: 'Bullshit. Who remembers? Who's left? Just Lincoln people remember.'

It was the afternoon of June 3, 2004. Miriam's father would disappear from her life on June 28.

6.

Months after the funeral, after Labor Day, when Star Lake emptied out and the downstate home-owners were gone, they trashed one of the new houses on East Shore Drive. Stoned on crystal meth like lighter fluid inhaled through the nostrils and a match lit and *whup! whup! whup!* it was like

288

a video game, wild. A replica of an old Adirondack lodge of the 1920s, except the logs were weatherized and insulated; there were sliding glass doors overlooking the deck and the lake. Maybe it was a house their father, Les, had worked on; the brothers weren't sure. Not Gideon – after the funeral he'd flown back to the Mideast; his duty had been extended – but Martin and Stan and some of their friends. Forced a back door, and no security alarm went off that they could hear. Trashed the place looking for liquor and found instead above the fireplace mantel a mounted buck's head, sixteen-point antlers; shining their flashlights, outraged to see a Mets cap dangling from one of the points, a small American flag on a wooden stick twined in the antlers, sunglasses over the glass eyes, so they pulled down the buck's head to take away with them, stabbed and tore leather furniture with their fishing knives, smashed a wall-screen TV, smashed a CD player, tossed dishes in a frenzy of breakage, overturned the refrigerator, jammed forks into the garbage disposal, took time to open cans of dog food to throw against the walls, took time to stop up toilets (six toilets!) with wadded towels, in the bedrooms (five bedrooms!) took time to urinate on as many beds as their bladders allowed. It had something to do with Les Orlander, though they could not have said what. Sure, they'd remembered to wear gloves; these guys watched TV crime shows. Martin wanted to torch the place, but the others talked him out of it. A fire would draw too much attention.

Miriam wasn't a witness to the trashing, had not been with her brothers. Yet somehow she knew.

7.

'My damn mother, I wish . . .'

This second time. The words came out sudden and furious. Whatever was in her bloodstream had got into her brain. And the music was hurting. It scared her, the way the blood arteries beat. '. . . wish somebody would put that woman out of her misery, she'd be better off.' What was his name, he'd been Gideon's close friend in high school, Oz Newell was Miriam's friend here. Oz Newell was protecting her. Leaning his sweaty-haired head to Miriam, touching her forehead with his own in a gesture of clumsy intimacy, asking what's she saying and Miriam says, 'I want somebody to kill my mother, like she killed my father.' So it was said. For months it had needed saying, building up in Miriam like bile, and now it was said and the guys stared at her but maybe hadn't heard her, even Oz laughing, so certainly he hadn't heard. Hay Brouwet was trying to tell him something. Nobody could talk in a normal voice; you had to shout so your throat became raw. Hay was cupping his big-knuckled hands to his mouth, so Miriam could see that Hay was shouting, but the music was so loud, must've been she was so stoned, she couldn't hear a thing.

Whatever is done. Whatever you cause to be done. It will have happened always. It can never be changed.

In that other time, before her father killed himself. On the drive home from Gettysburg. If Miriam had said . . . what words? If Miriam had said, *I love you, you are my father. Don't leave me.* Of course, she'd said nothing. Underlining passages in her earth science workbook as her father drove north on the throughway, home.

It was later then. They were somewhere else; the air smelled different. There was less noise. The vibrations had ceased. When they'd left the Star Lake Inn, Miriam didn't know. Possibly she'd passed out. An inky mist had come over her. She remembered laying her head down on her crossed arms on a table to which her skin was sticking. Though she knew better, there was the fear that her brothers would see her, drunk, disheveled, sluttish in the company of older guys, some of them bikers, stoned, excited, looking for a way to discharge their excitement, a dog pack sniffing for blood. In this pack, Oz Newell was her friend. Oz Newell swaying on his feet and oozing sweat would protect Miriam, she knew. There was an understanding between them. Miriam believed this. For Oz carried her to his beat-up Cherokee, lifting her in his arms. Miriam was limp, faint-headed, her mouth slack and eyes half shut; she could feel his arm muscles straining, the tendons in his neck. Oz's face was a strong face, like something hacked from stone. The skin was coarse, acne-scarred. The jaws were unshaven. It was late, it was past 2 A.M. Miriam had to be carried; her feet were bare, very dirty, the soles scratched, bleeding. One of those dreams where you have lost your shoes, part of your clothing, strangers' eyes move onto you, jeering. The stained red T-shirt and cord skirt riding up her thighs – Miriam tried to tug the skirt down, her fingers clutching, clawed. She'd been running in the gravel parking lot. Hair in her face, panicked. 'Don't! Don't hurt –' but no one was listening to her. Kevin had left the inn; the pack had followed him, Miriam clutching at Hay Brouwet's arm, but he'd thrown her off as you'd flick away a fly. Miriam had not remembered that Kevin was wearing a Yankees cap but this had to be Kevin, big-jawed boy with sun-bleached hair straggling past his ears, Kevin with the rich father, Kevin complaining of the sleek white sailboat, he was headed for a Jeep, ignition key in hand he was headed for a steel-colored Jeep parked partway in weeds at the far end of the lot when Oz Newell and Hay Brouwet and Brandon McGraw and their friends advanced upon him cursing – 'Fuckface! Where ya goin'!' – and Kevin turned to them with a look of utter astonishment, so taken by surprise he hardly had time to lift his arms to protect his head. The men were whooping and rushing at him, fierce as dogs in a pack; Kevin tried to run but they caught him, cursing him, slamming him against the Jeep, the Yankees cap went flying, Kevin's head was struck repeatedly, Kevin fell to the ground as the men circled around him, punching and kicking with their steel-toed workboots. Miriam clutched at their arms, pulled at them, begged them to stop, but they paid no attention to her, even Oz Newell shoved her from him, indifferent to her pleas. And a part of her was thinking, *Hurt him! So he will know.*

There was justice in it, such a beating. You felt this. Though you could not acknowledge it, not even to Oz Newell and his friends.

In the gravel, partway in the weeds at the end of the lot, the bleach-haired boy lay writhing and vomiting. His clothes were torn, his chest exposed. He had not been hurt. It hadn't been a serious beating. They laughed in derision, watching him crawl toward the Jeep. Bleeding from a broken nose, but a broken nose isn't serious. His front teeth were maybe loosened. The pretty-boy face had been roughed up; he'd had to be taught a lesson. Rich fucker. Rich guy's fucking son. Stay away from the Star Lake Inn, fucker. Stay away from our girls. Next time it's your head that'll be broke. Your brains you'll be puking. The guys were feeling good about this. They were grateful to Miriam, who was their friend Gideon's young sister, for needing them. For turning to them. The adrenaline high is the best high, the purest high. Laughing so tears stung their faces like acid. Except they had to get the hell out, fast. What if somebody inside the inn had called 911? Two or three of the guys had come on their motorcycles, some in pickups. Oz Newell had his beat-up Cherokee, which smelled like he'd been living in it. There was a plan to meet at another place a few miles up the road at the Benson Mines, open till 4 A.M. But Oz Newell said he'd better get Miriam the hell home.

On Salt Isle Road the wind was moving in the tops of the trees like a living thing. There was the moon sliding in the sky, about to disappear behind clouds. And the clouds so thin and ragged, like torn cloth blowing across the face of the moon. 'Look!' Miriam pointed. 'Makes you think there's some reason to it.' Oz glanced sidelong at Miriam, sprawled in the seat beside him. He'd had to toss soiled shirts, Styrofoam wrappers, beer cans into the back to make room for her. 'Like the moon makes a center in the sky. So the sky isn't just . . .' Miriam was losing the thread of what she was saying. It was an important thing she meant to say, might've said to her father; maybe it would have made a difference. The Cherokee was lurching along the narrow lakeside road. Whatever had gotten into Miriam's brain was making her feel like she wasn't inside her skull but floating a few feet away.

Oz Newell said, surprising her, his voice was so

deliberate: 'Back there, Miriam, what'd you say about your mother? I didn't maybe hear.'

So Oz had heard. Heard something. Miriam thought, *He will do it. For me.* It could be an accident. There were so many accidents with guns. All the men owned guns. Boys owned guns. Even off-season you heard gunfire in the woods. Les Orlander had not been one of those who'd owned many guns, just two. The shotgun, the rifle. The rifle taken into custody by the county sheriff's department, then released to the family, and Stan had appropriated it, and the shotgun, to take back to Keene with him. Oz could use a rifle. Oz could fire through Ethel's bedroom window. Oz could hide outside in the bushes. Oz could fire through the windshield of the Cutlass when Ethel was driving into town. It could be a robbery. A stranger. This time of year there were many strangers in the Star Lake area. There were many strangers in the Adirondacks. There were break-ins, burglaries, vandalism. There were unexplained beatings, killings. It would happen swiftly and then it would be over and Miriam could live with Martin in Watertown, where he was out of rehab now and working as a roofer, and he'd seemed lonely, and Ethel had said, Honey, come home, live with your sister and me, and Martin had pushed her off, saying he'd sooner be in hell.

In childish bitterness Miriam said, 'My mother. What she did to my father. She should be punished,' and Oz said, as if perplexed, 'Punished how?' and Miriam said, wiping her mouth on the shoulder of her AU SABLE BOATHOUSE T-shirt, 'Some way.' Miriam's brain was becoming vague again. It was like clouds being blown across the face of the moon; you couldn't see what was behind the rapidly flowing movement, if it was moving also. Oz, driving the Cherokee, braking at curves, said nothing. He was driving more deliberately now, as if he'd realized that he shouldn't be driving at all. Miriam could hear his panting breath. She said, 'I'm not serious, Oz. I guess not.'

Oz said, hunching his shoulders, 'Shouldn't say a thing like that. About your mother. See, somebody might misunderstand.'

Turning into Miriam's cinder driveway, Oz cut his headlights. Miriam saw with a pang of dread that the front rooms of the house were darkened but the outside light, at the carport, was on, and lights were burning at the rear of the house: kitchen, Ethel's bedroom. 'Miriam, hey! Christ.' Oz laughed; Miriam was clutching at him. She was kissing him, his stubbled jaws, the startled expression on his face. He pushed her away and she crossed a leg over his, jamming against the steering wheel. She was desperate, aroused. It felt like drowning, wanting so to be loved. Should be ashamed, but it was happening so quickly. Her mouth against the man's was hot and hurtful, her hard, hungry teeth. She had no idea what a kiss is, the opening of mouths, tongues, the softness, groping. Oz laughed, uneasy. Pushing her away more forcibly. 'Miriam, c'mon.'

She was too young, Gideon's kid sister. She was a sister to him, or she was nothing. He was sure she'd never had sex with anyone, and damned if he'd be the first.

'I love you. I want to be with you.'

'Sure, baby. Some other time.'

Miriam jumped from the Cherokee, made her way wincing, barefoot, into the house. So ashamed! Her face pounded with heat.

The kitchen was two rooms, one a former wash-room. Les had knocked out the wall between. There was a long counter with a scarred white enamel sink. The beautiful cabinets of dark, polished wood Les had built. On the linoleum floor were scattered rugs. Miriam saw that Ethel wasn't in the kitchen even as, in her bathrobe, a cigarette in hand, Ethel entered the kitchen from the direction of her bedroom. Ethel's eyes were brimming with emotion, fixed on Miriam in the way of one staring at a blazing light, blinding.

Miriam's heart gave a skid. She loved this woman so much, the two of them helpless together, like swimmers drowning in each other's arms.

Her voice was brattish, exasperated. 'Why aren't you in bed, Mom? I told you not to wait up.'

Now that Les was gone and would not be coming back, Ethel was in mourning. Her face was pale and puffy without makeup, raw. Yet strangely young-looking, her mouth like a bruise, wounded. In the chenille robe her body was slack, ripe, beyond ripeness. The loose, heavy breasts were disgusting to Miriam, who wanted to rush at her mother and strike at her with childish, flailing fists. Miriam, who was staggering with exhaustion, limping barefoot, hair in her face, and her ridiculous tight red T-shirt and white cord skirt stained with her own vomit. Wanting to hide her shamed face against Ethel's neck which was creased, smelling of talcum.

Somewhere distant, in the mountains beyond Star Lake, a melancholy cry, a sequence of cries. Loons, coyotes. Les had taken Miriam outside one summer night to listen to plaintive cries he identified as the cries of black bears.

Ethel smiled uncertainly. Knowing that if she moved too suddenly, Miriam would push her away, run from the room. Barefoot, wincing in pain. The door to her room would be slammed shut, it would never open. 'You look feverish, honey.' Ethel must have smelled male sweat on Miriam. She smelled beer, vomit. Unmistakable, the smell of a daughter's vomit. But shrewdly deciding not to go there, in that direction. So grateful that the daughter is home. Coming to press a hand against the daughter's forehead. Miriam flinched, dreading this touch. For hours she'd been dreading it. yet the hand was cool, consoling. Ethel said, her voice throaty, bemused, 'Where've you been, are you going to tell me?'

For a moment Miriam couldn't remember.

Where had she been? Her mouth was dry, parched as sand. As if she'd slept with her mouth open, helpless in sleep as a small child.

'Nowhere. Now I'm back.'

BLEED

Hadn't known the girl. He had not. All he knew was, she was the daughter of friends of his parents. Or maybe just acquaintances, for his parents had known many people in those years. First he remembered of her, a distinct memory, he'd been thirteen years old and in ninth grade and she'd been only five years old, a lifetime between them at those ages. One small child interchangeable with any other small child, girl or boy, and of virtually no significance to a boy of thirteen, for whom no one matters much except a select gathering of boys his age and older, and a very few girls. And there was his mother speaking to him in a voice frightening to him, impulsive, intimate, and her hands on him as if to restrain him from slipping away: 'That poor child! And her parents! Of course, they have to be grateful that she's alive, and that terrible man has been—' and he saw a shudder of revulsion in his mother's face, and quickly he looked away, for there was something wrong in this, his mother speaking to him in a voice he rarely heard except when his parents were speaking together in the privacy of their bedroom and the door was closed against their children; and Jess was the sort of boy lacking not curiosity exactly but the recklessness required for wishing to overhear exchanges between your parents you understand are not meant for you to hear. And so Jess resented this behavior on his mother's part. That look in his mother's usually composed face of revulsion tinged with excitement. For there was something sexual in this. Jess knew, and didn't want to know. For what could *terrible man* mean if the girl had not been killed, except sex? Jess was embarrassed and resentful, hotly his face pounded with blood, badly he wanted to escape. What had he to do with a child eight years younger than he was! And his mother saying, 'If you've heard anything, Jess, will you tell me? Tell me what you've heard.' (They were in the kitchen. Jess's mother seemed to have been waiting for him there. Had him trapped between the refrigerator and the stove.) At thirteen you no more want to speak of sexual matters with a parent than you would want to speak of God with a parent. And so, not meeting his mother's gaze, Jess mumbled that he hadn't heard anything about whatever this was his mother was telling him, whatever ugly and unspeakable incident wholly unrelated to him and to any of his classmates, Jess took care not to repeat the girl's name – the name of a five-year-old girl means virtually nothing to a boy of thirteen – assuring his anxious mother that no one at his school had been talking about it, so far as he knew. *So far as he knew* was possibly the truth. *So far as he knew* was, for a boy of thirteen being questioned by his mother in a way distressing to him, the most negotiable of truths. 'The worst of it has been kept out of the news, so far. Her name isn't being released and actual details of what he did except "repeated assault," "critical blood loss" – imagine! A five-year-old girl! Nothing about the family, and a picture only of the . . . "perpetrator."' Jess saw that his mother's mouth, which was usually a smiling mouth, was contorted. Harsh lines bracketed his mother's mouth. *This is the way she will look when she is old. When she is older*, Jess thought. Wanting badly to escape now, push past his mother and run upstairs to his room, shut the damn door behind him and burrow into his most secret and forbidden thoughts, sick thoughts, guilty thoughts, where neither his mother nor his father could follow him. For there are places in the world like secret fissures and fault lines into which we can burrow, and hide, where no one can follow. Stammering now, insisting that he hadn't heard anything about the girl, nothing at school, daring now to lift his eyes to his mother's eyes in a desperate appeal, and it was then that Jess's mother uttered the astonishing words Jess would never forget: 'I wish I could believe you.'

Not accusing so much as yearning, wistful. And

her mouth strained, ugly. And it was the final moment of Jess's childhood, as it was, for Jess's mother, the final moment of a phase of her motherhood. Though neither could have said. Though neither would have possessed the words to speak of their loss. At that moment in the gleaming and overlarge kitchen of the Hagadorns' 'classic contemporary' house on Fairway Drive overlooking the sculpted hillocks and sly sand traps of the North Hills Country Club golf course, it was clear that the mother could not trust the son even as the son, steeling himself against a sudden unwished-for gripping of his mother's hand on his shoulder or a caress of proprietary fingers at the nape of his warm neck, could not trust the mother.

'Go away, then. *Go.*'

That night overhearing her speaking to his father and her voice quavering in disgust, reproach – 'that terrible man,' 'terrible thing,' 'so close to home,' 'should be put away for life' – and this time Jess stood very still in the upstairs hall outside the closed door of his parents' bedroom, scarcely daring to breathe, needing to hear all that might be revealed. And more.

Why? It was the sex. It was the sex secret. That thrilled quaver in his mother's voice. That look on his mother's face. For now he would see his mother at a distance and recognize her as a woman, a woman among other women: female. In Health

303

Science you were taught that sex was 'normal,' sex was 'healthy,' sex was 'good,' sex was 'nothing to be ashamed of,' sex should be 'consensual,' sex should be 'safe,' yet the fact was, everyone knew that sex was secret, and sex was guilty, and sex was sniggered at by the guys, and sex was a wild roller-coaster ride you were scared to climb into yet had no choice about climbing into, soon. (How soon? Thirteen, in ninth grade, Jess was one of the younger and shyer and less experienced boys but he was determined this wouldn't last.) Sex was 'porn,' and sex was 'sex pervert,' and sex was 'rape-murder,' and sex was that 'terrible man' who'd done that 'terrible thing' to a little girl whose name Jess would try not to remember.

Another time. A few years later. Not the same girl. And not Jess's mother but Jess's father interrogating him, not in the kitchen but in Jess's room, from which there could be no escape.

'—know anything about this . . . abduction, do you?'

Quickly Jess shook his head: *no*.

'—boys in your class? Not friends of yours, are they?'

Quickly Jess shook his head: *no*.

It was so: Jess wasn't friends with the boys involved in the 'abduction,' and Jess didn't know the 'underage' girl. All he knew was what he'd heard: the girl wasn't a student at North Hills High, her parents weren't residents of North

Hills but of Union City. The rumor was, there was only a mother, an 'illegal immigrant.' The rumor was, the 'underage' girl was in eighth grade. (But 'mature for her age.') (Girls were maturing at an alarming rate in middle school; you heard astonishing things.) It was possible almost to think that this girl was the girl to whom the 'terrible things' had been done by the 'terrible man' when Jess was in ninth grade, but Jess knew that this was unlikely. (The other girl, such a little girl at the time, would still be in grade school. And anyway, her family had moved away from North Hills and no one ever spoke of them now.) Still, Jess had to suppose that the two girls were like each other in crucial ways. Circumstances were similar. For this time too there had been 'terrible things' perpetrated upon a young girl, and this time too there was talk of blood.

Bleeding on the mattress. Bleeding all over. And too drunk to give a damn how grossed out we were.

Jess hadn't heard these words of disgust firsthand. Jess wasn't a close friend of any of the guys who'd driven out to Bay Head. Though the guys were seniors, and Jess Hagadorn was a senior, and it was graduation week, and there were parties. Many parties, of which some overlapped on the same nights. And some of these were parties to which Jess Hagadorn had been invited, and some of these were not. For there were social circles – cliques – that excluded Jess Hagadorn, though the Hagadorns lived on Fairway Drive overlooking the North Hills golf course and Mr Hagadorn owned Hagadorn Electronics, Inc. And Mrs Hagadorn was friendly with many of the mothers of Jess's classmates. Jess was seventeen years, ten months old and still one of the younger, shyer, and less experienced members of his class, but Jess did have friends, Jess did get invited to a number of parties. He'd taken a girl to the senior prom. He'd been coeditor of the North Hills yearbook. It was an incontestable fact, Jess Hagadorn hadn't been one of the half-dozen senior boys who'd left a late-night party to drive twenty-eight miles to the beach house at Bay Head, at the Jersey shore, with the drunken underage girl. The beach house belonged to the family of one of the boys, who'd taken the key without his parents' knowledge. Jess wasn't even certain who'd gone on that drive: popular guys, jocks and rich kids. A Fairway Drive neighbor, three houses down. Maybe a few girls, in another vehicle. How many vehicles drove to Bay Head wasn't clear. The girls would claim to have left the Bay Head party after only about a half-hour. The girls would claim to have left when they saw 'how things were headed.' Meaning the drinking and drug-taking, and the deafening heavy-metal music. Meaning the underage girl. All that Jess knew, and was trying in a faltering voice to explain to his father, who stared at him with a grave gray gaze as if viewing him through a rifle scope, was that following the party at Andy Colfax's house

306

(to which Jess Hagadorn had not been invited, though, if he'd gone, like numerous others who hadn't been specifically invited but simply showed up, Jess would have been welcome, or anyway not made to feel unwelcome) the 'abduction' had occurred. It was an 'alleged abduction,' for the boys' claim was that the girl had gone with them willingly. She'd 'insisted upon' accompanying them, she'd 'practically begged.' And so the drive to Bay Head had been 'consensual.' Whatever happened at Bay Head had been 'consensual.' At least at the beginning, at the North Hills party, 'consensual.' If Jess Hagadorn had been invited to join the half-dozen guys and the underage girl on the drive in Ed Mercer's father's Chevy Trailblazer to the Jersey shore, possibly Jess would have been flattered, grateful to be included by such popular jocks and rich kids after years of being excluded. So maybe, yes. If he'd been invited, maybe he'd have gone with them; this was a possibility. This wasn't exactly what Jess's father was asking, but it was what Jess's father seemed to be implying. No matter that Jess would have been the only boy at the Bay Head house to be graduating summa cum laude. No matter that Jess would have been the only boy to be attending an Ivy League university in the fall. And maybe now Jess Hagadorn would be one of seven North Hills, New Jersey, senior boys arrested by Bay Head, New Jersey, police on charges of statutory rape, sexual assault upon a minor, providing a minor with alcohol, forcible abduction of a minor, resisting arrest. Except Jess hadn't been one of these boys. He hadn't so much as glimpsed the girl. He didn't know her name. (If he'd known, he had forgotten.) He'd heard that she'd lied about her age. He'd heard that she was fourteen. He'd heard that she was sixteen. He'd heard that she was thirteen. He'd heard that her birth date was unknown for her single parent, her mother, was an illegal immigrant and had no papers. He'd heard that the girl herself was an illegal immigrant and had no papers. He'd heard that she was 'physically developed,' 'mature for her age,' whatever her age was, as a white girl would not have been. Nor would any white girl, at least any white girl from North Hills, have climbed into a vehicle with a gang of drunken high school seniors on an impulsive drive some-time after 2 A.M. to the Jersey shore twenty-eight miles away at Bay Head. (And especially no white girl who was having her period – this is what Jess heard, at second or third hand – would've gone with the guys unless possibly, considering how drunk/drugged the girl was, she hadn't realized she was having her period and would in this way disgust the guys, or if she'd known, she'd forgotten. Another possibility, the girl began having her period at the time of the 'abduction,' 'assaults.') Jess knew nothing about any of it. Jess had not glimpsed the girl. Jess had not heard the girl's screams, and if he'd heard, Jess might have thought the girl was laughing. When girls drink, girls scream with laughter. Like birds being slaughtered, girls scream with laughter. Girls high on drugs scream with laughter. And when girls have sex, girls scream with pleasure, or so Jess had reason to believe.

Sex secrets. He'd heard his own mother scream not once but many times. He was sure this was what he'd heard, in the night, in the upstairs bedroom when the door was shut. As a young child, years ago. That was when he'd heard the screams, he believed. Not that he wished to think about it; he did not. He would not think about it. His mother and his father. He would not think of how profoundly they disgusted him, as he would not wish to think of how profoundly he would disgust them if they knew him. There was a chill solace in this, that Jess's parents did not know him. No more than you would know the heart of a stranger glimpsed on the street, at a distance. By the age of thirteen Jess could no longer bear to be touched by his mother; all that was finished between them. Jess's little-boy love for his mother, whom he'd adored.

And now Jess's father. It was hateful of Jess's father to enter Jess's room without being invited inside. Rapping his knuckle on the door and opening the door in nearly the same gesture. And now interrogating Jess. Grave gray distrustful eyes fixed upon Jess and both fists clenching, unclenching, as if of their own volition. 'You're telling the truth, Jess, aren't you? Look at me, son.'

'I am looking at you, Dad! I am telling the truth.'

Son. No one in actual life said *son*.

Son! Jess was no one's *son*.

Always now he would realize this: no one's son. For his father did not believe him, and his father did not love him. From this time forward, Jess would long remember.

Especially Jess could not have told his father about the blood. He had not seen any blood, that was a fact. That was the truth. Hadn't seen any blood smeared on the girl's body, the insides of her fleshy thighs and in her tight-coiled bushy pubic hair lavish as a strange wiry growth. And on her young round breasts, olive-skinned, with nipples like purple stains. So much blood, on the girl's legs, on the sheets, and on the mattress, on the guys' penises and groins. A wild crazy scene made deafening by high-decibel music. You couldn't have heard the girl screaming.

It was known that the girl was drunk, and drugged, and out of her mind, hysterical. Crying, and accusing. Making threats. Yet she'd been eager to go with the guys, she'd been flattered, made to believe that they 'liked' her. Maybe one of them 'loved' her. Maybe he'd be her boyfriend. (Maybe!) By that time no other girls remained at the beach house. All the white girls had left. These were senior girls, departed by 4 A.M. Originally a half-dozen vehicles had been parked in the coarse sand above the house. Bay Head police would determine from tire tracks, but by the time police officers arrived, summoned by Bay Head neighbors, at 4:40 A.M., only the Trailblazer remained. Jess Hagadorn had not been there, of course. Jess Hagadorn had not been within twenty-eight miles of the Jersey shore. This was a fact to be pledged to his parents: Jess had been home at that time, in his bed. Through the night sweating and sleepless and by 6:25 A.M. still awake in a misery of nausea and head-hammering pain, having stumbled into the bathroom adjacent to his bedroom not once, not twice, but three times to vomit into the toilet bowl. And with shaking fingers flush the seething vomit away. And Jess's parents had heard him, of course, and had reason to claim *Our son was home. Our son came home early from a graduation party. Not long after midnight, our son returned home. Our son is a good boy, a trustworthy boy and an honor student, we trust our son and had no need to wait up for him. Our son has said that he had a few drinks – beers – at one or another of the graduation parties, but he had no drugs. Not ever drugs. Our son has pledged to us: not ever drugs. Our son knows nothing about what is alleged to have happened to any underage girl, our son has pledged to us that he has told the truth, and we believe our son. Our son will be attending the University of Pennsylvania in the fall, an Ivy League school.*

Hadn't known the girl. He had not. All he knew was, he'd tried to help her. He'd been the only one to help her. Driving home, and his mistake was, he must've made a wrong turn off I-95.

311

Exiting in the rain at a place he'd never heard of, Glasstown, or Glass Lake, somewhere beyond Trenton he had needed to fill up the gas tank, in a 7-Eleven beside the gas station he'd bought a cola drink for the caffeine charge, needing to clear his head, badly he wanted not to be making this drive home, Thanksgiving weekend and his mother had insisted Jess you must come home, what will the relatives think, yet he'd delayed leaving campus, leaving Philadelphia in a stream of slow-moving traffic on the expressway, the drive to North Hills wouldn't take more than a few hours but he'd been awake much of the previous night and as he drove hunched over the steering wheel something fluttered teasing and tormenting at the periphery of his vision like those tiny white moths you see batting themselves against screens in summer in the night; in the grubby 7-Eleven store he'd been distracted by the TV set above the cashier's counter, a surveillance TV showing a fraction of the interior of the store, and Jess saw his own figure on the screen, his back to the camera, shift to the right and the TV figure shifts to the right, shift to the left and the TV figure shifts to the left, turn and walk toward the rear of the store and the TV figure walks out of the frame but (you have to assume) is picked up by another TV monitor in another part of the store. Except in the men's room there were no TV monitors. (Were there?) Leaving the men's room, he was surprised to see – at least he thought this was what he was seeing, happening so fast as these things do, you don't know how to assess what you are seeing, even to know if in fact you are seeing it – the door to the women's restroom was being opened and shut again, and opened and again shut, as if to tease, had to be a child playing, a little girl with shining dark eyes peeking at Jess from behind the door, giggling, Jess smiled at her but kept on moving for there was something strange about the little girl, quick Jess left the 7-Eleven store without a backward glance and immediately forgot the incident, if you could call it an incident; now having taken a wrong turn to get back onto I-95 he found himself on a narrow country road outside a small town (Glasstown, Glass Lake) and that hammering-harranguing pain in his head was beginning *Why! Why are you here!* waiting for a freight train to pass, long lumbering noisy train humping and hammering at his head, Jess's eyes ached as if he'd been staring into a blinding light, gripping the steering wheel of the Audi (his mother's former car she'd passed on to Jess when she bought a new one) waiting for the damned train to pass, badly he wanted not to be here, badly he wanted not to be driving home for Thanksgiving, he had disappointed his father by declining to study engineering, he had disappointed his mother by declining to be the reliable loving son his mother required; and in a nearby field a child suddenly appeared, a small figure running and stumbling in the tall grass, in the icy rain, out of a stand of scrubby trees the child seemed to have emerged, Jess stared blinking and incredulous: *Is that a child? A little girl?* She was lightly dressed for the chill dank air of November, in what appeared to be a dress with a short skirt, and over the dress a soiled sweatshirt, her legs bare, she was bareheaded and her small face contorted in a look of terror. Behind Jess the driver of a pickup leaned on his horn, for the freight train had passed, the last of the noisy lumbering cars had passed, red lights were no longer flashing but Jess had not noticed, and when Jess failed to move forward across the railroad tracks the pickup swerved around him in an explosion of pent-up annoyance, and other vehicles followed, for no one seemed to have noticed the child so strangely alone in the field, or if they'd noticed had not cared. Quickly Jess shifted to park, got out of the car, and ran into the field to approach the little girl asking what was wrong? had something happened to her? for clearly this was an emergency situation. Clearly the little girl was in distress and needed help. All this Jess would explain afterward and many times he would explain, though to be precise, what happened would have happened so swiftly, yet so disjointedly, like a badly spliced film, mysterious pleats and gaps in the narrative, and the figures blurred and not always fully within the frame. The fact was: a little girl of about nine had run out of a scrubby woods about fifty feet from the road where Jess Hagadorn had been waiting for a freight train to pass, near dusk and an icy rain was falling, the girl appeared to be desperate, ill-clothed in a pink cotton dress and a sweatshirt, her legs were bare, on her bare feet were filthy sneakers and in fact the girl's clothing was filthy, stained and covered in burrs, and her hair was disheveled and matted, her mouth looked soft and bruised like a fish's mouth after the hook has been torn out. Her hair was ashy blond, almost white, ghostly and luminous on this dark November day, and as Jess stooped over her he could decipher only part of what she was saying: '– want go *home*. Want go *home*.'

Was the child lost? Or had she run from a nearby house, or a car? Had she been injured? Had someone been chasing her? There was no one visible in the field; no vehicles parked on the road, except the Audi; no houses in sight. Jess asked the girl where her home was? where had she come from just now? where were her parents? was she hurt in some way? but the girl was too agitated to answer, whimpering, shivering, and wiping at her eyes. So Jess took her hand.

Afterward explaining he'd had no choice but to take the child's hand and lead her back to his car, no choice but to urge her to walk with him, assisting her, half lifting her over a ditch and into his car, and yes, Jess was wondering if this was the wisest thing to do yet under the circumstances not knowing what else he might do, what choice he had, for there appeared to be no one in sight, no one to flag for help, and no houses visible from where he stood. He thought, *The crucial thing is to help. To help her. To rescue her. That is the crucial thing.*

In the Audi Jess tried to comfort the girl, wiped at her tear-streaked face with a tissue, asking her in the calmest voice he could summon where she lived? had she wandered off from home? had someone brought her here, to this desolate place, and left her? Another time asking her, had she been hurt? For he saw that the little girl's clothing was stained with something darkish – was it blood? And her hair was clotted with – was it blood? He couldn't see any visible injuries, but he was hesitant to examine the girl closely, reluctant to lift the skirt of the soiled dress to examine her legs. 'Where is your mommy? Your daddy? What has happened to you?' Jess's heart was pounding rapidly in his chest and his mouth had gone dry. For he knew that there was danger here, even as he knew he had no choice but to seek help for the girl. All his senses were alert, like wires yanked tight. The girl was shivering convulsively, so Jess turned up the heat. He saw that the girl's eyes were an anguished blue, her nose was reddened and needed blowing. Her small angular face was dirty, the luminous blond hair disheveled and matted as if she'd been sleeping in the woods, or had been held captive in some terrible place, like a cellar.

All this while Jess had been fumbling with his cell phone, punching in 911, but the calls failed to go through. He could make no sense of the girl's stammered and incoherent words and so he made the decision to turn the Audi around in the road and drive in the direction of Glasstown, or Glass Lake, though he had no idea how far the town was. He assured the stricken girl that he would get help for her: he'd take her to the police, or to a hospital. He assured her that she would be safe, and taken care of, and no one would hurt her again, but instead of comforting the girl, Jess's words seemed to upset her, for she became more agitated, protesting, 'No – go *home*. Want go *home*. Go *home!*' And Jess said, 'But where is your home? Can you tell me? In this direction? Is this the right direction? Or—'

Jess was driving through icy rain that pelted the windshield and the roof of the Audi like a fusillade of nails while at the same time still trying to call 911 on his cell phone. In the little plastic window barely visible to Jess's squinting gaze were the discouraging words NO SIGNAL.

Afterward Jess would explain how reportedly he'd asked the sobbing child where she lived, what had happened to her, had she been injured, what was her name; and the girl answered what sounded like 'Dada and Mummy will be mad at me and hurt me worse if they know that I'm not—' but Jess couldn't make out the girl's final words, which might have been 'at home' or 'in bed.' Jess said, '"Hurt you worse"? Did your parents hurt you?' which seemed to upset the girl even more, so that

317

she kicked and threw herself about in the passenger's seat, crying, 'They will! They will! They will hurt me – worse!' Hoarse guttural sobs racked the small body. The girl's face was contorted, ugly. Tears leaked from her eyes and mucus from her nose. Jess was driving frantically in the rain, looking for the lighted windows of a house, or another vehicle on the road; he despaired of locating Glasstown, or Glass Lake; possibly he'd taken another wrong turn, or the road had forked and veered off in the wrong direction. *Life plus ninety-nine years* would be the sentence. *No possibility of parole* would be the sentence, to be begun shortly after his twenty-third birthday. Though he would try to explain, countless times he would explain the desperation with which he'd sought help for the distraught little girl, trying to reason with her even as he'd begun to see that it was hopeless, he could make no sense of what she was saying, needing to take hold of the girl's arm to restrain her, for she'd been flailing her hands in a way dangerous to the driver of the Audi; at once the girl gave a sharp little shriek like a cat being tormented, pushed Jess's hand away with the rude alacrity of a much older girl, she shrank from him and began crying harder, striking the side of her head against the passenger's window in an inexplicable and maddening reaction, provoking Jess to think, *That will leave a mark on the window, that will be evidence unless I wipe it away.* Though knowing that, in this nightmare unfolding about him like a deranged film, he would never have the opportunity to wipe the window clean.

Jess reached for the girl, to restrain her; didn't want her to injure herself. With unexpected fury the girl pushed at him as if he, Jess Hagadorn, were her attacker, as if Jess hadn't taken her into his car to find help for her but to attack her, as if Jess Hagadorn had in fact been her attacker, from whom she'd tried to flee. While driving his car at a slow jolt along the graveled road he tried to grip the girl in the crook of his right arm, for he was much stronger than the girl and was losing patience with her. How like a frantic little animal she was, giving off heat, her little body quivering with energy, with the wish to resist him. Suddenly Jess felt a sharp pain in the fleshy part of his right thumb, for the girl had bitten him; swiftly the thought came to him, *That will be evidence, they will match her teeth to the bite.* Jess cursed the girl, braking the car so that it skidded on the road as he seized the girl's head in his arm and pried open her jaws, holding her in the crook of his arm like a vise. Telling himself he had to restrain the girl to prevent her from injuring herself, but the truth was, Jess was frightened of the girl. Very possibly this was a dream of such anguish he could scarcely bear it, and yet Jess knew it could not be a dream, for you can determine a dream by its texture. Dreams are soft-edged as watercolors, while waking life is hard-edged as a photograph. Anxiously Jess peered through the rain-splotched windshield: trees, a galaxy of trees, leafless limbs, branches, twigs. So many! There could never be such complexity in a mere dream. And the sky was shot with fissures and cracks like aged skin. In three quarters of the sky it was dusk, a bruised-plum color, while in the west (Jess assumed it must be the west, though in his confused and disheveled state he had no idea where he was) there stretched a horizontal band of orange-red, blood-orange-red, beautiful amid gathering gloom. Jess thought, *If this was a dream, I could not see so much. It would be just her and me.*

And so this was not a dream. If not a dream, there could be no escape. Jess was holding the girl tightly, to calm her. For the girl had begun to squirm, writhe, kick. Savagely she kicked at the car dashboard was if she'd have liked to smash it. Kicked at the windshield as if she'd have liked to smash it, but Jess prevented her in time. 'Damn you! Goddamn you, *stop*!' Hot breaths in each other's faces, they were struggling together. Jess could not comprehend what was happening, why the girl had turned against him. And now suddenly clambering over him, a little wildcat digging her claws into him, laughing, straddling him awkwardly as he sat behind the wheel, her thighs bare beneath the stained dress. To his surprise, he saw that her wax-pale little-girl thighs were smeared with blood. So she had been injured, and had kept her injury from him, bleeding from a secret wound between her legs, and now there were blood smears on his trousers, and on the leather seats of the Audi; the front of the girl's sweatshirt was smeared with blood, and one of the cuffs soaked in dark blood. Furiously Jess thought, *Her blood will be all over me. That will be the most damning evidence.* With a part of his mind cunning and furtive and detached from their frantic struggle Jess calculated how he might clean himself of the girl's blood, where he might shower, in safety, in utter privacy, if for instance he could arrive home at the house on Fairway Drive overlooking the golf course in North Hills, if he could slip into the rear of the house without anyone noticing and quickly ascend to his room on the second floor; in a swoon of relief and gratitude he would enter his room, his boyhood room, the room he had come to despise by the time he'd left for college but the room that seemed to him now, in retrospect, a place of sanctuary, and if he could shower in his bathroom undetected and undisturbed he would cleanse himself thoroughly of the girl's blood, dark blood coagulated between his fingernails and in snarls in his hair, a difficult time he would have shampooing his hair and combing the snarls out of his hair but he was determined, and he would take away the soiled clothing, the stained and incriminating clothing including underwear and socks, all of his clothing contaminated by the girl's blood; he would destroy this evidence, somewhere – unable to calculate, in the exigency of this moment, in the front seat of the Audi, struggling with the uncannily strong girl, exactly how he would destroy it, for his heart-beat had doubled, tripled, as if he were approaching orgasm and helpless to turn back. The girl cried, 'Bad! Bad! Bad! Bad!' like a crazed bird, striking at Jess with hard little fists. Or was the girl laughing at Jess? Teasing, taunting? Was this a trick? For as Jess pushed the girl away the girl bobbed back at him, laughing, grinning into his appalled face, pushing boldly into his arms and again straddling his thighs, pressing and wriggling against him where he'd become aroused, helpless to stop her. For Jess didn't want to hurt her. Jess knew that he must not hurt her. Except to protect himself, he must not use force on the child, though clearly this child was older than he'd originally thought, older than nine years and very likely an adolescent girl, a dwarf female, small and stunted and with a flat chest, rounded little tummy, and no hips, soft-muscled upper arms and thighs, an angular face and those glittering blue eyes. 'Bad! Bad!' she was panting. Jess managed to push the girl aside and continued driving, not knowing what else to do; the Audi was weaving on the road, must've been that Jess had taken another wrong turn, for the road appeared to be narrowing, the road was deserted and dark except for the Audi's lurching headlights, yet the girl had lowered the window beside the passenger's seat to call out, in a plaintive child-voice, 'Help! Help me! He hurt me! Bad man hurt me!' Jess protested, reaching for her, had to stop her, wrestled her away from the window, trying to clamp his hand over her mouth, trying to grip her head in the crook of his arm as in a vise, but another time the girl kicked and writhed and bit at his hand, managing to slip from him and open the door and scramble outside. Jess cursed and braked the Audi, left the key in the ignition to follow after the girl, who ran screaming into a field, following a faint path in the direction of a landfill, or a dump; Jess's nostrils pinched at the smell of something burning, a garbagey-rubbery odor, he entered a clearing to see human shapes, derelicts beneath a makeshift shelter huddling together over a small smoldering fire. The girl ran screaming toward them, with Jess close behind her, a large whiskery man in army fatigues paused in the act of lifting a bottle to his mouth to shout at Jess and lurch to his feet; two other men roused themselves, advancing threateningly against Jess and giving him no opportunity to explain himself or the situation. So abruptly were the men struggling with Jess, cursing, striking, and pummeling him, Jess was taken by surprise, backing away and shielding his head with his arms; one of the derelicts struck Jess repeatedly with a broken umbrella, the skeletal remains of an umbrella, the staves raked his face, Jess snatched it from the man and struck him over the head with it: 'Damn you, I'll kill you!' As Jess struggled with the derelicts, the girl escaped; Jess broke away from the men, stumbling after her; for nothing mattered except the little girl in the bloodstained clothes, who would make such terrible accusations against Jess. The derelicts shouted after him but didn't pursue him as Jess tramped through a scrubby woods, now it was nearly night and the icy rain had turned to sleet, panting and miserable Jess found himself on a hill above a four-lane highway, the interstate he'd unwisely exited from what seemed like a very long time ago yet could not have been more than an hour ago. The girl was somewhere ahead; Jess had no choice but to follow, now stumbling down a steep hill, and seeing ahead the small furtive figure of the child, the little demon-girl who'd left her blood in his car and on his person, there she was limping in the direction of an enormous tractor-trailer truck parked on the shoulder of the highway with its engine running. The driver would be sleeping inside and the girl was determined to wake him, Jess had to stop her before she got to the truck to scream for help; he managed to catch up with her, grabbing her, clamping a hand over her mouth before she could scream, whispering, 'Stop! Please! You know I didn't hurt you! I am not the one who hurt you!' Jess pleaded but the girl didn't cease her struggling. He saw that her cotton dress was not only bloodstained but torn, she was naked beneath it, her hairless little vagina was bleeding, her legs sticky with blood, fresh blood leaked from her nose and her mouth where one of her front teeth appeared to be loosened

The girl must have done this to herself, for Jess was not responsible. Jess would plead, *I didn't want to do any of this, I was left no choice.*

Traffic thundered by on the highway, yet no one seemed to notice the struggle at the side of the road. Though it was night, reflected light from the highway made the surrounding area visible as if by moonlight, where Jess was dragging the girl into the underbrush, panting and grunting he managed to drag her into a clearing where he could restrain her, try to reason with her, they were in a picnic area beside the highway, there were tables, benches, the ground was littered, Jess had to press his hand hard over the girl's mouth to muffle her cries, like a maddened cat she fought him and so Jess had no choice but to straddle her, hold her down with his weight, squeezing her between his knees, Jess must have weighed one hundred pounds more than the girl yet was having trouble restraining her for there was an unearthly strength in her little body. He thought, *If there is snow now it will cover her,* but he felt little solace, for in the spring, or in another day or two, the snow would melt. In his hand was a chunk of concrete. He lifted it, and he struck with it, and he felt the child-skull crack. The child-skull was composed of soft bones that could not withstand an adult's blows. Blood rushed from a wound in the girl's scalp, an alarming cascade of blood. For head wounds are the bloodiest of wounds. The girl kicked more feebly now, shuddered, moaned

325

and went limp. Her angular little doll-face had grown slack, her eyes were open and staring and empty now of their demonic fury. Jess thought of giving the girl artificial respiration for he'd learned the rudiments of first aid in high school but he dared not press his mouth against the girl's open bloodied mouth as he could not bring himself to lift the girl's torn and bloodied dress to examine her wound, but instead pulled it down over her thighs as far as it would go. Who had dressed such a small child in such inappropriate clothes, a thin cotton dress, a sweatshirt of some coarse cheap fabric, and no socks, only just sneakers on the child's bare feet? The girl's parents were to blame. Jess was not to blame. Jess had wanted to help, and Jess's help had gone wrong. He was arguing his case, staggering to his feet in utter exhaustion. What now? What came next? He would try to remember: he covered the girl with leaves, lifting leaves in his clumsy hands, and he located a strip of rotted tarpaulin and dragged it to the limp little body and covered it. Jess then stumbled away to search for his car. Trying to retrace his footsteps through the woods. Shrewdly he was drawn by the smell of a smoldering fire, and at the dump there was the derelicts' makeshift shelter, but the derelicts were nowhere in sight. Jess made his way along a faint path, stumbling and limping and sobbing, and there, as if waiting for him, was a police cruiser, a vehicle with a red light on its roof, parked close by Jess's Audi, which looked as if it had skidded partway into a ditch; the derelicts were speaking with two uniformed police officers, these were New Jersey state troopers examining Jess's car, already they'd discovered the front seats smeared with blood and one of them was shining a flashlight into the opened trunk; by this time it was too late for Jess to turn and flee back into the woods for the state troopers had seen him and were shouting at him to come forward, lift both hands in the air they were shouting, their guns were drawn, Jess hesitated, wondering if he should try to run anyway, back into the woods where there might be a burrow he could hide in, headfirst in a burrow in some dark sheltering place, even as the state troopers continued to shout at him, advancing upon him with their drawn guns like a TV cop show of the kind Jess never watched any longer, shouting, 'On the ground, son. On the ground.'

VENA CAVA

Love you! they'd said.

Love you so much! they'd said to him, So happy to have you back with us thank God.

There were fierce hugs, kisses. Hot searing kisses of the kind to leave scars. He was in the midst of the hugs, choked for breath. He was in the midst of their fierce love, observing himself from a distance of approximately fifteen feet – the far side of the room beside the Christmas tree – noting how salt tears sprang from his mangled eyes and ran down the skin grafts of his cheeks like rainwater in rivulets eroding hard-packed red earth. Love you, Dennie, was said to him, Thank God home from that terrible place those terrible people like animals.

They did not call him Lance Corporal here. All that was left behind.

Who they'd hired to play him was winking at him over the heads of – who these were – 'family,' their names were known to him as his name was known to them, except in the excitement the names were like coins in his pockets he'd grope for, through holes in fabric they'd fallen down inside the lining of his jacket, not lost exactly but he couldn't get to the damned coins, not without ripping more fabric.

His voice was raw and lurching. Wait! I'm over here. This is Dennie here.

Except the actor or whoever it was had taken his place. So the Lance Corporal got drunk, sullen in a corner of the bright-lit living room beside the Christmas tree they'd been saving, they said, till he could see it. Not a real tree like you'd cut down in the woods but a Wal-Mart tree, 'syntheesic,' some soft white fluffy material like fur, shiny red bulbs that sent slivers of light like glass to hurt the eyes and a sparkle angel at the top – one of the fat women smelling of her body was earnestly explaining to the Lance Corporal tearing sparkle wrapping paper from a present to reveal to him plaid flannel pajamas. See Dennie, we waited.

We knew! You'd be back.

We knew! We prayed! We prayed so hard!

It was a long time since he'd been hugged like this. Kissed and clawed at and tears splotching his shirt front and the fly of his khakis. He had to resist the wish to fend them off.

The Lance Corporal wasn't sure if he was hearing these people speak to him directly or if the words were being channeled/monitored through the titanium implant in his (right) inner ear/cochlea. For it did seem to be – he had to concede – if he could not see the mouth. or if the mouth was contorted or mumbling, or a soft sunken mouth lost in fatty jowl ridges or obscured by straggly whiskers, he could not decipher the words and he was left resentful and anxious and alert to being mocked.

He was the sole bearer of the title Lance Corporal in all of Yelling County, North Dakota. He had served three tours of duty in the war. He had been honorably discharged. You can bet his hometown was damned proud of him.

By a special request of the Lance Corporal's family the local media was to respect his privacy. There would be no front-page photographs in the *Ashtree Junction Gazette* or on local TV. He had the ID on his (left) wrist. He had the dog tags. If he'd been shipped here this must be the address they had for him, in their records. Another proof of identity was, the Lance Corporal had been driven past the old high school on their way to the house. In his mangled right eye the Lance Corporal had been ingeniously fitted with an interocular implant lens of plastic guaranteed to withstand melting at temperatures below 1000 degrees Fahrenheit and through this minuscule lens the Lance Corporal saw vividly and in quivering color. Not just the crummy sandstone facade of the high school they'd all gone to but beyond the high school the gouged mountains and the abandoned blast pits and the open-pit mine filled with red-glowering dark water they'd all gone swimming in – these 'familiar sights' were glossy and one-dimensional like magazine illustrations. What the hell, the Lance Corporal said. That's really something, the Lance Corporal said uneasily, and Mack who was the Lieutenant's (older) brother said, Yeah, Den, thought you'd like a little detour.

There was a test here, the Lance Corporal supposed. One of them instructing, Shut your eyes son. Tell me am I lifting your arm or lowering it, and he'd concentrated with all his strength, not wanting to give in, to peek through his eyelashes, saying firmly, Lifting. And the doctor – if it was a doctor – said, And now what am I doing, lifting or lowering, and he'd said less firmly, Lowering. No – lifting.

Later he'd realized it was a trick: whoever it was had only been taunting him, neither lifting nor lowering his arm as there'd been the trick with the pin in his big toe – was it pricking? Or not? Or – which toe? The Lieutenant's feet were obscured from him, he couldn't have cheated if he'd wished to cheat.

So at the high school, some kind of vision test. Or the high school had been physically altered, repainted (but subtly, in a color near identical to the old) or (more ingenious yet) the building he'd been taken to see had not been crummy Ashtree Junction High they'd all gone to but an entirely different building on a different street; as the gouged mountains in the near distance hadn't been the old familiar Humpbacks mined to exhaustion by Delphic Ore, Inc., but photo-projection of some kind, triggered into 'virtual' existence by the approach of the Lance Corporal's brother's Bronco pickup. So shrewd was the Lance Corporal, he'd conned his brother into believing that he had been taken in by these tricks, he'd *reacted exactly as a normal returning vet would react in such circumstances.*

So long as the Lance Corporal took his meds. In particular the chalky-white Zomix tabs. And the red-jelly capsules that went down smoothest with cold Coors.

Dennie, look at you! Oh, honey.

They were proud of him. The females wiped at their eyes. The men tried not to stare. Noisily they passed around the medals, the citations. The stained and dog-eared photos. The Lance Corporal hoped to hell the animal-head photos weren't in that batch.

There was Maudie, his young wife. He'd been crazy for her in high school. There was Sadie, and there was Bessie, and there was Momma-Jeanne, and there was Grandma-Jeanne, sag-faced teary women in puff perms to make their small heads appear larger on their bulky bodies in J.C. Penney stretch Orlon pantsuits, observed from the rear you could not easily distinguish between those fat asses.

There was his brother Mack. Or whoever they'd gotten to play Mack – shit-colored goatee, hair beginning to thin at the crown of his head, the identical Harley-Davidson cap he'd been wearing since the Lance Corporal had seen him last, as if the Lance Corporal even with a steel plate in his (shaved) head was such an asshole to fall for *that*. There was the old man with the sour sag-face splotched with liver spots like dirty rainwater. There were his uncles. His brother-in-law with the beer gut. Guys from Ashtree High he'd swear were dead, like him. Blown up like him. But he'd been the Jokester and a Jokester doesn't stay dead.

Daddy! Dad-dy!

Trembling little four-year-old kid scared to death of the Lance Corporal, blinking in awe and fear of the Lance Corporal's skin-graft face and glaring plastic eye and the shaved head with the glinting steel plate in like a sliding slot of bluish hue. Poor pathetic kid sucking his snot forefinger urged by the shiny-faced woman with the great-looking boobs falling out of a scoop-neck peach-color Orlon sweater sprinkled with seed pearls – this wasn't Maudie, was it? This was the other one, not Maudie Skedd he'd been crazy for. But the one who'd been so sweet to the Lance Corporal after he'd been ditched by Maudie. The one who seemed to know a lot about him, laughing and excited in a way to put Momma-Jeanne's nose out of joint, the Lance Corporal knew. This one was so hot, she displayed her wifely right to touch the Lance Corporal, kiss him wetly and streak his graft-skin face with lipstick to prove *I am not disgusted or revulsed, I am the most loving wife as I am the most faithful wife and a damned devoted mother*. Many times in the course of the afternoon this one confirmed her wife status by running her red-painted plastic fingernails along the Lance Corporal's shivery neck, along his wasted arms and along his wasted thighs, and by whispering in his ear to provoke him to bare his teeth in a slow smile. Saying Dennie Junior had not seen his Dad-dy in XXX months and every night he'd prayed for his Dad-dy and been such a good little boy, his Dad-dy had come home at last and forever.

There was something about this statement that pissed the Lance Corporal, he wasn't sure what. In the war the Lance Corporal had assisted at interrogations in which enemy insurgents were closely questioned by the Lance Corporal's superior officers and the formerly naive Lance Corporal had acquired a bullshit detector suspecting now that no four-year-old could have uttered Daddy! Dad-dy! in such a seeming sincere manner without having been coached.

Say hi to Dennie Junior, Dennie! He's just a little scared, it's been so long.

So long was being put to him as a reproach – was it?

These tours into combat, the Lance Corporal had been serving his country. The Lance Corporal had been serving in the War Against Terror. The Lance Corporal took pride in this, and it would piss him grievously should his mission be challenged.

334

Sure he loved Dennie Junior. Just didn't know what you did with a kid so young yet not a baby, that can't talk to you or ask questions. People seemed to be waiting, watching. Like a spotlight making the Lance Corporal anxious. Not enough red-jelly capsules to make the Lance Corporal steely-calm. And the kid's slightly crossed eyes were freaking him. The pale blue-shale color of the Lance Corporal's own eyes in some long-ago time when he'd had what you would designate as *normal eyes*. That age, you want to crush them in your arms. You want to shield them from the hurt and evil that awaits them. You want to explain to these staring people, *Know what? – this was a mistake. None of this I actually meant.*

Not his life in the war was the mistake. But his life here. His personal life. His post-Lance Corporal life. That was the mistake.

Still – he was the Jokester. The wild things he'd said, crazier and cruder than the other guys and still the girls had been hot for him, a bad boy from Ashtree Junction.

All that was past now. They'd shoveled him up in bleeding steaming parts. They'd dumped these parts in Ziploc baggies labeled DONOR ORGANS. The bones were of no use except the marrow, said to be priceless on the Saudi black market.

Now it must've been a TV special, the young Marine Lance Corporal had been shipped back home to the (mostly ex-) mining town Ashtree

335

Junction, North Dakota. To the modest asphalt-sided ranch house at 89 Magnesium Street. Whoever was playing the Lance Corporal was fumbling his lines and sick-looking like he'd made the worst mistake of his dumb-prick fucking life only hasn't figured out yet what it is.

In the storage closet at the back of the house, his old twenty-two deer rifle. That was a solace. He knew the rifle was there, last time he'd come home he'd checked. But the stock was cracked, he seemed to recall. His own fucking fault he'd been impatient slamming the stock against a tree when he'd missed an easy shot at a buck. It was Pa's shotgun he was thinking of. The Remington 1100 twelve-gauge double-barrel with the bolt action, which felt so good in the hands. Birdshot was the ammo he'd use, not buckshot. Birdshot is small, you could say dainty. Birdshot will not cause the target to explode in guts, feathers, flying skeins of blood.

He'd had to turn in his own Marine-issue firearms. These had been taken from him.

Who they'd got to play the kids he could not guess. Maybe the kids were actual? The little boy bearing the Lance Corporal's old name and the little girl who was his sister Michelle's child, his niece? They'd coached these kids to call him Daddy and Uncle Dennie. It was sweet and cute and the love came so strong in him like that sensation before puking – 'nausseous' – that left him weak, unmanly. And he thought *This is where the Lance*

Corporal is known and loved. This is where the Lance Corporal can be forgiven.

Still he was not certain if this was an actual thought of his or a TV thought beamed to him through the titanium implant.

Sometimes through the implant, speech was provided him. Though it was not the Lance Corporal's native speech yet he had to be grateful to have such speech at all, for there were 'misfirings' in his cerebral cortex as in the 'brain stem' it had been explained to him. Saying *Proud to serve my. Sickness unto death. In Jesus' name. Will not die in vain.*

This was embarrassing! This sucked! How the fuck had it happened, the Lance Corporal was still wearing his ID bracelet from the hospital? Remembered clearly they'd cut the damned thing off his wrist, or he'd torn it off his wrist with his teeth.

Dad-dy, what is this? Dad-dy!

Wouldn't you know the kid would discover it. TV kid this had to be, following some sinister strip – script? – the Lance Corporal had not okayed.

So much of this, confused to him. In the dark half of his brain where things got lost.

One of the women was fussing, helping the Lance Corporal remove the telltale hospital ID. Eight-inch sewing shears, cutting through the plastic. If you try to tear the fucking thing off your wrist, you can't. Also there was secret code, to trip

337

off security alarms if you tried to walk out of the ward. Burn Ward, Psych Ward. Orthopedic. Surgery. They'd deactivated the Lance Corporal's ID for the Lance Corporal was discharged now from the VA hospital as from the Marine Corps 'with valor.'

Time to eat, Dennie! C'mon, let me help you.

Need some help, Dennie? Look here, son.

Your favorite pie, remember? Banana cream.

On the couch he'd been half asleep, the tall luke-warm Coors tilting between his wasted thighs, about to tip over and leak liquid onto him like warm piss. Shit-faced drunk on no more than three or four beers with the meds. Not supposed to drink with the meds but fuck that, the Lance Corporal was *home* where they respected him. Ashtree Junction where they knew the Lance Corporal from birth onward and must've said they'd forgiven him, or the charges were erased – 'zonerrated' – and the records sealed. The Lance Corporal was mistrustful of this but would not dispute it. The Lance Corporal was a *father* here. Must've been, there were special dispensations for *fathers, husbands.*

He was nuzzling the little boy's neck which was hot and smelled of something sweet like soap and the little boy was becoming uncomfortable in his daddy's arms, maybe his daddy's stubble-jaws against the little boy's soft skin, or some chill chemical/metal smell of his daddy's numerous implants and shunts, and therefore the kid began to become restless and squirmy and panting through his mouth and to tease him the Lance Corporal tightened his arms around him holding him captive *Gotcha!* making a sucking noise sucking with his lips against the blue-pulsing carotid vein in Dennie Junior's neck, thinking *This is my son! My life that has been given back to me.*

This is my son, I can do any goddamn thing I wish to do for which none of you sonsabitches is going to stop me.

Halfway through the meal the *nausseousness* came over him, he had to lurch from the table. And in the bathroom puking into the toilet. Okay he'd flush the toilet. Still more puking, then flushing. The more you heave up, the better you feel. Except the Lance Corporal had a taste of panic in terror of dislodging the shunt in his chest a thing like a catheter in the *vena cava* the large vein that returns blood from the body back to the heart. He'd seen diagrams and he had seen the actual shunt (steel, plastic) and he'd signed the papers he was okay with this for it had been explained *This is a medical miracle to save your life* but if something happened to the shunt, if it was dislodged by a sudden spasm of vomiting, coughing, convulsing, it was two hours to the nearest VA hospital, in Grand Forks. Thinking maybe it was a mistake to let them remove the ID bracelet how'd he get readmitted? Your ID is white/plastic/computer-generated. Your ID contains all vital information about you. Your ID contains surname/forename/initial/patient account #2938826–1822/date of birth 4/21/81/sex M/date of admission 8/19/07.

A rage came over the Lance Corporal at the need to be grateful for such shit. The need to crawl like a kicked dog licking the boots of 'superior officers.' Or, grateful at these people – 'family' – fussing over him calling him Dennie like they had some claim on him. Like they knew *him*. Thinking of his old man's Remington 1100 in the back closet, the sight of which would calm them down quick.

No he was okay. This was a 'transition time' – he knew and he was okay with it. Just very tired, sulky, and bored. *Nausseous* so much to eat heaped on his plate. Drinking, time to drink. Then there were the tricks.

How after supper there were these new people in the house with faces that resembled faces he'd known. Except the names were lost, like lost coins he'd hear rattling inside the lining of his fleece jacket. Keys too, slipped through the holes. These were 'neighbors,' saying his name like they knew him and had the right, but that wasn't the trick, the trick was how they disappeared right in front of him, in an instant. One of his uncles crossing in front of the Lance Corporal past the TV where the football game was on and in that instant the uncle was gone, vanished; then a few minutes later the Lance Corporal sighted that same uncle just a few feet away.

Where were you? the Lance Corporal asked.

You – where'd you go? I'm talking to *you*. Couldn't remember the uncle's name or even if for sure this fat bald guy was his uncle. The Lance Corporal spoke hoarsely and not altogether coherently so there was difficulty in comprehending his speech but the Lance Corporal took care to smile to show that, hey, he was okay with this kind of weirdness, this tricky shit, maybe they were all drunk and that was the circumstance so they could laugh at it but the Lance Corporal did not want anyone laughing at *him*. Sure he could take a joke. He was the Jokester. How'd you make yourself disappear like that he was asking the fat bald guy. All of them were looking at him with uncertain smiles. It was well known the Lance Corporal had been the Jokester but that was a long time ago and they could not be sure if the Lance Corporal was joking now. How the hell d'you make yourself disappear, he asked. He was asking politely. Civilians tended to be fearful of the Lance Corporal and his kind. In uniform they were a sobering sight! They could be hotheaded. They could be cruel. They could be inventive, impulsive. The goats they'd run into on the road, that first full day when the Lance Corporal had been new to the war in the time of his first tour of duty (in fact not a lance corporal then but only private first class) some of them – the goats – they'd decapitated. For the hell of it. So nerved-up, and they hadn't yet engaged the enemy. The thing is dead what's the difference. Also a dog, which had not been completely dead though run over by Jeeps. Not people, they had not cut off any human heads in the Lance Corporal's battalion, though there were rumors. The goat or maybe two goats and the dog with mange all over his body like scabs.

The goat with the deep-socketed eyes like female eyes brimming with hurt and reproach and just slightly crossed. The dog with doggy mongrel eyes. Coarse sand-colored fur but the fur of the insides of ears was silky fine, feathery. Eyes that were opened wide in terror and astonishment and something like recognition. These they'd brought into the barracks. Not the Lance Corporal but some of the others. These were slightly older guys of whom the Lance Corporal was fearful but knew he dared not reveal it.

Dennie Junior was feverish past his bedtime. The little girl-niece had been taken home. The men were drinking. The TV was on loud but no one was listening. Dennie Junior was saying Daddy you won't go away again will you anxious and sucking at his fingers and Daddy slapped the fingers away from the sucking fish-mouth and said No.

Whoever it was that was playing the Lance Corporal/Daddy said no in a firm voice like a fist coming down hard on a table.

Civilians you can't tell apart. Dark-skinned, rat-eyed. *Kill them all let God sort them out.*

That night it seriously pissed the Lance Corporal how the kid too, which so much fuss was made of was the Lance Corporal's own *flesh and blood*, had started playing that same trick disappearing into the left side of . . . whatever it was – a sudden deep hole like a cellar or a pit, a gouged-out mine pit in the side of a mountain, where things went in and were gone. In a slow voice of the kind required to speak to morons and/or the brain-damaged the *nerowlgist* had explained to the Lance Corporal that he had a *nerowloggical deficit*. See, sometimes that part of the brain is shut down. Like a light in a room, switched off. As soon as the light is *off*, you can't see. You can't see that the light is *off*. You can't see the dimensions of the space the light would illuminate if there was a light because once the light is *off* the thought of the light is *off*. The very word 'light' is *off*. Civilians who risk stepping into that darkness disappear. Sometimes they reappear but most often they do not.

> *All a man truly craves is the respect of his fellow men. And women too of course. The respect that is due to him. And this is the respect due his country. God will sort out the rest.*

Dennie! No, honey, it's just a dream.

The mother hurried to the child's bed. In the night cries and gasps for breath and choked screams. The Lance Corporal rarely slept through a night even with his numerous meds swallowed down with Coors, but when the Lance Corporal

343

at last drifted off into an exhausted sleep like discolored froth-surf on a beach thinly covering the raddled sand, the Lance Corporal was often wakened by the child's cries and the commotion of the woman comforting the child. Dennie, honey! Mommy has you, honey, it's just a dream.

Now the Lance Corporal was home in the house on Magnesium Street, Ashtree Junction, North Dakota. The Lance Corporal was home permanently and except for his twice-weekly therapy sessions at the VA Hospital at Grand Forks, to which he was driven (usually by a volunteer relative), the Lance Corporal did not often leave the house. The Lance Corporal was left to ponder how it had happened he had been honorably discharged from the most revered of the U.S. armed services and yet the son the Lance Corporal had been given did not appear to be a well child.

Bad dreams in the night and sometimes while watching TV and videos with Dad-dy. The child who'd been potty-trained began to soil his bedclothes and sometimes – the most shameful times, which threw Dad-dy into a rage – his daytime clothes, for he could not control his *pee* which leaked out of him as out of a drippy faucet that no matter how hard you twist shut will yet drip.

The Lance Corporal's young wife was not the one the Lance Corporal had been remembering in the hospital, which was a sharp disappointment. That was a separate disappointment of which the Lance Corporal (who was a realist in all things)

344

saw no purpose in speaking for the Lance Corporal was a mature man now twenty-seven – twenty-eight? – years old. Three tours of duty he had served his country in the war, this now the Lance Corporal could certainly endure.

Yes there was sex between the Lance Corporal and his wife. Yes if you are wondering.

At the therapy clinic the Lance Corporal's wife attended crucial sessions to acquire certain skills. And so there was sex between the Lance Corporal and his wife, to a degree.

Yes we are happy together, we are man and wife. Yes if you are wondering.

Yet the Lance Corporal insulted the wife, calling her by another's name. In the extremity of his passion, not knowing what the fuck he was saying, or moaning. This is not right, the wife protested. I'm the one who loved you, I was the one who married you, not her, the wife protested piteously and hours were required late into the night to placate her and these hours were exhausting to the Lance Corporal who would come to realize shortly, like so many others, that it is easier to erase some problems than to solve them, or even to make the effort to solve them. In the back closet the bolt-action shotgun, a single barrel for the female and a single barrel for the fretting pissy-smelling kid and a quick reload for himself.

It was a well-publicized fact, meant to dissuade young males: the leading cause of death in such western states as Wyoming, Montana, Idaho,

Utah, and the Dakotas among young males sixteen to thirty is (1) vehicular accident, (2) suicide by gun.

It was a well-publicized fact meant to dissuade but a fact to give solace to most who hear it. *Your gun is your friend. Your gun won't let you down when you need it.*

Shrewdly the Lance Corporal had devised a way to drive any vehicle, even the Dodge pickup standing high from the ground. It was an ingenious technique involving one of his old boots, the handle of a ten-pound sledgehammer, and an oversized leather glove. His brother Mack whistled through his teeth Jez-zuz, Dennie! Got to hand it to you, you are one smart dude.

Or, you are one smart fuck-ass.

(In such ways the brothers communicated. Since boyhood, in such ways. Often Mack would slap Dennie across the shoulders, or against his head but gently now, for there was the steel plate. There were the implants you could not risk dislodging.)

On his restless drives mostly into the country-side through the ravaged landscape and into the Hump foothills past slag heaps, open-pit mines, and lakes smelling of sulfur – where in a long-ago time the Lance Corporal's daddy and granddaddy and who the fuck all else in the family the Lance Corporal had to assume worked for Delphic Ore, Inc., which mined ore – whatever fuck ore the Humps had, Delphic Ore, Inc., mined – you knew that, and you'd know that Delphic Ore, Inc., was bankrupt and shut down and whatever the Humps had to yield to mankind was long since yielded, sold and consumed and gone; and the Lance Corporal knew this and did not contest it. Thinking *I have served my country, this is a good thing. This is my country.*

Pa's old Remington 1100 he took with him. This was not illegal, this was not a concealed weapon. The Remington 1100 is one of the great guns though this specimen had to be forty years old, the nickel-plate barrel scratched and the maple stock worn smooth.

Just birdshot he'd loaded. In case from the pickup he might see a flock of mallards or snow geese and have the opportunity for a good clear shot – this was a wish of his.

In the TV version Maudie Skedd would arrive in the house on Magnesium Street. Maudie crying and her crimped yellow hair in her face. Maudie on her knees begging forgiveness. Maudie shamed, for all of Ashtree Junction knew of her betrayal. And the Lance Corporal said calmly *All that is past Maudie. I am in love with my wife who is the mother of my son. I forgive you Maudie this is my new life now.*

In the TV version, a handsome actor like the young Brad Pitt would play the Lance Corporal. For you could not portray the Lance Corporal as the Lance Corporal's actual self which no TV viewers would wish to see and the truth is, the actual Maudie Skedd is twenty pounds overweight and not so great-looking any longer.

If there was the TV version, there would be the Lance Corporal/Daddy with the beautiful little boy too. A little boy not so fretful always sucking his snot forefinger so you wanted to slap him.

The Lance Corporal loved his son more than his own life. The Lance Corporal played video games with Dennie Junior, watched TV cartoons, and repaired his broken toys. The Lance Corporal spent time with his son for the wife was working at Pennysavers at the mall where employees are offered such discounts, you'd be a fool not to take advantage.

Momma-Jeanne came over, also Aunt Sadie, Aunt Bessie, and Grandma-Jeanne. Helping the Lance Corporal with his little boy, for there was the realization *This is a transition time for all.*

Sometimes they prayed together. The Lance Corporal came to believe that he could sleep a purer sleep after prayer.

The Lance Corporal had killed in the war. The Lance Corporal had no idea how many of the enemy he had killed in the war. Though some of the enemy he had seen die – he had seen actual heads explode – so there was no ambiguity. Civilians he had seen, children and females of all ages he had seen, and these were bodies he could not recall having been upright and living before they'd become bodies. It was easier to recall them as bodies. The Lance Corporal had followed orders given to him by his superiors. The Lance Corporal had followed orders without regret or reproach. In the dark half of the Lance Corporal's brain figures were gathering. There was whispering, muffled voices. There should be a balance they were saying. The Lieutenant realized *It's in their language.* For this was the other language, of the enemy. The sinister guttural language no one could speak nor even comprehend. Saying *If you give us yours.*

My what? Give you my – what?

Yours.

Waking tangled in sweaty bedclothes or sprawled in sweat-soaked T-shirt and boxers on the couch and the TV on mute a few yards away in the night the Lance Corporal groped in panic for the box cutter he kept by his side at such times, carried in the pickup and Pa's old Remington 1100 in the back seat (of the pickup) – a man had to be armed at all times. This was post-9/11 U.S.A. This was a time of terror stalking the land. The Lance Corporal with the shunt in his vena cava wakened with the knowledge that the enemy dead had not said *If you give us your son you will be forgiven.* They did not say that. He did not hear that. For these were but civilians and not empowered to make such proposals. They did not say *If you give us your son as you have taken our sons from us you will be forgiven* but the Lance Corporal understood, that was the promise.

Where is Dennie Junior? In sudden fear for the

child the Lance Corporal woke the snoring woman and stumbled into the child's room where the child had wakened in fear of him and he saw – it could not be for the first time he saw – that this child was not Dennie Junior but another child, scrawny, undersized, with deep-socketed, slightly crossed eyes. These eyes shone with feral cunning like a creature's eyes glaring up beside the highway in headlights. Where is Dennie Junior? the Lance Corporal demanded, and the woman said, This is Dennie, this is our son, and the Lance Corporal said, This is not our son! This is not my son! Where have they taken my son! And the woman comforted the crying child, saying that Daddy was having a bad dream, Daddy did not mean what he was saying, and the Lance Corporal backed off in fear of the misshapen child with the large rat-head and staring eyes in which there glared that look of recognition, of the damned. And the woman said, Of course this is Dennie Junior, don't scare us like this, honey, please, it's one of your nightmares, and the Lance Corporal said hesitantly, Is it? That's what it is? A nightmare, and the woman said, Yes, it's a nightmare, now come back to bed.

Twice weekly he was driven to therapy in Grand Forks. More frequently now his brother Mack drove him, for other relatives had ceased volunteering. The Lance Corporal did not now have a driver's license for his license had been taken from him, for 'disability.' The Lance Corporal yet persisted in driving the Dodge pickup into the countryside when he wished, making his frequent stops at taverns where the Lance Corporal was likely to be known and drinks bought for him, and if the Lance Corporal required assistance out to the Dodge pickup, there were volunteers to assist him. If Yelling County sheriff's deputies sighted the disabled war vet driving his Dodge pickup on local roads they were inclined to look the other way, but there was no question the Lance Corporal dared not drive on the state highway to Grand Forks where vehicles sped at beyond eighty miles an hour and eighteen-wheelers careened heedless and headlong through the waste landscape like banshees.

On TV these trips to Grand Forks would be deeply moving for the intimacy springing between the Lance Corporal and his brother driving alone together to Grand Forks and back in Mack's SUV, but in actual life the brothers did not much speak. There was so much to speak of! and yet the brothers were frequently at a loss for words. Mack wore his grimy Harley-Davidson cap pulled low over his forehead, sucked at cigarillos with a clamped jaw exhaling smoke sideways from his mouth in the shape of a single errant tusk as his (younger) brother the Lance Corporal tried to summon forth boyhood memories to share with his brother yet lost these memories in the very instant of recalling them as, like the tusk-smoke drawn out the opened window of the SUV, the boyhood memories vanished. So much was shifting into the left side of the Lance Corporal's impaired brain, he wondered how he could bear it. Saying one day in a voice of hoarse raw boyish grief, Mack, they took my son from me, the one they left isn't mine. I know that I am meant to accept him, I am meant to love the little guy and I do love the little guy, but Jesus, Mack, it is so unfair. I thought I deserved more respect, Mack. Quietly beginning to cry, tears like warm pee leaking from his mangled eyes. Mack said, Jesus, Dennie, hey – c'mon. Mack was shocked, embarrassed as hell, a hot blush rising into his face, That's not so, Dennie, Dennie Junior is your son for sure. That's crazy talk, Dennie. And the Lance Corporal said, Is that so, Mack? Tell me, Mack, is that so? I will believe you, Mack, and Mack said, staring straight ahead at the state highway bland and featureless and empty as the pavement of hell and groping to lay his hand on the Lance Corporal's wasted arm, Jez-zuz, Dennie, sure, why'd I lie to you?

Because you are one of them, you bastard. That's why.

In the war there was not always combat. There was boredom as well as combat in the war and as danger came in streaks and streams and deafening explosions so boredom came like lava slow and suffocating and like sand filling the

352

moist crevices of the soul. The decapitated goat, the decapitated dog. Later, there were other decapitated bodies. Exploded heads but also rescued heads. Heads in jars fitted with sunglasses and helmets and cigarillos between the jaws and the eyes glazed and empty at first until maggots began to fester and writhe with a look of inner crafty life. In the barracks there was laughter, these sights were so funny! In this recovered life *back home* he heard their laughter and was roused and frightened by it and fumbled for his weapon. Sometimes in the night when the child woke in terror the child's choked cries sounded like laughter of a jeering sort. The Lance Corporal took his meds as prescribed and these he supplemented with Oxies and Percs he'd scored at one or another of his frequent stops in town and along the state highway (Friday's, Wineberie's, Starburst Lounge, Pussy a Go-Go) but after a while the Lance Corporal gave up the quest for sleep was a vanity of the long-ago life he had renounced. Upright he sat in a chair facing the muted TV. Lately he dared not lie on the couch for he'd felt the shunt inside his chest begin to shift just perceptibly from the vena cava and there was the risk of sudden breakage, leakage, and death.

This will save your life, son. Have faith.

Goddamn, he did! He had plenty of faith.

Therapy was working. There was 'progress.' He struggled to walk in baby steps, he lifted

353

twenty-pound dumbbells that left him dazed and breathless and the dark side of his brain enlarged. There began to be talk of his former job being returned to him. There began to be talk of promotion to store manager. The North Dakota governor spoke passionately of the war and of those 'sons of the state' who had sacrificed. The president was optimistic about the war. On TV the president was optimistic and bravely smiling about the war. The president had sent by certified mail a personal letter thanking the Lance Corporal for his 'selfless service' in the war as well as a color photograph of the president with his optimistic and courageous smile and the photograph was inscribed to the Lance Corporal and signed with the president's signature. There was a gold seal of the United States of America. This the Lance Corporal presented to his parents, Momma-Jeanne and the old man, Pa, whose lungs wheezed and whistled like air escaping from a balloon from forty years in the Hump mines but the old bastard was proud of his son, and that was something. What guts he had, it was said of the Lance Corporal. What courage. Yet there were those who yawned rudely and in the mirror beyond the massed whiskey bottles and the blaring TV there were knowing smirks, winks. *What a sucker to enlist. What a total fuckhead asshole sucker to enlist. Now you aren't even him. You aren't Dennie Krugg.*

Where Dennie Junior was, Lance Corporal/Daddy didn't know. The child was hiding from him beneath

354

the bed. The child was whimpering, crying. The child's pajamas were soaked in pee. The dimensions of the house were askew and mocking, not rectangular but a parallelogram the Lance Corporal recalled from high school geometry. The bathroom faucets (sink, tub) had been switched, to confuse him. Where *hot* had been now there was *cold*. In the hospital they'd tested him: do you feel *heat* do you feel *cold*. There was never any clear answer, for whatever he said the response was *Good!* He could not bear it, how the child cringed and hid from him. Seizing the child in his arms that were unexpectedly strong he had no choice but to haul the child into the bathroom and into the tub making Daddy-cooing noises of comfort. On one of their drives to Grand Forks he'd begged Mack to tell him, how do you bear it, being a father, and Mack said, Hey dude – you just do. You learn, and you do.

But how, Mack. Tell me fucking how.

You learn. You get used to it. You get cool with it, see? You just do.

Mack, I don't know. I don't think so, Mack.

A baby crying you get used to it. You tune out. Worst case, you walk out. Every guy does. As long as you don't, you know, do anything. And you won't.

Okay, dude, see what I'm saying? You won't.

Every guy is scared he will. But it passes. You won't.

This night though, this was a bad night. The female had been at him and he'd had to deal with her. And the child, which was not his child (he knew) but was his responsibility. In the tub the child was screaming, the child with the misshapen head and crazed eyes. This was not a child but a goat – a goat carcass. The heads were wrapped in plastic bags from Pennysavers, he'd used double bags to catch the drippage. Such strain, and a coughing spasm he was in fear the shunt would slip from the vena cava bearing used and despoiled blood into his heart to be cleansed of impurities. He'd thought it had to be his own blood his bare feet were slipping in. On the bathroom-floor linoleum, and on the stairs. The phone had been ringing he'd knocked to the floor. The woman's cell phone he had demolished with the heel of his foot. Their noise had been silenced, the Lance Corporal was feeling good about that. The Lance Corporal was feeling hopeful about that. He'd washed his bloodied hands, forearms, and his face and he'd felt the steely stubble on his jaws. In the pickup he'd wrapped the tools – the hand ax, the saw – in garbage bags. He would carry the carcasses and the heads out to the pickup when he'd rested. He was very tired, his blood sugar was low. Dennie? Hey. Somehow, Mack was with him. Must've driven up in the SUV and the Lance Corporal had not heard for he'd dozed off Or, could be the fucking titanium implant in his inner ear had lost its charge. A tiny battery in the implant, it had lost its electrical charge. So much had been swallowed up in the dark side of his brain. He had appealed to the officer who'd discharged him *Don't send me back to them. I am not ready to return to them yet. I can't live with civilians. I am afraid that I will hurt civilians.* The Lance Corporal was asked why would he hurt civilians of his own kind who loved him and the Lance Corporal said *Because that is the only way to stop them loving me sir.*

How was this? The Lance Corporal was unarmed. Dozing and waking abruptly and unarmed and barefoot and in his bloodstained T-shirt and boxers in his own house. Goddamned Mack was the one with the shotgun not the Lance Corporal who was unarmed. Mack had not yet made the discovery in the cold scummy bathtub water nor the other on the floor of the bedroom. Yet grimly Mack spoke, Don't do this, Dennie, back off. As in a nightmare in which you are stark naked the Lance Corporal was without a weapon. It was astonishing to be without a weapon at such a time. Sheila? Mack was calling. Hey, Sheila? It's me, Mack. You could see Mack's hands shake. You could see that Mack would not have the courage to fire. For Mack was a civilian, he had not ever fired any discharge of any weapon at any other person. The sight of his Lance Corporal brother covered in blood and barefoot and stark-eyed was terrifying to him, he could not possibly aim true. He was saying Dennie? Where's Sheila? Where's Dennie Junior? He was pleading, begging. He was holding his shotgun which had a short grip and a short barrel for bird-hunting and was not a shotgun the Lance Corporal believed he had ever seen before. His own shotgun he'd taken from Pa was on the kitchen table not yet loaded. A pack of birdshot he'd opened but had not yet loaded. Step back, Dennie, Mack was saying, but the Lance Corporal had not traveled so far, across so many oceans and galaxies, a steel plate in his skull and a miracle shunt in his heart, to be told what to do by a civilian. Calmly the Lance Corporal reached for the shotgun that was aimed at his heart and with all his fingers seized the barrel.